Other Titles by TW Brown

The DEAD Series:

DEAD: The Ugly Beginning
DEAD: Revelations
DEAD: Fortunes & Failures
DEAD: Winter
DEAD: Siege & Survival
DEAD: Confrontation
DEAD: Reborn
DEAD: Darkness Before Dawn
DEAD: Spring
DEAD: Reclamation
DEAD: Blood & Betrayal
DEAD: End

Zomblog

Zomblog
Zomblog II
Zomblog: The Final Entry
Zomblog: Snoe
Zomblog: Snoe's War
Zomblog: Snoe's Journey

That Ghoul Ava

That Ghoul Ava: Her First Adventures
That Ghoul Ava & The Queen of the Zombies
That Ghoul Ava Kicks Some Faerie A**

The horrors of the past meet the brutality of the present!

Dreadland Chronicles: ALL ROADS LEAD TO TERROR — Richard Schiver

Dreadland Chronicles: The Reaping — Richard Schiver

They offer hope in a hopeless world!
Available in print and e-book format

Onset

(Book 1 of the New DEAD series)

TW Brown

Estacada, Oregon, USA

DEAD: Onset
Book 1 of the New *DEAD* series
©2016 May December Publications LLC

The split-tree logo is a registered trademark of May December Publications LLC.

This book is a work of fiction. Names, characters, businesses, organizations, places, events, and incidents either are the product of the author's imagination or are used fictitiously. Any resemblance to actual persons living, dead, or otherwise, events, or locales is entirely coincidental.

This book is protected under the copyright laws of the United States of America. Any reproduction or unauthorized use of the material or artwork contained herein is prohibited without the express written permission of the author or May December Publications LLC.

Printed in the U.S.A.

978-1-940734-57-6

My *DEAD* world gets reset.

Welcome back. First, a few things should be cleared up. If you are already a fan of my *DEAD* series, then you know what you are stepping into here…almost. And if you are new, then I hope this series becomes part of your "must read" collection.

When I wrote the original *DEAD* series, I had so many "grand" ideas. I was going to give zombie fans a visceral and all-encompassing series that would re-define what fans of this genre could expect. Yeah…well, in the first three books, I learned A LOT. I almost regret the entire *Vignettes* portion of the series. Oddly enough, that section produced some characters that were fan favorites. "Tight like a Tigah!" belonged on a tee shirt. That is also where I got my collection of hate mail and (yep…true story), death threats.

There were a lot of people who just could not get into all the one-timer characters in *Vignettes*. My idea behind that entire section was to give the reader a global look at the world of the undead. Those were the "cartoons" between the *Steve* and *Geek* chapters. All they did was muddle things up for a lot of readers.

You will not find any of my multi-character narrative style here. This is the story of one person in one part of the world. I have no idea how many of these books will eventually make up the entire series. I am not setting a specific number just because I think I hamstrung myself in the original series by saying I would be done at twelve books.

Because I had an endgame with the DEAD series, I had to stick to my guns. Also, I have edited for other authors in this genre. One writer in particular wrote a solid six-book series. He went on to other things and I continued to edit them. One day, I received book seven of his six-book series. I shot back an email asking what was up. His words were basically, "My new stuff isn't making the money that *Series X* was making (sorry, no names), so I am continuing the series." I thought that was a bit of a slight to the fans.

What that did do for me was remind me that, while I am doing what I love, this is still my job. This is what I do for a living. That is why I started the ***DEAD: Snapshot—{insert town here}***

i

collection of stand-alone books set in my ***DEAD*** world. The regular response was, "But then what happens?" after each of the *Snapshots* (Portland, Oregon; Leeds, England; & Liberty, South Carolina). And for those of you wondering…yes, the *Snapshots* will still be written. Up next: Las Vegas, Nevada.

Writing a series is what I do best. I chose to return to the world that I created with my twelve-book ***DEAD*** series. I want to go deep into a single character and the people he encounters. I also want to give you a person that can be anybody. No super prepper or military badass.

So, here we go. This is still a ***DEAD*** book, but I hope that it gives you something different. I also hope that it brings back some of the readers who just could not get through the original series because of the epic number of characters that populated one page and were gone.

Another thing I want to do is share with you the location of this tale. When I write about places I have little or no actual familiarity with, I use Google Earth to take me down to the street level as well as give me an overview. So, if you are curious about the general area where much of this story takes place, I include the Google Earth page that stayed up on my computer the past few months:

https://www.google.com/maps/@45.4563507,-122.5649157,264a,20y,270h,44.98t/data=!3m1!1e3

Naturally I took certain creative liberties, but this should at least allow you to drop into the location of the story and "see" what Evan and the others see. Since this is not far from where I live, I had the advantage of driving over and checking it out on foot.

I hope that you enjoy this new series. Whether you do or you don't, I invite (beg is perhaps more accurate) you to leave a review. Those are the lifeblood of us writer types. Especially those of us in the Indie scene. I can't tell you enough the importance of your reviews.

And now, let me wrap up with a few thank you notes. To my amazing Beta reading team, YOU make this a better book.

Your honesty when I miss the mark is so vital: Debra, Sophie, Todd & Amy, Cassie, Malik, Andrea, Caron, Hope and Terri. Each of you has my deepest thanks. To my wife, Denise, you pushed me to chase my dream. Every single time I think I am not doing it well enough, you smack me on the back of the head and tell me to get back to work. Last but not least, each of you who picks up this book and gives it a shot. It is no lie when I say that I see you as my employer. You pay my salary. You allow me to do what I love. When I meet you in person, I never understand why some of you get so excited. I see me every day and am just not as impressed. So, if we meet, just relax. Let's enjoy a cup of coffee and talk about zombies, dogs, music…whatever. And feel free to drop me an email. I answer them all myself just like I read EVERY review. And if you have endured this rambling intro, I guess it is time for me to step aside and let you get on to what you are here for…ZOMBIES!

I just wanna be somebody!
TW Brown
October 2016

*The REAL Evan Berry…
Thanks for "Shaking us all night long!"*

Contents

1	The First Few Hours	1
2	Legacy	19
3	The Punch in the Gut	39
4	Martial Law	57
5	No Rest for the Weary	75
6	Day Two Begins	93
7	The Journey to Safety Begins	111
8	Out of the frying pan…	129
9	…and into the fire.	147
10	The Dog	163
11	Discoveries	179
12	The Children	195
13	Noise	211
14	"Hate to say I told you so."	225
15	Bad Man	241
16	A Time to Kill	253
	Paul Stokes is Dead	269

1

The First Few Hours

"Evan? Are you up?"

I spat out the mouthful of toothpaste and cupped my hand to my mouth. "Just getting ready to shower, babe," I called back.

As I rinsed the sink, I could hear Stephanie, my fiancée, padding around upstairs. I was almost done washing my hair when the curtain opened and Steph popped her face in.

"You should leave about ten minutes early," she said and then took a sip from her coffee. She closed her eyes and gave a slight moan of pleasure, taunting me with the fact that I hadn't had my first cup yet.

"Is something wrong?" I asked as I patted down my body to make sure I'd rinsed off all the soap and then shut off the water.

"I guess the police have a section of Powell blocked off. Something about a homeless person or something wandering around in traffic." She stepped back and handed me my towel.

As I dried, I could hear the Channel 8 morning news team discussing the road closure. I tuned it out and went about gathering my things for my first day of work. Granted, I was only going in as a substitute, but the principal had made it clear that he believed there was a place for me in the music department. I would finally be a full-time school teacher by next year!

As I zipped my bag, my eyes drifted to my heavy tool belt.

DEAD: Onset

I'd worked the past few years in construction while I finished school to be a music teacher. It was hard work, but I didn't mind it knowing that it was only temporary. Also, if not for that job, I would've never met Stephanie Strasdin.

I took one last look in the mirror on the back of the door to be sure I was ready. My straight dark hair fell just past the shoulders. I'd been pretty happy when I was told that I didn't have to cut it. I had on a simple black pullover shirt with the long sleeves pushed up just above the elbows and my favorite pair of black jeans. I'd actually debated on which shoes to wear. I loved my Doc Martens. The toes were a bit scuffed, but Steph had nudged me towards the fairly new docksiders.

"You want them to take you somewhat seriously," she had quipped. "That is going to be hard to do if you look like just another student."

She had a point. I'd always looked young for my age. Chances are, I would end up being carded well into my thirties which were only three years away.

As I shut the closet door and prepared to head into the kitchen, I paused to watch the bedroom television that had on the local morning news. The footage was being taken from the Channel 8 helicopter. Sure enough, Powell Boulevard was a parking lot for as far as the eye could see in both directions.

The picture swung around and zoomed in on a group of police cars with their lights flashing. A tighter zoom brought a few of the officers into focus. It looked like they had their weapons drawn. I had a feeling that scene wasn't going to end well.

Grabbing the remote, I shut it off. I didn't want that kind of negativity bouncing around in my head on the first day. Sub or not, this was my first teaching job. I didn't want anything to take the shine off this morning.

"Didn't you say there was just some mentally ill person wandering around on the highway?" I asked as I walked into the kitchen where I could smell toast and coffee in that perfect marriage of morning fragrances.

"I thought it was a homeless guy," Stephanie said as she slid a small plate containing two pieces of toast slathered with butter

The First Few Hours

and honey.

"Wow...wonder why the cops feel the need to pull their weapons? You'd think they would learn from all the others showing up in the news these past few years." I took a bite of my toast and shoved that story out of my head for good. Today was my big day and nothing was going to ruin it.

"I will probably have to stay late at work today," Stephanie said over her mug of coffee. "So how about you grab some pizza from the take and bake around the corner? We will celebrate your first day and you can tell me all about it when I get home."

"That new girl didn't work out?" I pushed my plate aside. I'd only eaten half a piece of toast, but I was just too excited to eat.

"She has called in or left early every day for the past week."

I got up and moved around the breakfast island to kiss Steph. She leaned up and kissed me on the tip of my chin. It was one of those things that had a story to why she did it. Too bad I couldn't actually remember it.

"Chewie!" I called.

There was a long pause and then I heard the dull thud of my Newfoundland as she slid off our bed. There was a jingle of her tags and the sound of her big feet padding down the long hallway. I knelt down to greet the big, black dog as it plodded into the room.

"You be a good girl for me, okay?" I grabbed her by her jowls and kissed her cold, wet nose. I looked up at Steph who was holding my denim knapsack out, waiting for me to take it as I headed out the door.

"She'll be fine. All she does is curl up under my desk and snore." Steph gave the dog a pat on the side as I stood and took my bag.

I opened the door and stepped out into the misty morning. A solid blanket of high clouds was providing a steady mist. That was one thing about spring in Portland, Oregon...it was not much different from fall or winter. I reached in my pants pocket and grabbed my keys as I tried not to leap down the stairs and sprint to my car. A fresh surge of excitement churned in my

DEAD: Onset

stomach making me glad that I hadn't eaten much or downed a full cup of coffee.

I reached my door and paused. My nose wrinkled and I habitually checked my shoes to ensure I hadn't stepped in a Chewie landmine. They were clean. I sniffed again for some stupid reason and almost gagged.

"Smells like something died," I choked out.

"Probably Mr. Bickford's cat," Steph held a hand over the lower part of her face to try and block the smell that was almost so thick that it seemed as if I could taste it in the back of my throat. "That silly animal keeps killing squirrels and then leaving them on the porch. I think it has a crush on Chewie."

"It'll be anarchy…dogs and cats living together," I said in a poor Bill Murray from *Ghostbusters* impersonation.

"You are such a dork," Steph teased.

"You're marrying this dork," I called back as I slid into my beat up old pickup truck.

I turned over the engine and bumped the lever to get the windshield wipers to do a quick sweep across so that I could see. I backed out and heaved the wheel around to aim me towards the exit of our quiet little cul-de-sac. As I dropped into drive, I glanced over one more time at Steph who was standing on the porch with Chewie at her side. She brushed a lock of her dark hair from her eyes and raised that hand in a wave goodbye. I waved back and headed to the first day of what I was sure was going to be the most memorable day in my life.

Today…I was going to be the music teacher at Franklin High School. As I pulled out and headed over to Foster Road, I switched on my radio.

"…unconfirmed reports of the entire town being quarantined—"

I gave my CD a nudge and smiled as it slid into the player. Seconds later, the opening chords to AC/DC's *Highway to Hell* blared in my cab. The news had been pretty dismal as of late. There was some new flu or sickness or something that had everybody in a tizzy. Personally, I could care less. I never understood why folks got so bent out of shape over a sickness

The First Few Hours

that killed a handful of people when there were literally billions in this world. The news always made it seem worse than it really was and did a hell of a job scaring the gullible general public.

I sang along with Bon Scott all the way to work. As soon as the big brick building came into view, I had to fight the urge not to stomp on the gas. When I pulled into my parking space, I had to just sit for a moment as the excitement swirled around inside me. I watched groups of kids as they trudged to the main entrance of the high school before I finally got out of my truck. That is when I saw another teacher giving me a questioning look.

"Can I help you?" the older woman said.

She was probably in her fifties and had hair that had turned a very unflattering shade of gray. The wrinkles around her eyes, the crevices in her cheeks, and the lines at the corners of her mouth gave her away as a smoker before I got close enough to pick up on the telltale stink. She was maybe a shade over five feet and far more than a shade over two hundred pounds. Her eyes were dark and piggy and the frown she wore so naturally had me thinking of every teacher that I'd despised when I was in school. I could just imagine the life being sucked out of a room whenever she entered it.

"Name's Evan Berry. I'm the music teacher?" I hated that my voice quavered just enough to make that seem like a question.

"Mr. Poole is the music teacher here," the woman said with a snort.

"Yeah...I'm his sub."

"Oh...well then, you aren't *really* the music teacher, are you." There was no quaver in her voice, so her words came across as a statement and not a question.

I opened my mouth to say something that I would probably regret later when the sounds of a police car's siren erupted on Powell Boulevard just a few yards away causing me to jump. I looked over to see the squad car speeding away with lights and siren in full effect.

"Not from around here, are you?" the woman sniffed as she

waddled past me and headed toward a side entrance to the school.

I felt a bit of my earlier exuberance trickle away and quickly made the decision that I would not let some sour old lady ruin this day. If everything that I'd been told in my final interview was true, then this would be the end of my days in construction.

"I'm the music teacher, dammit," I whispered as I took a deep breath and pulled open the door.

This may be my first day, but I was familiar enough with Franklin High School to notice that there was something a bit off. There should be more kids walking the halls, hurrying to class, or just hanging out by their lockers. As I made my way to the teacher's lounge, I began to notice something else on the faces: fear.

I made my way down the hallway of hushed conversations and teenagers that were acting more like frightened children being dropped off for their first day of preschool. I pulled up by a fountain a few feet away from a trio of girls.

"...says that her mom made them help tie her dad down to the bed because he kept trying to attack them," one of them was saying in a hurried whisper.

"Jessie said that she saw a man behind the Dumpster in the Safeway parking lot, and that he was eating what she swore looked like a dog!" another girl exclaimed.

"He was probably one of those gross homeless people all spun out on meth," the first one tried to insist.

"Yeah, well my dad says that this is something worse than the news is letting on. He is home right now packing things into the RV. He says that we are leaving this afternoon for someplace in Eastern Oregon where he goes during hunting season," the girl who had told about the supposed dog eater commented.

I decided that maybe I should just head to the faculty lounge. Teenagers—especially the girls in my experience—love to over exaggerate and overdramatize.

I was anxious to get to my classroom, but it was obvious that something odd was going on here. For the first time ever, I was beginning to wonder if maybe I'd become too cynical when

The First Few Hours

it came to the news. After all, it seemed there was always some sort of illness that they would pound into the public's consciousness. I just could not get worried when some bug or another would be claimed as being responsible for the deaths of nine people in some backwater province in China. I knew that there had been a lot of talk the past few days, but I'd ignored it.

I was a little disappointed when the first person I saw as I opened the door just happened to be the unpleasant woman from the parking lot. I stepped inside and shut the door behind me. A handful of other teachers were clustered around a table that had a ratty looking coffee maker sitting on it; that seemed like the place to be.

"Evan," a man's voice called from my left. I glanced over to see Principal Julian Gordon poke his head up from behind a newspaper.

"Principal Gordon," I returned the greeting and adjusted my course to head over to the collection of chairs and a loveseat that had a rip where some of the stuffing poked out.

"Looks like your first day is going to be a short one." Principal Gordon folded his paper and tucked it into a small pouch sewn to the side of his chair.

"Why is that?"

"Where have you been?" he said with obvious surprise at my ignorance of whatever this bug was that had everybody so worked up.

"You guys are talking about this Blue Plague thing that the media is blowing up and scaring folks with?" I tried not to sound too derisive, but I really did not have much faith in the spin machine that was our so-called news media.

I looked around the room and suddenly realized that everybody's attention was now directed at me and the principal. I felt my mouth grow dry at the ominous feeling that filled the faculty lounge. A bell rang signaling the start of class, but I wasn't the only one to jump at the sudden sound.

"The rumors are that it is some sort of human rabies that is spreading like wildfire," Principal Gordon said with a grimace once the ringing stopped. "Riots were reported this morning in

DEAD: Onset

Tokyo, but the worst is North Korea. They just went dark about twenty minutes ago and the president is calling some sort of security council meeting."

"The internet is saying that a town in Kentucky is being completely quarantined and that the citizens have all turned into crazed, blue-faced lunatics that are acting like gee-dee zombies just like you see in the movies," a man wearing a red flannel shirt and faded jeans growled from where he stood staring out the window on the far side of the room. Easily over six feet tall and with reddish-blonde hair that had him looking like the man on the Brawny paper towel packages if you added in a well-groomed and impressive beard that rested on his barrel chest, Carl looked exactly like I thought a shop teacher should.

"Carl, don't be ridiculous," the principal scolded. "Carl is our resident conspiracy theorist…and when he isn't filling that role to the fullest, he is our woodshop teacher."

I laughed and then wagged my finger around the room at all the assembled teachers. "This must be some little ritual or something that you folks do to the new guy."

"You really think the media is just making this stuff up?" the parking lot lady said in total disbelief.

I was about to say something about how they'd blown up things like H1N1 and West Nile when my phone buzzed. I was still getting used to having a cell phone and it took me a few seconds to realize the source of the tingly buzz in my pants pocket.

"Excuse me, just a second," I said, holding up a finger as I saw Stephanie's name on the screen.

We had a standing policy about calling each other at work: we didn't. When you were on the clock, your time belonged to your boss. If she was calling me, then it had to be an emergency.

"What's wrong, Steph?" I asked in a loud whisper as I stepped back out into the almost empty hallway.

"There is a man in our backyard and he is trying to get in the house!" Stephanie sobbed. "He tried to attack Chewie…she managed to get away, but he bit off a piece of her tail, Evan."

My mind quickly replayed the snippet of conversation I'd heard from the girls gathered by the water fountain. I shook my

The First Few Hours

head to clear it and was about to speak when I heard the sound of glass shattering.

"Steph!" I shouted, already my feet had me moving towards the parking lot.

"Evan, he's trying to come in through the back door...he broke the window!"

I heard the deep bark of Chewie, but it didn't really sound like her. This dog had a ferociousness that was not something that I could accept as being from my sweet girl. This was the opposite of my gentle giant. There was the sound of something cracking followed by Stephanie's scream.

Then the line went dead.

The door to the faculty lounge opened and the principal stepped out. "Is everything okay, Evan?"

"No...I don't think it is," I heard myself say. The thing is, I felt like I was outside of my body for some strange reason. Whatever this was, it couldn't be happening.

"Evan?" Principal Gordon said in a loud whisper.

"I have to go," I mumbled as I started for the exit.

I could hear the principal calling me as I sped up from a fast walk to a jog and then a run. I reached the exit and slammed the door open so hard that the clang made me jump and caused some nearby dogs to start barking.

I was just reaching my truck when a voice called from almost directly behind me. I spun, a fist raised as if I felt like I was about to be attacked.

"I'm coming with you." It was the woodshop teacher, Carl. "That phone call sounded serious. If it's one of them things, you might need some help."

"One of what things?" I snapped as I jerked the door to my truck open and jumped up into the cab. "I don't have time for this crap." I slammed the door and was more than a little surprised to see the burly man stalk over to the passenger side and give the handle a tug.

Exasperated, I leaned over and flipped up the lock as I turned the key in the ignition. I didn't actually wait for him to get all the way in as I dropped the lever into drive and punched the gas. I was less than ten minutes away, but that could be an eternity if somebody was breaking into my house.

"Thought I heard something about your dog being attacked," Carl said as he grabbed the dashboard to brace himself while I swerved around a car that was waiting to make a left turn at the intersection that I flew through.

"You were listening in on my call?"

"Friend, your lady was screaming. Everybody in the lounge heard."

I hadn't thought of that. The light a half a block away turned yellow. I stepped on the gas knowing that there was no way I would reach it before the light turned red. As I shot through, I heard the honks of angry drivers in my wake.

"You get us killed and you won't be doing the little woman any good at all, friend," Carl said through clenched teeth as I practically drove up onto the sidewalk as I reached the next intersection where I had to turn right.

The truck bounced a bit as it took the corner and I fought the steering wheel to straighten us out. I eased up a little on the gas pedal, but I still had to weave between traffic. At last, I saw my street. At the entrance to the cul-de-sac were a half dozen or so people. They were all just standing in a group. A few were pointing or craning their necks to get a better look. I smashed down on the horn as I approached and was briefly grateful that they at least moved out of the way. I recognized some of the neighbors and made a mental note that I would be in a few people's faces when this was over. How the hell could they just stand there while Steph was in obvious trouble?

Almost on cue, I heard a scream coming from the direction of my house. It started like a regular scream...but then it changed. This was like nothing I'd ever heard in my life, and it almost made me sick to my stomach just hearing it and knowing the source.

Carl was already out of the truck before we'd skidded to a complete stop. I jumped out right on his heels and sprinted for my front door. He didn't wait for me and burst into my house. I noticed that he was pulling something from his hip that looked

The First Few Hours

like one of those extending police batons.

Just as I stepped through the doorway, I heard another scream. It was so blood-curdling and terrible. It hurt me deep inside to hear somebody make that noise; knowing that it was Steph caused that pain to burn itself into my soul so deeply that I did not believe the feeling would ever go away even after this was over. A second later, I was hit by the smell. It was the same as I'd detected this morning when I'd left for work, only much stronger and mixed with something coppery.

I had no idea what to expect when I followed Carl down the hallway and to rectangle of light that was the entrance to our bedroom. At first, my eyes could not really comprehend what they were seeing. A dark splatter of blood had sprayed one wall and the drips were making their way down as gravity took charge. There was a strand of black fur on the floor at the foot of the bed that looked like Chewie's tail. The dog was on the far side of the bed and standing between this man who was covered in filth and where Steph had retreated. Somehow, I'd taken the lead from the woodshop teacher and led the way into the room.

Steph was on her knees on the bed, clutching at her left arm that was gushing blood all over her precious white comforter. For some reason, all I could actually think in that second was how angry she was going to be at having her favorite comforter ruined. There was no way all that blood was coming out.

"Hey!" a voice shouted from just behind me and to my left.

Carl shoved past me and was waving that baton in the direction of the man who'd assaulted Stephanie. I climbed up on the foot of the bed, momentarily cursing the fact that she'd insisted on that pedestal which made the bed sit uncommonly high.

The horrid smelling man brought his gaze up to Carl and what I saw made me pause. His eyes were all covered in a sick yellowish film. It reminded me of this lady down the street with really bad cataracts. Only...there was more to it than that. Besides the hideous film that coated them, they were shot through with black tracers. His mouth was coated in red; obviously from having taken a bite out of Stephanie's arm.

Those two things were enough to convince me that something was very wrong with this guy. My eyes tracked down to his right side. The coat and shirt he'd been wearing was shredded and I could see his bare skin underneath. I had no doubt that I was seeing his actual rib bones where the flesh had been savaged.

Are those bite marks? I wondered as Carl swung his baton and connected to the side of the guy's face. I'd just grabbed Steph by the hand of her uninjured arm, but my eyes were focused on a single tooth that I saw fly through the air. I heard it land on our floor with a 'plink' sound and I shuddered involuntarily.

The man was now turning all his attention on Carl. He was reaching for the person who'd just struck him and the mangled mouth opened to emit a low groan. Carl swung again, this time connecting with the upper arm. I heard a nasty crack, but the crazy son-of-a-bitch didn't even appear to notice. He staggered towards Carl and tried to grab the retreating woodshop teacher.

"You seeing this?" Carl grunted as he swung again.

This time I was certain that he'd broken the man's arm as the baton connected with the right wrist. Still this guy gave no indication that he'd been hurt. He staggered another step towards Carl who was now back-pedaling to get clear of the clutching hands that reached for him.

Chewie had jumped up on the bed and come over to me. I saw a nasty trail of blood following her, and I could now confirm that she'd indeed lost most of her tail.

"Evan," Steph cried, "what's happening? What is wrong with that…lunatic?"

"It's just like I was saying." Carl took a few steps back, putting more space between him and the reeking lunatic that I was now certain had to be on drugs in order to take that kind of beating and keep coming.

My mind tried to make sense of Carl's statement. I knew there should be some sort of meaning there, but all I could process at the moment was Steph's crying and obvious need for a doctor, and Chewie's terrible injury.

At last, the fog clouding my brain seemed to clear a bit, and

The First Few Hours

I pulled Steph with me as I made for the doorway. Just as we reached it, I paused long enough to yank open my closet and pull out a couple of belts that were hanging up.

"You paying attention?" Carl called out as I pushed Steph out of our room and then proceeded to back out as well.

I watched as he swung that baton again. This time he struck just above the knee. I heard the crack and saw the leg bend inwards at an unnatural angle.

"What the…" That was all I could manage. This was just not possible. That guy should be on the ground, howling in pain and maybe clutching his ruined left knee. Still he came at Carl; although, he was now titled to one side very noticeably as he staggered forth.

Chewie had squeezed past me, and now Carl and this intruder were the only two people in the bedroom. The amount of blood everywhere gave me pause. Looking at this poor man, I tried to figure out how we would be able to explain this to the police. After all, despite his having attacked Steph and my dog, we (and by "we" I mean Carl), had shattered this guy's wrist, done terrific damage to his knee, and I was almost certain that his one arm had been busted above the elbow.

"C'mon, Carl," I urged. "We need to get out of here and call the cops."

Carl paused, leaned forward, and then gave the injured man a hard shove back before turning to face me. "Do you not see what is right here in front of your eyes?" I opened my mouth to respond, but he talked over me, shutting me up. "This ain't no damn rabies. This is some gee-dee George Romero zombie shit. If'n you're too stupid to see it…let me demonstrate further."

I once again tried to speak, but Carl had already turned his back on me. In a flurry of blows, I watched him shatter bones in the arms and then take out the legs. I wanted to stop him. Part of my brain was screaming at me about the wrongness of what he was doing. I backed away with Steph, moving up the hallway, but still able to see what Carl was doing to Steph's attacker.

"You see what I was saying about this being a gee-dee zombie like in the movies?" Carl called out to us.

DEAD: Onset

It was all just too much. I turned, scooting Steph along towards the front door. She was bleeding, and I needed to get her to the hospital. Something in my head reminded me that I'd had the presence of mind to grab a pair of my belts from the closet.

Turning to Stephanie, I think I registered for the first time just how bad off she was. Her face had drained of all its color and she currently had her eyes squeezed shut.

"I'm gonna get you to the doctor," I said in a rush. I could hear the heavy thuds as Carl continued his merciless beating of the sick man in our bedroom. All of this was reminding me of some bizarre scene from a Tarantino movie. "Before we go, I just want to put this on your arm to hopefully slow down or stop the bleeding."

I had already made a loop with the belt, but now I looked down at her wound and my vision swam for an instant. I bit the inside of my cheek to keep from passing out and then I fixed the belt on her bicep, just a few inches above her elbow. The rip on her forearm was jagged and nasty. I could see flaps of skin and strands of muscle all slick and lubricated with a crimson sheen.

"Steph?" I realized that she'd stopped crying hysterically at some point. I gave her a gentle shake and her eyes flitted open.

I stumbled back out of reflex. Her eyes, once beautiful and shiny...always hinting at mischief, were now unfocused and staring straight ahead. Also, I could see the capillaries darkening almost as I watched.

"We need to get moving, friend." Carl was now standing beside me.

I started to look over my shoulder to the bedroom and he moved into my line-of-sight to keep me from actually seeing what he'd done. But I knew. Yes...in the back of my mind, the knowledge that he'd just beat a man to death in our bedroom was there, and the reality of it was growing. He reached out to guide me the rest of the way up the hall and I jerked from his touch like it scalded my skin.

"I can manage," I said, although I doubt he hardly heard me. My mouth was so dry that the words were more of a rasp than actual intelligible sounds that conveyed how I did not want his

The First Few Hours

help.

I nudged Steph and she took one slow step after another. I was almost to the door when something bumped into my leg hard enough to cause me to stagger. I looked down to see my dog Chewie staring up at me with her big brown eyes.

I felt myself tearing apart from the inside. There was a trail of blood where she'd walked and her tail was dripping. Steph was bleeding from her forearm and had apparently gone into shock.

"I need your help," I said to Carl.

"Your little lady needs the hospital." I thought I heard him mutter *'For whatever good it'll do her now'* under his breath. "I think I'm just gonna walk home."

"Wait...what? You're leaving?"

"I gotta get home and take care of business. If I was you, I'd..." His voice faded and he glanced back over his shoulder. At last, he turned back to face me. "Look, I know you gotta take her to the hospital. I ain't gonna try to talk you out of it." I opened my mouth, but he motioned me to be quiet. "I can tell you ain't ready to believe me yet...but I think you will before long. Just don't wait until it's too late. If I can impress upon you how important it will be to get your missy there checked in and then maybe you come home once they take her in back. Come home and see to your dog maybe."

I glanced down at Chewie. She wagged what was left of her tail and blood splattered the sofa and the television screen with gruesome results.

"I'll patch her as best I can and get that fella out of your bedroom—" That snapped me out of my haze for a moment.

"What about the police?" I blurted.

"I can call 'em, but I don't think they'll be coming too soon. Sounds like they got enough troubles at the moment."

That was when the sounds of sirens filtered in and registered in my consciousness. How was all of this happening so quickly? Maybe I was still asleep and would wake to my alarm any moment now to start my first day as a teacher.

"You need to hurry up and get her to the hospital if there is gonna be any chance at all." Carl was now herding Steph and me to the front door. "You hurry...and don't stop for anybody. When you get to the hospital..." He stopped again and I could tell he was struggling with something as he stared at Steph. "Just you try to remember what I was saying about all this. Nobody is gonna want to believe it. Nobody will accept it for what it is until it's too late. Sad thing is, I think we already tipped past that point and are sliding head first into a big shit storm the like of which none of us are ready to face. Hell, I barely believe it myself."

Somehow, as he'd spoken, Carl had managed to get us to my truck. I thought I saw a few of the onlookers from that crowd at the corner standing in the neighbor's yard. Honestly, if you asked me five minutes from now, I don't know what I would remember.

The truck almost seemed to be driving itself as I made my way to Legacy Hospital. I was oblivious to anything but reaching the beacon of help that the hospital represented.

"Just stay with me, Steph," I kept repeating every few blocks...or maybe it was every few seconds.

Each time I glanced over at her, she was simply staring straight ahead. I doubted that she was seeing anything. Seven times I had to pull over for emergency vehicles of all sorts. Also, I drove past one apartment complex that looked to be swarming with police as well as three ambulances. It was around then that I realized I kept hearing the *pop-pop-pop* of small arms fire. That was when it became clear to me that maybe Steph wasn't the only one in shock.

As I sat behind a Tri-Met bus and waited for the light to change, I physically slapped my face a few times. The first two times barely registered, but by the third time, I felt clarity return. At least I was hoping that was the case.

At last, I pulled into the emergency entrance and miraculously found a place to park. My eyes took in the surroundings and I realized that there were two ambulances in the bay. Things were compounded by the fact that the parking lot looked to be nearing capacity. I wasn't a regular at hospitals, but that seemed

The First Few Hours

to be a bit much.

I climbed out of the truck and made my way around to the passenger side. I opened the door, but Steph was still just staring straight ahead. I undid her seatbelt and took her good hand. She was like a robot, but she climbed out.

"It's a surprise," she said when her eyes finally looked up at me. Tears added some of the shine back, but those dark tracers seemed to be growing darker and lacing her normally beautiful hazel eyes with something terrible.

I was taken aback by her words. They'd been the first she'd uttered since the house where all she had basically done was scream hysterically.

"What's a surprise, Steph?" I asked.

We stood that way for a while, but she had slipped back into shock or whatever it was that had her acting like a…

Zombie? Was I really about to use that word?

I shoved that out of my head along with all the nonsense that Carl had been spewing. Hell, that was probably why that word came to mind. Well, I'd be giving him a dose…if the cops didn't arrest his ass. I wasn't sure they would be able to overlook the fact that he'd busted up that guy so bad despite the fact that the bastard had attacked Steph.

What about those other injuries? the voice in my head piped up, but I shut that down fast as well. I wrapped an arm protectively around Steph as we made our way to the entrance of the emergency room of Legacy hospital. We were almost there when she began to slump against me.

I felt her knees go and moved to scoop her into my arms. Her head lolled back as I began to carry her as fast as I could to those twin sets of double doors. I stepped on the electrical pad that cause the doors to swing open and I rushed inside.

"Help!" I croaked.

DEAD: Onset

2

Legacy

I sat beside the bed and looked down at the still form lying there. The slow but steady beep of the heart monitor was the only thing providing me with any strength at the moment. The last few hours had been a blur of signing forms and answering questions.

When I'd told of the attack, the doctors had barely flinched. There was no look of surprise or astonishment at the fact that a strange man had broken into my house and bitten my fiancée. I'd felt obliged to tell them about Carl and what he'd done. I might not have given every single detail, but I'd told them I was pretty sure that he'd killed the guy.

As they treated Steph, I was asked to wait in the lobby. I'd been certain that the police would come. They would start asking me questions, and then they would go and probably arrest Carl. My mind was already putting things in order as best as possible to hopefully minimize the trouble that the crazy woodshop teacher would get into. After all, he'd taken down the animal that had attacked Steph; that was the least I could do for him.

But they never came.

Every single time those double doors opened, I expected to see men in blue uniforms. They would go to the front desk, ask a question of the intake receptionist and she would point at me.

DEAD: Onset

They would come over and start asking about the murder.

But they never came.

Eventually, a doctor stepped out of the entrance to the emergency room's treatment area and called my name.

"Evan Berry?" the haggard looking doctor shouted over the din of a waiting room that was becoming more crowded by the minute.

I stood and followed him back to the cubicle where they had treated Steph. I'd been told that she was sedated and that a doctor would be coming to talk with me soon.

"You're a doctor," I'd snapped. "Why can't you tell me what is going on? She is going to be fine, right? I mean…people don't die from a bite on the arm no matter how nasty that one happens to be."

"I'm just an intern, and I have no idea about your wife's condition," the man replied flatly. I didn't bother to correct him about our marital status.

He'd swept open the curtain and ushered me inside. I'd stepped over to her bed and then turned to ask another question, but the intern was already gone. I didn't know what else to do, so I just held her hand. The beeps of her monitor my only reassurance as I waited.

And waited.

And waited.

Twice I pulled myself away from my beloved to pull aside the curtain that was our partition. I watched as harried doctors and nurses scurried about like ants in a hill that had been kicked. I knew there was no sense trying to slow one down enough to get any answers. I heard enough yelling and demands being shouted by other frustrated people who were as in the dark about the condition of the person they were with as I was with Steph.

"I don't understand," I whispered, squeezing her hand. "This is all wrong. I just want you to open your eyes and tell me that you are going to be okay."

But she didn't. The hours continued to tick by. I must have slipped off to sleep, because a scream very similar to the one I'd heard from Steph caused me to start. My first reaction was to

Legacy

jump up from my chair and look her over to ensure that nothing had happened during my slumber.

That was when the next sound registered. My mouth went dry as my eyes flashed to the heart monitor whose comforting beeps had acted as the lullaby that sent me to dream land. It had to be wrong. All the numbers were at zero, there was a light flashing, and this annoying buzzer was blaring. I have no idea how long that had been going off or why it hadn't snapped me awake instantly unless it had just started. Honestly, I was so disoriented that I could not be sure.

I quickly turned and ripped open the divider curtain. What I saw was an impossibility. The central nurses' station was empty. There were doctors and nurses fighting with patients all around the emergency room area. I watched as one doctor went down under a trio of patients in their flimsy gowns. A geyser of blood sprayed in syncopation with the failing heartbeat up as the scream turned to a gurgle. A smear of blood at my feet drew my attention to the left where what looked like a paramedic was sprawled flat on her back. A woman was hunched over her and the noise I heard made my stomach lurch. Her gown was gone and she was squatting rather obscenely, her nakedness apparently not something she cared about in the least.

My eyes refused to look away as I shifted just enough to look around the hunched over shoulders of the woman. I guess I had to confirm what my brain was trying to tell me. I watched as blood slicked hands reached into an open cavity that had been torn in the paramedic's abdomen and pulled out strands of things that, up until now, I'd only seen in biology textbooks.

The sounds of screams were coming from every direction and they were of a nature that I'd never experienced. Coupled with the thick and pungent stench that was very much like what I'd smelled from that man in our house, my senses were simply too overwhelmed to allow me to do anything. All I could do at the moment was stand rooted to my spot in the opening to the cubicle where my Steph was lying on a gurney with a monitor that was screaming an unanswered call for help.

Something caught my attention out of the corner of my eye

and I'd forced myself to turn back around. "What the…" My disbelief caused my mouth to go even drier, if that were possible, and my words died deep in my throat as it felt as if my esophagus had shrunk to a pinhole.

Steph was sitting up. Her face was slack and void of any emotion. That normal golden olive tone was gone. Her flesh appeared to be a bluish-gray. Her hair was an unkempt nest that hung lifelessly past her shoulders; but it was her eyes that had me unable to look away. It was the eyes that told me that this was not my Stephanie…my beloved…my fiancée.

Her normally bright hazel eyes were now covered with that same ugly film I'd seen in the eyes of the man who'd attacked her. The black tracers were etched deeper and darker now…a true black.

"No…it isn't possible," I managed past a tongue that felt like sandpaper.

What felt like another person moving fast collided with my back and sent me sprawling into the cubicle. I ended up partially laid out across the foot of the gurney that held Steph. The struggle behind me was a mix of grunts and moans that somehow managed to make it to my ears despite the awful screams and symphony of discordant alarms. It was all becoming just more of the ambient noise that I imagined a person heard when they first arrived in Hell.

Something cool slapped down on my left arm and I turned my head to see that it was Steph's hands. The thing is, I knew her touch. I'd felt it a million times in these past years that she and I had spent together. That touch I was feeling right this moment was *not* her in any way, shape, or form. The feel of her hand on my skin never failed to give me chills. It was having that very same effect; but now it was for an entirely different reason.

I shoved myself away, feeling the tips of her fingers as they lost purchase just as they were about to close over my forearm. The struggle behind me shifted from eerie moans and labored grunts to a whimpering.

"No…no…Marty…it's me!" a voice cried.

Legacy

I looked down to see a young girl no older than fifteen as she pawed at a woman who looked to be in her forties. The girl was on top and looked to be trying to lean in and take a bite out of the woman who lay on her back. I heard the click of teeth snapping together and was about to step in and yank the crazed child off the woman.

Then, a sound made the hairs on my arms and the back of my neck stand up on end and I jerked my head over to where Steph was now struggling to get off of the gurney. *That sound could not have come from her*, I told myself. Then...her mouth opened.

The sound of a baby's cry came from her as she reached for me with both hands and plummeted to the floor when her balance shifted too far to one side. Out of reflex, I lunged to try and catch her. In the process, I stumbled over the two figures that were wrestling on the floor at the entrance to our cubicle.

I ended up in a heap of bodies as the sounds of screaming and begging crashed down on me. Something tugged on my side and I pushed away. It was worse than any nightmare I could recall as I managed to reach a sitting position.

Stephanie seemed to have forgotten about me as she struggled with the flailing arm of the woman who had been trying to fend off the girl she'd identified as 'Marty' a moment ago. That girl had been knocked back against a cabinet and was now on her hands and knees as she crawled back towards the poor woman who was now shrieking as Steph leaned in and took a bite from the arm she held onto.

I could actually see the skin stretch and then rip as Steph's teeth found purchase. Blood welled and then sprayed as a large chunk of meat was torn away. That was when I heard "the scream" again and knew what it signaled.

I'd seen the movies. Oddly enough, I was actually a bit of a fan. Granted, I was a bit more into the more recent titles like the 2004 Zak Snyder remake of *Dawn of the Dead*, but I'd never once considered the possibility. It just wasn't...realistic?

The woman screamed again, her register going from high to ear-splitting in seconds as Steph leaned in and tore away another

DEAD: Onset

chunk of her arm—this time a piece of the bicep. By now, Marty was there at the woman's side and her hands were ripping at the black button-up shirt. The sounds of the plastic buttons bouncing off the tile floor found a way into my ears despite the cacophony of noise.

I started to stand and Steph's head rotated in a slow series of bird-like jerks and fits until her horrifying gaze met mine. There was nothing of her in what I saw. In fact, I could not even look at this thing with the blood dripping from between its lips as it chewed on the raw meat of the shrieking woman's arm and recognize even a hint of the woman I loved with all my heart.

For a split second, I worried that the two creatures crouched on the floor would come after me, but apparently they were content with ripping that poor woman apart. I took one slow step after another as I backed away from the cubicle, but now my head was searching from left to right as more of the fresh Hell that was Legacy's emergency room came into view.

I saw a man on the floor just to my right as he started to sit up. The rip on his belly allowed for a variety of things to come spilling out across the floor as he rolled to his side and onto his knees in order to stand.

The taste of bile was already building in the back of my throat, and my mouth filled with saliva in anticipation, but I forced it down and moved away. My eyes found the 'EXIT' sign across the room. If there was a place I could have been that put me farther away, I didn't know of its existence. A cry for help to my left turned my head, and I watched as a doctor went under two men and a woman who all had the same skin discoloration and tracer-riddled, filmed-over eyes.

I saw a way across the room if I moved now. With one final look back, I had to battle past the pain in my heart as I saw that thing that had once been my Stephanie. She was pulling out a strand of what I had to guess to be intestines from the gaping rip in the soft belly of the woman who was no longer screaming or struggling as she was fed upon by the two figures hunched over her splayed form.

It was tearing me up inside, but my brain was already

screaming for me to run. I took off, planting my hands on the counter of the nurses' station and vaulting over it. At least, that had been my intention.

My right hand found a few pieces of paper that had been left on the counter and it shot out to the side. I slammed into the counter, a stinging pain shooting down my right hip where the bone slammed into the hard, flat surface. I stifled a cry as I threw my right leg up and onto the flat counter space. Heaving myself up, I was about to climb over when the body of what I guessed to have once been a nurse sat up and tilted her face up at me.

Her death had been horrific…but then, which of the ones happening all around me at the moment weren't? Her attacker had taken a bite out of her face, ripping the entire nose away to leave a cavernous hole in the middle. A patch of scalp had been torn away as well, and that had allowed for copious amounts of blood to pour down and create a crimson mask that was now turning dark brown or even black in places. When the mouth opened, a low guttural moan escaped that seemed odd coming from such a petite woman.

I brought my other leg up and around so that I was now seated and facing this thing. As it reached for me, I kicked out as hard as I could and sent it toppling over on its back. Not waiting to see how much the blow affected it, I vaulted off the counter and to the floor where I ran along the large circle with computer monitors and file holders strewn all about my path.

By the time I'd gone halfway around the giant circular station, a few of the mangled occupants had turned to me and were shambling in my direction.

Zombies.

Carl's voice came back to me. *"This ain't no damn rabies. This is some gee-dee George Romero zombie shit. If'n you're too stupid to see it…let me demonstrate further."*

I'd been horrified by what I'd witnessed him do to that…man. Only, now I was surrounded by virtually irrefutable proof of exactly what he'd claimed. Sure, I knew all about the classic zombie of the older generation. In the newer renditions, many of the movies had the zombies coming after people at a full-on sprint. *Thank God that wasn't holding up*, I thought.

I pushed open the small gate that allowed me to exit the nurses' station and started for the doors. I had to be careful not to step in and slip in the blood that was all over the floor, but at last I reached the way out of this terrible place.

When I'd gotten far enough away from the closest zombie, there was an odd peace that settled in my mind as I came to grips with calling these poor souls by the Hollywood name of zombie. Of course, they were really much more than a simple zombie. I'd actually had a friend in my college classes at Portland State who came here from Haiti. One Halloween, he and I had gotten into a conversation about zombies. Needless to say, our ideas were greatly different on what made up such a creature. For one…his weren't actually the dead come back to life. That seemed like a lifetime ago now.

So much was happening so quickly that my mind was having a terrible time coming to grips. I knew that I would probably collapse into a ball and cry my eyes out once I got a few moments to let things sink in. I had just lost the woman that I loved with all my heart, yet, I could not mourn. It was as if my brain was overriding everything as it increased in focus on doing the things that I needed in order to stay alive.

I burst through the double doors into the lobby of the emergency room area. If I'd thought that I was going to find safety or any sort of salvation, I was gravely mistaken. The lobby was almost as much of a nightmare. Just across and to my left, a little boy was on his knees over the body of what I was going to assume had to be his mother. He had a large chunk of something that was jelly-like and almost a purplish color dangling from his blood smeared mouth.

A man was stumbling along between a row of the anchored plastic seats and promptly fell over them when he turned my direction and tried to lunge at me despite being several feet away. There were overturned plants whose dirt added in with the blood on the carpeted floor to create huge, dark stains of nightmarish mud. The entire area was littered with magazines and even a few purses that must've belonged to people who'd either fled in a hurry or become one of...*them.*

"Say it!" I hissed out loud to myself. "It's exactly what that crazy bastard Carl was saying. These are zombies."

My voice drew the attention of a few more of the undead that were wandering around the lobby. It was time for me to get the hell out of here. I could still hear the screams coming from behind me, but they were growing fewer and farther between.

From where I now stood, I could look out the main entrance doors. I was stunned to discover that it was night. A car had crashed in the entrance and was doing a great job of blocking the way out. Darkness had thrown a blanket over the city and I'd spent the entirety of this day in the hospital at Stephanie's side. I took a few steps toward the doors, my eyes darting around the open area to keep tabs on every one of the zombies present—there were currently seven—and make sure that they were not going to get ahead of me and cut off my exit.

As I neared the exit, I could see a large SUV in the drop-off area. It was sort of parked at an awkward angle and the doors were wide open, but there was no sign of anybody. I glanced around wondering if maybe the driver and/or passenger might be one of the poor souls now stumbling after me. That look back also revealed that the mother who had just moments ago been on the floor being chomped on by that little boy was now struggling to her feet. She was just joining in the slow-motion pursuit of me, but oddly enough, the child appeared to be hanging back. It was clear he had his eyes glued to me, but he was just standing there.

I snapped my head back around at the sounds of sirens coming from out front. No sooner did I refocus my attention on the exit when the red and blue strobes of police vehicles began to dance before my eyes.

I think I'd been moving so slow because my unconscious mind was none too eager to step outside despite what was happening in this hospital. With the arrival of numerous Portland Police vehicles, suddenly my legs found a new speed. I made a run for it and scrambled over the car that was jutting through where it had crashed into the entrance. I was only vaguely aware that there was at least one occupant inside, but I didn't care.

I slid across the hood and down the back. Coming to my feet on the trunk, I began to wave my arms wildly as over a dozen squad cars now occupied the driveway to Legacy Hospital.

"Please!" I managed. Honestly, I was simply unable to think of anything else to say.

"Step this way, sir!" a voice boomed from the PA of the closest squad car.

As I did, I could see police officers piling out of the back of a huge van. They were all dressed like some sort of assault team with guns poking up over their shoulders as well as helmets that had little spotlights on them. One of them rushed past me and I could hear the tinny crackle of the radio in his ear.

"Bravo Team assembled at the emergency room entrance and preparing to enter," the man said as he broke into a jog towards the hellscape I'd just exited.

I staggered past another trio of armed and armored personnel who were walking into something I did not feel any amount of training could prepare them for. In that instant, I regretted any and all thoughts I'd had about police officers and their media foibles when it came to the use of force. Suddenly, I thought that just maybe, these past few years, we had been taking the teeth out of the one thin veneer we had as civilians to protect us from the monsters—in whatever form they might appear.

An officer in the standard blue uniform stepped to me and threw a blanket over my shoulder as he ushered me to the back of another open van with a huge Portland Police Special Response Team logo and shield on the side. A moment later, another person stepped up and shone a light in my eyes.

"Are you injured?" a female voice said with clinical sterility.

"What? No...I don't think so." I doubted they wanted to hear that my soul was shattered and my heart obliterated.

"Are you certain?" came the clipped reply.

I looked up in the woman's face and was about to tear into her when my mouth actually snapped shut. I did not need a flashlight to see the black tracers in the woman's eyes. It was not a trick of the lighting for her skin to be the pale and sickly color it appeared. My eyes tracked down to her left arm where a bandage peeked out from the cuff of her sleeve.

"You're bit," I rasped.

She glanced down at her arm and then back at me. "Just a little rip above the wrist. Barely broke the skin," she said dismissively, but the squint of her eyes gave away her discomfort.

"Maybe you should be the one sitting here," I tried to joke, but her expression did not register even the slightest tinge of a smile.

"No, we are understaffed as it is." She gave a dismissive wave. "Now, if you are sure that you are okay, I will head over to the triage tent they are setting up. Looks like this is going to be a long night."

The EMT or paramedic or whatever she was turned and walked away. My eyes tracked her, and I saw her pause once and lean on the hood of a nearby parked car for a moment. Her head drooped and I waited to see if she would collapse. After a moment, she stood and continued on towards what appeared to be a white tent that was going up much faster than any tent I'd ever pitched while camping.

I sat a few moments longer just to try and catch my breath. The first time that I tried to stand, my legs shook so bad that my knees started to buckle. I looked down at my hands and they were trembling in a way that cold had never caused. The more I tried to get them to stop…the worse it got.

The sounds of gunfire made me jump, and I decided that, shakes be damned, I was leaving. I forced myself to stand and started for my truck. I was briefly reminded of popcorn popping as the gunfire would come in waves of furious activity and then die down to a few random pops and bangs.

When I climbed into the front seat, my nose was assaulted by the coppery smell of blood from where I had to imagine Steph had been slowly bleeding out. I shoved that thought away and rolled down my window. I pulled out of my space and wove through a parking lot that looked like a wrecking yard in places. I could see where numerous vehicles had crashed into or bumped off of each other in peoples' haste to get here.

As I made my way onto MLK Boulevard, I began to notice something. There was almost no automobile traffic. As for pedestrians, they were out in numbers that seemed way out of the ordinary.

I passed by a pair that were on the sidewalk in front of one of those open bay car washes. The bright fluorescent lighting washed out their skin complexion, but it also made the dark stains on their clothing stand out all that much more. I did not need to get close to know that I was seeing bloodstains.

One of them turned towards me and stumbled out into the street. The entire front of him was darkened with blood, be it fresh or old, it was impossible to tell. His arms extended, and he was grasping at the air like he thought he could just grab my truck and capture it with his bare hands. I had to swerve at the last second to avoid hitting him. He passed by my driver's side and I could see that his throat looked like little more than a big black hole underneath his chin.

As I turned up Powell, I spotted a roadblock made up of large military trucks and a single police car. I did not feel like dealing with that just yet. I wanted...no, I *needed* to get home.

I yanked to the right on my steering wheel and drove into the residential area. Streetlights were hit and miss in this neighborhood. To add to the eerie quality, many of the houses were shrouded in darkness. Whether it was due to the residents trying to hide their presence or because they were gone, I had no idea. Whatever the case, there was no lack of cars parked along the curbs on both sides making my navigating just a bit more precarious. Twice, something stepped out of the shadows and bounced or collided off the rear section of my truck.

My instincts always caused me to take my foot off the gas for a few seconds, but the images of what I'd witnessed induced me to accelerate sooner rather than later. I turned left to try and make my way back to the main road and get out of the maze of confined spaces and found myself almost bumper-to-bumper with a large olive-colored troop transport truck.

"Stop your vehicle!" a soldier called as I started to shift into reverse.

For a split second, I considered slamming into reverse, punching the gas, and trying to escape. The biggest obstacles to that were the confined space I was already in which severely limited my ability to maneuver, and the fact that driving backwards looks really cool on TV and in the movies, but doing it well at any speed faster than a crawl is not in most people's skillset. That would certainly include me.

I rolled down my window and leaned out. "I'm just trying to get home, sir," I called out. The soldier stepped forward, his features coming into better focus. I'd just called a kid that looked like he might've just graduated high school last year 'sir.'

"We can't let you through this way," the soldier said as he approached my window. "Nasty business up there just block or so."

"What sort of nasty business?" I asked.

"Can't really say," the soldier replied.

Can't, or won't, I wondered.

"Also, you may want to turn on your radio, there have been announcements the past few hours about civilians getting off the streets." The soldier took a step back and gave me a nod.

I sighed as I backed up and crept further into the darkness of the Southeast Portland neighborhood. I punched the button and turned on my radio.

"…reports now coming in from all over the city that more widespread violence…"

I hit the button to another station.

"…out of Washington that the president has sent a detachment to Ohio where his daughter is enrolled in college…"

Another.

"…that no communication has come out of Japan in the past several hours is certainly cause for speculation that…"

And another.

"…fires reportedly burning out of control as emergency crews are stretched beyond capacity prompting the mayor to issue a plea for citizens to refrain from using the 9-1-1 service until…"

DEAD: Onset

Click.

I shut the radio off.

My head was spinning. How could this happen so fast? And then I began to recall the little stories popping up over the past several days that told of illness spreading in a small town in Kentucky to the point where the CDC sent in a team and was shortly joined by a National Guard detachment. I'd simply ignored them. For one…they were in Kentucky. How did that have anything to do with me here in Oregon and the beautiful Pacific Northwest?

At last, I pulled into my cul-de-sac. What I saw almost made me drive up onto the curb. The houses on either side of mine were dark and the driveways empty. The house across the street was in stark contrast with every single light on. The front door was wide open and it looked like the resident was moving with all the boxes loaded into the back of a trailer that I'd never seen before.

I pulled into my driveway and shut off the truck, climbing out into the chilly spring air. That was the first time in a while that I could recall having been aware of anything so mundane as temperature.

"Evan?" a voice called from behind me. That would be my across-the-street neighbor, Grady Simons. I think he's lived in this neighborhood since the Seventies or something. He was always the first one outside to start cleaning up after a windstorm or show up at your door if he saw you doing something that might benefit from another set of hands.

"Grady," I said in greeting.

"I heard that something happened to Stephanie earlier."

My mouth went dry and somehow I ended up sitting on my butt in the middle of the road. Hands were on my shoulders and I had to blink a few times before my vision cleared enough so that I could see. It took me a few seconds to realize that my eyes were filled with tears.

"Jesus, kid, you okay?"

"No…I'm not," I managed. I looked up into the dark-skinned man's face, not at all embarrassed about the fact that I was suddenly crying like a baby. "She's…she's dead."

"What?" I heard the incredulous tone, but it was fading to more of a buzz as he continued to speak. "Are you sure? Crap, of course you are, sorry."

It was like saying those words ripped off all the blinders that shock had put on me the past several hours. Somehow, I think I had simply managed to put that single very important fact out of my head up until now. The problem with that was that time seemed to have acted to concentrate my pain into something that stole my breath and reduced me to the blubbering mess that I was at this moment.

"Let's get you out of the road," Grady said as he pulled me to my feet.

I could hear an urgency in his voice that sounded totally foreign. Grady Simons was a lot of things, but I don't think "in a hurry" had ever been used in a sentence with him for as long as I'd known him.

As if to provide context to this abnormal behavior, a soft, low moan carried on the air. It was answered by a series of agitated barks from a dog somewhere close. I followed Grady to his house and looked over to see the neatly stacked boxes that had about two-thirds of his trailer full.

Once inside, it looked like no kind of packing that I'd ever seen before. There were boxes everywhere, many partially full without any apparent rhyme or reason. The one closest to me as I took a seat on the couch was a perfect example. I saw boxes of bar soap, unopened packages of underwear, and several assorted canned veggies and tins of sardines.

"Goin' on a trip?" I asked as Grady pulled his door shut and then peered out the open curtain of the huge picture window that dominated his living room.

"You gotta know what's goin' on out there," Grady said absently as he continued to look out into the relative darkness.

"How bad?" That was all I could manage.

"The reports are lagging, but it is on every channel. And when I say that, I'm talking all the way down to the Cartoon Network. They stopped running warnings about disturbing content a few hours ago because there was no longer any content that wasn't disturbing." Grady moved away from the curtains. "Funny thing is that the government is still in full denial mode. They got some prissy bitch named Linda Sing from the CDC claiming that we ain't looking down the barrel of a zombie uprising."

I noticed he hadn't used the word 'apocalypse' just now. Did that mean there was still hope?

"I heard that Japan went dark," I offered.

"Heh…" He made a funny sound in his throat that could have been a laugh. "That's the tip of the iceberg. Japan, China, Indonesia, and both North and South Korea have not returned any attempts at communication for the past several hours. Of course, the media isn't making that a big part of what they are telling. That is mostly being shared on the internet…least it was 'til the damn thing tripped offline. Supposedly you can still get on, but it is jammed up more often than not if you try, and all you get is anything from the page not being found to your little hourglass just turning over and over and over."

I glanced over at the television and saw the name Dr. Linda Sing on the banner at the bottom of the screen. I looked around for a remote but had no luck spotting one.

"Can I hear that?" I asked.

Grady turned to the television and made a disgusted sound in his throat. "They been running that clip since this morning." Grady walked over to the television and pushed a button to send the volume bar creeping across the bottom of the screen.

"… to address the issue of a peculiar illness that is apparently sweeping the country. While we are still in the preliminary stages of trying to figure this out, I want to make one thing clear." The woman leaned forward at the podium a bit and made it a point to almost glare into the camera. Her mirthless face looked as if she had perhaps not allowed a smile to creep across her lips in many years. The bright lights only washed out her features that much more. "Those rumors of the dead coming back and attacking the living are beyond ludicrous. Ignoring the pure physiological impossibility, there is simply no way this can

Legacy

be considered with any seriousness." A chorus of voices off camera began shouting questions, but the doctor held up her hands. "There is nothing further to report at the moment, but I assure we are working hard on the issue, thank you."

Grady thumbed the button again and turned the volume down as a talking head appeared on the screen and began to speak as an image appeared over his right shoulder of what looked to be helicopter footage of a riot in downtown.

"They ain't gonna cop to this until it's too late," the man said with a tired sigh. He shook his head and turned back to me. "That's why I'm heading out…tonight. And I would suggest you do the same."

"Where are you headed?" I asked, genuinely curious.

"Out of the city."

I guess that was as good of an idea as any. Still, despite all I'd seen, I wasn't exactly ready to abandon everything and run for the hills.

"I wouldn't hold off for too long," Grady said as if he could read my thoughts.

I sat silently for a moment. Grady gave me a sad look and then disappeared into his kitchen. I heard the sounds of pots and pans being thrown about. Actually, it literally sounded like he was throwing them around the room.

My eyes returned to the television and I saw that they were rolling footage of what looked like one of those more upscale apartment complexes. An entire three-story building containing several units was a raging inferno and there was not a single fire truck in the picture. The reporter was well down the parking lot from the building and the camera kept scanning the scene. I pushed myself up from the couch and knelt in front of the TV, bumping up the volume just enough so that I could hear what the reporter was saying.

"…over an hour now, and there has still been no response by the local fire department. Even more telling is the complete lack of any police presence. While we have seen a few cars zip past with lights and sometimes even sirens blaring, not one has bothered to stop here as the Lakeside Apartments continue to burn…"

I turned the volume back down and stuck my head in the kitchen to see Grady on his knees under the sink. He was tossing things out over his shoulders for the most part. Occasionally he would set something down beside where he knelt.

"Take care of yourself, Grady," I called.

He banged his head coming out from underneath and I winced. He moved around until he was seated on the kitchen floor with his legs out in front and he rested his back against the cupboard doors to the right of the open cabinet he'd been ransacking—for lack of a better description.

"I'd tell you to do the same, Evan. But I see a look in your eyes that tells me I might be wasting my breath." I cocked my head at him and raised an eyebrow in what I hoped would be seen as an invitation to elaborate. "That pretty little gal of yours is gone, and you don't see what else there might be worth fightin' for. And I can tell you this…a fight is a comin' and it ain't one nobody is ready to take on."

That all seemed a bit over-dramatic for somebody as laid back as Grady. Not too many folks were as easy going…especially in these days where everything moved at light speed and constantly threatened to sweep you off your feet if you stayed put for too long. For just a moment, I thought he was finished with what he'd been saying; then he resumed his micro-lecture. "That gal wouldn't want you to just roll over, and I gots me a feeling that is exactly what you'll be tempted to do. If not now, then soon. And often."

I was pondering his statement when an explosion sounded from frighteningly close by. I ran for the front door and threw it open. A chemical smell filled the night air and I turned to the left towards what I knew to be Foster Road. A roiling cloud of black smoke and flames reached achingly skyward.

"The Space Age," Grady's voice came from just behind me.

That was the closest gas station, and one that I'd probably stopped at a couple hundred times in the past few years. I wasn't sure how it had started or what had managed to get past all the safety measures and such built in at most modern gas stations. I knew there were supposed to be kill switches or something to prevent such a thing from happening. I did know one thing for sure, and it was Grady who voiced those thoughts out loud.

"Wind is blowin' this way, and ain't no firemen coming to put it out any time soon. This little neighborhood is toast."

DEAD: Onset

3

The Punch in the Gut

I'd almost been afraid of what I would find when I walked in the front door. Carl had been true to his word in that he'd disposed of the body. What he hadn't bothered to do was tidy up afterwards. A nasty, dark smear ran from our hallway to the side door that opened out into the little covered awning over the head of the driveway.

My curiosity got the best of me and I found myself following the trail. I stepped back outside and marched like a lemming to its doom as I approached the metal shed where our bicycles and all our yard tools were stored. Pulling the aluminum door open, the stench of hot death roiled out and went up my nose in a rush of foul unpleasantness that had me fighting back the urge to be sick.

I slammed the shed closed and returned inside. I could hear the occasional sounds of cars honking their horns or people shouting. That was mixed in with sporadic gunfire and I must have just stood in the middle of my living room…our living room…for what seemed like forever but was likely just a few minutes.

I could feel a bout of hysterics trying to build and made every effort to force it down. Maybe a time would come that I could allow that, but if the dam broke now, I might not ever be able to repair it. I would sit here in my living room as the flames from that gas station fire engulfed me, the house, and put an end to it all. I had to tell myself that such an outcome was not acceptable.

I walked into the kitchen and looked around. If I was leaving for good, then what was tops on my priority list of 'must have' items? My eyes drifted to the wall beyond our tiny kitchen table. They came to rest on a framed picture of me and Steph taken at Timberline Lodge. That photograph had been my favorite picture of her. It captured her most perfect smile, she had rosy cheeks from the cold and her eyes sparkled. The white background of the snow-covered lodge set off her dark hair seamlessly. I grabbed it and tucked it under my arm.

Food and all that would probably be easier to find than things like clothes and other items. I headed down the dark hallway to our room, doing my best to ignore the dark trail that ran the length. When I reached the bedroom door, I paused.

Had I been imagining things? I could've sworn that I heard something. Whatever it was had a deep resonance to it. I froze, standing stock still, every nerve in my body seeming to thrum with electricity. I was rewarded seconds later when I heard the sound again; this time certain that it had come from my room.

That was when I realized I wasn't carrying a weapon. Whether this was the honest-to-goodness zombie apocalypse or not, being without a weapon right now was foolish.

The problem existed in the fact that the remedy was in our bedroom closet on the top shelf, behind all kinds of crap. I was about to take a very stupid risk when a voice in my head reminded me of the variety of tools in our shed.

I hurried to it as quiet as possible. Opening the door to outside was a reminder that I needed to act with haste. The fire was spreading. I was seeing little orange embers drifting to the ground as nearby trees had now become part of the conflagration. I held my breath as I opened the shed once more and was thankful that I'd been so insistent about everything being put in its place. A hand axe hung above the multi-drawered tool box and I grabbed it.

Heading back inside, I froze for just a moment when the

The Punch in the Gut

sound of one of those terrible screams cut through all the other general racket that seemed to be growing louder and more discordant with each passing minute.

I headed back up the hall and stopped at my door once more. Forcing myself to try and calm down just a bit, I held my breath and listened for that sound. I was rewarded almost immediately as the low resonance drifted to my ears.

Being as careful and as quiet as possible, I pushed the door open slowly. Despite the time that had passed and the fact that the body had been moved outside, the bedroom had a foul stench that made my nose wrinkle. Dark stains were on the walls and the once pristinely white bed was a sight out of a horror movie.

Curled up in the middle of it was a huge dark shape. The sound I'd heard came again from the dark form and I felt my body slump as I recognized the sounds of snoring that Chewie was so famous for.

"Hey, girl," I whispered.

The massive head lifted very slowly and craned around to regard me. When the head tilted to the side and a low rumble came from deep in the chest of my Newfoundland, I froze.

Did dogs turn? I wondered briefly.

I reached over and flicked on the light switch for the room and instantly regretted it. The dark stains were much more terrible in the light. Chewie sort of crawled towards the foot of the bed and I was able to see strips of cloth wrapped around and secured to the small bit of tail that remained.

I walked over and was greeted by Chewie rising up and slathering my face with her huge, sloppy tongue. That was the one thing we'd been warned about when we first looked into getting a Newfoundland; they are sorta famous for their drool. Chewie was no exception. I remembered many nights when she would sit just a few feet from the dinner table and stare at me and Steph as we ate. There would literally be a puddle of drool at her feet as she regarded us hopefully, waiting for the tidbits that she knew were sure to come.

"How you doin', girl?" I said in a hoarse whisper as I knelt down and grabbed her huge head in my hands and put my forehead to hers. She tilted up and gave me another lick on the face as if to say, *I've been better, but I am sure glad that you're home.*

As much as I wished that I could simply flop down onto the floor and hug my dog, I needed to get it in gear. I would not be able to load much, but I could at least grab a few things before getting out of here ahead of the approaching fire. I gave Chewie a pat on the head and walked into the kitchen. When I passed through the living room, I switched on the television.

"...have lost that feed," the reporter was saying. I paused to get a look and was a little surprised by what I saw.

One thing about the people on television news that you could usually count on was an immaculate appearance. Their hair was always neat and their clothes were clean. The man staring into the camera was none of those things. His washed-out features led me to believe that he hadn't gone to the make-up chair. I could see stubble beginning to darken his jaw, and his hair looked like he'd been running a marathon before sitting at the desk. It was plastered to his forehead, and with the advent of HD, I had no trouble seeing the sweat trickling down his temples.

"We here at Channel Eight wish to send our hopes and prayers to field reporter Michele Takimi and her cameraman, Steve Herns." He sat up straight and leaned forward as if he might be straining to read something. After a few seconds, he gave a nod.

"We have been told that our duty here is now at an end. This network will be switching to the Emergency Broadcasting Network in just a moment. As we do, I want to wish you all the best and hope that we will overcome this terrible event. God bless the people of this state, the United States, and the rest of the world."

There was a moment where the man just continued to stare into the camera, and then the screen filled with a symbol noting that the Emergency Broadcasting Network was now active and that a message was forthcoming.

I headed into the kitchen and grabbed the large plastic container that we kept our empty soda cans in so we could collect

The Punch in the Gut

the deposit. It felt strange when I tipped the container and let the cans spill across the floor. After wiping out the inside, I went to the cupboard and tossed in all the dry and canned foods. Sadly, the container was less than half full when I finished.

An idea struck me and I rushed back out to that horrible shed once more. Our large cooler that we used for camping was sitting in the corner. I had to step over the dead zombie to do so, and that made me pause for a few heartbeats as I gathered my nerve and triple-checked to make sure it was truly dead-dead. I snagged it and turned to go back inside the house.

The smell hit me first, even stronger than that put off by the body already on the floor here in the shed. I'd been to focused on my task and ignoring my surroundings. If I wanted any chance at survival, I needed to get my head on straight.

Standing in the doorway and blocking my exit was a dark figure. The beehive hairdo told me it was our neighbor at the head of the cul-de-sac.

I stepped back and almost tripped over the dead body already littering the floor. The dark form advanced and let loose a low moan that I heard echoed from not too far away. That meant I had even less time than I'd thought.

In the movies, people usually have no trouble flipping that switch that turns them into some sort of badass zombie killer. In that moment, I wished I could find that switch. Twice I batted the reaching hands aside, unable to put the axe I held in my hand into play.

I felt a cold dead hand brush my cheek at the same time my back found the wall of the shed. That was apparently what it took to flip the switch. I raised my arm and brought the axe down hard right in the middle of my funky-haired neighbor's forehead. When she fell, the axe pulled free and I stood there over the body for an indeterminate amount of time. I might have prayed for forgiveness…honestly, I couldn't say. My brain was getting fuzzy, but eventually I collected the cooler that I had obviously dropped at some point and headed back to the house.

My gaze drifted to my right and I saw that Grady had left at some point. His house remained open, but the truck and trailer in

DEAD: Onset

the driveway were gone.

"Good luck," I whispered.

Up the street I could see a few forms moving along. The fire over on Foster was drawing closer, and the flickering light was casting everything in dancing shadows that amped up the creepy factor.

I went inside, determined to be loaded and on the move within the half hour. Chewie was waiting at the door. The fact that she wasn't jumping and barking at all the strange activity was evidence to me of how much her tail injury must be hurting.

"I'll take care of us, girl," I said as I passed by and gave her a pat that was probably more for my own reassurance than hers.

As I passed the television, I noticed that somebody was talking. I paused to listen despite the fact that the voice in my head was urging me to hurry and get out of here.

A man in a rumpled suit came to a podium. The American flag hung on one side. The man wiped his hand down his face and then looked up at the camera.

"My fellow Americans, we are currently dealing with a situation that is unprecedented. As I address you, the president and several key members of the cabinet are en route on Air Force One to a secure location. They will be working endlessly with the CDC until a solution to this strange epidemic is found. We ask that you please heed the announcements from your state and local officials as we take the steps to stem this horrific tragedy that is being suffered around the world.

"In a moment, your local emergency broadcasting systems will inform you of what to do. Afterwards, the president will address the country. God bless America, and the rest of the world, as we can hopefully come together and resolve this crisis."

There was an instant as the man gathered whatever he had brought to the podium where the camera lingered on his face. Just like the local reporter I'd seen a few moments ago, I saw the sweat running down in rivers. This guy was just as afraid as everybody else.

The screen returned to the EBS test signal. The ticker informed me that an announcement from the local network would

The Punch in the Gut

be carrying region-specific information in one moment. Time felt sluggish, but at last there was a camera shot of a large desk. The Oregon state flag was on one side, the American flag on the other. A gray-haired man in a suit sat behind the desk with a few sheets of paper. He seemed surprised by something and then looked up at the camera.

"People of the Portland-metro and surrounding areas, we are facing something that is unique in our history. There is a terrible virus or contagion that is sweeping through not only our city, but the world. As reports flood in from around the world, the symptoms are consistent.

"This is what we know for certain. Those infected are currently described as hostile and displaying violent, cannibalistic characteristics. The CDC has confirmed that this disease is communicable. There is no known prevention other than to avoid contact at all costs.

"Local hospitals have ceased accepting victims of attack. You are directed to bring any person bitten but still alive to stations set up by the police and National Guard. Currently in the Portland-metro area the following locations are set up as monitoring sites: The Rose Quarter, PGE Park, Roosevelt High School, Beaverton High School, Gresham High School, Tigard High School, Forest Grove High School, and Franklin High School. Be advised that more sites are planned, and that those who must use the Rose Quarter or PGE Park will be directed to a FEMA-run emergency shelter where they will be asked to provide information on the person or persons they delivered. At each high school, that information will be obtained at a designated checkpoint established in the vicinity. There will be signs clearly designating routes to take. Also, be advised that you should only use the Rose Quarter and PGE Park if you're in the immediate vicinity."

I had to admit, that last bit made perfect sense. While some people might actually feel better in one of those larger facilities, an influx of people heading downtown would create a nightmarish gridlock.

"Additionally, the president is expected to speak at seven

Pacific Time, approximately eighteen minutes from now. Martial law is expected to be declared on a national level, and Portland is already in the process of recalling all members of the National Guard.

"I ask you now to please follow the instructions you will see on the screen and do your part to keep the peace here in our beautiful city. If you are listening on the radio, this message will be repeated on a loop until the president speaks. After his address, your local stations will be broadcasting continuous updates of what to do. We will get through this, but only if we stick together as a community."

The man smiled and tapped the pages on the desk as if to signal that he was finished. There was a flash, and then the EBS pattern returned. The crawler began scrolling the high points of the national and local addresses as well as the locations to bring those who were infected.

"Wow," I breathed. "I guess it's official."

Honestly, to have it all said like that suddenly made it real. I'd been doing my best to come to grips with the idea of zombies like the ones in the movies, but now a person behind a desk wearing a suit—no matter how rumpled—had just given this a solidity that it had lacked.

As much as I'd dismissed the media and its overblown hype machine…there was power in seeing this announcement on the television.

"We need to get moving, Chewie," I said.

As if she understood exactly what I was saying, the big Newfoundland lumbered to the front door and sat down beside where her leash and collar hung from a peg. I made a whirlwind tour of the house and grabbed the things I felt most essential. I was in the process of grabbing a stack of blankets when I heard a tremendous crash from out front.

I hurried to our living room window and peered outside to see Grady's house in flames. A tree in his backyard had fallen across the roof and caved in the far end of the house where the bedrooms were located. The heat was now something I could feel. Like it or not…ready or not…it was time to go.

The Punch in the Gut

I told Chewie to stay while I hauled the pitifully few boxes and stacks of things I thought I might need into the back of the pickup. The two things I'd been certain to take on the first trip were the picture from the kitchen and the box in our bedroom closet that held the case containing my Ruger .357. The three boxes holding a hundred rounds each suddenly did not seem like much. Still, it was better than nothing.

I ran to the bathroom with a pillow case. I figured that I would just grab everything in the medicine cabinet and our toothbrush drawer and be ready. I was scooping things into the open cloth case when my eyes registered something sitting on the counter. I might have stared at it for several seconds, still just grabbing everything and dropping whatever my hands clutched into the opening, my actions slowing incrementally until at last I stopped.

The realization of what I was looking at gave me a sick feeling. I set the partially full pillow case down and then just stood there with my hands on my hips. Suddenly, I felt like Brad Pitt at the end of *Seven* when he kept pleading with Morgan Freeman.

"What's in the box?"

I reached down and picked up the object. Turning it over in my hands, I felt my throat tighten once more. Tears were already welling in my eyes. But they were not so bad as to keep me from seeing the little "positive" in the window of the pregnancy test.

"It's a surprise."

Steph had uttered those words in her delirium. This had to be what she'd been referring to when she'd said them. I staggered back against the wall and slid down to the floor.

"Noooo," I wailed and threw the little plastic wand.

It hadn't been bad enough that I lose the woman I love? I looked up at the ceiling, my eyes boring a hole straight to the heavens. I couldn't be considered a religious man, but if there was a God, then it was to that entity that my scream of rage was directed. I heard something and felt the nudge of my faithful dog as she came to see what could possibly be causing her master this much distress.

I felt more tears trickle down my cheeks and closed my eyes

as Chewie's tongue wiped them away as fast as they could appear. I threw my arms around her neck and I bawled. At one point, I briefly wondered if I would be able to stop. It truly felt as if something inside of me had shattered into a million unrepairable bits.

I don't remember her disengaging, but at some point she had done so and was now in the living room, barking and whining. I could smell smoke now and knew that my time here had come to an end unless I wanted to just give up and die.

Now it was Grady's prophetic words that came to mind. *"That pretty little gal of yours is gone, and you don't see what else there might be worth fightin' for. And I can tell you this...a fight is a comin' and it ain't one nobody is ready to take on."*

The thing is, fighting was never my thing. Not that I allowed myself to be pushed around, but I simply was not the kind of guy to go looking for a fight. Being punched sucked. I'd been in a scrap shortly after Steph and I had started dating. One of the guys on the construction crew I was with had made a lewd comment about her. I'd politely explained that I did not appreciate what he'd said and asked that he not do so again. He had not accepted those terms.

The actual fight had been brief. Supposedly, I'd been considered the victor due to him ending up out cold. I'd managed to land a lucky shot right on the point of his chin. Still, my hands had been swollen and sore for a week. Also, my busted lip and black eye hadn't felt much like what I imagined winning should feel like.

By the time I'd finished loading and brought Chewie out to the truck, one of the bushes in my front yard was smoldering and threatening to go up at any moment. I gave one last look back at the house where so many of my hopes and dreams would go unrealized.

"I am going to fight my hardest," I vowed. Whether it was to myself or something that I put out in the cosmos in the hopes that Steph would know, I have no idea.

I climbed into the cab and looked up to the end of the street where the exit of the cul-de-sac emptied onto the main road. The

The Punch in the Gut

fire had already jumped across the street, so both sides were sporting twin pillars of smoke and flame. It was gonna be warm on the way out, that was for certain. Add in the dozen or so figures that were limping and shambling with apparent aimlessness and this was going to be an exit worthy of any action hero.

"Hang on, Chewie," I whispered, giving the dog a scratch behind one ear.

The engine turned over and I noticed all of the closest walking dead turn as if they heard me. I would file that away as the first item to get confirmation of when I had the time and opportunity: *Zombies react to sound.*

I shifted the truck into drive and eased out onto the street. I hadn't really been paying attention when I got home, but the whole block was strewn with debris. There were loose articles of clothing tumbling in the breeze that was driving the fire this direction. I also noticed that two of my neighbors' houses looked abandoned, but their front doors were wide open.

The second house on the left is what made me apply the brake and pause despite the urgency that churned in my belly. All the lights appeared to be on and the curtains open wide. At the front room window, a figure stood, pawing at the glass.

"Missus Browner," I said to the night air.

Mrs. Browner was in her early fifties. Her husband had died from a heart attack about five months ago and there was a lot of speculation that her constant screaming and nagging that could be heard all up and down the street was likely the greatest culprit.

The woman, at least on the surface, was absolutely beautiful. Sadly, her core was toxic. She was always complaining that somebody's garbage had been knocked over and blown into her yard, or scolding people for not keeping their yards and flowerbeds in the same immaculate shape that hers were in—at least until her husband died. If not for the kindness of others, it would've been hard to tell where her lawn ended and the rose garden along the front of the house began before long.

Ever since her husband passed, she had rarely been seen or heard. The only reason her yard had been mowed was because of

DEAD: Onset

Grady. He'd done it one Sunday while she'd been at church. That was the only day of the week you might catch a glimpse of her, and then only as she walked to and from her car.

Her left arm came up to slap at the window and I could see the fouled bandage that was now only still in place because of the dried blood that had it cemented to her skin. I could not recall the number of times I made snide and nasty remarks about that woman. Now...I felt pity. She had died alone, probably scared, and in a lot of pain most likely.

I eased past the flames and looked around at the destruction caused and likely to worsen with the fire raging out of control. Houses and small businesses were adding copious amounts of fuel. This neighborhood was packed in nice and tight. Add in the fact that we loved our trees, and it was all too easy for the unchecked blaze to hop from one building or residence to the other.

Once I managed to get away from the worst of it, I decided that it might be best for me to head over to Franklin High School. It had been listed as an emergency shelter location.

As I drove, I was seeing a lot of empty police and assorted other emergency vehicles parked askew here and there. None of them showed signs that their occupants were anywhere nearby.

I pulled up to a pair of squad cars and put the truck in park. My throat tightened reflexively and my stomach turned at what I saw. Sprawled beside the open passenger door was what remained of a policeman. I could not begin to imagine the pain he must've endured.

His left arm was a few feet away from what remained of the upper half of his body. Just across the street, I spied a pair of the undead hunched over what had to be one of his legs. His insides were in a gory heap around the mangled and broken remains of his torso. What added to this macabre scene was the fact that the policeman had turned and his head was aimed at me. His dead eyes were locked onto my pickup and his remaining arm was reaching impotently for me despite the fact that the truck was a good ten feet away.

My eyes drifted to the pistol sitting just a few feet from him, basically in the middle of the road. Just past that was a section of

The Punch in the Gut

his belt with a small oblong case that I was guessing held a few spare magazines.

Scattered not too far from all that were four zombies that had obviously met their end here when this poor guy made his last stand. I considered my chances and took a look around to ensure that, other than the leg-munchers just across the street, there were no other zombies wandering around.

"You stay put, Chewie," I said to the big dog that seemed just as interested in what was going on outside the relatively safe confines of the truck's cab as I.

As quietly as possible, I pressed the lever and eased my door open. The rush of sound was surprising and made me realize how insulated I was against the world while in the cab of my pickup.

Now that I could hear more clearly, I almost wished that I'd stayed in the truck. Screams carried on the night. They were all terrible in their own way, but some stood out. When the source of one scream or another managed to include a few words of obviously unheeded begging and pleading, it made me want to be sick. I heard cries for mothers, fathers, God. As far as that last one, I just don't think He is listening anymore.

Scattered amidst the cries, I could hear the short, staccato bursts of small-arms being fired as well as the resonant crack of rifles and the thunderous booms of shotguns. It was all there.

The Pacific Northwest is often called an outdoorsman's paradise. Hunting is such a big deal that some schools actually plan for it and anticipate the absentee rate increase. There is no shortage of guns. That is something that I would be keeping in mind as this scenario unfolds. If things look like they are going the way of the pulp fiction and midnight movie renditions, then at least I know I shouldn't have any problem finding weapons once the worst of the chaos has subsided.

Somewhere close, I heard the sounds of screeching tires followed by a terrific crash. There was an explosion that I recognized as a transformer blowing. Sure enough, a split second later, the lights all up and down this section of road flickered and went out. The area was plunged into an eerie quasi-darkness that was only pushed back in pockets where fires burned unchecked.

I did not want to be out here any longer than necessary. I was thankful that I'd had the presence of mind to point the headlights of my truck in the general direction of the pistol. I suddenly felt a bit foolish coveting it so much as I hurried over and grabbed it.

I hustled to the belt and my fingers clutched it. I stood to turn and run…and froze like a deer in the headlights.

The belt had been just a few paces from the rear bumper of the squad car. It never occurred to me that there may be a zombie lurking behind it. After all, I would have been able to see anybody standing there…right?

True…unless the thing waiting on the other side of the police car was in a condition similar to the poor officer that had been ripped in half (and then some). Sprawled on the ground, lying on its belly, was a woman who looked old enough to be my grandmother. Like the poor officer, she had also suffered the terrible fate of being ripped in half. Unlike him, however, she still had both arms and was now using them to drag herself towards me.

Her mouth opened and closed as she gurgled and hissed. The ambient spillover from my headlights provided a little bit of illumination to see the horror all too clearly. I was having a difficult time tearing my eyes away from the wet strands of her insides that were dragging behind her ruined lower abdomen. I just wish that was the worst of what I was seeing.

There was a little boy who couldn't have been any older than four. The dark stain down his right side from where his little arm had been brutally wrenched off made my heart hurt in sympathy. He was sitting on the curb, his one good hand holding a fistful of something I was grateful I could not see clearly. It was bad enough to see it being shoved into his mouth. More darkness dribbled down his chin and added to his filthy tee shirt.

As soon as he saw me, he paused in his feasting. Very slowly, his one hand lowered and he cocked his head to regard me with what seemed like a peculiar degree of interest. Unlike zombie granny, the boy made no move towards me. He simply

The Punch in the Gut

continued to stare with eyes that, even in the shadows, I could see were laced with the dark tracers.

I took a step back. That seemed to almost frustrate zombie granny as she made very slow progress in her pursuit of me. She began to mewl and moan even more intensely. Her hands slapped the pavement impotently and nails broke as she clawed at it to try and close the distance between us.

My eyes flicked from her to the child. He still showed no signs of moving, but there was no doubt that he was watching me. His head would tilt first one way, then the other. I continued to back away slowly until he vanished from my line of sight; then I broke into a run. I had no idea why that zombie kid hadn't made even the slightest move for me, but I was in no mood to push my luck.

I reached my truck just as another horrific shriek of pain came from nearby. I was almost in the driver's seat when the next scream came. This one was not in the register of those I was now associating with individuals who were being ripped apart and eaten alive. This was…well…it was just a regular scream. Fear, horror, futility. It could be any, or a combination of each. What I was certain of was that this person was close and, as of this second, not bitten. At least I was pretty sure.

"Stay," I commanded Chewie. I doubted she needed any coaxing to stay put, but I'd felt the need to at least say something to her before I shut the door and went in search of the source of that scream.

It had sounded like it came from just across the street…and in the direction of the leg munchers. Crap.

I felt my grip tighten on the hand axe that I actually kept forgetting was in my hand. I took a deep breath and then started towards the darker shadows. The building looked to be housing some sort of small bakery. I suddenly craved donuts and had to concentrate to keep my mouth from filling with saliva as my stomach reminded me that it was long past when I should've eaten something.

As I dipped into the darkness, I paused to let my eyes adjust. To my right, the leg munchers had apparently grown weary of gnawing on that mangled limb now that something more substantial was presenting itself. Before the closest one could stand, I moved over and brought the axe down hard on the crown of its head.

"Dammit!" I hissed. I jerked my hand away leaving my weapon jutting from the top of the zombie's head. I shook the hand that had wielded the weapon as if that would make the terrible stinging sensation just magically go away.

Now I had no axe with one zombie still getting up to come for me and began to fumble for the pouch on what was left of the belt I'd recovered. I could've tried for the axe, but that meant going towards the still animate ghoul.

My hunch proved correct and I pulled out a magazine for the officer's M9 Beretta nine millimeter. Slamming it into place, I let the slide do its job and brought the weapon up just in time to jam it into the forehead of the zombie and pull the trigger. The skull acted as a pretty decent sound suppressor, although the noise still echoed up and down the street.

The body dropped like somebody had just pulled the plug. Without seeing if I'd drawn the attention of any other zombies in the area, I snatched my hand axe free and ran to the shop where I heard a crash that sounded like a bunch of metal pans being thrown to the floor.

Another scream came and I plunged forward...like an idiot. I reached the glass-paned entry and saw a young man standing up top of a counter. He had what I first mistook to be a massive club like you would imagine the cartoon cavemen carrying. When a shaft of light caught it, I realized it was just a very large wire mixing whisk. That explained why it was doing little more than knocking the large female zombie backwards a few steps each time he swung and connected.

I tried the door and made a hissing sound between my teeth out of frustration when I discovered it was locked. Seeing no other recourse, I stepped back, aimed the pistol at the glass door right by the handle, and pulled the trigger. A neat hole appeared, along with a few cracks. Using my elbow, I gave the window a good bang and was rewarded with my fingers again going numb

The Punch in the Gut

as I hit my not-so-funny-bone flush with the still unyielding glass.

Something made me look up as I was dancing around making all kinds of noise from the stinging pain shooting down my arm, and I saw that the large female zombie had obviously heard me and decided to come check me out. She was at the glass already since the front area of the shop was so small.

This was actually the closest that I'd been to one other than Steph back in the hospital, and back then, I'd been trying to escape with my life. Now that I had this miniscule bit of safety between me and this member of the walking dead, I could not help but try to take a closer look.

Her face was slack. That was definitely something that added to the creepy factor. Despite her obvious desire to get at me and eat me alive, there was no anger or malice in her facial expression. She simply stared out at me as she tried to bite through the glass. Her mouth left an ugly slime trail of gray and yellow mucus flecked with bits of black. Seeing no other alternative, I pointed the gun at the woman's forehead after taking a step back, just in case.

The gunshot was just another joining the chorus that could be heard coming from all around, but that didn't make me feel any better about being out in the open after making so much racket.

On the good side, I must've hit the perfect spot, because the window blew into a bunch of tiny shards and the zombie toppled back, landing on the floor with a meaty slap. I leaned forward and found the little twist knob that acted as the old-fashioned kind of door lock and turned it.

"Are you okay?" I asked as I squeezed in past the fallen corpse to at least get off the street for a moment. As soon as the words came out of my mouth I felt like an idiot. Who, at this moment in time, felt okay about anything?

"You shot Miss Crebbs," a shaky voice replied.

At first I thought this person was going to deny the fact that Miss Crebbs had just about been ready to eat him like one of the cupcakes that I saw on the last remaining display shelf that hadn't been knocked over with its contents trodden underfoot. Then the young man I pegged to be in his very early twenties jumped down and flung his arms around me.

"As much as I appreciate the gratitude, we need to get out of here." To emphasize my point, several seconds of what sounded like automatic weapons being fired came from an uncomfortably close distance.

The two of us exited the cupcake shop and were halfway to the truck when a car came barreling around the corner. Perched outside the vehicle and seated in the open rear windows were a pair of individuals wearing bandanas around the lower part of their faces. Each had a rather military looking rifle pointed skyward.

We were out in the open with no place to run and I felt my blood chill as both rifles lowered to point in our direction as the car skidded to a stop. As I saw flame belching from the barrels of both guns, all I could do is close my eyes and wait for death to come in a hailstorm of flying lead.

4

Martial Law

"Run!" a voice shouted as soon as the gunfire ceased.

I opened my eyes and was amazed to see that I was still alive. Not a single bullet had touched me. I glanced over to the person I'd just basically rescued from the bakery to see that he was also unharmed.

The sounds of moans from behind me caused me to stumbled forward out of reflex and I turned to see a dozen walking dead stumbling towards me. They were less than a half a block away and very intent on adding me and my mystery friend to their numbers…or at least their menu.

I grabbed my companion's hand and ran towards the car. I could tell as I approached that it was already too full to allow even one more person, but that wasn't my ultimate destination anyway.

"Thank you!" I shouted, giving the guy closest to me a sloppy salute.

"Best get off the street!" one of the car's occupants called after us. "Word is that the military is shooting everything that moves…living, dead, or otherwise."

My new cohort raced around my truck without being told and was waiting for me to unlock the passenger side. By the time we got in, our unnamed rescuers had mowed down the majority of that group of zombies and were speeding past the downed bodies that were scattered all over the street.

I decided that they probably knew better about which direction to go than I did; and besides, that was the direction that I'd been headed. It would take me to my ultimate destination of Franklin High School where there was supposed to be a FEMA or Red Cross station of some sort.

"Name's Morey Reynolds," my passenger said, leaning forward around Chewie to try and make eye contact.

"Evan Berry," I answered, jerking the wheel hard to the right to avoid a zombie that staggered out from between a pair of parked cars.

"I really want to—" he began, but I cut him short.

"We can do this later," I said, not liking how sharp my tone sounded, but really couldn't help it since I was now banking hard to the left to avoid the bumper of a car that had been flipped on its side and took up almost half of my side of the road. "I gotta watch where we're going just this minute."

To Morey's credit, he didn't say another word. Chewie was a different story. She kept whimpering and whining as she lost her footing on numerous occasions and almost ended up on the floor. Once, when I had to slam on the brakes, she conked her head hard enough against the windshield to crack it. After that, Morey tried to keep a handle on her which made things considerably easier on all of us.

We were about six blocks from the high school when I turned a corner and slammed on the brakes throwing all of us forward hard. I winced as my ribs connected awkwardly with the steering wheel. *I guess that's why we are supposed to wear seatbelts*, I thought as I tried to suck in a breath past the pain.

"Is anybody in your party bitten?" a voice called from behind the dazzling spotlight that was now hitting me square in the eyes and basically blinding me.

Party? I thought. *There are only two of us and a dog.*

"Are you bit?" I asked Morey.

"No...Miss Crebbs gave me a nasty scratch on my arm, but I'm not bit." I could hear something in Morey's voice and I

Martial Law

turned to look at him. I shaded my eyes from the beam that had the entire cab bathed in fluorescent white.

He looked really pale, and that was beyond what the light was doing. Sure enough, there they were…those damn black squiggles in his eyes that made them look like they were bloodshot. His straight brown hair was a bit greasy, matted; and sweat had it plastered to his forehead. He had an unfortunately abundant degree of acne scarring on his cheeks that stood out in purplish hues under the spotlight.

"You sure?" I asked.

His head jerked around to me and those dark tracers weren't the only thing that I saw in his eyes. I also saw fear. He might not be bitten, but he was infected with whatever it was that was turning normal people into flesh eating monsters from all those horror movies, and I think he knew it.

"Yeah, see?" He pulled his shirt sleeve up and showed me a set of furrows in the meaty part of his forearm.

"And that's it?"

"Jesus, man…I think I'd know if I was bit."

I stuck my head out the window. "Nobody in here is bit," I shouted to the handful of soldiers standing in front of a trio of Hummers that blocked the road.

Now that my eyes were adjusting somewhat to the glare as well as the fact that the spotlight had moved just a bit, I could see three large machine guns, one mounted on top of each of the Hummers. No surprise, they were trained directly on us. I could also make out at least two dozen bodies sprawled on the road. A couple of them were missing their entire head; no doubt they'd taken a couple of rounds from one of those wicked .50 cals.

"We need you to exit your vehicle with your hands in the air." A trio of soldiers were now headed for us, their weapons not actually pointing at us, but they were slung in front and I doubted they had the safeties engaged. I was pretty sure they were all carrying M4s.

As they neared, I spotted little red pinpoints dancing on the ground. Laser sights. Yeah, there was not going to be any resistance from me. As crass as it sounded in my own head, if they said they were taking Morey to some sort of quarantine, or worse, killing or simply not allowing him in, then that was his problem. I'd done my good deed when it came to the guy.

"We need you to step out of the truck," one of the soldiers said. Funny thing was that it really did sound like more of a request than an order.

"Stay here, girl," I said to Chewie, then opened my door and climbed out.

I was sort of anxious for a moment as Morey appeared to hesitate, but relaxed just a bit when I heard the door open on the passenger's side. I closed my door just to make sure that Chewie stayed put.

"Can you take that weapon and set it on the ground and then walk three steps past it, please." That wasn't a request, and I spied the man who'd spoken as he advanced ahead of the others. He looked to be about my age and the oldest of the bunch when it came to the soldiers manning this post.

I did as I was told and set my axe on the street. To hopefully gain a bit more trust in the eyes of the man, I carefully pulled the remnant of the belt which had luckily held the holster—where I'd slid the Beretta—as well as the magazine pouch and set it down beside my axe. I glanced up and saw the look in the soldier's eyes. It was a mix of gratitude and annoyance, which might've been at me for having the weapon, but I think was more directed at himself for having missed it, slung sort of over my shoulder like it had been.

"You need to strip down," the soldier said. Again, this was not a question.

"Why?" I asked, although I had a good idea.

"We are just performing random checks to make sure that people who are claiming not to be bitten are telling the truth."

"Random?" I scoffed.

"Believe it or not, a few hours ago it was totally random. We had such an influx that we would've lost half of those waiting in line to the zips if we'd checked every single person," the soldier informed me.

Now that he was up close, I could see his eyes and the tre-

Martial Law

mendous amount of fatigue in them. In the ambient light from all the vehicles and the spotlights, I could see that they were a steel blue. The lines etched around them were made even darker in contrast, and now I was not as sure that we were so close in age. He looked to be at least ten years older up close.

I peeled off my pants and shirt and was going for my boxers when he held up a hand. "If you're bitten there, you wouldn't be standing," he said with a weak chuckle that showed his attempt at humor.

"Hey, Sarge?" one of the soldiers called from over where Morey had stripped down.

"Yeah?" He turned and I scooped up my pants and shirt and began getting dressed again, although I continued to pay attention to how this was about to play out.

"This guy has a nasty scratch...no bite, but that scratch apparently came from one of the zips."

"We were told to watch out for bites."

I had to bite my tongue. Honestly, did they not see his eyes? Still, it wasn't my place. Besides, these guys were running the show and had to know what was going on better than I did. Maybe just getting those tracers in the eyes is not the official sign that you're infected like I had led myself to believe.

A voice in the back of my head started to scold me for being an idiot, but I was suddenly feeling as tired as that sergeant looked. I just wanted to get inside the secure area, find a place to hunker down, and then get some sleep and figure things out tomorrow.

"You two can go ahead and go inside," the sergeant told us. "Drive to the football field and park the truck there. Either of you familiar with the school?"

"Actually, today was supposed to be my first day there as a teacher," I replied.

Holy crap! Had it just been this morning when I'd pulled in all excited about my new job?

"Well then, you need to go to the gymnasium and check in. From there you will be assigned to a bed. They will explain the way everything works once you get inside." He glanced over to my truck. "Unfortunately, the dog can't go in."

"Say what?" I snapped as I picked up my axe and the belt with the Beretta.

"Resources are not set up for animals. Food is already a concern if this goes longer than just a couple of days. And that stays as well." He nodded to the handgun I'd slung over my shoulder.

"I have her food, and as for my weapons, I don't see just going in there and waiting like a cow at the slaughtering pen. If things fall apart—" I started to argue.

"You got a permit to carry?" the sergeant said in a voice that was equal parts tired and annoyed.

"Actually…" I fished out my wallet, but he was holding up a hand.

"I don't care. But we just can't allow civilians to all be jammed in there with a bunch of weapons. Nerves are frayed and people are already on edge. The last thing we need is for folks to add weapons to the mix."

"What if I promise to keep it in my truck?"

"You turn them in to us and we give you a ticket. When we break down this camp, you can check in with the supply officer and he will return your firearm." The words rolled out of the sergeant's mouth like he'd said them a thousand times; and maybe he had by now.

The fact remained that I did not see anything good coming from me not having a way to protect myself if things went bad. I glanced at Morey and then back at the sergeant.

"Maybe I'll try my luck out here," I said.

If he picked up anything in my glance at my human travelling companion, he didn't let on. "Actually, that is not really an option."

"Excuse me?"

"Martial law was instituted and nobody is allowed out on the streets at this point. You can either enter of your own will…" There was an implied threat in his voice.

"Or?" I shot back. If this guy was going to act the part of the big, tough army man, then I wanted his to say the words.

Martial Law

"If you attempt to leave, we will detain you."

"And if I resist?"

"You do understand the concept of martial law, don't you?"

"I just want to hear you say it."

"Say what?" Now he was starting to falter.

That's the thing about fiction. In the books and movies, they always like to paint the military and police as power hungry lunatics. Sure, there are always a few bad apples in the bunch, but just like the general population, most are good down deep. They would have to be to volunteer to do things like go into collapsing towers, burning buildings, and foreign countries where the enemy comes in every shape and size imaginable.

"Say that you will shoot me if I attempt to leave." I held my breath.

I've played a bit of penny and peanut poker with friends. Bluffing was never something I found that I had a skill for like some folks. This was a bluff I did not want called. If he said he would shoot me, I had no idea what I would do. On one hand, there was absolutely no way that I could leave Chewie; on the other, I didn't want to be shot either.

"Look, if you promise to keep the dog in the truck, and..." he glanced over at my vehicle, "...I'd tell ya to try and keep it hidden, but I don't see how you will pull that off. Maybe by the time somebody sees it—"

"Her, Chewie is a her," I offered, hoping to do like what they say you should do if you are ever taken hostage. If I gave her name and gender, maybe it would soften things up a bit.

"I don't give a good goddamn. Just try and keep the dog out of sight. And I can't vouch for what will happen if she is discovered," the sergeant snapped back.

I nodded and set down the weapons. I paused, figuring the unasked question would do me no good. "If I put it in the cab, how about I keep my axe?"

"Sure, just get a move on, you've attracted zips and my boys have work to do."

I turned to look and saw a handful of dark forms staggering our direction. That was enough for me tonight. I hurried to the cab with my axe in hand.

I climbed in and smiled when I noticed the box tucked in behind the front seat. I still had my Ruger .357. What they didn't know wouldn't hurt them, I guess.

One of the Hummers inched back to allow me to pass. I gave the soldiers a wave and received grim nods in response. I couldn't blame them.

I headed up the street and noticed that every single house on both sides had the doors open. Stakes with white streamers were planted in the front yards. I guess that meant those locations had been searched and probably emptied of anything worth a darn.

That assumption was confirmed when I turned the corner to see a pair of the big military transport vehicles parked sort of staggered and across the street from each other; each pointing the way I was coming from, which I found a bit odd. Soldiers were walking out of the houses carrying plastic containers full of stuff. That was stranger still.

I understood the basics of martial law probably as much as the next person. I was pretty certain that it did not give the military the right to basically loot private residences. Not that I was gonna make a fuss, but I would remember this if we came out the other side. Somebody would be held accountable for what I was witnessing if I had anything to say about it.

Once I passed the trucks, I could focus on the here and now. I glanced over at Morey who was leaning with his head against the window. His eyes were shut and I very carefully let my foot off the gas as I clutched the axe.

"Are we there?" he mumbled.

"No." I accelerated just as carefully. "Just getting a look at something."

It wasn't a lie. Of course *he* was what I was getting a look at now that I was driving through a neighborhood with regularly spaced streetlights. I was not confident that he wasn't infected. I know what I'd seen in his eyes and still couldn't believe that the soldiers at the checkpoint hadn't stopped him or whatever it was that they were doing with those who'd been bitten. I was guessing they either turned them away…or worse.

When I finally reached the school, I felt the cramps in my fingers and realized that I'd been white-knuckling the steering wheel during the short drive the past few blocks. I also realized that a lot of people had flocked to this location in hopes of finding safety. The streets were jammed with cars and there was no way in hell that I would be able to park anywhere close.

A thought came and I turned left and doubled back a few blocks. While it was clear that all of the residences in this area had been gone through (by the military I assumed), the vehicles in the driveways were left unmolested. I chose one and pulled in.

"What are you doing?" Morey asked, his voice sounding raw and tired. "That soldier told us to get to the school. I don't think he would be okay with you not doing what he told you."

"I'm parking here. The lot is full at the school. I think it is better to be on the outside edge of things…just in case." I waited for him to ask what just in case scenario I might be thinking about, but he didn't.

I climbed out of the truck and watched as Morey seemed to not realize that he needed to get out of the truck as well. The man just sat slumped over in the passenger seat. Chewie did not seem to want to have anything to do with the man all of a sudden. I felt my stomach tighten and hefted my hand axe.

"Morey?" I called softly.

There was a heartbeat or two of silence, and then his head sort of lolled over to me. When it came up and the eyes opened, I was already pulling Chewie towards me by the scruff of her neck.

"Whoa!" he squeaked as I cocked my arm back and prepared to end this poor man's existence with a blow to the forehead.

"Are you going to stay in the truck, or can you walk to the school. It's only a few blocks."

The truth was that now I just wanted this guy out of my truck. I didn't care what the soldiers were screening for, Morey was infected and probably ready to turn into one of those things within the hour. There was no way that I would leave him in the cab with Chewie.

"Yeah…sorry…must've dozed off for a moment."

He reached over and, after three or four failed attempts, eventually managed to get the door open. He suddenly vanished from sight and after I helped Chewie back into the cab and shut my door, I went around to find Morey sprawled on the ground. His left arm was extended out above his head and kept flexing and twitching—opening and closing to rip away tufts of the grass that was growing in the little strip between the sidewalk and the house.

Despite my misgivings, I couldn't just leave him there on the ground. Moving to his side, I knelt and helped him to his feet. I leaned him against the side of the truck and cracked open the passenger side door. After getting my face slathered with drool from Chewie who was acting like I'd been gone for a week instead of just long enough to walk around the truck and help Morey up, I slid the box with my Ruger under the seat and kissed my dog on the bridge of her large, flat nose.

I had to figure something out. Were the soldiers so blind to simply following orders that they refused to see what I thought was so clear? And if I brought Morey to the shelter, would I be unleashing a monster? Perhaps I could find somebody there and very covertly hand Morey over to them, explaining that I was almost certain the tracers were a sign of the infection. If nobody would take him, then perhaps I could just stay with him until what I felt had to be the inevitable occurred. All I would need to do then was have the stones to finish him off.

I moved over beside Morey and slung his arm over my shoulder since he basically seemed out on his feet. We started up the road with the sounds of gunfire at our backs. I had to guess it was the picket sentries taking down all the zombies that had been drawn during my time talking with the sergeant.

At last we arrived at the rear entrance to the school. Another pair of military Hummers were parked at this entrance as well. The soldiers waved us through without a word and we were directed to a cluster of white tents that were in place on the tennis courts. I could see the football field bathed in the brightness of a series of spotlights in place all the way around the perimeter.

Martial Law

We were about halfway to the tents where I could see men and women bustling about in white coats. There were even a few in what I had to guess were HAZMAT suits. They looked like spacemen as they wove in and out of all the madness.

Morey stumbled and then collapsed. I hadn't been paying attention, and so I ended up tripping over him and falling hard on the pavement of the parking lot. I heard Morey land with a nasty crunch and splat. Getting up to my hands and knees, I rolled him over and saw that his face was a dark mess. It was too dark still in this section of the parking lot to see clearly, but I knew that his face was covered in blood. When his mouth opened, I heard something plink on the ground. He must've busted out a few teeth, and I was certain that his nose was destroyed.

"Can I get some help?" I called.

I reached over to see if I could help Morey when the first hints of that smell hit my nostrils. I recalled it from the emergency room. It isn't a smell you can really equate to anything else, and I was certain that I knew what it meant.

No sooner had I scrambled back when I saw one of Morey's arms start to twitch. The fingers spasmed a few times and then began to clutch slowly at the air. When his head turned, I could see well enough to know that his eyes were open. A low moan escaped his lips and I backed even further away.

"How the fuck did one of those things get in?" I heard a voice snap from behind me.

I glanced over my shoulder to see a woman in one of the white coats standing there with a pair of soldiers who were not carrying rifles, but I did notice leather holsters on their hips. One of them was already drawing his pistol.

"Step back, sir," the man said as he strode past me.

Without hesitation, he brought the gun to bear and fired a round into Morey's forehead.

I couldn't help but wince. Maybe some of it was from the sound of the pistol being fired, but I think that, deep down, I was still not totally okay with seeing what basically looked like a human being shot in the head. Despite having put a couple of the things down myself, there still seemed to be a part of me that wanted to refuse this new and harsh reality.

"We need you to get on your feet, sir," one of the soldiers barked.

I looked up to see all the weapons now pointed at me! "Wait a minute! I'm not bit," I started trying to explain.

"If you and your friend were supposedly clean, then maybe you can explain what just happened," another soldier growled as he produced a zip tie and approached me. "Now turn around and place your hands behind your back."

"But I'm not—" I started, but was cut off when the butt of the soldiers' rifle caught me in the gut.

I dropped to my knees and struggled to get air into my lungs which had been so suddenly and unexpectedly emptied of any and all oxygen. My mouth opened and closed like a fish out of water and tears blurred my vision as I struggled to try and get even the slightest breath.

"Private Nagel," a voice barked. "You will step back from that civilian and turn yourself in to the MPs right this minute."

A hand gripped my shoulder and I looked up to see the distorted features of what looked like a woman's face as she knelt in front of me. I opened my mouth, but still nothing came or went.

"I want to apologize for the private's behavior, sir," a female voice spoke, confirming my guess.

I blinked and some of the tears cleared. I could now make out the very pale features of a woman who looked to be in her fifties. Wisps of gray hair poked from beneath her military cap and her eyes were highlighted by deep creases and the corners of her mouth had serious frown lines.

"No...problem..." the words slid from my mouth, but I wasn't sure they were actually understandable.

"Now, we need to get you to the indoctrination tents for an exam before we can allow you into the shelter. Can you stand?" the female soldier said. I noticed little metal bars pinned to her shoulder lapel and figured she must be an officer of some sort, although my lack of military knowledge kept me from having

Martial Law

any idea what her rank might be.

"We have zips over by the fence again, Captain Peele," a voice from the direction of the tents shouted.

"And your yelling won't help the situation," the female officer said between clenched teeth. "Get some personnel over there to put them down so they don't build up at the fence and knock it over."

I made my way to my feet, but my knees were still a bit wobbly. The first step was the hardest, but it was becoming slightly easier to breathe. I followed the small group of doctors and soldiers to the tents and saw rows of tables and curtained off areas that I assumed were for exams.

"We've had word that the shelter at Tigard High School already fell to these things," the female officer said conversationally as she escorted me to one of the curtained exam areas and held the flap open, indicating that I should enter. "We only got the message that anybody bitten, no matter how minor, is a candidate for the infection. We are trying to get a quarantine set up here because there were a number of people earlier today who arrived with injuries that were allowed in."

I didn't know why she was sharing all of this with me, but it was interesting information. I kept my mouth shut so that I wouldn't break her flow and stop her from talking. I had no idea what sorts of information she might let spill, but it would be more than I'd had earlier today. The problem I had was not just blurting, *'Hey, you people have seen zombie movies, right?'*

"Of course, we're just the local National Guard Unit. Word has it that regular army is on the way. We will probably all be shuffled out to the perimeter when they arrive." She laughed bitterly. "Well...not me. I'm an officer, but I am sure they will have no problem finding some sort of shit job to stick me in like they will my men and women."

She stopped at the flap to my little cubicle and told me that somebody would be in soon to see me. She started to exit and then paused, turning back to me. "I'd stash that little hand axe if I were you. If you try to go inside with it, it will be confiscated."

After over two hours, I had to wonder what her idea of

DEAD: Onset

'soon' might be. A last the flap opened.

"So, do you have any bites or injuries inflicted by an infected individual?" the elderly man asked as he continued to stare down at the clipboard he was making notes on.

"Umm...no...that was established at the checkpoint." I didn't bother to mask the annoyance in my voice.

"Yes, well it seems that the orders were not transferred out to the sentries until just a few hours ago," the doctor said, not seeming to notice or care that I was well past the point of impatience.

"So can I go?" I asked.

"What?" The doctor's head suddenly popped up. "Goodness no. I need to have you strip please so that I can inspect you and confirm your status."

I opened my mouth to say something rude, but just as quickly clamped it shut. It wasn't going to do me any good. And honestly, I just wanted to get in and find someplace where I could relax for a couple of hours and try to get my head straight.

After the most intimate physical in my life which had me on the verge of asking if maybe he would be sending me candy or flowers later, I was told that I could dress and that I was now required to report to the school's cafeteria with the piece of paper he handed me stating that I was inspected and found to be clean.

I walked out of the tent and paused to get a look around. I spotted a trio of Dumpsters and paused long enough to slip my axe underneath the middle one. I pushed it just far enough back that it wouldn't be easily spotted, but not so far that it would take me too long to retrieve. Of course, I had no idea if I would ever be able to grab it. But at least I knew where one available weapon existed if things started to go bad. It was something.

The school grounds were barely recognizable from what I'd known just this morning. Military trucks and a handful of the drab, tan Hummers with the machine guns mounted on them were parked around the lot amidst all the cars that were crammed in as tight as possible. The spotlights added an even more surreal atmosphere as they all pointed down to the football

Martial Law

field. And then I spied it. A large structure at the far end of the field where I knew a massive Walmart Supercenter sat just on the other side of the fence that ran along the southern border of the campus.

I could not help but veer that direction to take a look. I was almost to the lip where I could get a better view of what was down there when a voice froze me in my tracks.

"That's far enough. You need to return to the main building or I am going to shoot." There was an edge that was more fear than authority in that voice.

I turned around with my hands in the air. "I was just curious," I said with a forced chuckle. "Sorry...didn't realize there were any out-of-bounds areas."

"Nobody is permitted down there near the pens," the young man replied. I could see as well as hear him relax when he realized that I wasn't going to try and challenge his authority.

"The pens?" I asked. If I couldn't go see for myself, then perhaps he would confirm what I thought I'd seen.

"We've had to put a few of the people who fell to the infection down there in the pens. Gotta keep them away from the rest of you for your own good."

"Hey, sounds like a great idea. I've seen them things in action and would just as soon not get torn apart."

"You'd be surprised at how many people can't stop seeing them as their friends and loved ones." He paused and let out a long, tired breath that had no business coming from somebody so young. "Sad really. One lady threw herself at one of those things, insisting it was her husband and that he didn't have a mean bone in his body."

"Didn't end well, I take it?"

"Zombies don't see us as anything but something to eat."

I cocked my head at the word. I'd thought it...and of course Carl had thrown it out there without hesitation, but this felt different.

"Zombies?" I let that question sound just a bit skeptical, but not enough that I might embarrass the young man. I wanted him to talk...maybe defend his position.

"What else can you call something that actually and literally died, and then gets back up and attacks the living. And no, they don't attack each other. Hell, they walk in little groups and barely notice each other. But let some warm-blooded, living person cross their path and it's game on."

I nodded.

"Now I think you should go inside, sir."

I'd been called 'sir' more in the past few hours than I think I had my entire life. I decided that I didn't care for it very much.

"The name's Evan." I stuck out a hand. At first I didn't think he was going to shake it, but at last, the kid stepped forward and clasped my offered hand.

"Brian McGrady."

"Nice to meet you…just lousy circumstances," I said, repeating a phrase I remember hearing my grandfather use a lot.

I turned and headed for the main building. I was pretty sure that every light in the place was on. I hadn't really paid that much attention, but now that I did, I was able to see a lot of movement. The place was well past the fire marshal approved capacity, of that I had no doubt.

I climbed the stone step to the metal doors and opened them to find a half dozen soldiers standing around with their weapons slung across their bodies. The halls were full of people and I was hit by the overwhelming heat and mugginess of so many bodies confined in this building.

I could actually see some people stretched out on bedrolls on the floor of the hallway. Despite there being so many people, it was actually pretty hushed as folks spoke in voices that were barely above a whisper.

"You need to report to the cafeteria," one of the soldiers said in a bored, monotone voice.

I began to weave through the throng of people. As I did, I found myself pausing from time to time. At first I thought it was just my imagination, but after the third or fourth time, I was certain. I could smell it.

The smell of infection.

I paused once to try and casually observe a group of people

Martial Law

all clustered around a lone figure lying on a cot. I could hear their hushed whispers. They knew, and yet they were trying deny what was right before their own eyes. That is just one problem with us as a species: we always believe right to the very end that it certainly "won't happen to me" when bad things crop up. It is always going to be somebody else. *Not this time, folks*, I thought as I moved on.

Changing my focus, I started scanning faces. More specifically, I was looking at people's eyes. I was almost positive that was the sign. By the time I'd reached the cafeteria, I had spotted seven people with the tracers starting to show. Once, when I made eye contact with one of them, they looked away hurriedly and I was almost certain that person knew.

That started to make me angry. If somebody knew they had this…this…whatever it was, how could they allow themselves to be around other people?

I finally reached the cafeteria, but I'd already made up my mind that I was going to be finding a way out of this place as soon as I could. I fell into one of the five lines and prepared to wait my turn when I heard a familiar voice.

"Hey, friend."

DEAD: Onset

5

No Rest for the Weary

I flopped down on my assigned cot and looked around the gymnasium. The faces all around me wore expressions of fear, loss, confusion, and uncertainty. Personally, I just felt numb. I don't know if I have had time to truly digest the past day.

That realization was a punch in the gut all by itself. It had taken less than twenty-four hours for my entire world to be turned upside-down. No matter what happened next, I did not believe that it was possible for me to ever recover from this day.

"I brought you some water and a peanut butter sandwich." Carl's voice arrived at my ears from a million miles away and I looked up, surprised to see him standing over me.

"How?" I had to struggle just to get that single word out, but now that I did, I felt like I was going to collapse in on myself; as if that single word had been the last thing holding me together.

"Who knows. If somebody in the government has any ideas, they ain't talking. And I don't think anybody is ever gonna be able to tell us." He looked around and then knelt down so that he could keep his voice at just above a whisper. "Asia is just plain gone. I'm talking China, Japan, both Koreas…fucking India. That is close to three billion people, and there has not been a peep from that part of the world for most of the day. Damn Russians went through the looking glass if you can believe the internet rumors…before that crashed."

"What?" None of this was really making sense. Obviously I'd missed a great deal while I'd been in the hospital. "What are you talking about?"

"Moscow dropped a nuke on itself. That is sixteen million souls just gone. And if you can believe it, their president stayed at freaking ground zero and made some sort of final broadcast begging China and the United States to do the same. It was all over the internet before it crashed. Whether it is just overloaded with folks trying to figure out what is going on or our infrastructure is already crumbling, you can't log on to anything." Carl looked around the room and dropped his voice just a bit more. "And I don't think being here is the best idea anymore. They already had at least a dozen people turn in here."

"But they are screening people at the checkpoints," I said weakly. I'd already watched firsthand as they allowed a person who was infected pass through their security perimeter, so I knew even that was not a guarantee that we were the least bit safe.

"That didn't really start until late this afternoon. Until then, they were putting the injured in a group of classrooms in the southwest corner of the school. And they weren't really making people stay there unless their injuries were critical."

"It is more than just the bites," I said, surprised that I was able to actually find my voice. "I was with a guy who just ended up being scratched, but he turned. I saw the black squiggles in his eyes. When we reached the checkpoint, the soldiers let him pass because he wasn't bit."

"If this is blood-borne, it might be worse than just a bite or a scratch." Carl noticed that I had yet to touch my peanut butter sandwich and licked his lips. I handed it over and he started to wolf it down.

"Worse how?" I asked when he seemed to become too engrossed in eating.

"Hell, it might pass if you get some of the infected blood in an open cut. Sorta like when people contracted the AIDS virus from their dentist and shit," Carl answered around a mouthful of peanut butter and wheat bread. "This could be way worse than the movies." A look passed over his face and he appeared to have a bit of difficulty swallowing that last bite. "Did you return home after the hospital?"

It did not go unnoticed by me that he made no mention of Stephanie. He'd known her fate the moment he'd seen her injury. He'd even tried to warn me without coming right out and saying that she was a goner.

"Yeah, I grabbed a few things and loaded them into the truck. Not much, but better than nothing."

"The dog..." Whatever he was trying to say died on his lips and he looked away.

"Chewie?" I asked, curious as to his sudden apparent discomfort. "She's fine for the most part. They wouldn't let me bring her in, so she is in the cab of the truck. I will have to get out there first thing in the morning. Not sure what I will be able to do, but I sure as hell ain't just abandoning her."

"Wait...she's okay?" Carl seemed genuinely surprised.

"I'm sure a vet should get a look at her tail, but I don't see that as likely. I'll just have to keep her injury clean and—"

"You're sure she's okay?" he blurted, cutting me off and causing a few nearby heads to turn our direction.

"Umm...like I said, as well as can be expected." I got a strange feeling that there was something he wasn't saying.

"You need to put her down."

"What?" Now it was my turn to raise my voice and cause people to look over. "I won't do any such thing."

"This...whatever it is...it's turning dogs, too." The words had come out in a rush, and it was a few seconds before they fully sunk in.

"But she's fine. I just left her."

"When you go out there tomorrow, you may not like what you find."

I listened as he recounted a run in with a mutt of a dog that had obviously been attacked. It was on three legs, but there was no doubt in his mind that this abomination was just as much a zombie as that man he'd killed in my bedroom.

DEAD: Onset

I had nothing to say in response to this revelation. I didn't want to believe him, but I'd also seen with my own eyes the very things that he'd been warning me about in the faculty room earlier this morning.

My God, I thought. *Had it just been this morning?*

At some point, Carl wandered away. I wasn't sure if I was happy about that or not. Eventually, I stretched out on my cot and stared up at the ceiling. My thoughts drifted, and I was so tired that it seemed impossible that I could not fall asleep.

Yet, as the minutes crept past and became hours, I became resigned to the fact that sleep would elude me; at least for the time being.

At last, I sat back up. Suddenly I was regretting having given away my peanut butter sandwich. My stomach growled its agreement with that sentiment as I made my way to the bathroom. A line at the door gave me time to sort out my head and make some decisions. The biggest was that I was not going to stay here. I had no idea where I might go, but something about this place was eating at me.

The man in front of me was rubbing at his hands like he was trying to wash something from them. I looked closer and saw a dark stain on his right arm. At first, I thought he might be bitten, but then I realized his shirt was intact. That was somebody else's blood.

We inched forward one agonizing step at a time. I'd only headed over to the bathroom because I was not sure what else to do, but now that I was here, I realized I had to go pretty bad.

"Now we know how the women feel," I tried to joke to the dark-skinned man in front of me. I saw the briefest hint of a smile tug up at the corners of his mouth, but it was as if gravity refused to allow him such a luxury.

"My Randi has been in line for over ten minutes," the man said. There was a deep sadness in his voice, and I did not need him to tell me that he'd lost somebody in this madness.

"You folks been here long?" It was a pretty lame question, but I didn't know what else to ask this man who gave off the feeling that he was carrying the weight of the world on his shoulders.

"Got here an hour or so ago. Came on a military transport truck that went through our neighborhood and picked folks up." He paused and turned sideways enough so that I could see his face. "Had to drag my Randi…she wouldn't go."

His eyes drifted over to the girl's bathroom where the line was easily twice the length of ours. I followed his gaze and saw a tall woman who stood with about as much life in her eyes as those things…the undead…that were roaming the streets. The woman stood in the queue and seemed to just trudge forward whenever the line surged.

"Barry Jenkins," the man said as he offered a hand.

"Evan Berry." I shook the man's hand and gave him a closer look.

His skin was the dark brown of a chocolate bar, and his brown eyes still had a bit of a sparkle that told me this sadness that I was seeing was not his usual demeanor. He was balding, and single silver strands could be seen sprinkled amidst his black, tightly kinked hair. It dawned on me that this man and his wife were on the cots right by my own.

"A pair of berries," I chuckled at the similarity of his first and my last name.

"Yeah…but I'm a blackberry," he guffawed, a smile able to finally overcome the downturn that I'd seen in full control of his mouth just a moment ago.

"So, are you two sticking around…or…" I didn't want to broadcast the fact that I had no plans to remain here, but I thought it would be good to hear what other folks were thinking and feeling.

"Not sure…still trying to get my head around what is going on." Barry looked around again and his eyes settled on something, tightening slightly.

I followed his gaze. At last, I discovered what I was pretty sure had his attention. A woman that I was guessing to be in her twenties was kneeling in front of a little girl no older than ten. She was using a wipe or cloth of some sort to dab at the girl's left arm.

"They stopped letting in those who have been bitten. Heard they've even shot a few. An hour ago, soldiers started wandering through the crowd. They've escorted a dozen or so to someplace else. Not sure I want to know where."

Barry seemed happy to talk, and I was ready to let him. I had been so focused on what happened in the hospital that my mind was not yet ready to try and fully process everything happening around me. I was still stuck on how I'd barely gotten away from my neighborhood which was likely nothing more than a charred mess now. I'd had that encounter when I'd attempted to save Morey. I could no longer credit myself for actually saving the man since he'd turned and been gunned down.

"...heard those screams, and I doubt I will ever get them out of my head," Barry was saying. "So I can't imagine how my Randi will ever get over seeing them things attack our little girl."

"Oh, man...I'm so sorry." And I was, from the bottom of my heart.

Yes, I'd lost the love of my life. That loss had been compounded by the discovery of her pregnancy that she was obviously going to surprise me with when I got home from my first day as a teacher. Still, I did not see how I could compare it with the loss of their child. And to have witnessed it?

At last a stall occupant emerged and Barry ducked inside to take his turn. I relieved myself as soon as the next stall opened up and then wandered the gymnasium. I noticed the soldiers were not allowing anybody to venture down one hallway. I also noticed that a dozen people were being kept on cots that lined a separate corridor. None had any visible injuries except for one who had a nasty scratch down her face. Her cheek was terribly inflamed, and when her head lolled my direction, I saw the dark tracers in her eyes. She didn't seem to be looking at me as much as through me, and I quickly grew tired of wandering the halls.

I returned to the gymnasium and paused at the sandwich line long enough to grab a replacement for the one Carl had consumed earlier. I spotted him on the far side of the huge open gym. He was standing amidst several of the teachers that I recognized from this morning including Principal Gordon.

I decided to veer over there and see what was going on. As I arrived, I spotted the dour, unfriendly woman from when I'd first pulled into the parking lot this morning. Her face was puffy and it was clear that she'd been crying. My animosity quickly transformed to pity.

"…they won't even let me see him," the large woman was whimpering.

"Won't let her see who?" I whispered to Principal Gordon.

"Her husband. He showed up with the first groups this morning. Didn't have a bite, nothing…but a few hours ago he started acting strange…got really sick and was doubled over. The soldiers grabbed him and threw him on a gurney. Didn't even bother to check him out first."

I considered my words carefully before I spoke. "You didn't notice if he had black tracers in his eyes, did you?"

The principal seemed to think hard for a moment before he finally spoke. "Come to think of it…there did seem to be something odd about his eyes." He looked at me with genuine interest. "Is that something we need to be worried about with this infection or whatever it is?"

I told him about Morey, including his unfortunate ending outside. I explained that, despite him only having been scratched, it looked like he had become one of the infected. I didn't say "walking dead" because I'd seen how dismissive they'd been with Carl earlier.

"Jesus." The man ran his hands through his hair and looked around the room. "I know for sure of at least five people who were scratched. Maybe we should wander around and get a better look?"

I heard what he wasn't saying. He now saw this as a problem much like me and Carl did. He might not be ready to say the "Z" word yet, but if he saw what I'd seen, I think it was not too much of a leap of faith.

After our little social tour where we stopped to talk to four of the people he knew for a fact had some sort of injury at the hands of the walking dead, we had more fuel to burn in our speculative fires.

"So the soldiers took one of them and two of the four have…did you call them tracers?" I nodded. "Two of the four have those black tracers in their eyes."

"Maybe we should stick close together," I suggested. "We may have to leave here in a hurry. I have a vehicle parked not too far from here."

I didn't know why, but I still wasn't really ready to share the location of my truck with anybody. A small voice deep in my conscience said that I was being selfish. I saw it more as cautious. I'd seen a few movies…and it always seemed like the worst in people came out in these situations. It wasn't like regular disasters where people went above and beyond to help. I think there is something about the fact that we skip all the stages and end up smack dab in the middle of hopeless. That, and when there is no framework…no infrastructure or mode of accountability, people become more of that raw essence of their being. Sadly, all those who have any good in them likely die early on doing what their nature drives them to do: help others. That leaves all of us who live in the gray area…and those who are black in the pit of their soul.

"I think one of us should be awake at all times. Sort of a watch over the group. If something bad looks like it is about to happen, that person can rouse the rest of us and we can be better prepared in case we need to make a run for it," I suggested.

The principal nodded, and then I saw his expression change so suddenly that I thought he might be one of the infected. His face turned a shade of crimson and he clenched his fists tight, holding his breath as he did so.

"I am so sorry, Evan," he gushed. "I didn't even think to ask how things went at home. Your wife…?" He left that last bit open in question as his voice rose in pitch just a bit.

I shook my head and had to bite the inside of my cheek to keep my tears at bay. If they came and I was offered any form of sympathy, I might very well not be able to stop crying…ever.

"I am so sorry."

I looked up and saw the raw emotion in his eyes as well as

what I now identified as shame. He pressed his lips together tight and I thought he was done until his next statement came out of his mouth.

"Your sudden departure with such minimal knowledge on my part…it's just…"

I listened as he hemmed and hawed over the words before I realized what exactly he'd been trying to tell me.

"You were going to fire me." It wasn't a question. And then I started laughing. Something about that bit of information struck me as funny.

"Things just happened so quickly, and we didn't quite catch up until…" the principal's voice faded and his red face gave away the embarrassment that he obviously felt.

"I think we can forget all that stuff," I said, placing a hand on the man's shoulder. "It is not like anybody expected Carl to be the voice of reason."

We shared a laugh at that, and I noticed a couple of the others nearby join in. All of a sudden, I felt exhausted, it was as if all the adrenaline that had kept me going these past several hours simply drained out through the soles of my feet. I excused myself and headed over to my cot.

I had no idea how long I'd been away from my little area, but in that amount of time, either we'd had in influx of people seeking shelter, or else everybody else was just tired and coming to bed at the same time. I did not see one empty cot in my area. Just as I arrived, I saw Barry escorting his wife to their spot just a few beds over from mine.

I gave Barry a wave as he guided Randi down to her place beside his. I watched as he covered her up, whispered something in her ear and then kissed her on the cheek. He gave me a nod before lying down. I noted that he did not close his eyes, but rather, they were locked on his wife who had not so much as twitched since he tucked her in.

A part of me longed to have the hand axe I'd stashed under that Dumpster outside. With a yawn, I stretched out, certain that despite my bone-deep fatigue, there would be no way I would fall asleep.

DEAD: Onset

***

"...repeat, we need everybody to assemble in the hallway. We apologize for the inconvenience, and we will let you all return to your area as soon as possible," the voice was blaring through a bullhorn.

"Not my favorite way to wake up," I grumbled. Sitting up, I looked around to discover almost everybody else up was already shuffling for the exits. "Nobody bothered to give me a shake?" I groused.

I slipped on my shoes and followed the mob. Looking around, I was struck by how much we sort of resembled the undead. Almost everybody was looking at their feet. It was as if we were already beaten. This only reignited the idea that I needed to get out of here. These people were the walking dead; they just didn't realize it yet.

I fell in and made my way to the hall. I still wasn't sure what was going on, but the mystery was solved as soon as the doors shut. I heard the pop of a weapon being fired. Several people jumped or started like they'd been hit with a jolt of electricity; but more simply stood in place, continuing to stare at the ground.

"This place is not gonna last long," a voice whispered in my ear. I wasn't surprised to turn around and discover Carl standing there, arms folded across his chest.

"On that we can absolutely agree." I gave a nod as my eyes continued to scan the huddled and shivering masses.

My eyes came to rest on a little boy. I figured him to be maybe five or six. He was wearing a jersey sporting the logo of the local pro basketball team. He also had a long sleeve shirt on, but I could see the outline of what I figured to be some serious bandaging on his right forearm.

As I studied the boy, he had been just as focused on the floor as the woman holding his hand. His straight, blonde hair hung down in his face just a bit, but something prompted him to lift his chin. Maybe he'd sense me staring at him. Whatever the

No Rest for the Weary

case, when he looked up, I wasn't surprised to discover that he had the first showings of the black tracers snaking through the whites of his eyes.

"Sooner than later," I whispered to Carl.

"What?" He shook like I'd just roused him from a dream.

"I said the sooner we get out of here, the better. If we wait too long, we might not be going anywhere."

He followed my gaze and I heard him swallow audibly. Then he tapped my shoulder and pointed out three more people in just our immediate vicinity that showed the symptoms I now equated with the infection.

"Why aren't the soldiers doing anything?" I whispered.

"Nobody has given them any orders. They are doing exactly what they were told to do," Carl replied. "And I wouldn't count on them much longer anyway. I heard one of the men saying that a quarter of the troops assigned here have already just up and left. Two entire sentry units never came back. Their reliefs went out and found the posts abandoned."

"How the hell is this happening so fast?" I breathed as my gaze returned to that little boy. I was staring intently when he suddenly stuck out his tongue at me, and I decided that maybe being this obvious was not the best idea.

"Simple." Carl looked me in the eyes, and his gaze softened. "How did you finally deal with your lady?"

"I didn't." As soon as the words came out of my mouth, I understood what he meant.

"I will grant that I am sure a few people have watched the movies or whatever, but nobody believed this could happen. And seeing something on the big or little screen is not the same as real life. That person you love…that child you brought into the world…can you really just shoot it in the head or bust it open with a bat? Most of us probably can't. Then we end up bit. We join the numbers." Carl's logic seemed ironclad.

He had a point. Yeah, I'd taken down a couple of the walking dead, but in the hospital, I'd just run. The thought of putting Stephanie down for good never crossed my mind. I'd run…gotten away from her as fast as I could with no thought of ending her existence. If she'd gotten her hands on me, would I have been able to do anything to fight her?

"My truck is just a couple of blocks over—" I started, but a soldier on a bullhorn cut me off.

"Okay, ladies and gentlemen, you all can return inside to the gymnasium." A trio of men in uniform stood in the double doors to the gym. They stepped out of the way and began ushering people inside.

"You think they'll just let us leave?" I asked.

"Martial law is in effect, but last I heard, it was from sunset to sunrise," Carl offered.

"Then I say we get the hell out of here now."

We headed inside with the idea of grabbing a sandwich and heading out. I told Carl I would meet him at the doors, I wanted to go tell Barry that I was leaving and perhaps ask him if maybe he and his wife would like to join us.

I reached my area and saw the man sitting beside his wife, he had her head on his shoulder and he was stroking her hair, whispering to her as tears trickled down his face. For just a moment, I considered simply ducking out. If his wife was this much of a basket case, did I really want them tagging along? I mentally slapped and scolded myself before taking a deep breath and approaching them.

"Hey," I said in greeting. Barry looked up, his free hand brushing away the tears. "So...me and this other guy are thinking about leaving. I was wondering if you'd want to join us."

The man glanced over at his wife, then at me again. He shook his head.

"I don't think we're ready to do that just yet," he said sadly. "I think I am going to hold onto my hope that things will right themselves for just a little while longer."

"Okay..." I leaned over to shake his hand. "Just don't wait too long. You don't want to be the band playing on the deck of the Titanic."

"I'll keep that in mind," he said with a laugh. "You watch out for yourself."

"Hey?" a voice said from behind me. "Is that cot open?"

No Rest for the Weary

I turned to see the unlikely trio of a man holding the hand of a young Hispanic girl with a teenage girl at his side. The man had dark circles under his eyes and looked like he was carrying the weight of the world on his shoulders like so many others in this room.

"Yeah…I was just checking out of this hotel," I said with a nod.

"Steve?" the teenage girl hissed. The man turned his head, but I caught his eye roll. "Thalia needs a bathroom unless you want to have to mop the floor."

"The facilities are right over there," Barry called from behind me.

I watched the two girls hurry off. The man, Steve according to the impatient girl, watched them head over to the bathrooms. While I did not think he was their father…at least not the young Hispanic girl, there was something very protective in his gaze.

"You can have my bunk," I told the man as I started for the exit. I heard his muttered thanks and knew his eyes were still locked on the door that the girls had vanished through. I was very glad I didn't have that kind of responsibility. I had a feeling it was going to be hard enough to take care of myself, much less a child.

I grabbed my bag and was almost to the doors when I saw a group of people gathered around a television that was on one of those rollaway carts. I recognized Carl in the rear of the crowd and headed over to see what all the fuss was about.

"I guess this ran last night…the station has had it on a loop," a woman said, her voice straining as she fought not to cry. "One of the soldiers just pushed this in and told a few of us we should probably watch it. He had all his gear thrown over his shoulder…I think he was getting ready to leave."

I moved closer to hear what was being said.

"…have been informed that the president's plane is reported to have crashed. No further details are being made available at the moment. However, we have been instructed by representatives of the United States Army to issue the following statement that reads as follows…" The man seemed to lean forward at the

DEAD: Onset

desk for a moment and squint. He looked past the camera. "Are you serious?"

A voice could be heard in the background, and the reply was loud enough to be heard clearly. "Read the teleprompter exactly as it is written."

"The dead are returning to life. The CDC has confirmed that a living person bitten by one of the undead, or zombies as pop culture would call them, will turn within seventy-two hours, but some have done so in as soon as just a few minutes. There is no way to determine how fast or why there is such a disparity in what are now called "turn" times. However, if a person has been bitten, you are required to either bring them to the nearest military-manned FEMA shelter or dispose of them yourself.

"There is to be no mistake, these are not your friends or loved ones. They will not recognize you in any manner or for any reason. Dr. Linda Sing had this to say…"

There was a flash on the screen and a poor-quality video showed a doctor's office that looked like any that a person would walk into. There were shelves of books in the background and several certificates or diplomas adorning the walls. Seated behind a desk was Dr. Linda Sing, the same woman who had gone on camera earlier to discredit any reports that the dead were returning and attacking the living. She looked tired and her uniform was a blood-stained mess; she was wearing dark sunglasses.

"Am I on?" the doctor asked whomever was operating the shaky, handheld video device.

"Yeah." It was one word, but the voice made it clear that whoever was holding the camera was agitated.

"Good. To whomever is watching, I am Dr. Linda Sing of the CDC. I am here to reverse my earlier statement that these people that are instigating attacks are not the dead come back. After detailed observations of a specimen that had no vitals and had been declared dead, I was witness to that individual sitting up and attacking another person.

"There can be no doubt that this individual was dead only moments before. However, after the specimen was restrained, numerous things were done that a living person could not endure, much less remain conscious during. Additionally, I can confirm that massive brain trauma seems to be the only method of dispatching these…individuals—"

"They're fuckin' zombies, you stupid bitch!" somebody off-camera yelled.

Dr. Sing glanced to the left and pursed her lips before continuing. "Simple decapitation is not entirely sufficient. While the body will become inert, the head still seems to function and a bite that transmits the infection can still occur."

With that last statement, the doctor removed her glasses and leaned forward. It was not a necessary gesture. The dark tracers in her eyes could be seen quite clearly.

"One of the telltale symptoms is the appearance of the darkening of the capillaries in the eye. If you are infected, I suggest you turn yourself over to the nearest FEMA center or military checkpoint. The only chance we have to contain this rests in your swift response—"

"That went out the window a long time ago while you fucking scientists sat on this information, you stupid bi—" another voice off camera hollered, but was cut off as the video ended abruptly.

The man behind the desk appeared on the screen once more. He was still looking past the camera in the studio, a look of what could very well be fear was etched on his face.

"Umm…yes, well." The man on screen looked past the camera again and seemed to grow even paler. A commotion could be heard in the background that ended with a woman's shriek and a nasty crash.

"Read the teleprompter like you were told, or she endures more of the same," a voice came over the broadcast clearly. The menace dripped from it with open hostility and no attempt to mask the threat.

"The United States Army has been given permission to…detain any person who shows signs of this infection. All such persons are to be removed from the general population until a remedy can be found. Currently, there is no known cure and

DEAD: Onset

the mortality rate appears to be at one hundred percent. If you are known to be harboring somebody who is infected, you face detention and will be considered to have violated the tenets of the amended martial law." The man gulped and wiped the sweat from his forehead. "The armed forces and law enforcement have been granted the right to execute any and all persons who show signs of infection…as well as those who harbor them."

A murmur rippled through the group gathered at the television. I saw a few spots where people distanced themselves from individuals. I didn't even need to look into their eyes to know why.

"Time to go, friend," Carl said as he grabbed my arm and began to lead me to the door.

We exited the gymnasium and found ourselves in a hallway bustling with activity. Several soldiers scrambled past with their gear. I watched as they hustled out the door.

"Aren't we gonna stop them?" I heard a voice from the stairwell to my left.

I leaned forward far enough to see a small cluster of men in uniform standing around a guy who sported more than a few stripes on his arm. I took him to be the man in charge. Despite the situation, he was in a pressed uniform and his face was clean shaven.

"I don't think so," the clean-shaven soldier replied. "In fact, I am telling you all now that your continued presence here is strictly voluntary. I know that many of you have families, and there is little confidence that we will see the relief promised us. The regular troops are in the wind. Nobody is answering at Fort Lewis, and while my last orders were that we maintain our presence here until troops from Lewis arrive, I now doubt that anybody is coming."

"Are you telling us to abandon our post?" one of the men asked hesitantly.

"No, I am simply telling you that your staying here is a choice. It is no longer an order. That useless officer they sent us yesterday was one of the first to vanish, which effectively put me in charge. I am not going to make anybody stay who does not want to, and if this ship does right itself, I will take the heat."

"Are you staying, Sarge?" one of the female soldiers asked.

"I will remain for the time being," was the clipped response. "Who will stay with me?"

One by one, I heard each of the young men and women gathered around all voice their desire to remain. Once again, I was in awe of the dedication these men and women had…despite the likelihood that the country they were sworn to "protect and defend against all enemies, foreign and domestic" was about to dissolve. As a nation, we'd been pretty resilient. We'd endured all manner of wars and terrorist attacks in our short existence. I don't know why, but something told me there would be no coming back from this one.

DEAD: Onset

Day Two Begins

"Jesus," I gasped.

In the less than twenty-four hours that I'd been inside Franklin High School, the world looked to have gone, for lack of a better term...to absolute crap. I could see plumes of smoke rising into the sky from almost every direction.

What was missing were the sirens of emergency vehicles rushing to respond and put out the fires. The sounds of gunfire came from all around, as did screams. Some of them were just the garden variety type, but every so often, I heard what I now termed as *the* scream. It was unlike anything I'd ever heard until yesterday, but there was no mistaking it.

Carl, Principal Gordon, and Betty Simms—I'd finally learned the name of the unpleasant woman that I'd met in the parking lot yesterday—all stood with me on the steps behind the school. This side of the campus was bordered by a massive open air mall. There was a multiplex, Walmart Superstore, a few restaurants, as well as a strip of several small shops and a military recruiting depot.

The sky was a bit overcast which amplified the smell of smoke and something else...something rotten. I was pretty certain that I knew what that might be. Not having been too familiar with the smell of death, I had been surprised when Carl told me that this stench was something very different from just death. I would have to take his word for it.

"So where do we go?" Julian Gordon asked. It felt strange not calling him Principal Gordon anymore, but he'd sort of insisted we drop that title.

"My truck is just up the road," I said.

I didn't want to think about the possibility that my beloved Chewie was now a monster. Maybe Carl was wrong. Maybe he just encountered a wounded animal that lashed out due to the pain or something.

As I tried to rationalize away the possibility that my Newfoundland might be waiting for me in her undead form, the four of us started up what I now saw was 86th Avenue. It quickly became clear that the military had been hard at work. Not a single house remained without the spray-painted 'X' and a small stake with a streamer planted in the middle of the front yard. I now wondered if maybe those individuals I'd seen emptying out the residences were part of the group that had deserted earlier.

The other thing that was impossible not to look at were the bodies scattered everywhere. Most had neat bullet holes in their foreheads, but some looked to have been crushed, a few blasted apart—most likely by a shotgun—and then there were the ones that were completely decapitated. And those were where we confirmed perhaps the most gruesome discovery so far.

The first severed head that we came across had belonged to a woman. Her long, flowing hair was fluttering in wispy strands as the morning breeze kicked up and brought the smells of fire and undeath wafting to our nostrils despite all of us having an arm slung across our faces to try and block some of it out. The filmed over, tracer riddled eyes were fixed on us. This was made extra creepy by the fact that the head was almost entirely upside-down. I most likely wouldn't have noticed if those terrible eyes had not blinked.

"You have got to be kidding," Julian choked out around his sleeved forearm that was pressed to his face in what I was discovering to be a futile effort.

The mouth began to open and close as I neared the head and

Day Two Begins

knelt in front of it. I picked up a twig from the street and poked the thing. The mouth snapped in a harsh clicking of teeth.

"That should not be possible," Julian breathed as he stepped up beside me.

"Actually, back in the days of the guillotine and the fall of the French aristocratic society, Marie Antoinette and that gang, it is said that the head remained cognizant for minutes after the decapitation. That is why the executioner often held it up and turned it to see the body so that it would presumably suffer just a few more seconds before death finally brought relief." Carl took a spot between me and Julian and then toed the woman's head with one booted foot.

I glanced up at him expecting to see a smirk but saw that he was being totally serious. His grave expression and pressed lips were pinched tight as he examined the head. As soon as I stood and stepped away, he stomped repeatedly until there was an ugly, pulpy squish and crunch.

We continued up the street and at last arrived where I'd parked my truck. From about a block away, I was able to see inside the cab. There was definite movement, and I felt the acidic juices in my belly start to multiply with each step until it felt as if a hole would burn through.

A few paces away, I stopped and held up my hand. The group paused, all of them looking at me with varied degrees of concern, confusion, and, in one instance, pity.

"Just wait here," I managed around the massive lump growing in my throat.

My hand felt numb as I pulled out the hand axe that I'd retrieved on our way out of the school parking lot. I found myself squeezing the rubber-coated grip in anticipation of what I would find. When I got closer, I saw her massive head bob up and down and then swing over to the driver's side of the truck where I was approaching. The window was covered in slimy film, keeping me from being able to see inside clearly.

Taking a deep breath, I stepped closer and gripped the door handle. The black head appeared to track my movement as it dipped up and down. I heard a deep rumble and huffing noise followed by what sounded a lot like Chewie's bark of excitement.

Did zombie dogs bark? I wondered.

I opened the door and brought the hand axe up in preparation for what would have to be done. I was hit by the coppery smell of blood and the thick musk of dog, but none of the foulness I'd been experiencing. Were undead dogs different?

I didn't have time to find out as Chewie lunged, her huge mouth aimed at my face.

The warm wetness of her tongue told me she was not undead, but that didn't stop an unfortunate squirt of urine from dampening the crotch of my jeans. I threw my arms around her thick neck and hugged Chewie until she finally pulled away and began to sniff in the direction of my companions.

"She seems fine," I said, my gaze pausing on Carl for just a moment. Maybe he didn't know everything. Maybe.

"I don't think all of us are going to fit in the cab," Betty sniffed.

She had a point. There were the two main bucket seats and then the space behind them with the pair fold down seats on each side that were a tight squeeze even for a child. Julian would fit, but it would be tight since he would be sharing space with Chewie. Good thing I didn't have to worry about being pulled over for unbelted passengers.

"I'll ride in back," Carl announced. Without waiting, he climbed into the cargo bed.

Julian, Betty, and I all piled into the cab with Chewie. She made the rounds, sniffing each person. Julian was given a proper swabbing with her massive tongue, but it did not go unnoticed by me that she had very little interest in Betty. When it came to new people, I usually followed her lead. I found dogs to be much more intuitive when it came to people and whether or not I could trust them.

Just before Stephanie and I got together, I had a mutt that I'd rescued from the local shelter. He was an older dog and was missing his right rear leg. When we went on walks, I always let him set the pace. Once he'd discovered the nearby park, he

Day Two Begins

would make a beeline for it as soon as I clipped on his leash and opened the front door. People would often wander up to see the three-legged dog as he bunny hopped after the ball we would play fetch with during our little excursions. For the most part, Pedro—that was the name he had when I got him and I saw no reason to change it—would happily pause in his game of fetch to let a stranger scratch him behind the ear. Those he really took a liking to were greeted with a full body wiggle that ended with him rolling onto his back for a belly rub. But sometimes he would shy away from a person. I usually would use that reaction as my cue to steer clear of that individual; and it wasn't confined to just men. Pedro shied away from his share of women…and even a few rowdy teens. Chewie's snubbing of Betty gave me a bit of confirmation when it came to my belief that maybe she was not a pleasant individual. I wonder what that said about me…that I would judge people based on my dog's reaction to them.

"So…" Julian turned to me, "…where do we go from here?"

I thought it over. In the movies, it seemed to be pretty common to run for a mall. That was a good reason *not* to do that. Besides, I wasn't entirely sure that I was ready for looting. That seemed to be a bit premature.

"I say we head to the house of whichever one of you is closest. We load up with everything we can fit into the truck. Pack like we are going camping," I offered.

"Do you really believe it is as bad as all that?" Julian said.

There was a plaintive tone to his voice that I did not expect from somebody who I saw as an authority figure. I guess I had my hopes that he would be some sort of leader. I was beginning to think that perhaps that was not the case.

I switched on the radio, hoping for something that would send us on the right path. All that I heard was a replay of that poor Doctor Sing. She had denied that the dead were returning and feasting on the living. By now, if somebody hadn't put a bullet in her head, she was probably one of them…a mindless eating menace. I turned the radio back off and indicated to Julian with my chin.

"Where to?" I asked.

"My house is right off of Holgate and 97th Avenue," Betty offered.

"That seems as good of a place to start as any." I pulled out onto the street. A few heads turned our direction and I saw a dozen or so more figures come stumbling out of the bushes of a house just a couple of doors down.

We turned left on Holgate and had to stop immediately. A military truck was parked crosswise, preventing us from moving past it unless I drove up on the sidewalk. The problem with that came in the form of the several undead crouched in a cluster around something on the ground on one side, and a lone zombified soldier standing in the middle of the sidewalk on the other.

I was about to shift into reverse when Carl banged on the rear window. Julian reached over and shoved it open.

"We got about thirty coming from behind. Get us outta here, friend," the man said in a voice that was much calmer than mine would have been given the situation.

I looked in the rearview mirror and, now that the bright white of my reverse lights were on, I could see a group of dark shapes coming our way.

"Everybody hang on, this is going to be unpleasant," I said through gritted teeth.

I cranked my steering wheel to the left and rolled up onto the sidewalk. I could already tell it would be a tight fit between the telephone pole on my right and the rock terrace that bordered the front of the house on my left. That did not include the soldier who continued to stand in the middle of the sidewalk and regard us with those vile, filmed eyes.

As soon as I was pointed straight and relatively certain that I could make it through the narrow opening without getting stuck, I gave my gas pedal a tap. We lunged forward and the bumper of my truck hit the soldier. The zombie fell back and vanished from sight. I applied a bit more pressure to the accelerator and felt us lift up. There was a sound of crunching and squishing and then we had all four wheels on the ground for that brief span before

Day Two Begins

the rear wheel rolled over the downed figure.

I heard a retching sound and then the splatter as Betty vomited all over the floor of the passenger side. Chewie made a huffing sound and I quickly rolled down the windows to at least vent out some of the stink of her sick. Unfortunately, Julian was not made of stronger stuff because he quickly followed in the purge. Unfortunately, he had shoved his face to the small portal of the window at the rear of the cab.

"Holy crap!" a voice hollered from the back of the truck.

I glanced in my rearview mirror to see Carl slinging his left arm around in an effort to rid himself of whatever had apparently splashed him. I had very little opportunity to observe all this as a pair of undead stumbled out from behind a parked van and into the path of my rugged little truck. I jerked the wheel to try and avoid them, but still managed to clip one and send her spinning away until she fell awkwardly on the curb.

By the time we were able to veer back onto the road, we had a dozen or so zombies still trailing after us. I couldn't really gun it and take off because the streets were a mess. There were bodies sprawled on the road and cars abandoned all over. Twice we had to edge around a wreck…and then we reached the overpass that would take us over Interstate 205.

A Tri-Met bus was sitting diagonally across the northbound lanes we were in which forced us over to the southbound lane. A motorcycle had obviously collided with the bus and was in pieces all over the southbound lane. The bike's driver was on the street about ten yards away and currently the focus of three of the undead who were ripping out strands from his insides. The fact that I could see his legs still twitching told me that this had to be a recent accident. Something had shattered the entire front windshield, leaving a massive and gaping hole.

A scream from inside the bus made me hit the brakes. I tried to get a look inside, but the windows were too high and we were already too close. I shifted into park.

"What are you doing?" Betty managed around a mouth that was still leaking drool and bits of what I had to guess were the rescue station-issued peanut butter sandwich she'd consumed

DEAD: Onset

earlier.

"Somebody in that bus needs help," I answered, surprised at my own amount of calm.

"They are probably already infected. We need to move." Betty looked over her shoulder and out the rear window of my truck's cab. "More of those things are coming."

"Maybe you'd like to get out and walk the rest of the way to your house," I snapped.

The problem at this exact moment rested in the fact that I wasn't sure that Betty was not correct in her assessment of the situation. But the fact that she was against this idea suddenly made it seem like the right thing to do.

I shut off my truck and made an exaggerated point of stuffing my keys into my pocket. I reached under the seat and had to fight back the urge to gag as the smell of Betty's vomit hit me in the nostrils with all its acrid force. I pulled out the box with my Ruger, checked to ensure it was loaded, and then dumped a handful of bullets into my palm as I climbed out of the truck and was able to stuff them into my other pocket.

"What are we doing?" Carl asked, sounding more curious than concerned.

"You had to have heard that scream on the bus," I said as I headed for the massive vehicle where the sounds of a struggle could easily be heard.

I broke into a run deciding that it would suck—at least for that person inside—if I were to arrive right *after* he or she was bitten. The doors took a bit of effort to pry open. As soon as I had it open, Carl was right beside me with a knife that would impress Crocodile Dundee in his hand.

I hurried up the few steps and looked down the length of the aisle. There was a body a few feet away that I recognized as being the driver based on the uniform. He was currently the source of attention for a pair of zombies that looked to be in their late teens. One of them had several piercings in her face that kept snagging on the tattered jacket worn by the driver. I watched as a ring above the right eyebrow snagged and tore free. A dribble of dark blood oozed like maple syrup in December from the fresh

Day Two Begins

rip in the zombie's face. She came up with a mouthful of flesh that dripped red and sent a rivulet down her chin.

The pierced zombie seemed to regard us for a moment, but then returned to the feast at hand. The other apparently decided that it wanted the fresh stuff for himself and began to rise to his feet. It was this scene that sat squarely between me and the young boy at the rear of the bus that was using his backpack full of what looked to be schoolbooks to fend off the two zombies swiping at him. Both of these undead looked like they were refugees from some local senior center and their advanced age was probably why the boy was having any success at staying alive and unbitten.

I raised my pistol, but Carl reached over and lowered my outstretched arm. He gave a shake of his head and flashed his massive blade before edging around me. He let the zombie get up and then reached out, grabbed a handful of hair, and drove his blade up under the jaw. He gave his wrist a violent turn and then jerked his hand free and shoved the inert corpse over and onto the pierced zombie that was still eating. Like a snake, he lunged in right behind it and drove his blade into the temple of the feasting female.

"Please!" the boy grunted as he slammed the closest zombie in the side of the head with his pack.

The only real effect this had was to wobble the creature. Whether it was because the boy lacked any real leverage to get off a good shot or the fact that the zombies were basically impervious to pain—or a combination of the two—the zombies were not disengaging from their attempts at the kid.

I moved forward and pulled my axe from the loop on my belt where it was beginning to feel like an extension of my person, and I brought it down hard on the back of the head of the closest of the two senior citizen zombies.

The kid cringed back and shrieked in horror as I jerked my axe free. At first I thought that it was due to his not understanding exactly what he was facing, then I saw the splatter of gore that had splashed his arm and exposed hand. He was frantically wiping the offensive fluid on the back of the seat he'd been cowering in as I grabbed the second zombie by the back of the head. I jerked it away and finished it as well.

Just as I pushed the body down to the floor, I heard the sound of my truck horn blaring. Looking over my shoulder, I could see out the front window of the bus, but that only gave me a very small view of the road since the bus was stopped all catawampus across the street. Apparently, Carl's view was better.

"We need to move!" he barked.

I reached back and grabbed the kid by the arm and slung him past me. He stumbled, but to his credit regained his footing and quickly scrambled after the man who was making a hasty exit. By the time I was within the first few seats and able to see outside, I understood the urgency.

The street back towards the way we'd come was thick with the walking dead. It was a pack that had to number over a hundred. They were all sizes and ages, male and female. And they had one thing in mind: get us and eat us alive.

I jumped from the bus and sprinted to the truck. Carl had the boy by the hand and was swinging him up into the back of the truck by the time I reached the driver's side door. I jerked the handle and almost broke my fingers.

"Unlock the damn door, Betty!" I shouted.

She started and then leaned over and hit the button. I opened the door, still nursing the bee sting sensation in the fingertips of the hand that had tried to open the door. Climbing in, I had to shift around to get at my keys and struggled because Chewie was now expressing just how much she missed me in the less than three minutes I'd been away.

Jamming the key in the ignition, I turned the truck over. Just before the engine roared to life, my brain played out the scenario where, for some mysterious reason, the truck refused to start. I would turn the key in futility as the horde drew near and only get it started as the first dead hands slapped against the rear bumper. But no; the truck started like a champ and I floored it as I shifted into drive.

"Turn right," Betty called as I approached 97th.

I floored it to the next intersection and then yanked the

Day Two Begins

wheel left, skidding around the corner. My fishtail turn elicited cries of alarm as well as a few expletives from Carl in the back.

"I said left back there," Betty insisted.

"Yeah, I heard you." I slowed and glanced in my rearview. Sure enough, the leading edge of the zombie mob were rounding the corner in pursuit. "And I will circle around once I know that the pack is moving this way. Otherwise we would be leading them to your doorstep."

That comment earned an audible gulp from Betty and she sat back in the seat, her lips pressed tight. I could tell she wanted to say something, but she could not find a flaw in my logic and was reduced to annoyed silence.

I let the truck roll another two blocks. As we crept along, I did not see any new walking dead; except, in one of the houses that we passed, I was certain that I saw somebody peering out the window and then jerking the curtain shut.

I circled back just as I said I would, and by the time I'd gone through Holgate and then another block before turning up 97th, I was convinced that we'd lost the zombie tail. I rolled along until Betty pointed to a small tan home on the left side of the street next to a townhouse duplex. I debated leaving the engine running, but decided against it as everybody piled out.

Chewie made to follow and I realized that it had been a while since she'd had a bathroom break. Besides, I doubt that she wanted to sit in the cab with all that vomit on the floor.

"Grab everything you can from the kitchen first, then work your way through things like hygiene, blankets, and anything you think is vital," Carl was saying as everybody headed for the front door.

I looked up to see the young boy still sitting in the back of the truck. His eyes were glazing over and I had to imagine he was in a state of shock. I considered checking on him, but decided that maybe his being somewhat catatonic was not necessarily a bad thing at the moment.

Chewie and I trotted across the street and she went about doing her business. As soon as she finished, we headed back to the truck. She surprised me when she changed course and went to jump into the back with the boy. I started to call her to me, but before I could open my mouth, she was already snuffling the youngster. I saw his face change from absolute shock to one of relief.

"You stay here and be a good dog," I said, giving her a pat on the head as I opened the passenger side and began scooping out the slurry on the floor. Eventually I gave up and just pulled out the floor mat and tossed it aside. That took care of a majority of the problem. Open air would have to do the rest for now.

That finished, I made my way to the house. I reached the door and paused, looking back at the scene playing out in the rear of my truck. My brain was wired to all those terrible movies. I would step inside the house, and as soon as I did, that is when the zombie that has been hiding unseen in some nearby bushes will come out and stagger over, attack the kid and my dog, and we will all rush out at the last second to see the carnage or make a rescue just in the nick of time—depending on how sadistic the movie's director might be.

Taking a deep breath, I stepped inside and allowed the flimsy screen door to shut on my heels. Looking around, this was exactly how I would have pictured Betty's house to look. There were shelves of those ridiculous figures of small children doing things like fishing with cane poles or swinging on a tire swing. I don't think kids have done that for the past several years.

One wall was lined with rows of *commemorative* (and I use the word very loosely) plates with images of cats on them. And the television was one of those ancient models. The kind that was built into a massive wood cabinet that had a turntable, radio, and cassette player built in.

There was a bookshelf, and I was guessing that not one of those books had ever had its spine cracked. It was a plethora of biographies and a vast array of the popular self-help philosophical crap about how to succeed, be a better person, and make the most out of yourself. In just my brief exposure to her, I knew she hadn't done much on that second item.

"We have all the blankets and towels in the hall closet," Betty called from somewhere out of sight.

Day Two Begins

I headed to that closet and opened it to find that it was indeed packed with a variety of towels, blankets, sheets, and comforters. I grabbed a stack and decided that it would be better to just start toting things out to the truck. I might've been a little influenced about my earlier premonition regarding monsters arriving just as I went inside.

Stepping out onto the single step landing, I looked around to discover that not one thing had changed. The boy was still hugging Chewie, and she was rewarding him with a generous if not slobbery swab of her tongue every so often. I dropped my load in the open cargo area and rushed back inside. While the situation seemed calm, I had no desire to tempt fate.

It was as I came out with my third load of towels and blankets that I was finally rewarded (such as it was) with a single zombie shambling towards my parked truck. It was coming from the direction of the neighborhood away from Holgate. And I wasn't the only one to notice. Chewie was on her feet in the back of the pickup and looking forward in the direction of the zombie. The hackles on the back of her neck stood on end, and she had taken a position between the boy and the approaching threat.

Grabbing my axe, I started towards the creature. It had been a man in his fifties or so by the looks. He had a fringe of gray hair that looked like a wreath as dead as he was; and he somehow had managed to still be wearing his glasses. There was a nasty rip on his right shoulder that left a dark stain down the front of his hideous checker patterned button-up short-sleeve shirt. His tan khaki shorts were kept up by a tightly cinched black belt and he wore black socks with sandals. The more sarcastic part of my brain said that maybe this guy was better off dead. There was a dark stain around his mouth and all down his front which told me this guy had already gotten his teeth into somebody.

I shoved that aside and moved in to end the man's existence once and for all. Just as I got to within a step or two, the report of a rifle made me flinch and duck for cover. The man toppled and fell face first on the street, his head cocked my direction.

DEAD: Onset

There was a nasty exit hole in the man's face that had obliterated most of his nose. Somehow, his glasses had stayed mostly in place, although one lens had shattered and the other had apparently popped out. I don't know why, but for some reason, I was fixated on that fact.

At least I was until I heard the crunch of approaching footsteps. I cursed myself for leaving my pistol on the front seat of my truck and prepared to lunge out and cleave whoever this person was that had just damn near killed me.

"Hey…whoever you are…sorry," a timid voice called.

I peeked up over the top of the hedge that I'd dove behind for cover to see a very young girl standing in the middle of the street with a rifle almost as big as her slung over her shoulder.

"It was a bad angle and I swear I didn't see you until it was too late," the girl apologized.

"You coulda killed me," I snapped, tucking my axe back in its loop and dusting myself off. Just as I did, I heard the screen door slam open behind me back at Betty's house.

"What's going on?" Julian was yelling.

"Hey," I whisper yelled, "can we quiet it the fuck down before we bring every zombie in a hundred-mile radius down on our heads?"

I turned back to the girl. "And you…how old are you? Eight? Nine?"

Her expression switched to that of youthful indignance. "I'm eleven and three-quarters…almost." That last word was added rather sheepishly.

I glanced to the corpse in the middle of the street with a near-perfect shot to the center of the back of its head, then back to this waif of a child. "Where did you learn to shoot?" Honestly that was the only thing that I could form up and push out of my mouth.

The reaction I received caught me totally by surprise. It was almost instantaneous. Tears welled up in the girl's eyes and began streaming down her cheeks.

"What in the world is everybody doing just standing out here on the porch?" Betty's voice cut through me and caused me

Day Two Begins

to snap around.

"Can you people just shut the hell up and get the truck loaded. What part of this whole zombie apocalypse thing are you missing?" I took a few steps toward the house and forced myself to lower my own voice. "Just finish grabbing whatever you can and then we have to go. I'm pretty sure every zombie for blocks around is heading this way."

I was almost certain I heard derisive comments regarding the gunshot being much more likely to be the cause, but I didn't care and already turned my attention back to this pre-teen version of Annie Oakley. She had wiped at her tears, making a dark smudge across her face that only emphasized her youth.

"I hate to bring up something bad, but I am guessing that, by the way you're reacting, your parents are gone." I couldn't bring myself to say the word 'dead' to the girl. No sense hitting her in the face with what looked pretty obvious.

"Mister Wills did it." She shot a look over her shoulder and even from just the profile of her face, I could see the eyes tighten and the lips press together in fury as she glared at the corpse. I guess I knew who Mr. Wills was without it being much of a stretch.

"I'm sorry." *Damn, what else can you say to an eleven-year-old kid who probably saw her parents eaten alive?* I thought. "Look, we have a small group, but we have room for one more if you want to join us."

The girl sniffed, and then she took a step back. I was caught off guard when the rifle slid from her shoulder and was in her hands.

"You're a stranger." That one statement had all the suspicion a person might've expected a day or two ago if they'd approached a strange child and invited them to just jump in their vehicle with them and take off. The problem was, this was suddenly a very different time. New rules were going to be written on the fly. People would have to adapt.

"Yes, I am. And so are all the people with me, but if both of your parents are…" I didn't know how to finish that statement.

"My mom is in the bathroom. She's just sick. As soon as the

ambulance comes, they will take her to the hospital and she will be all better. My dad…" And that was where she burst into tears again.

Suddenly, she looked every bit the eleven-year-old girl. Rifle slung in her arms or not, this was still just a scared child.

"Listen, umm, I don't know your name…" I left it open and waited to see if she would answer.

If anything, she now appeared even more dubious and suspicious of my motives. How could I blame her? The news was a continuous parade of terrible things happening to youngsters. The "Don't talk to strangers" mantra was preached heavily and with good reason.

"Okay, but I am going to say something that you are not going to like or want to hear." I took a step back to give her a little more space when I noticed her hands grip her rifle just a bit tighter. "Your mom is more than sick." I made it a point to look down at the corpse on the street. "She probably has the infection Mister Wills had, and there is nothing that will make her better. Also, the ambulances aren't coming anymore."

I thought back to my own experience at the hospital. If what I saw there was happening elsewhere, and I had no reason to think that it wasn't, then hospitals are the last place a person would want to be.

As I said those words, I saw the girl's face crumple. Her tears came in a steady stream now, and her body began to shake with sobs. I didn't know what to say. My mouth opened and shut a few times, but no sound came out.

I felt a hand on my shoulder as somebody eased me aside. The last person in the world that I expected to see was now kneeling before this shattered little girl.

"Hi there, my name is Betty Simms. You're Trina and Ray's little girl Selina DuBois, aren't you?" It wasn't really a question, but the girl nodded. "And you know me, I'm Missus Simms, I teach at the high school. Had both your mama and your daddy in my classes when they were younger. Now, I know this is really scary, but I think it would be best for you if you came with us. There is a bad sickness that is making people do strange things."

Day Two Begins

"Mister Wills ate my daddy and bit Mama really bad," Selina said through hitched sobs. "Daddy tried to make him go away, but he wouldn't and he pulled Daddy down the stairs. He hit his head and just laid there while Mister Wills ripped him open. That was when Mama sent me to my room, but I heard the screams. Finally, my mama made him go away, but he stayed at the door and we went upstairs where Mama said she had to go into the bathroom and that I wasn't to let her out no matter what."

Betty stood and extended a hand to the little girl. Selina sniffed, and then very slowly took the offered hand of Betty Simms and the pair started for the house. I still stood by my assessment of the woman and her relatively unpleasant demeanor, but I amended it to apparently pertain to adults and dogs.

I rushed inside and began to help carry out more supplies from the woman's home. Twenty minutes later, we had pretty much most of what anybody deemed useful loaded into the back of the pickup. When I went to climb in, I noticed that Chewie had curled up across the lap of the boy who had not moved or said a word during the entire process. I left her there in back which freed up enough room in the cab for Selina to squeeze in between Julian and Betty.

"Now where?" I muttered as I turned the key.

DEAD: Onset

7

The Journey to Safety Begins

"This is stupid!" Julian hissed as I jerked the wheel of the truck and turned left.

"I told you all that going to this Walmart was a bad idea," I said between clenched teeth as I avoided the pair of undead that lurched out in front of us as I turned into the huge, mostly vacant parking lot.

The front of the store had been devastated by a tow truck that had smashed through the entrance. I could see zombies roaming in and out of where the large bank of doors used to exist.

"So where do you suggest we go?" Betty said in a voice that was perhaps the calmest of us all. Something about having this child to watch over had practically transformed her into an entirely different person.

I thought it over. I knew that we needed to get out of the city. There was simply too much chaos for us to have any chance at survival. We needed to be out in the boondocks. We needed to be someplace where we were remote enough to avoid the worst of this, but still close enough to the populated areas to be able to scavenge for supplies if this did indeed turn out to be the actual zombie apocalypse.

An explosion nearby made me jump. I looked that direction

DEAD: Onset

and saw a plume of black, oily smoke rising skyward. Between the undead, the possibility that some of the living may not be anything we would want to encounter, and then all the fires, we needed to find a location to hunker down for a while.

An idea came to me. It was probably not the best choice, but it would at least allow us to catch our breath. All I had to do was hope everybody else would see the logic.

"Milo McIver Park," I said.

There was a moment of silence when I thought everybody would start laughing me out of the cab. My eyes were fixed on the zombie laden parking lot as I drove for the exit, but I caught movement out of the corner of my eye. I glanced over to see both Julian and Betty nodding.

"That is not a bad idea," Julian murmured.

The only difficulty now would be getting there alive. I pulled out of the parking lot of the Walmart and made my way to Interstate 205. Merging onto the freeway, I don't know what I expected. Nothing could prepare me for this new look into Hell.

"Oh, my God," Betty breathed. I noticed that she sort of pulled Selina in close and acted as a shield to try and prevent the young girl from seeing what was out there.

The first cars we passed were a mangled mess of what had been a nine-car collision. It looked like one of the vehicles had decided to go the opposite direction as everybody else. The mini-van facing the wrong way was the worst part. The side door had been ripped off in the accident and there were two children's car seats in the back that were an absolute nightmare. The dark stains were bad enough, but one of them still held most of a limbless, headless torso.

I was regretting our decision to take this more direct route almost immediately. We were just passing over what was known as the Springwater Corridor when I heard a loud staccato burst of what I instantly recognized as gunfire. A second later, the truck lurched and shimmied as at least one tire on the driver's side exploded.

"Hang on!" I called out as I slowed us in the middle of an overpass.

The Journey to Safety Begins

There was a series of shouts and screams as everybody reacted to the truck's erratic movements. As we came to a stop, I could feel the uneven wobble and lurch from the flat or flats.

Looking out the windshield, I could see them coming. Several undead had turned our direction, most likely drawn by the sound of the metal rims grinding on the asphalt. Looking in the rearview mirror, I could see that we'd sort of attracted a long trail of zombies *a la* Pied Piper style.

"Everybody out!" I barked.

Opening my door and stepping outside, I could now hear the assorted moans of the undead. But there was something else, and if I'd not heard it come from the mouth of my beloved Stephanie, I might've been draw to investigate.

"Is that a baby crying?" Julian gasped, looking in all directions as he sought the source of that horrible sound.

"You would think so…but you would be fatally wrong," I said as I clipped the leash onto Chewie and then pulled out my Ruger and shoved it in the waist of my pants. Last but not least, I slung my bag over my shoulder with my picture of Stephanie inside.

"I don't understand." Julian was edging close to the railing of the overpass, his head cocked as that sound drifted to us again.

"Me either," I admitted. "But some of the zombies make that sound."

"That's ridiculous," Betty hissed, covering Selina's ears like that would do any good considering the volume that she used when she spoke.

"Maybe, but I saw it for myself at the hospital."

"Really?" The doubt dripped thickly from that single word as Betty's eyebrows rose in emphasis of her opinion on this matter.

I did not have time for this crap. Stepping towards her, I leveled what I hoped came across as a very stern gaze. "It is the exact same sound that came out of Stephanie's mouth when her eyes opened and she reanimated as one of *them*." That last word was accompanied by a few flecks of spittle as I had to strain to force the words to come out of my mouth.

Betty's face paled some, and I saw understanding dawn in her eyes. "I'm...I'm sorry, Evan. I just don't know what to do, and I'm so terribly afraid." She paused and dropped her gaze. "I think we got off on the wrong foot. I'm really not such a terrible person."

"Fine," I said, cutting her off before she could launch into whatever she felt she needed to get off her chest. Here and now was not the time or place. "We need to get moving."

"Where?" was Julian's plaintive moan as he looked around and realized that we were discovered.

I was about to answer when another burst of gunfire sounded. I heard the rounds smashing into the side of the truck, puncturing the metal and creating what was almost like a metallic echo of the gunshots. Instinctively, I dove for the ground. Chewie's instincts were different and she tried to bolt, but thankfully I had a good grip on her leash. I dragged me forward a bit until I could yank her back and tug her down with me.

Looking around, I saw that Betty had the sense to do the same thing I had. She'd also kept presence of mind to pull Selina down with her. Carl peered at me from the rear of the truck where he was pressing up against the rear wheel...or what was left of it. Both front and back tires on the driver's side were gone and only the rims with fragments of rubber remained. The boy we'd rescued was with him and had his hands over his head as if that might magically stop a bullet.

The only person still on his feet was Julian. He was just standing there, his gaze looking in the direction that I was pretty sure the bullets had come from.

"Julian, get the fuck down!" I hissed.

He looked down at me with a confused expression; then his hands came up to his chest and I saw the dark bloom spreading across his shirt. He crumpled to his knees and his chin came to rest on his chest as he let out one long, rattling sigh. I knew instantly that he was dead.

"We need to get out of here," I whispered.

"Ya think?" Carl sniped sarcastically.

The Journey to Safety Begins

"What about all the stuff we have in the truck?" Betty's voice sounded dangerously close to tears.

"We're screwed in that department," I said bluntly.

Looking around, I could see legs as I scanned underneath the numerous vehicles stranded—likely for eternity—along this stretch of the interstate. There were too many to count as it seemed like a veritable forest was shambling our direction from all sides. No matter which direction we went, we were going to have to fight our way out.

Scanning my companions, I realized that only Carl and I had any sort of weapon. Not that I felt Betty would be any help, and the two kids even less, but we were not getting out of this without killing a bunch of zombies.

My brain scoffed at the idea of killing something that was already dead, but I quelled that voice and gave the current situation my full attention. The idea wasn't perfect, but there was no time for planning.

"Betty, you and Selina stick with me. Carl, you keep the boy close. Each of us should take opposite sides of the road here to try and split up the zombies coming our way."

"Stop calling them that," Betty hissed.

I ignored her. We could discuss the proper terminology later. Right now, I just wanted to get out of here alive and unbitten. I rose, but stayed hunched over. I was almost certain that our sniper probably only wanted whatever he or she thought we might have in the truck. Well, I had one last surprise in store for that asshole.

"We will take that side." I pointed to the side of the overpass closest to where the shots had come from.

On the plus side, we would have fewer zombies…on the negative, we would be closer to the shooter. If my plan worked, none of that would matter in a minute.

"Is the plan still to head for McIver Park?" Carl asked, keeping his voice low, but loud enough for me to hear.

"Yeah, if we get split up, that is still where I plan to head."

Carl gave me a salute and then got up on his hands and knees and started for the nearest car. He whispered something to the boy who made no indication that he heard, but as soon as Carl was a few feet away, the young man followed on his heels, staying down just like Carl as he crawled away.

I turned to Betty. "Okay, you and Selina move over by that car." I pointed to the one I meant for them to head towards.

"What about you?"

I was stunned. It was the first words that I'd heard Selina utter since we'd first met.

"I will be coming in just a moment."

Betty opened her mouth, but we simply did not have time as a luxury where I could explain everything. I crawled to the rear of the truck and then slid into the cargo area. Chewie was right behind me.

"Down," I commanded. I was so relieved when she did as she was told. That would earn her a treat…one of these days.

I had to tip a few boxes over to find what I wanted, but at last I had a book of matches. Glancing around at all the stuff we would lose, I wanted to cry. Next, I made my way to a box that had the word "clothes" scrawled on the side and tipped it. Grabbing the first thing I saw, it took me until I was out of the truck and around to the far side before I realized it was a gigantic pair of granny panties. I started chanting the mantra, "Don't look at the crotch!"

"Nasty," I breathed when my eyes did exactly what I had told them not to do.

I flopped down on the pavement and pulled out my trusty hand axe. It took a few tries because of the bad angle, but finally I managed to strike the gas tank with enough force to puncture it. That ever-present voice in my head returned to tell me that I was lucky there hadn't been any sparks. As was becoming the habit, I shoved that voice away and continued with my mission. Sopping the panties in the leaking fuel, I dragged them a few feet away, making sure to leave a trail. The voice started to weigh in again and I screamed in my head for it to shut up.

Once I was a few feet away, a distance I was in no way comfortable with as being far enough, I pulled the matches out and struck one on the cover. Inching the tiny flame close, I jerked my hand back when the fumes caught in a miniature explosion. A second later, the panties were ablaze and, just as I'd hoped, the flames began creeping along the ground towards my pickup.

Getting up into a crouch, I sped over to Betty and Selina and grabbed them both by an arm and jerked them after me. We hurried as best we could towards the far end of the overpass. I wove us around cars every time the way was blocked by one or more of the undead that were now converging with purpose towards the truck.

Eventually we found ourselves creeping between an old station wagon with occupants that were slapping impotently on the glass windows of their tomb and the concrete wall that marked the edge of the overpass. A zombie lumbered for me down one side. That was preferable to the five coming down the other.

I was just about to strike when a loud 'whump' sounded behind us. While not as spectacular as I'd seen in movies and television, the truck still went up in a ball of fire and black smoke.

"Go now!" I barked as I jumped up and brought my axe down on the top of the head of the business suit zombie.

Betty let out a yelp, but she did as she was told, dragging Selina along behind her. I was impressed with how fast the larger woman moved as I rushed to catch up. The sounds of our would-be sniper's shots plinking off of several of the cars we were leaving in our wake helped spur us on. I glanced down and had to almost laugh. Chewie was galloping alongside me, her tongue lolling out one side of her mouth, creating a massive doggie grin.

I was pretty sure that I heard somebody screaming a string of obscenities at us as we beat feet. Twice, I had to veer away from Betty and Selina to take down a zombie that would have likely made it across our path as we ran.

Once, I glanced over to the far side and ahead to see Carl engaged with a zombie. He had that huge knife with him and had to get much closer to the zombies than I think I would've been comfortable with, but he dispatched them in a way that was video game worthy.

I was amazed when we reached the far end of the overpass unscathed. Carl had already yanked open a car door and stuck his head inside. When he came out, I saw the look of disappointment on his face.

"We might get lucky if we check every single car, but…I have a feeling that a lot of these cars were abandoned while they were still running. They are bone dry. At least this one is. We are going to have to make it out of here on foot. Going back down into one of these neighborhoods is too big of a risk, and I'm not talking about the undead. I'll take my chances with them at this point." He gestured to the zombies coming from all over, drawn by the amazing amount of noise that we'd been a part of between the gunshots, explosion, and periodic screams. (I was almost glad in a way that every single one of us had yelped or out and out screamed at some point during our escape. If it had been just me, I would have been embarrassed. If it would have been just Betty, I think that would've driven the split between us even wider.)

"You can't mean for us to stay on this freeway," Betty exclaimed.

"It ain't like you gotta worry about traffic," Carl snapped.

"Let's just stay close and get moving," I said before this could escalate. I had a feeling there was no love lost between these two.

We started along at a brisk walk. To our right were the tracks for the light rail. We spotted one train ahead and I began to dread our reaching a point where we could see inside. Even from a distance, I could see dark stains and smears on the windows.

The sounds of screams were back in full force as well as that of gunfire, and even the occasional explosion as neighborhoods filled in the vista on both sides of the interstate. I was just starting to appreciate how sounds that were even the slightest bit muffled while we rode in the truck could be pushed almost entirely out of my consciousness. Those first few minutes out of it had been somewhat frantic, so all the peripheral stuff had been

The Journey to Safety Begins

shoved aside. Now we were faced with the hellish nightmare that was falling over the entire city; and the world by the sounds of things.

As we wove in and out of cars, things thinned out for a bit and we were almost able to relax. Most of the zombies we began to encounter were belted securely within their defunct automobiles. *Thank God for click-it or ticket*, I thought as we passed cars, many with open doors where the occupants reached for us impotently, unable to release themselves from their self-imposed bonds.

We neared a green sign on the side of the road that read "Happy Valley Next 2 Exits" but some clever person had spray-painted the prefix "un" in front of the word Happy. Apparently, Selina thought that was the funniest thing in the world and began to giggle like a fiend. The more we told her to quiet down, the worse it got, until she could barely walk.

"Hysterics," Carl whispered as he sidled up beside me, his face a grim mask of disapproval. "If she don't snap out of it, we may be in trouble."

"I'm pretty sure she'll mellow out eventually." I tried to hide my eye roll by looking the other way.

That was a mistake.

We'd come up alongside that light rail train by now. It was worse that it had looked from a distance. It wasn't the dozen or so zombies wandering around inside the cars, and it wasn't the smears and splatters of blood that were on every single window.

"What the hell?" Carl whispered as he actually veered towards the side of the road and closer to the scene.

Staring out at us from the three windows towards the back of the last train car were perhaps two dozen children. Correction…zombie children. Their filmed over gazes were locked on us and I had no doubt that, unlike the adult versions inside that seemed oblivious, these were very much aware of our presence.

I grabbed Carl by the arm and pulled him back. He started and looked around as if he hadn't realized what he'd been doing. After a sheepish grin, he simply stood with his hands on his hips and stared at the bizarre sight.

"It's like the little sumbitches are thinking," Carl said as he pointed unnecessarily towards the cluster of zombie children.

Something tickled the back of my mind, like perhaps I'd seen something before. Unfortunately, at least at the moment, my brain was too scrambled to pick anything out of value. By the time we made it across the next overpass of sorts, we had thick trees on either side of the interstate. I'd hoped that it would muffle some of the sound, but that was not the case. In a world this dead—no pun intended—every sound seemed to be magnified exponentially.

We were moving along at a steady pace when we heard the sound of an approaching vehicle. Because we were in a bit of a dip, our visibility was somewhat limited, and so we could not tell if it was ahead of us on our lane or in the other lane across the divide that existed between the north and southbound lanes.

"Everybody down," I said, pulling the group towards a flatbed truck hauling a very long trailer with a trio of forklifts strapped into place.

We all huddled together and waited. Eventually, the vehicle grew close enough that we were able to tell that it was in the northbound lane as opposed to our southbound one. It wasn't moving very fast, and that really amped up the level of anxiety that I was feeling with each passing second.

We continued to sit still, each of us with our backs pressed against the wheels of the flatbed. A single zombie had spotted us and was heading our direction, but it was moving so slow that I was confident that the approaching vehicle would be past us and beyond the hump of the northbound lane before we would have to take it down.

When it did come into view, I saw that it was a green SUV. It obviously had a sunroof, because a lone individual was poking up through it with a gun to his or her shoulder as they apparently swept the road ahead. That was not the soundest strategy in my opinion and showed a lack of understanding that enemies could easily lie in wait and ambush them from behind. After all, they'd driven right past us. If we'd been bent on attacking others, we would've been able to snipe them with no trouble.

The Journey to Safety Begins

I'd just given the word for us to move out when I heard gunfire back in the direction the SUV had disappeared. A tinge of guilt pasted my conscience a bit as I realized that I'd made no effort to warn those people about what waited for them from back the way we'd come. Looking around, I saw that I was not alone in that sentiment. Even Carl had a downcast look to his expression. For some reason, that made me feel good. I think, up to this point, I'd believed he was all about himself and to hell with anybody else.

"You think those bad people got them?" a small voice spoke from beside Carl.

I jumped at the unfamiliar sound of the young man's voice. My reaction apparently scared him a bit as he ducked behind Carl for protection.

"Maybe," Carl answered, gently steering the boy back out to the group and from behind his legs.

I caught the look of disapproval in Betty's eyes, but I had to agree with Carl's approach. I didn't think we had the luxury any longer of protecting the children from certain aspects of the truth. That thought made me sad, but it was a reality of what was happening around us.

"I hope they were smart like Evan and got away." The boy looked up at me, his eyes squinting as the sun hit his face.

I hadn't even known that he'd known my name. Maybe it was time that I learn his. "Okay, everybody, I think we should all know each other's names since it looks like we will be together for a while. I don't wanna be sayin' 'Hey you!' every single time I need to get somebody's attention."

We went around one by one and gave our names. When it was over, I now knew that I was travelling with Carl Higgins, Betty Sims, Selina DuBois—age eleven and three-quarters, and Michael Killian—age nine (no fraction given). The two children seemed to be the only ones interested in Chewie enough to ask her name. I winced when they didn't get the reference to my favorite Wookie.

"Okay, so the first thing we need to do is obtain weapons for everybody. Carl and I can handle a lot, but if you get trapped, then you are going to need to protect yourself," I announced.

"You want to give weapons to the children?" Betty gasped.

"I hate to say it, but the mindset of as recent as yesterday has to go. If we want to survive, all of us are going to need to be able to fend for ourselves," I answered, then realized that Selina's rifle was back in the truck and lost to us forever. "As unlikely as all this seems, the dead are getting up and attacking the living. They get up and kill...the people they kill get up and kill." I channeled a little snippet of a speech I'd heard in the original *Dawn of the Dead*. "And as sad as it seems, I believe there are going to be a lot of people who take advantage of the chaos. They will be more dangerous than the walking dead. Trusting people is going to be difficult. I think our best bet for the time being is to avoid any other survivors."

"What if somebody is in trouble?" Betty challenged. "Are you prepared to simply walk away and leave them to whatever terrible fate they are facing? Is your ability to care restricted to just the children?"

"I think they are the least likely to turn around and stab us in our sleep." I gave a shrug. The reality was that children might be the least dangerous to us as a whole, but they would also be the largest negative draw on resources without offering a return in labor or security. "I will be the first person to tell you that I'm not much of a hero. I am not some military-trained type who has all the answers. I worked in construction to get myself through school to be a music teacher. I am winging it and playing it by ear. I am going to make mistakes. Also, I am absolutely not the leader. We are a group and everybody has a say in what we do. If it gets to a situation where we have strongly opposing views, we can take a vote." I glanced at the kids. "Sorry, but that will only be the adults."

I saw Selina scowl, but Michael didn't seem to care. In fact, he wasn't really paying attention to what was going on here. His gaze was fixed back the way we'd come. I glanced over my shoulder to see what had him so captivated.

"Okay...first thing I want to make clear," I said as I started ushering our group onwards, "is that if you see something like a

The Journey to Safety Begins

pack of zombies coming our direction…you tell the group right away." I fixed Michael with my gaze, but it did not seem to matter to him in the slightest.

We started walking again. The undead were really spread out on the interstate at this point. But they were still in numbers that made us have to weave and duck around the assortment of vehicles that would never move again for the most part.

As we walked, I kept looking over our shoulder at the zombies that were now starting to fall in together and form a pretty large horde. I was not all that keen on leaving the interstate, it was a nice straight shot to our destination for the most part. Also, the sounds of people dying, the sporadic gunfire, as well as more than just a few fires burning out of control had me uncomfortable with the idea of venturing into the neighborhoods. Those were basically war zones. If I was travelling by myself, I could slip in and out of places. Run, hide, and do whatever I needed to do as the circumstances warranted.

With these kids in tow, the reality was that we were severely handicapped. I hated even thinking it, but having them along might hamper our chances for survival. It was something that I would have to take in a moment-by-moment basis and see what might arise. Again, I hated myself for even thinking this way, but I don't know if I will let myself die to save somebody that would then have no chance of survival in my absence.

"You're thinking them kids is a liability," Carl whispered as he moved up and matched my stride.

"How the hell…?" I started, but then clamped my mouth shut.

"For one, you keep shooting them looks and your face just goes pale as one of them deaders. I kept thinking you would start crying." Carl clapped a hand on my shoulder. "And you ain't alone. In fact, if it woulda been solely up to me, I might've left 'em behind a while back. This ain't some damn show where things look bleak and then we magically come up with the answers. The dead ain't gonna give a rip about our best intentions and good deeds. They will tear us apart without hesitation."

"Are you saying we need to abandon them?" I whispered,

fighting myself to keep my eyes forward and not to look back where Michael and Selina were now both walking with Betty.

"No. Not now. Sorta like farm rules, you don't name the animals you plan to eat. Them kids have names...can't just up and leave 'em to be zombie snacks."

I wasn't sure how to feel about Carl. The biggest problem was that he was actually saying out loud many of the things I was thinking. I didn't recall that sort of thing coming up in any of the movies I'd seen. At least not from the folks I would've considered the so-called good guys.

"Morality is gonna be something each of us will have to struggle with as this goes on." I glanced over at Carl and saw that he was looking over his shoulder. He turned back to me. "Each of us is about to find out who we really are. And I will be honest with you, I am not sure what that means for me."

We walked in silence for a while. As we approached a zombie or zombies that we could not avoid, one or both of us would move to take it down. At last, we came to an exit that gave me an idea. The Johnson Creek Boulevard exit would drop us pretty close to 82nd Avenue. There were shops and stores all along that strip. While the cars on the highway were problematic and risky, I was willing to bet we could find one in a parking lot.

I explained my idea to Carl. He nodded and we waited for Betty and the two kids to catch up.

"Okay, so we are going to go down there and find ourselves a car," I explained.

"And steal it?" Michael said with an odd lack of emotion. I glanced over at him and he was just staring at his shoes.

I noticed that Betty was looking at me, then the boy, then raising her eyes like she thought I should know something. Well, she would need to be more specific. I did not have any idea what she was trying to signal to me with her eyes.

"Yeah, I guess you're right. But I don't think the owners will be missing it," I said as casually as possible.

"Because they got ate up."

I did a double-take. Michael still continued to just stare at the ground. I looked at Betty and she was almost leaning for-

The Journey to Safety Begins

ward as if she thought I was about to answer the million-dollar question. I hated to disappoint her, but I had no clue.

"This just keeps getting better," Carl leaned over and whispered to me.

I shot him a questioning look, but he just turned and started walking towards Johnson Creek Boulevard. I was confused and frustrated.

After a moment, I jogged after him. Chewie was not all that happy with my jogging and made an agitated huff to let me know that this sort of thing would only be tolerated on a limited basis. "What the hell are you talking about?"

"Look, I hate to say it, but I'm not gonna hang with this group. I want to survive, and if you want to do the same, then I suggest you just cut the cord and let them drift away. They don't stand a chance. Maybe you haven't noticed, but Betty can barely keep up. The reason she is walking with the kids is because they move closer to her speed and don't care if she stops to catch her breath every few hundred yards. The only reason they are still even with us is because you and I have been clearing the path."

I turned back to Betty and the two kids. Selina was staring at me, one eyebrow raised like she was waiting for me to say something. Michael continued to stare at the ground. Betty stood between them with a look on her face that I could not even begin to read.

"So you're just gonna bail?" I asked incredulously.

"No, I am gonna survive. And if you want to have even the slightest chance of seeing the sun come up tomorrow, I suggest that you do the same."

With that, he turned around again and started walking. I stood there, unsure of what to do. One voice in my head told me to pull my gun and blow the creep away. The only thing stopping me was that I wasn't a murderer. There was seriously no way that I could just shoot a person. Not a living one anyway.

I stalked back the few yards to Betty and the kids. As I did, I could see that our zombie mob was still coming. They were like the tide. And like the tide, it could come and sweep you away if you did not pay attention.

"So, what's the deal?" I asked as I motioned with my head that they needed to get moving.

Betty glanced at Michael and then back to me. She mouthed something, but I was not proficient at reading lips.

"Just spit it out," I snapped. I didn't have the patience.

"Autism," she hissed in a voice that was barely above a whisper.

It took me a moment, but then I realized that she was telling me that Michael was autistic. I knew next to nothing about autism. Okay, that wasn't true…I didn't know a damn thing about autism.

"We can worry about that later," I said. "right now, we need to get off the interstate and check out the possibility of grabbing a car. Walking to McIver is just asking for us to end up dead. Also…I don't know about you, but I am thirsty, hungry, and I need to use the bathroom."

Michael made a snort and giggled, covering his mouth with his hands and then just froze. All my earlier thoughts came back to me and I glanced over my shoulder to see Carl vanishing around the bend as he continued his way along the Johnson Creek exit.

"Are you gonna leave us?"

I snapped back around to see Betty with tears in her eyes. Selina apparently picked up on the emotion quickly and her eyes were close tearing up. Michael just continued to stand there with his hands over his mouth, his gaze fixed firmly on his feet.

"I know I'm slow…and I also know I'm not an easy person to get along with. I'm set in my ways and not always accepting of others," Betty managed while still sounding somewhat out of breath. "But I can't do this alone. I'm afraid, and I honestly have no idea what to do. I don't know why we are going to McIver, and I don't know why we are talking about stealing a car. Honest to God, I could just sit here and wait for those things…" she shot a look back at the approaching herd of walking dead, "…and just let them have me. But I've heard those screams—"

Without warning, Michael shrieked. It wasn't exactly like the one you heard from those who were being ripped apart, but it was a damn good impersonation.

I took a deep breath. It was in that instant that I knew there was no way I could desert these three and leave them to almost certain death.

"I'm not going to leave you."

DEAD: Onset

8

Out of the frying pan…

After it was made very clear to me that neither of the children would swap holding Betty's hand for mine, I took position a few yards ahead and led my unlikely band of potential survivors along the Johnson Creek Boulevard exit ramp. We finally reached the end, and I felt my heart jump into my throat. Echoing my feelings, Chewie let loose with a soft rumble that was part growl and part whine.

If Carl had gone into the chaos I saw laid out before me, then he was either crazy, dead, or a freaking beast. The undead were wandering the streets in singles and groups everywhere. The orange sign of the big-box hardware and home repair chain was only a hundred or so yards away, but it may as well be on the moon.

I knew that there had to be at least a few vehicles in that parking lot. And it would be likely that one of them would be an older model. That was crucial if we were going to be able to hotwire it. New cars had too much going on, and I didn't feel confident that I would be able to get one of them started. I just knew an older model pickup would be sitting in that lot.

"We can't go back the way we came," Betty cried.

I turned to see the leading edge of our zombie tail coming down the exit. Our only choice was to hurry across this intersection and make our way back up onto the interstate.

Or…

I looked to the left and up the gradual slope. We could get across that overpass that crossed over Interstate 205, and if my memory served me correctly, there were a few small strip mall locations as well as the fringes of a residential area over there. It wasn't the packed in scene like the Portland neighborhood we'd left behind. While certainly not rural, the neighborhoods out here were simply not anywhere near the levels of congestion.

It was a coin toss, but my dry throat and the rumble in my belly won out. I turned left.

"This way," I insisted when Betty did not immediately follow.

"Why wouldn't we just try our luck back up on 205?" she asked. "We've been doing fine."

"Yeah, but without some food and water soon, we may start running into trouble."

I glanced down at my big Newfie and was so proud of how well she'd endured thus far. Her mouth was a foaming mess, and I knew right then that my mind would not be changed. She absolutely needed water. And then there was the fact that this day was passing and I had no desire to be out in the open when darkness fell. Sure, it was still hours away, but I had no idea how long it would take us to walk the entire distance to McIver if that ended up being our fate.

"I think we need to get off the street for a day or two. There is too much going on right now." As the words came out of my mouth, I became convinced that was the right choice.

Betty nodded. "Yes, perhaps that is for the better." I saw a shadow cross behind her eyes.

"I'm not gonna bail."

She actually started and I was pretty sure I'd just hit the nail on the head with what had been passing through her mind. I couldn't blame her. The past several hours had been madness, and it wasn't like there was any sort of bond between me and her…or those kids for that matter.

"You're gonna steal a house now," Michael said those

Out of the frying pan…

words with the same emotionless tone he'd used when stating that I had planned on stealing a car.

"We are just borrowing it," I tried to assure him.

"I don't think the owners will come back. Probably eaten," he said with the flat calm that apparently always permeated his voice.

"Let's go." I did not want to keep standing here while that herd coming off the interstate drew ever nearer. Also, we'd been lucky up to this point, but I was not willing to continue risking that stroke of luck as all the zombies off to our right continued to do whatever it is that zombies did when they weren't eating people or following them.

We started up the road, and when I reached the overpass and could look back in the direction we'd come, I felt a queasy feeling in my stomach. I knew that there had been fires burning, and I'd obviously been aware that a growing number of the undead were following us. I was not prepared for the at least mile long serpent made up of what must be hundreds of zombies that were coming along and picking up stragglers as they went. It was a cartoon snowball, growing to something indescribable.

Then there were the fires.

The dark fingers pointing skyward in the form of the pillars of smoke rising into the late morning/early afternoon sky were almost as numerous. In some cases, the plumes were so massive that they had to encompass entire blocks. I thought back to my house and the encroaching fire that had chased me from it.

"This is so bad," I said needlessly. "So much worse than any movie."

"What movie?" Betty asked, her breathing already coming in labored gasps as we resumed our trek up the long and gradual slope.

I glanced over at her and realized that maybe not everybody had a glimmer of an idea as to what might be going on. While I had certainly seen the classic Romero flicks, I never considered that I was perhaps the minority. Horror was sorta like comedy when it came to the general public. It was segmented at best and some folks snubbed it out of hand just because they would not ever "lower themselves" to such things. Betty was probably one of *those* types.

As we made our way towards a parking lot where I saw a sign that read "Biscuits Café" in bright red letters, I gave her the briefest of rundowns regarding the zombie genre. I told her about movie zombies (or ghouls is what would have been the name we'd be calling these things if the original label given to the undead by George Romero had stuck). I told her about the way the infection was spread.

"That is ridiculous," she managed to wheeze as we stopped at the door to the small café.

I looked inside and breathed a sigh of relief when I saw that the place looked untouched. Then I looked back at Betty and the kids. "You got a better explanation for what is going on? That doctor for the CDC changed her tune. She saw it for herself…before she got bitten." I paused and recalled her broadcast. "Only, this thing with the eyes is different. Those dark squiggles seem to be an indication that a person is infected. I'm no doctor, but I know what I've seen."

"Blackshot," Michael whispered loudly.

I considered his statement and thought that was as good of way to describe the symptom as any. I returned my attention to the door. I was not versed in picking locks. It always looked easy on television or at the movies, but I had no clue. I'd also noticed that this small parking lot was empty of cars, which was a bit of a bummer.

Looking at the other businesses that made up this little complex, I spotted a dentist, an optician, and an insurance agent's office. Food and beverage were the priority. We needed to get inside this café. I could see a cooler on one wall that was filled with soda, sports drinks, and, most importantly, water.

"Everybody keep a lookout." I scanned the area and could not believe that there was not one single rock or brick lying about.

From where we were located, I could look back towards the interstate. I was relieved to see that the horde had not turned our direction. The only problem would be the moment I found some-

Out of the frying pan…

thing to break into this place. Noise was travelling much farther these days with the relative quiet.

I jogged the length of the building and was about to round the corner in my search when I heard Betty call out from behind me. "Evan?"

I turned to see her standing there with the door open. The kids had already ducked inside. Feeling like a total idiot, I rushed back.

"Michael just walked over and pulled," she said with a sheepish grin that let me know she felt just as silly for not even bothering to try to open the door either.

I gestured for her to enter and that I would follow. As soon as I stepped inside, my hand went for my axe. The very identifiable smell of the undead hit me right in the nose. Kids being kids, they had not even bothered to pause and rushed for the cooler, jerking the door open and grabbing sodas.

I hurried past and climbed up on the counter. There was nothing on the floor, but there was a door to the back—the type with the small, square window that was in place to hopefully prevent collisions as people came and went. I saw a head move past in a slow manner that told me what I needed to know.

"Everybody stay back from the counter," I hissed. Scanning the room, I saw an area that was at least partially out of sight of possible passersby out front—and well out of sight of the little door window. "Over there." I pointed.

Betty, to her credit, grabbed the kids and ushered them to where I indicated. Chewie padded along, apparently content. Of course, it could have had something to do with the bottle of water that Selina had opened and offered.

Once they were out of the way, I lowered down to the floor and crept to the door. Peering inside, I saw the kitchen side of this little café. My heart just about did a flip when I spied all the shelves loaded with canned goods. Also, there were at least two walk-ins. I was betting one to be a freezer and the other to be for produce and the like. This was the zombie apocalypse equivalent of hitting the lottery. All I needed to do was take down the one…damn, make that three zombies in the back.

"Okay, here is the deal," I said in a voice that was barely a whisper when I returned to where Betty, Chewie, and the kids waited, "I have to go in there and take down the zombies."

"Now you are going to murder," Michael said in a voice that was not even close to a whisper. It was loud enough that it made me jump.

"That's not—" I started, but the thud of something bumping into that door to the back of the restaurant shut me up and made me spin around just in time to see one of the zombies stagger out.

It could have been funny if I'd been a spectator rather than actively involved in the situation. This one zombie was a girl in her teens by my best guess. She was wearing a blue pullover shirt with the restaurant's logo on the left breast. Her neck was a mangled mess, ripped out badly enough that her head sat tilted to the right on her shoulders like she was examining something. She had frizzy dark hair and what had probably once been freckles were now just ugly dark blotches all over her skin.

This zombie almost seemed to take her place behind the counter like she was waiting to take an order. Her body had to turn for her to actually put us in her field of vision…provided zombies really could see. Her mouth opened and the hairs on my arms and the back of my neck stood up when that awful baby cry sound came from her.

Unable to help myself, I turned to Betty. "See? Not all of them make those low groans, some of them make that noise, so be careful. You may think you are rushing in to help, when really, you are going to your possible doom." I didn't mean for it to sound so ominous to the point of being cliché, but it was the truth.

"Stay put," I said as calmly as possible, and then I approached the female zombie.

As I neared the counter, it fixed its rheumy gaze on me. The body jerked and twitched a little as it re-oriented on me and then lunged, its arms swiping at air. Since I was still a good several feet away, all it managed to do was topple forward against the counter. This sudden movement caused its head to loll forward

Out of the frying pan…

and now it sat awkwardly with the chin almost nestled between the girl's breasts.

Before it could recover, I moved forward and brought my axe down on the crown of its head. There was a now-familiar jarring sting that shot up my arms as the hard skull cracked under the force of my blow. A second later, there was an ear-piercing scream from behind me. I spun, not sure what I would find or have to face.

Michael had pulled away from Betty and was pointing at me, screaming at the top of his lungs. Betty had instinctively recoiled and moved away, shielding Selina from him.

"Michael," I hissed, hurrying over to the child.

Like a switch was thrown, he stopped. His hands folded in front of him and his gaze returned to the floor. "You murdered."

That single statement was not spoken with any emotion. He was reporting what, at least to him, was a fact. Being totally ignorant, I could only assume that this behavior had something to do with his autism.

Chewie had risen from where she'd sat beside Selina making a mess as she did her best to drink as much of the water being poured out as possible. The dog seemed to sense something and went to stand beside the boy. As soon as she did, Michael plopped down on the floor and began to scratch her chest and pet her down the length of one leg.

There was no chance for me to try and make sense of anything as the door banged open and the other two zombies appeared. I was now pretty sure which of these had been the root of the problem here. There was a boy with a nasty rip on one arm about the same age as the girl I'd just ended and a woman I guessed to be in her thirties. Her mouth was a dark smear of dried blood.

I hurried to them and, after glancing over my shoulder where Michael continued to sit beside Chewie, I took each down with a single blow to the head. There was no scream, and I breathed a sigh of relief as I returned to my little group. Chewie looked up at me as the boy continued to stroke her soft, black fur with a look that was like, '*No worries, I got things covered here*

DEAD: Onset

with the boy.'

"Okay…who's hungry?" I asked with a smile.

Selina was the only one who raised her hand. I followed Betty's gaze and realized that she was fixed on the corpse of the girl sprawled over the counter. Drops of dark fluid dripped from the gaping divide I'd created in her skull, forming a large puddle on the floor.

Looking out front, there was still no sign of any activity. That scream had not brought anything down on us; at least for the time being. I very unceremoniously grabbed the girl and dragged her over the counter. That proved more difficult than I'd imagined. A dead body seems to weigh an awful lot.

It seemed to take forever, but at last, I got the three bodies out the front door. I had sort of stacked them off to the side of the entrance and then returned inside and went straight to the men's room. I felt like I should strip down and wash every inch of my body, but I settled for my arms and scrubbed from just above the elbows all the way to my fingertips.

After the first cleaning, I noticed some black under one finger nail and had to dig furiously to get it out and then wash my hands again. As I did, I imagined Adrian Monk in my place and started to laugh at the thought of how my once favorite television detective would have probably walked right into that zombie horde and called it quits. Of course, he would've offered the zombies proper napkins to wear as bibs before they ate him. I exited the bathroom still chuckling which earned me raised eyebrows from Betty and a demand from Selina to fill her in on what was so funny.

"We heard you laughing out here," the girl snorted.

"Betty said you must have gone crazy," Michael deadpanned.

I tousled his hair as I passed and he jerked away from me like I'd just slapped him. Chewie moved between us and nosed the boy, calming him just as fast as I'd agitated him.

"Okay. Now who's hungry?" I asked again.

The response was much more positive, but I noticed Betty could not stop glancing out front as she walked through the

Out of the frying pan…

small café and made her way to the back. There was still a lingering stench from the undead, but, luckily, there were a bank of windows up high along one side. I had to climb up and open them all, but with a breeze blowing through the kitchen and the grill turned on, that stink was either slowly pushed out, or we just became numb to it.

In moments, I had patties from the walk-in that had obviously been pulled for the upcoming day's shift sizzling on the large grill. While I flipped the burgers, Betty helped by pulling out baskets and prepping a series of buns. She asked each of the kids what they liked on theirs and then me.

"Pretty much anything," I said as I flipped each burger and started to peel slices of cheese to finish them off with.

"Even monkey butt?" Selina giggled.

At first I was caught off balance by the question. When I looked over at her, I saw a crooked smile on her lips, but hesitation in her eyes. It hit me right then what these kids—or at least her since I had no clue as to young Michael's mindset—were experiencing and how frightening it had to be. She wanted to laugh and have a moment of normal.

"Especially monkey butt," I replied, giving her a big wink as I did.

"Eww, gross! Evan likes monkey butt," she squealed.

My eyes flicked to the open windows as a moan drifted on that same breeze that had been cleansing our air of undead stink. She saw my glance and shut down instantly. Her face was crumbling on itself as that single moment of levity was shattered.

"Better than skunk butt," I whispered as loud as I dared.

That made her giggle and I breathed an inner sigh of relief. I pushed away thoughts of what sort of world these two children—and any others that might be fortunate enough to survive—might have to look forward to.

At last, the burgers were ready and we all sat down on the floor to eat. To their credit, the kids never asked why we could not go into the dining area. I took my first bite and froze as I watched Michael open his burger and lick all the ketchup from one side and then fling his leaf of lettuce away. He pressed the buns together again and took his first bite. With a nod that I took as satisfaction, he started eating.

Betty had managed to find plastic cups and filled each with water. When Selina asked for soda, she was told that she could have some later if she ate all her burger and finished her water. That actually seemed to satisfy her, and she began to eat with gusto. Betty caught me staring and gave me a slight nod.

Chewie had a trio of patties as well as a carrot from the chiller. That last bit of her meal seemed to surprise everybody and more than once I noticed Betty and Selina gape as the big Newfoundland gnawed on the orange vegetable like it was a huge, meaty bone.

"She also like apples and watermelon," I said after swallowing a bite of what might've been the best burger I'd ever eaten. It sure felt that way as I licked a trail of grease that began to drip down my arm.

When the last bites had been taken, everybody leaned back with content yawns. I saw eyes closing as Selina and Michael's head drooped, his chest already rising and falling in a slow, steady rhythm.

"Maybe we can take a break here," I whispered to Betty. I saw the obvious relief on her face and realized that I was exhausted myself.

I motioned for her to stay put and crept to the door to the front part of the café and peered out. A pair of zombies were wandering across it at that exact moment, and I unconsciously held my breath as if they might be able to hear it. My eyes drifted to the door we'd come in and I saw that single oval knob gleaming as if the very heavens were shining on it.

The lock.

If I could go turn that without being noticed, we'd at least be safe from any zombies wandering in on us. I was now realizing how tired I was from the day-long surges and recessions of adrenaline coupled with a lack of any quality sleep.

I stood there watching the zombies for what seemed like an eternity before they finally shambled out of sight. As soon as they were gone, I cracked the door open, making a point to stay

Out of the frying pan...

crouched behind the counter for a few seconds until I felt like it was safe to go lock the door.

Scurrying across the open diner floor, I reached the door and turned the knob, then dashed back to the counter and ducked behind it once more. After a few deep, steadying breaths, I peered over the counter to see that the parking lot was still empty.

Satisfied that we were at least somewhat safe for the time being, I joined Betty and the kids in the back. Sliding down the wall, I saw that Chewie was curled up around the feet of Michael. Part of me wanted to be jealous, but it was impossible for that emotion to gain any traction. One of the things that Chewie had done since she'd been a pup was to go to pediatric centers and assisted living centers.

Newfoundlands were famous for being companion dogs. She obviously sensed that her skills were needed for that boy. Hell, maybe she knew something was different about him. Whatever the case, my eyes closed, lids fluttering down like fall leaves. My last recollection was of Chewie snuggling in closer to the boy as his hand absently stroked the length of her neck.

***

I opened my eyes to almost perfect darkness. I say almost because there was a silver glow from the moon coming in from the windows high up in the wall directly across from me. It was probably that light in my eyes that woke me.

I looked around and could barely make out shadowy forms of my fellow survivors. Something warm and wet ran up the length of my arm and I recognized Chewie's massive and somewhat prickly tongue as it swabbed at me. I reached over and gave her head a rub, kneading her ears like I knew she loved. She pulled back and made a high-pitched whine in response.

"What's the matter, girl?" I asked as I stretched and stood up.

A snort from one of the dark lumps got my attention. It took me a few seconds to realize that I was missing something important. I cleared my head of the last vestiges of sleep and tried to figure out what I was missing.

"Dammit!" I swore in the darkness.

A snore cut off midway and I heard Betty mumble and then moan. "What? Huh?" she slurred.

"Michael is gone," I said over my shoulder as I headed for the front of the restaurant.

I whisper-called his name a few times but did not trust that he would actually answer me, so I searched every dark corner and looked under every table. After checking the bathroom, the sick feeling that was rising in my throat had become a burning sensation that tasted like sour mustard and charred beef.

Like the condemned being led to the gallows, I walked to the glass door. My hand fumbled around until I found the knob of the deadbolt lock. It was up and down. I remember very distinctly that it ended sideways after I locked the door.

Pushing it open, the chilly night air caused my skin to pebble. The silence was broken by a distant burst of gunfire punctuated by a boom that I took to be a shotgun.

Moans of the undead reached my ears from almost every direction. None of them seemed terribly close, but none were far enough away not to fill me with a sense of dread.

My conscience stabbed me in the heart as it reminded me of some of my earlier musings about the children being a liability, and that burning in the back of my throat became something else. Staggering a few steps out into the parking lot, I bent at the waist, my hands slamming into my knees as I vomited violently. The wet splatter of chunky liquid on the asphalt sounded like Niagara Falls in the relative silence. The smell came on the heels of that sound and compounded my purging reaction.

When I was finished, I stood and turned to see Betty standing in the doorway. I made my way back to the café on wobbly knees.

"You found him?" she asked, obviously mistaking my reaction.

"No, but he definitely left," I whispered. "I locked that door, and now it is unlocked."

Out of the frying pan…

Betty stifled a sob and threw her hand to her mouth as that slight noise echoed around the open inside of the restaurant. A low moan from somewhere close elicited a squeak and she plugged her mouth with two fists instead of just the one.

"We have to find him," she finally whispered once I shut the door.

"And how do you suggest we do that?" I shot back, failing at hiding my own anger. She didn't have to know it was directed more at myself than at her. "It's pitch black out there."

And that was when a new realization struck. I turned and looked outside again. While I could make out a distant glow in the direction of Portland, the power was out in this neighborhood. None of the streetlights were working. Also, I now realized that the low hum of the cooler where the kids had grabbed that first soda was now gone. It was as quiet as the tomb here in our little sanctuary.

"Can't your dog sniff around for him or something?" Betty asked.

"She isn't a tracking dog. She would just as likely lead us to a zombie as she would the boy if I let her out and followed her lead."

"But I thought dogs had excellent noses." The desperation in her tone is the only reason I bit back a harsh response.

"Tracking is a skill. Chewie is a registered companion, and she was even certified at the first level of water rescue," I answered. "Tracking a person is something else entirely."

"We can't just do nothing," she insisted.

"Until the sun comes up, that is all we can do," I answered.

I turned back to the front windows and scanned the parking lot, hoping beyond reason to see a small shape skip past. Not even a zombie wandered by.

I continued to stand there with no idea how much time elapsed. Eventually, the darkness began to ebb and I started to make out shapes more clearly. Out on Johnson Creek Boulevard, I saw a few dark figures moving along in both directions. The undead paid each other no mind. That they did not all seem to be moving in a single direction, as if in pursuit, was some small comfort. Also, I did not see any clusters gathered around something on the ground. I was taking solace in everything I could at the moment.

The door to the kitchen area eventually opened and Betty appeared with a bleary-eyed Selina. The lack of questions told me that the girl had probably been informed in some nature as to the fact about our missing group member.

Betty had a burlap shoulder bag over each arm and I mentally smacked my forehead. She'd thought to gather at least a few supplies. It was good to see she was starting to figure out how dire our situation was and that she needed to step up her game.

"We need to get moving." I indicated outside the café. "Things are a bit busy out there. We may have to fight off a few of the zombies, but if you two stay close, we should be okay."

"How are we gonna fight?" Selina asked, a slight tremor in her voice.

She had a point. We'd taken care of hunger and thirst, but I had not thought to find them any sort of weapon. Before we walked out this door, there had to be something in this place that each of them could carry.

I walked back to the door leading into the kitchen. If they were going to be any help, I had to find them something that allowed them to attack from a distance. The idea dawned that perhaps they didn't have to actually kill a zombie if they could just keep it at bay long enough for me to take it out.

I found a push broom. "Selina?" The girl came over to me. "If one of the zombies came, do you think that you could shove it away with this?" I handed it to her.

She looked at it with obvious confusion. "How will this help?"

"Pretend that I'm a zomb—" I didn't finish getting the words out of my mouth when she whirled the broom around and clocked me with the heavy brush end of it.

"Like that?" she asked innocently.

I rubbed my shoulder and nodded. "Pretty much."

"Okay." She seemed satisfied.

Now all I needed was something for Betty. I looked around

Out of the frying pan...

at all the cutlery, but that meant she would be fighting the undead up close. I didn't see that as likely.

"How about this?" Betty said and I turned to see her holding a short metal paddle.

"What the heck would that be doing in the kitchen?" I asked.

"Maybe for that huge mixer over there?" She pointed to the largest mixer that I'd ever seen in my life. It was in a back corner and easily a foot taller than me. The bowl for it looked like Selina could climb in and hide inside it.

"Okay." We all gathered together and I opened the door to the front of the café. I must've been talking louder than I thought, because apparently we'd drawn some of the nearby undead to the glass-fronted entrance.

"No time like the present," I muttered. Turning to Selina and Betty, I asked, "Are you ready?"

There was a pause and I became more and more tense with the sound of each hand slapping on the glass. Selina was looking dubiously at her broom...and I didn't blame her. What the heck was I thinking?

"We can do this," Betty spoke up. She sounded resolute and certain.

"Just stay with me. If we start to get separated, make a hissing sound or something...just don't yell, got it?" I made eye contact with each of them to be certain there was no misunderstanding.

Both of them nodded.

Through this entire experience, I'd managed to save that one small carry bag. I knelt, moved my picture of Stephanie aside and rummaged through the miniscule number of items that I'd managed to save thus far. I shoved one of the boxes of bullets in one pocket. I opened the other and dumped the contents into the other one so that I had a ready supply of loose bullets that I would not have to fumble around with if the need arose.

I could feel my hands starting to tremble and realized that I was suddenly scared out of my wits. There would be no way out of this place without taking down a good number of the walking

143

dead. Despite what they were, it was still a little difficult not to see them as people. The early morning gloom only made it worse since it masked their inhumanity. At the moment, they just looked like very anxious patrons wanting in. The problem was in what it was they were hoping to feast on.

After taking one more deep breath, I went to the door, turned the lock, and shoved it open. The zombie that had been directly in front of the door tumbled backwards and knocked another one over like a pair of bowling pins. I stepped out and brought down my hand axe, cleaving the skull of the closest zombie.

Betty was right behind me and jabbed out at a zombie that was trying to come at us from the left. As soon as it fell back, she moved in with a vengeance and brought the end of the paddle down on one of the two zombies that I'd knocked over when we exited.

I felt something against my back and then Selina was at my side with her broom. She poked at a zombie on the ground. It reached for her and she screamed. I froze as heads turned.

The day was just breaking and the sun was spilling across the scene. I had not really been able to see much past the parking lot. The road had been in shadow, and I'd seen a few figures moving out that way. What I had not been able to see were all the zombies milling about just down the road at that overpass we'd crossed. For some reason, there were still a whole lot of them clustered around down there.

"Run!" I hissed, shoving the next zombie aside, no longer concerned with dropping them. If we stopped to fight here, the wave coming up at us would wash over us within minutes.

Chewie shoved past me and bowled over a zombie policeman. I noted that his holster was empty, but I doubt it would have mattered. The moans of the undead were growing in volume, and looking to our left, there were more spilling around the corner by the insurance agent.

Our only real option was to run out onto Johnson Creek Boulevard, turn right, and continue up the long and gradual hill that led into a residential area. I felt that Chewie I would be able

Out of the frying pan…

to make it just fine if we ran hard. I was less confident that Betty or Selina would fare as well.

DEAD: Onset

9

…and into the fire.

I spun to see a zombie with an unyielding grip on the broom that Selina was supposed to use to try and shove the undead back while we made our escape. That, however, was not what was making her scream. Another of the zombies had moved in beside her and had a handful of her hair in one fist as it did its best to jerk her towards it.

It was sooner than I'd hoped, but there was no way around it now. I stuffed the axe in the loop at my belt as I drew my .357 and stepped to the zombie that was just about to try and bite into the top of Selina's head.

Jamming the barrel up against the temple, I fired. There was very little muffling of the sound. My arm snapped up with the recoil but I was able to recover fast and move to the one holding the heavy end of the broom. This time I put a shot into the forehead.

I grabbed Selina and pushed her towards the street. "Right…go right and just run!"

"But—" she started to protest. I shoved her in the direction she needed to be going.

"GO!"

Turning, I saw Betty heave one zombie away with her free hand and then jab at another as she backed towards me. I rushed to her side and kicked the zombie moving in from her right. She acknowledged me with a grunt as she brought the paddle up and then thrust out with a firm two-handed grip on the shaft. The end of it smashed into the open mouth of a zombie, shattering teeth and rocking it back and away.

With a small clearing created, she was able to disengage and turned to follow me. I ushered her past, intent on bringing up the rear. Chewie had bounded after Selina and was currently crouched and growling at a pair of zombies approaching from down the road. That was not so much the problem as the fact that this pair were only the very leading edge of a mob that had been wandering around on the overpass just down the slope from us.

I almost tripped stepping down from the curb and onto the road, but it was Betty who was suddenly at my side and grabbing my arm. She helped keep me on my feet, and together, we started after Selina.

"Chewie," I called. Obediently, the dog broke of her confrontation and bounded after us.

An open grassy area was across from us on our left and another big series of buildings was on our right. There was also a road leading between the café complex and what the lettering on a rounded brick wall identified as the Mt. Scott Professional Center. As we passed those buildings, the words "MEDICAL CENTER" on the side caught my attention. I made a note of this place as I felt it might be beneficial to perhaps try and come back here for supplies if we ever get a vehicle again.

The four-way intersection gave us a moment on flat ground to gather ourselves as Betty and I caught up with Selina who was now crying so hard that I had no idea how she was able to see through all the tears. My eyes instantly scanned her for any signs that she might be bitten or scratched, but she seemed fine.

"It's okay," I said in as soothing a tone as I could manage while I sucked in gulps of air.

"M-m-my hair," the girl whined.

I looked closer and saw that a large chunk of her hair had indeed been ripped away and she was left with a jagged bald

...and into the fire.

patch towards the back. That was also when I noticed a bit of blood running down the back of her neck. I felt my own blood run cold. Was it possible that she was infected now?

Doing my best to remain calm, I gripped her shoulders and turned her towards me. I looked into her eyes, but all I saw as the shimmer from her tears.

"I know it hurts, but we have to get moving," I said, still not confident that she had not become infected.

Could I kill this child if she turned? I thought as I nudged her onwards and we resumed our uphill trek.

There were zombies on the road ahead, but not in the numbers or concentration that existed behind us. The two lanes on either side were separated by a raised divider with plenty of small shrubs that would trip up anything attempting to cross. I just wished that maybe there had been some sort of actual barrier dividing the lanes. The one good thing was that there was a steep, grassy hill on our left once we cleared the pine trees that lined the sides of the road. We had perfect vision of anything that might come from that way. The left side was even better. Again, there was a grassy slope, but the bottom of the hill that bordered the road had a three-foot-high rock wall. Any zombie coming down from that side would likely fall rather unceremoniously to the sidewalk and be easy to outdistance.

On both sides, at the tops of those slopes, I could see some very expensive looking houses. They were not necessarily good choices since they looked to have an extremely large number of windows, many going from the ground up to the second or perhaps third floor.

I don't know how many times over the years that I have driven along this same road. I never once thought about how steep it was if you are on foot. In a car, I could just cruise along with no worries. If I was already starting to feel a burning in my lungs as well as my quads, I had no doubt that Betty was in pain. Yet, she was keeping her pace constant and steady.

As we reached a long, arcing bend in the road, we also reached the end of the bushes serving as the divider between the two lanes on each side. Now there was just a raised concrete sidewalk of sorts. Also, on our side, the grassy slope was replaced by a tiered rock formation that reminded me of the side of a pyramid. On our left, the slope was still all grass, but there was not a single zombie stumbling down it. We were actually reaching a spot where there were only a few of them ahead, and those few were spread out enough that we would probably be able to get by them without too much effort.

Glancing over my shoulder, I saw that the mob from the overpass was still in pursuit. There would be absolutely no way we could backtrack if something came up in front of us. I had to hope that a bit of luck would fall in our laps.

Jogging ahead, despite the fact that my jog was almost slower than our fast walk, I approached a pair of the walking dead that we would most likely not be able to avoid. I tucked the pistol away and pulled out my trusty hand axe.

The first one almost made me laugh. He had easily been over three hundred pounds in life. His walk was much more of a drag-step waddle and I could imagine him scooting around in those little electric carts. His face was a hideous mess as dried blood had caked and crusted over in his unruly bird's nest of a beard. He would be the easiest to evade as I took down his companion. Still, judging by his beard, he'd managed to get his teeth into at least one victim. His only visible injury was a large black smudge on his right forearm that looked more like a bruise than a bite.

His companion was his polar opposite. She looked like perhaps she'd been out for a jog when she'd been attacked. Most of her right arm was shredded and destroyed from the elbow to the wrist. You could actually see both bones of the forearm quite clearly. Her mouth was still clean, which meant that she'd yet to feed; although, there were at least a dozen bullet holes in her upper body.

I took her down first, sweeping her long, slender legs out from under her in one movement, my hands checking her at the shoulders to send her onto her back. Placing my foot on her chest, I whispered an apology and then split her face almost in two.

...and into the fire.

Not taking even a moment to really allow myself to see what I'd done, I focused my attention on Big Boy. He was wearing coveralls and a red tee-shirt with the logo of some sports team on it, but so much blood had run down his chin and beard that the lettering was obscured by a huge blackish stain. I decided to use his size against him and made a feint to his left. As soon as he started that way, I juked to his right and brought my axe up.

He was like a cruise ship in that he was not designed for hairpin turns or sudden stops. Still, he made his best effort. That caused him to lose his balance and he tumbled. When his feet got tangled, it actually sent him falling sideways...in my direction.

Now it was my turn to try and dance around. Unfortunately, my swing was already committed and I was moving into him as he fell into me. His side hit me hard and his enormous hand managed to be dangling in the perfect spot as his knuckles acted almost like the head of a whip and struck me squarely between the legs.

I barely managed a yelp of agony. Perhaps I should at least be thankful for that as I would not be drawing still more attention our direction. Sadly, the pain proved to be too much for me and I found myself on the verge of blacking out. When his massive frame landed on me, I was certain that my end was here. The wind was literally crushed out of me in one massive exhale as the weight of his body forced all the oxygen from my lungs in one huge whoosh.

Then the world went dark. I wasn't unconscious because I could hear Chewie barking furiously which pretty much negated my having not screamed when I took that nut-shot from Big Boy. For some reason, I couldn't see anything, plus, now that I had the wind basically knocked from me in addition to the pain radiating in huge waves from my groin region, I began to panic. Worse still, I could not do anything about it. I was basically immobile.

Finally, I registered the fact that I was lying pinned beneath the massive figure of Big Boy. I got flashes of daylight as it moved and squirmed on top of me, obviously seeking to get its head around so that it could gobble me up. I just knew the bite was coming and my journey was about to come to a gruesome end. There was a loud pop that sounded like a gun, but I could not be sure.

I would have gotten sick if I had anything left in my stomach, but since it was empty, all I could do was gag. That only made things worse as I wondered which I would die from first: lack of oxygen or being eaten? The body shifted, and suddenly I could see. I was staring straight up at a partly cloudy sky. Betty's face came into view and she reached out a hand.

"Get up, Evan. We need to move, that huge group of zombies is coming around the bend."

I looked up and could make out Betty's round face looking down at me. There was a dark splatter across her shirt, but it was the pistol in her hand that really drew my eyes.

"It fell out of your pants or whatever," Betty answered my unasked question. She looked back the way we'd come from again and then back to me. "Now you *have* to get up."

I tried to move but my legs would not budge. I had to struggle to muster the strength to look down. Having the wind knocked from me was not going to just clear up. The problem with that was not just in the feeling that I might never be able to draw a full breath again, but in the fact that it almost paralyzed a person.

Moving my legs with the wind knocked from me would be a struggle, but with that huge corpse sprawled across them, I wasn't going anywhere. Betty's gaze followed mine and she tucked my pistol in her waistband and then bent to try and move the offensive carcass. She grunted with the effort, but not much changed.

Fear was not doing my ability to recover any favors. I could now hear the moans increase in volume. The chorus was punctuated with plenty of the baby cries to add to the creepiness of the hellish choir.

I was a goner. There was just no way that I would free myself and make it to my feet in time. Betty could hardly haul

...and into the fire.

herself up this slope. It was not reasonable to believe for a moment that she would be able to drag my sorry ass or even help me limp along.

"Get moving, Betty," a voice growled. "I got Pretty Boy here. Watch your step, but these rocks ain't that hard to climb. You too, little missy."

I turned my head and spotted Carl as he came sliding down the pyramid-esque rocks on his rear end. That was enough to make my heart just about burst, but the small shadow I saw at the top of those rocks was all it took to etch a smile into my face despite my grimace of pain and discomfort.

"Remind me to never hire you to babysit if I have kids, friend," Carl grunted as he pulled me from under the massive coverall-clad body that was almost my doom.

I managed a pitiful squeak as he hauled me to my feet. He looked around and then scowled. We started up the road. I saw the rock formation slide by, but he continued to force me to limp up the gradual slope. Every so often, he would pause and look over his shoulder, curse under his breath, and then force me to continue on.

Very slowly, I began to regain the ability to draw in the most miniscule amounts of oxygen. A little further, and I could almost suck in a breath.

"The moment you think you can run, you just say so," Carl panted as we continued our hike up this steep section of road.

It took more effort than I expected, but I finally chanced a look behind us and was amazed to discover that the undead were apparently moving faster than we'd been going. That gave my recovery a boost and I nodded, picking up my tempo to a fast walk.

I finally felt like I could manage a word or two. "Why don't we head up the hill?"

"Because those bastards are too close and will follow. They may stumble and fall, but I found out the hard way that they just don't stop. Eventually, they will make the summit, and with a herd that size, we are fucked seven ways to Sunday, friend."

That made sense. Of course that was the only thing that did

at the moment. I had no idea where he'd actually come from. And I was willing to bet that small shadow I'd seen was our Michael. Had he found the boy like he did us, or vice-versa? Did it matter?

I decided that it did.

"The boy." It was a statement and I felt confident that Carl understood.

"Damn fool was out wandering the street. I kept hearing this voice, and so I came out from where I was hunkered down. It was pretty dark, but the moon was bright enough that I made out this little figure running around in the damn road." Carl paused and actually chuckled. "He was telling the zombies that they needed to run and hide or they were gonna be murdered. The thing is, he was apparently smart enough to know that they couldn't touch him because he ducked and dodged out of their attempts every time."

I didn't know what to say. In a way, it all made perfect sense. At least it did when I confined my thoughts solely to Michael.

"I thought you left us for dead weight," I finally said.

It wasn't that I was ungrateful for being saved. And it wasn't that I wanted to pick a fight with him, but Carl had bailed on us. Why had he come out and obviously saved the boy, and then me?

"I got to thinking while I sat all by myself and listened to the moans of the undead. Like we said, this situation will define who we really are. There won't be any pretenses because there really aren't any consequences or accountability when it comes to our actions. Oh sure, we can screw up and end up zombie chow, but all the rules of the world we knew just a short time ago are gone…history." He paused and I thought that was his entire answer. "I decided that I'm not *that* guy. I'm not the uncaring asshole I believed myself to be. My conscience was eating me alive the whole time…at least once I'd found someplace to hunker down."

By now, we had rounded a sweeping bend in the road and, after taking a look over his shoulder to confirm that we were out

...and into the fire.

of the zombies' line-of-sight, he started us up the slope. The footing was a bit treacherous, and more than once I ended up on my knees. By the time we made it to the top, I glanced back to see the zombies rounding the corner. It didn't appear to me that we'd been spotted.

"They just go along until something else distracts them," Carl whispered. "Sorta like a girl in a jewelry store…fixated on that one thing until another shiny object is dangled in front of her."

Okay, I thought, *Carl is a bit of a dick, but at least he had enough of a conscience to go down after little Michael and then basically save our butts.*

We made our way to an enormous house. It looked like it cost well over a million dollars. The cars parked in the big, turn-around driveway looked like they cost more than I would make in a lifetime.

"Down at the end of the driveway is a gate. It was open when I got here, so I pulled it shut, but the damn electric lock won't engage, so I had to use some wire to keep it closed. I doubt it would hold up to any serious pulling or tugging," Carl explained. "When I got inside, there was one of them things locked in a bathroom. Easy enough to put down, but that was it."

We reached the stairs that led up to the main doors and I was amazed that any single person or family could afford something like this. I felt a little guilty when I took a bit of happiness in the fact that these people had bailed on a location that was actually not a bad candidate for holing up and waiting things out.

It was set back from the street by a long entry drive. It had a gate and five-foot-high wall encircling a good-sized yard. Sure, the lock wasn't engaged at the moment, but I bet we could find something better than a bit of wire to keep it secure. Sitting on a hill and being three stories high, we would have an excellent vantage to see the surrounding area.

Then I walked inside.

It was like something out of an episode of *MTV Cribs*. In the entry was a massive fountain and there were stairs that wrapped around this huge circular foyer along the walls. Straight ahead was an arched opening that revealed a living room that was probably the size of my house. The far wall was floor to ceiling windows that looked out onto Johnson Creek Boulevard. I could see just bits and slivers of the actual road from this far back. It was disconcerting to see that many of the walking dead plodding past from such a relatively close distance.

There were also exits on either side and three doors spaced evenly around this entry hall. A stack of suitcases and a safe on wheels were on one side of the fountain which still had water gurgling from the tipped pitcher the fat little cupid was holding. It was obvious that the suitcases had been rifled through.

"It seems the former occupants left in a hurry," Carl said, noticing as my gaze lingered on all the open luggage with clothes strewn about. It was easy to envision Carl just tossing all the expensive looking blouses, slacks, dress shirts, and ties over his shoulder as he went through everything.

"Evan," Betty appeared, peering down at me from the railing above, "Michael is here." The relief in her voice was obvious, and she even managed a hint of a smile.

A moment later, the boy appeared beside her. Selina moved up behind the boy in what looked to be a rather protective stance. I doubted that she would let the lad out of her sights for a while.

"There is food everywhere," Selina crowed, and then looked around as if she expected a zombie to materialize out of thin air and attack her. "They even have a kitchen up here," she added with a loud whisper that echoed off the domed ceiling above.

From somewhere in the house, I heard the deep 'woof' of Chewie. Instantly, Selina turned and dashed from sight with Michael on her heels. I saw a look of worry cross Betty's face as well.

"Chewie, come," I said in a voice that was just a shade over conversational tone. Within seconds, I heard the click-clacking of claws as she emerged from wherever she'd been rooting around upstairs. As soon as she saw me, she reared up on her hind legs a bit like a horse and then swaggered to the staircase, descending them with her rolling gait.

...and into the fire.

She reached the bottom and trotted over to me. I accepted my wet swabbing of her massive tongue. After I ruffled the fur around her neck, I pointed to the floor. Obediently, she flopped down and then stared up at me with her dark brown eyes.

I let the small bag drop from my shoulder. I found it a bit strange that the contents of the bag represented everything I now owned in the world. When I set it on the floor, I heard the distinctive jangle of busted glass. Kneeling, I unzipped it and saw that the picture frame had gotten shattered. Probably when that mountain of undead flesh fell on me.

"Dammit," I breathed.

A shadow fell across my bag and I looked up to see Carl standing over me. His eyes drifted to the picture and then back to me. I saw what almost looked like condemnation cross his eyes, then it was replaced by something else.

"If you try to hold onto the past, it might eat you alive from the inside." Carl's words were not harsh, nor were they steeped in pity. It sounded like he was honestly just trying to give me some good advice that he felt might help me.

I pulled the busted frame out and shook the rest of the glass free. Without acknowledging him or saying anything, I got up and ventured into the house. I was pretty sure that I could find a frame somewhere in this mansion that would hold my picture of Stephanie.

***

I stood on the balcony and stared out into the distance. Fires still burned everywhere, but I could also detect clusters of light that seemed too coordinated to be just random lights or fires. To the right of where we were currently located, there was a sprawling complex of houses.

It was one of those types where every house looked almost identical to the ones on either side. There might be subtle differences, but you could be assured that the identical floorplan existed someplace else in the little pop-up neighborhood. All of the so-called yards were about the size of a postage stamp and the backyard was pretty much confined to the deck.

From that direction is where we heard the most noise. Since darkness fell, I'd heard a variety of shrieks and screams that gave me the chills. They weren't the "I'm being eaten alive" sort; nope, these were the kind that indicated something dark and sinister might be happening. Sometimes, there was the pop of a gun, and the scream was suddenly silenced.

I noticed that the zombies were drawn to all this noise. A steady stream of them stumbled and shambled along up Johnson Creek Boulevard. While it was clear that they were drawn to the sound, I was a bit surprised that they did not necessarily try to take the shortest route. They followed the path of least resistance versus direct lines.

That proved true until about an hour ago. I'd just finished taking a shower. I don't think warm water ever felt so good. Carl explained to everybody that we might not want to get used to it. With the power out, the hot water heater would not be providing such luxuries any longer. More good news came in his revelation that it would not be long before the systems of pumps and such that circulated water throughout the city would be going away soon as well.

I was slipping into some clean clothes courtesy of the former residents when I heard a chorus of moans that told me there was a rather large mob approaching. I'd watched them as they appeared to home in on all the sounds coming from over in that little neighborhood. Unlike the singles and smaller groups that had passed, this group made a beeline for their ultimate destination. When the first of them started up the hill, I felt my heart leap into my throat.

The moon above was peeking through a few drifting clouds, but it was easy to watch this huge pack of walking dead as it mowed down everything in its path to reach the houses where all the noise came from. Eventually, I began to hear what sounded like wood snapping and cracking. It took me a moment to realize that had to be the sound of fences being folded over like so much balsa wood.

A short time later, there was a flurry of gunfire. Shouts and

...and into the fire.

screams began to erupt from that area. It wasn't long before I began to hear *the* scream. And not just one or two. There were several, one piled on top of the other to create a chorus straight from the darkest nightmare.

I kept thinking that it would have to stop...there should be an end. Could there really have been that many people that close? But that made me wonder just what kinds of people they were. There is no way they didn't hear me, Betty, and Selina as we almost met our doom. What did that say about them as human beings? That they could hear us in obvious danger and simply ignore it.

Hypocrite, the voice in my head chimed.

And it was correct. I was listening to people being ripped apart and eaten alive by a horde of the walking dead, yet I did nothing. I stayed put on this balcony and just wanted it to be over. I wanted the screaming to stop. I wanted that last person to die so they would be quiet. So what did that say about me?

There was a roar that almost sounded like a bear, then a barrage of gunfire. The smaller pops of handguns, the low booms of a shotgun. Then, for just the briefest of moments, there was silence.

And then *the* scream.

My mind painted a variety of pictures that would illustrate what I'd heard. But unless I actually went over there, I would not know. A peculiar sense of curiosity overwhelmed me. I knew right then that I would have to go over there and see for myself.

Certainly not right this minute. I would go in the morning when it was light out. We'd already discussed the fact that this was a pretty good place to ride things out. At least for the time being. We would need to venture out to some of the surrounding neighborhoods and hunt down supplies. The bright yellow Hummer in one of the bays of the six-car garage would serve nicely. We could bring back a decent haul in that vehicle and also not have too much concern if we had to go off the beaten path such as it was.

At last, the final scream faded and I was standing there

alone, on the balcony, staring towards the dark outlines of that nearby neighborhood. I could see flames flickering in the darkness and I hoped that it would not be blown this way if it grew into something larger.

"You should murder the sick people."

The voice from behind me made me jump. My hands were patting all over my body for a weapon that I was not carrying. It took me a few thundering heartbeats to realize that it had been Michael speaking. His dark shape was standing in the open door to the room I'd chosen for the night.

"What?" I wasn't sure that I'd heard him correctly.

"They are bad, and if you don't murder them, they will eat us." The boy continued to stare at the floor as he spoke, but his words were crystal clear.

"Okay?" It came out almost sounding like a question. Still, that seemed to satisfy the young man. He gave me a nod and walked away.

I stood there for a moment, debating on whether to go after the boy and maybe see if I could get him to talk. In the end, I decided to just let it be. I turned back to the neighborhood and discovered that there were now at least three houses ablaze.

I could feel a sense of growing concern. Those houses were now massive fires with the flames shooting skyward several feet. Perhaps it would be best if we began making preparations for a hasty exit. I knew all too well just how fast a fire could close in and force you out.

There was a good-sized grove of pine trees between the houses and our stronghold, but I did not think it to be a good idea to wait for them to go up before we reacted.

I was not even two steps out the door when Betty appeared from a few doors down. Selina was beside her holding a well-worn and faded stuffed giraffe. The woman was wearing some sort of nightgown that did not look at all comfortable. It was clearly a few sizes too small.

"Evan?" It was just my name in the form of a question, but it spoke volumes.

"Let's change plans," I said, trying to sound calm and cool.

...and into the fire.

"Instead of picking through this place tomorrow, I say we do it now and start packing things in the Hummer. Make food and water a priority."

"We'll get dressed and be right out."

I shook my head after she and Selina disappeared into the bedroom they'd claimed. I had donned a pair of sweats with the local soccer team logo emblazoned on them. Green wasn't my favorite color, but clean clothes were nothing to scoff at. Besides, beggars can't be choosers.

I headed down the stairs to discover that Carl was stacking plastic container boxes by the door. He set down the one he'd been carrying and then stepped aside. I was surprised to see Michael toting a much smaller box and setting it alongside everything Carl had stacked and ready. Carl looked up and saw me coming down the stairs.

"I was up and started getting some essentials when those yay-hoos started carrying on. Thought they might bring trouble, so I started loading up early." Michael gave the man a tap on his side. "And this little guy decided to help."

I stared down at the unlikely pair for a moment before shaking my head and joining them. "Should I start taking what you have here out to the Hummer?" I asked.

"It wouldn't hurt." Carl gave a nod and then headed back into the depths of the house and areas I had not yet even begun to explore.

For the next hour, I loaded the large containers into the gigantic H2 Hummer. I'd never seen the logic or reason for owning something like this. I was certain that it devoured gasoline like nothing else, and that would be a problem once we left and took it on the road. It had been a relief to discover that the tank was full, so at least we had that much fuel to get us someplace when we bugged out of here.

Eventually, Betty and Selina arrived. They did a mix of helping me and loading more boxes. I think Betty just wanted to be sure that a few of the discoveries that she'd made in the kitchen found their way into this loadout.

She'd been like a kid in a candy store as she'd gone through the pantry. And I had to admit, whatever it was that she'd whipped up for us to eat earlier this evening had been beyond amazing. She'd admitted to being a bit of a Food Network addict. Apparently she'd attended a few culinary classes over the past few years.

As the sun began to peek it head up and push some light through the scattered clouds, we had managed to load a considerable amount of supplies into the Hummer. And when I say 'We' I mostly mean me. I was just shutting the door when Selina bounded out to me.

"Carl says we can relax," she gushed, almost out of breath and panting heavily.

"What?" I had no idea what she was talking about.

The front door opened a bit further and Carl stepped outside. "The fires are burning out, and the wind is keeping them away. It looks like we will be okay. Plus, when the rain gets here, I think it'll settle things down."

I looked to the sky and then back at Carl with a perplexed expression. From what I was seeing, the clouds were clearing. Carl must've caught my look and understood my doubt.

"This baby never lies." He pointed to his right knee. "Messed it up real bad about ten years ago. Hurts like a sumbitch sometimes, but it is the best barometer that I've ever known. Never been wrong so much as once. When she gets to singing, I know we'll have rain within about six hours."

I wasn't gonna argue. And, truth be told, I was glad that we weren't leaving this place just yet. I still felt like I could use about another week's worth of sleep. And Chewie had been in heaven once we discovered the indoor pool downstairs.

"If you say so," I said with a shrug, and then headed inside. Less than four hours later, the skies opened up and let loose with a downpour of almost biblical proportions.

10

The Dog

I looked out the window and allowed at least a small sigh of relief. The housing development that had been swarmed over by the zombies early this morning was only smoking in a few areas. For the most part, it looked like the fires had died down, largely due to the torrential rain that had swept through the area. At the very least, they weren't spreading.

Everybody had gone off to their own separate rooms at some point. That left me alone with Chewie. As I stared out the window, she sat beside me. Every so often, she would whimper. That made my next task very clear: I needed to find a veterinary clinic. I wasn't sure what she would need, but hopefully I could figure out what sorts of medications were antibiotics. Also, she needed that tail cleaned and bandaged properly.

I realized in that moment that, just a day ago, I'd bemoaned being burdened with two children. Yet, it wasn't for either of them that I was about to set out into the Portland Hellscape on a mission.

I knelt down and brought her large, broad head around to me and looked into her eyes. "I'll take care of you, girl," I promised.

Her response was the anticipated swabbing of her tongue across my face. I hugged her, and felt her body lean into mine. It was a display of mutual love and comfort. It is also what obliterated the emotional dams I'd hastily thrown up since this nightmare began.

I felt the first tears trickle down my cheeks, and then the floodgates opened and I began to sob unlike any time I'd ever experienced in my life. I honestly have no idea how long I cried.

At some point, I'd pulled out my newly framed picture of Stephanie. Not that I could actually see it through the tears. I held it in my lap, then I hugged it to my chest. Those two actions were repeated countless times as I wept for everything that I'd lost.

It wasn't just my future wife; she'd been my friend, my companion, and fellow adventurer. Add in the fact that she'd just discovered she was pregnant with our child, and there were actual moments where I did not know if I would be able to catch my breath from crying.

Eventually, and after however much time had passed, the tears lessened. Whether it was from the fact that the well had run dry, or if perhaps my psyche was now ready to begin the slow healing process, I have no idea. What I do know is that the tears eventually abated.

Chewie had sprawled out on the floor just a few feet away, her muzzle resting on her massive paws. She was regarding me as if to ask me if all that crying nonsense was over.

"I think I'm done for now, girl," I whispered.

She seemed to understand, and gave a loud huff before her eyes shut. A moment later, her snores competed with the sound of the rain. Eventually, they won.

I got up and scoured the room that I'd chosen. Apparently it was the master bedroom. There was an enormous closet that was probably as large as Stephanie and my bedroom had been. Most of the clothes I found were useless…unless I was going to be attending a board meeting sometime soon, which I seriously doubted.

On one of the shelves, I spotted a box stenciled "Ski trip" and pulled it down. There were plenty of snow suits and gloves, all things that would come in handy, but not quite what I was searching for. One of the vehicles that we'd discovered in that

The Dog

massive detached garage had been a custom-made Harley Davidson motorcycle. Again, I was guessing it to be valued at well over two or three years' worth of what I made as a salary. Somebody with a bike like that had to have leathers. I just did not see how they wouldn't.

In the third box that I pulled down from the shelf that ran around the perimeter of the closet, I hit pay dirt. The bonus came when I was able to confirm that this guy and I had been very close to the same size.

It took some work and a bit of baby powder on my skin that I'd spotted on the master bedroom's personal bathroom, but at last I was outfitted in a full set of biker's leathers. There were even riding goggles, gloves, and boots. All of which I donned.

I stepped out into the bedroom and threw my arms out wide. "What do ya think, Chewie?"

The Newfoundland lifted its head and regarded me with bleary eyes, then dropped her head back onto her paws and resumed her nap. I gave her a dismissive wave and then turned to check myself out in the mirror. I looked like much more of a badass than I knew myself to be. Still, I also felt like I had at least some minimal protection from the walking dead. Maybe a set of chomping teeth would grab hold, but perhaps they wouldn't tear through the leather before I could pull away.

That was the hope.

After pulling out my few meager belongings from my carry bag, I attached my Ruger's holster to the belt I was wearing. It wasn't perfect, but at least now I had easy access to my handgun. Also, I'd been able to fashion a better loop for my hand axe which now hung from my right hip, opposite my Ruger.

I found a small box and dumped in all my loose bullets and then slid that into a large pocket inside the heavy leather jacket I now wore. Now it was time to go find Carl. I wanted him to know that I would be slipping out to try and locate a veterinary clinic.

He ended up being easy to locate. The man had set up a hammock in the main entry hall. It had a metal frame and actually looked rather comfortable. Curled up underneath it was

DEAD: Onset

Michael. The slow and steady rising and falling of his chest indicated that the young boy was probably asleep.

"I'm going to slip out for a bit," I whispered.

"Out?" Carl opened his eyes and regarded me with a look of curiosity. "You think anybody can just go *out* anymore?" The word 'out' was heavily emphasized with a sincere dubiousness. It was obvious that he thought I was not playing with a full deck. "Them folks in that housing development are all probably getting up right about now. Least, any of 'em that's got enough left to come back."

"I need to find a vet and get Chewie cleaned up properly," I insisted.

"And what do you think is gonna happen when you don't come back?" I noticed that he did not say 'if'. "Who's gonna take care of that dog? These kids? You think I'm gonna do it? And if I up and leave, Betty and these youngsters are as good as dead."

"Yeah, but you aren't that guy. Remember, we talked about that just a bit ago."

"That's because I have you on hand to take the brunt and the burden for the most part. I'm just here as backup."

My eyes drifted down to the boy sleeping under his hammock. Carl shot the boy a look over his shoulder and then returned his gaze to me, a hint of red creeping into his cheeks.

"I can't control where the boy sleeps." His protest was sheepish enough that he and I both knew right then that he was full of it.

"Look, that dog probably means more to me than any single one of you people," I said evenly. It was time that I made a few things clear. "If I was on the roof and could only drag one of you up or my Chewie, you'd all be screwed. And it wouldn't even be close."

Carl seemed to consider my words for a moment, then nodded. "Fair enough. Always good to know where a person stands. So, you say you're going out for supplies at a vet. You know what to grab? You know what sorts of things are to help fight off infection? Bigger question, you even know where a vet is from

The Dog

here?"

"I figured that I could just grab one of the Harley's from the garage."

"Ever ride a Harley?"

"No." I added hastily, "But I have ridden a bike, so I don't imagine there is that much difference in the operation."

"You ever *heard* a Harley?"

I opened my mouth and then closed it just as quick. I knew without him saying just what the flaw in my plan would be. I would be ringing a dinner bell for the undead that would be heard for miles in this new, relatively silent world. For as smart as I thought I was, that topped the list of things that idiots would do in the zombie apocalypse.

"You're gonna have to go on foot. But before you do, I suggest you figure out where the hell you're going."

I stood there like an idiot for several seconds. How would I find a vet nearby? And just wandering around was asking for trouble.

"There is a clinic just down the hill in the direction you came from," Carl finally offered. "Might not be such a bad idea to hit it now. It probably ain't high on the looters' lists. We should be able to slip in, grab some useful supplies and be back here within a few hours."

"We?" I arched an eyebrow.

"You don't think to go out there alone do ya?" Carl challenged.

"And who is going to stay here and watch over the others?" I'd had my mind made up that I was running this mission solo. I'd fully convinced myself that I would be faster if I was alone.

"The others are not entirely helpless," a voice came in a loud whisper from the top of the stairs. I looked up to see Betty coming down. Her lips were pursed and she was obviously agitated. What was new?

"I may not be able to do much, but I am certainly not an invalid. I will get up to speed and do what needs to be done. Obviously this is something that I don't understand, but that does not mean I can't be helpful." The woman reached the bottom of the stairs and fixed both Carl and me with her beady eyes, her chin thrust out in challenge.

"You think you can hold this place down, keep it looking like nobody is here, but be ready to fight off a living person if they come through our gate?" Carl stepped up to Betty. "There ain't no 9-1-1 if somebody comes trying to kill you. And if you don't think that is a possibility, then you weren't listening to what was going on just up the hill."

I saw Betty's face pale. She'd obviously heard.

"Look, I can't tell you that I would be able to kill another human being—" she started, but Carl cut her off.

"Then you aren't ready."

"Wait a minute." I felt the need to interject here. "Just because she isn't Gung Ho to start killing the living—" Now it was my turn to be cut off.

"You better start paying attention to what is going on around you. We got stranded on the interstate because somebody probably just wanted what we had. They shot at us. Then they more than likely took out that vehicle we saw heading back the way we'd come from. And you think those folks in that fancy little pre-fab neighborhood wish maybe they would've been quicker on the trigger when whoever it is that showed up and did whatever was causing all them screams we heard before the zombies came?"

I didn't think Betty could grow any paler. I'd been wrong. She swallowed hard and twice tried to speak before the words actually made their way out of her mouth.

"You don't think I know that bad things are happening? Well I do. But I also refuse to believe that we are the last decent human beings alive," she finally managed to spit out.

"Yes, and you are probably right, but I would say that the burden of proof is going to have to be on a stranger. I won't allow anybody near these little ones until I feel I can be in the same room as they are and close my eyes." Carl moved closer to his hammock as he spoke.

He'd just revealed more about his true nature in those few words and that single action than I think he realized at the mo-

The Dog

ment. I also knew without a doubt that Betty and the kids would be safe with him if something happened to me. Unfortunately, I was not as confident when it came to my dog. That made my decision easy.

"You aren't coming." The statement hung in the air for a moment, then dropped hard on the room. Carl whipped around to me, but I held up a hand. "You just made the case for why you need to stay. Betty may be ready for a lot, but if she had to actually kill another living, breathing human being, I doubt she could do it. You need to stay here and watch over her and the kids."

"You can't think to go out there without backup," Carl argued.

"I'll bring Chewie."

"The dog?" He started to laugh, apparently thinking that I was joking. When I continued to stare at him without flinching, he sobered up in a hurry.

"She will let me know if trouble is close, and if something happens to me, then she won't be a burden to you."

"Evan, I agree with Carl here. I don't think that is a good idea." Betty stepped up and joined in on the debate.

"And you think you are gonna go with me? How long will you last if I have to make a run for it?" As soon as the words came out of my mouth, I wished I could get them back. She was just expressing concern. I'd returned that display by taking a shot at her. "I'm sorry, Betty," I apologized, and I meant it. We hadn't started off on good terms, but, like it or not, we were in this together.

"No need to apologize," Betty said softly, the hurt coming through clearly in her voice. "I know what kind of shape I'm in. And no, I doubt that I would be a good candidate for you to bring along. I just happen to agree with Carl that it is not a good idea for you to go out there alone. I'm sure your dog is wonderful, but she is no substitute for another person watching out for you."

"We can run this conversation around and around until we are blue in the face..." I don't know why, but that single phrase suddenly struck me as funny and I started to chuckle. Carl soon joined in, and then, at last, Betty. Pretty soon, all three of us were laughing like idiots.

"Shut up, I'm asleeping!" a small voice groaned from under Carl's hammock.

We all clamped down suddenly but then that made us start laughing even harder. We managed to make our way into the gigantic living room, each of us with our hands over our mouths which only reduced our laughter to explosive bursts of air accompanied by the occasional snort. Once we were able to regain our composure, I looked at the pair with as much sobriety as I could manage though my tears and flushed face.

"I will be as careful as possible. Perhaps if I take a car from here and then park it a few blocks away when I come back with all the goods. Then we can slip out and bring in whatever I find bit by bit without me actually driving back to the gate."

"And you would be leaving whatever you find in this car where just anybody could walk by and take what they want?" Betty said.

"I think it will be safe enough until we can go out there and grab whatever I manage to scrounge up."

"Cars bring zombies and people…this has to be on foot. So maybe we should make a bit of a priority list," Carl offered.

The three of us sat down and came up with a bunch of necessities. Once we had our list, we prioritized it and that meant that it was too dark by the time we had it all finalized. At some point, the kids had both woke up and come to see what we were doing. I saw the relief on Selina's face very clearly when she discovered that the adults were still present and had not abandoned them.

"You get some sleep," Carl insisted. "If you are making this run, then you need to be at the top of your game. Betty and I will hold things down."

He made a good point. I went upstairs and, after laying out everything that I would be bringing with me tomorrow when I left at the butt crack of dawn, I stripped down and crawled into bed. I knew that I was exhausted. Chewie climbed up on the bed with me and flopped down. Making herself comfortable without

The Dog

showing the slightest concern that she almost shoved me out of bed. That single moment actually felt normal and I fell asleep with my hands knotted up in her fur as she commenced snoring almost immediately.

* * *

The rain had passed through and washed some of the stench out of the air. I moved through the knee-high grass slowly and carefully. There was a blessing and a curse to having this undeveloped plot in between our potential stronghold and this neighborhood. The good was that it gave us a natural and open clearing that would make approaching us without being seen next to impossible. The bad was why I was now being so careful; it was largely due to the creepy-crawly that pulled my foot out from underneath me and managed to gnaw on the toe of my boot before I drove my knife through its temple.

So many people had been either ripped in half or lost their lower limbs. At least that is the way it seemed. I sure as hell don't recall seeing so many in that kind of shape in the movies.

I reached a fence that had sectioned off the backyard of one of the houses and could actually peek into that open area. The fence itself had been reduced to splinters in this location. From the looks of things, it had been crushed inward. I had to assume the zombies had done this with the sheer weight of their numbers.

All these houses facing this side had steep slopes to their yards. I hated being at the bottom. My line-of-sight would be hampered until I got up there. In this one yard I counted three of the undead. They were all gathered at a small doghouse. One of them was on its hands and knees with its upper torso crammed in the opening. Maybe it was stuck. That would be nice.

I slipped in and crept as slowly as possible so that I would not alert them to my presence. Already, I'd shifted to my hand axe. For some reason, that weapon felt natural in my hand now. There had been the opportunity for me to swap it out with a rugged machete Carl had located with some impressive gardening tools, but I had grown strangely attached to this particular weapon.

By the time I'd gotten within striking distance of the first zombie, I could see that the one on the ground had indeed gotten stuck inside the small dog house. That left the other two. The first had obviously been an employee of a fast food chain. The shirt with those all-too-familiar Golden Arches was a mess, but the logo was very recognizable. The poor kid looked to have been pulled down and feasted on. His lower body was an absolute wreck, and there were parts and bits hanging out of him that certainly should not be. My axe came down, and I caught him solid on the crown of his head.

One of the skills that I was learning and becoming more adept in was the quick pullback after a strike. If I didn't, the body could fall and pull the weapon from my hand in the process. There was no way to avoid the sting that came from the sudden and violent contact, but if I braced for it, then it seemed not to hurt quite as much.

The second was just some random female. I didn't bother to get that close of a look. In fact, I was trying not to look too closely at any of them. That seemed to humanize them a bit too much for my liking. Maybe the day would come when I would be okay with this, but for now, it was too soon. These had been regular people as recent as maybe even yesterday. The fact that they were the walking dead was perhaps something that I could come to terms with over time. For now, I needed to act fast.

I glanced at the one stuck in the dog house and decided it was definitely not worth my time to screw with it. If it somehow managed to dislodge itself, and I ran into it on the way out of this place, then I could deal with it at that time.

I jogged up to the house. The rear sliding glass window was completely destroyed. The stench from the house was so bad that I did not know if I could endure going in. I pulled out the wads of cotton that Carl had given me and swabbed them all across my upper lip and under my nose. They were coated with Vick's Vap-O-Rub and flooded me with the smell of chemically reproduced eucalyptus.

The Dog

I stepped inside and saw bits and pieces of human remains all over the place. That was in addition to the fallen corpses with various severe and traumatic head wounds. A few had taken shotgun blasts up close and were missing large portions of their heads. In a few cases, the dark, chunky spray that had dried to the walls told me where the shots had taken place.

I stopped in the kitchen and began to go through the drawers. This idea had come from Betty. While many people had long since stopped needing phone books, that did not stop them from being delivered. Some people disposed of them right away, but others shoved them in drawers. Maybe it was out of habit, but she'd made a good point about that possibility being our best bet for finding the exact locations of a lot of things we might need. Also, I was to check around for maps—another dinosaur that was fading into extinction. Still, if I was going to find an atlas or something of that nature, checking around in the kitchen area was a good start.

I was thrilled when I struck pay dirt on the first try. In a drawer of the island counter structure in the center of the kitchen, I found a local directory and stuffed it into my empty backpack. My pack had been in the garage with a bunch of other high end and very useful camping gear that we'd loaded the majority of into the Hummer. The pack would allow me to carry more stuff easier than just a simple duffel. It would allow me to keep my hands free in emergencies in addition to being a much quieter way to transport goods.

The next thing I did was head down the hall for the bathroom. While we'd found a few basic things in the house we were staying in, there had been a pitifully short supply of actual first aid gear—which I found strange considering some of our other finds that indicated the individuals who lived there were obvious outdoor types.

This house had what I expected I would find in most of them as I did my search. There was a bit of isopropyl alcohol, some hydrogen peroxide, and even some antibacterial ointment. There was a box of Band-Aids, but there were only three left in the box and they were the smallest ones that are barely good enough for a paper cut.

Upstairs, I found another bathroom, but this obviously was the one used by a teenager. There was absolutely nothing of use unless I counted the half a roll of toilet paper and the almost empty tube of toothpaste. I decided to stop long enough to scan the book for vets in the area. I found one. Now I needed a proper map to show me the best way to get to it.

After making a note of some of the things that would be useful for us to come and grab, I moved on to the next house in hopes of finding a map. I had to creep along behind the car parked out front and then climb through the hedge that acted as a natural barrier between the residences. I made it to the side entrance to the garage, but discovered that it was locked. Creeping along the side of the house, I peered over the fence around the backyard. It looked clear and I hurried through the gate, closing it behind me before I allowed myself to exhale.

I stepped up on the small porch and a sound from behind me made me pause. It was coming from the yard of the house that I'd just left. Turning, something in my gut told me that whatever I was about to see…it was very bad.

Apparently, at some point, the zombie that had been stuck in that small dog house had managed to free itself. That had allowed what I was now seeing to also come out of the small, igloo-shaped piece of plastic.

What had once been one of those little yipping dogs that I personally never had any use for was now a matted mess of blood and gore. This poor thing had been ripped into at the belly and now dragged most of what remained of its insides behind it.

It sort of waddled as it made its way across the yard. When it reached the stairs leading up to the back porch, it paused and seemed to regard those stairs for a while before trying to climb them one at a time. As it scrambled up to the second stair, that trail of its guts got caught on the lip of the lower wooden step and eventually pulled most of the strand free.

Carl had been right. The dogs turn just like people. But then why hadn't Chewie done so? My mind recalled having heard something about it taking as much as up to seventy-two hours.

The Dog

That would mean anytime now she should be hitting that mark. Part of me wanted to abandon this quest right here and now. If she turned while I was gone, that would put the burden on Carl most likely. He would be the person to put her down. In my mind, that needed to be me. Period.

I looked into my pack and saw the few meager things that I'd managed to grab and realized that returning now simply was not reasonable. Despite the fact that Chewie meant more to me than any of those people, I needed to make this run outside the relative safety of our walls count for something.

I could not help myself as I watched that pathetic creature climb those stairs and make its way inside the house. Was it operating on instinct like we assumed the undead were doing? Was it hoping to find the zombie versions of its master inside? And if it did eventually come across its former owner, would it then follow him or her around?

I shook all that from my head and ventured into the next house. The sliding glass door was intact. I could see one zombie roaming around in the living room through an arch that separated a dining room with a beautiful cabinet that had miraculously remained intact so far. I could see a fancy gold-trimmed china set on display inside.

Giving the sliding glass door a tug, I was hit with an overwhelming wave of stench when I managed to get it open. Staggering back, I turned just in time to lean over the rail and be sick. I heaved twice more before I could get myself together. When I turned around, I almost fell over backwards. As it was, I basically stumbled into that rail I'd just been leaning over with enough force to cause my back to pop loudly.

Standing in the frame of the sliding glass door was a zombie. She was completely naked. I averted my gaze out of reflex as my brain still issued commands from an old world where modesty existed. Still, I'd noticed bindings dangling from both her wrists before I'd done so. That added more depth to the nightmare I'd been hearing unfold in this little housing complex before the zombies came and busted up the party.

I reminded myself that this creature was no longer living. I doubted she was experiencing any sense of embarrassment or shame at her nakedness. I turned back to this creature as it slapped feebly at the glass. I saw what looked like phone charging cables still tied around each ankle. They had cut deep into the flesh and left a nasty stain from where the blood had dried and then flaked away.

With the door open just a crack, I could hear the moans as the creature gnawed impotently at the glass. A disgusting smear of thick mucus and blood fouled the glass as she continued trying to get at me.

Steeling myself, I jerked the slider the rest of the way open and stepped aside as she tumbled out and landed hard on the wooden deck. With one stroke, I brought the axe down onto the back of the zombie's head, ending its suffering once and for all.

Now that she was dead and no longer a threat, my eyes made a cursory inspection. What I saw sickened me. I had no doubts as to what her fate had been before the undead arrived. Part of me believed that perhaps the zombies had been a bit of a mercy. I also had the time to hope that her tormentors and captors had suffered a gruesome ending.

Stepping into the dining room, a noise to my left caused me to glance over into the kitchen which was just through another archway. On the floor was a man who'd met just the sort of grisly ending that I'd wished for just a handful of seconds ago in regards to the raiders or whatever they were that had descended on this little community. His left arm had been wrenched off, leaving a nub of bone sticking out where it had once been connected to the shoulder. His throat was a gaping black hole and his nose had also been ripped off his face. His right leg was missing and his stomach had been ripped open so that the zombies that had feasted on him could get at the soft inner bits. The finishing touch rested in his being naked from the waist down. There was nothing but copious amounts of dried blood down below the waist, and I didn't have to look too closely to know that he was missing his twig and berries.

Still, it wasn't that sight that had me frozen in place. Sitting beside the sprawled figure was a zombie child. I guessed him to

The Dog

be perhaps four or five. He was holding a large two-pronged fork that had probably once been used at the barbecue grill or to hold a roast in place while it was being carved. I quickly noticed a few dozen punctures up and down the little boy's arms that probably matched the spacing of the tines on the fork he was holding.

Currently, that fork was plunged into the left eye socket of the zombified man on the floor. A viscous goo trickled down the man's cheek. I waited for the child to get up and come for me, but it simply stared up at me as it pulled the fork free and then slowly plunged it down again. This time, it punctured the man's cheek causing the moan to be cut short and transform into more of a gurgle. I could actually see one of the tines stick out near the back of the jaw.

I stepped away as I heard noise from deeper within the house. I did not think it was worth the risk to venture in any further. I made a very slow retreat out the sliding door, pushing it shut once I was back on the porch. That entire time, the child had made no move for me. He'd simply continued to watch me with what almost seemed like curiosity and fascination.

As soon as I was over the back fence of this house and in the yard of the next one, I took a few minutes to settle myself down. Both my hands were trembling and I felt like I would hyperventilate soon if I didn't get my breathing under control.

At last, I was able to approach the next house. It actually looked totally untouched. I didn't see anything moving around through any of the windows as I drew closer. Once I reached the small back deck, I eased a covered barbecue out of the way and cupped my hands to the window so I could get a good look.

Nothing.

I tried the door and it was locked. I moved around to the first window I came to and pressed my palms flat against the glass to try and open it. No luck. That would mean exiting the backyard and trying the garage or perhaps the front door. That last one was the least enticing choice as far as I was concerned.

I opened the gate and slowly stuck my head out to get a look. I didn't see anything, and the moans I did hear were not close. I stuck near to the side of the house as I moved to the front. Once I reached the corner, I had to actually work up the nerve to look around it.

The street was littered with debris. Also, the gentle breeze would occasionally shift and send a streamer of smoke wafting past from two of the houses smoldering across the way. A single zombie was standing in the middle of the road about two houses up past me. It seemed to be staring up at the sky for no apparent reason.

I eased around the corner and ducked behind the car parked in the driveway. Once I reached the end of my cover, I took another good look around. I had about five long steps to get me to that front door. I made sure that nothing was looking my way and then scurried to the door. I reached it, turned the knob and felt a surge of relief when it opened.

I slipped inside, shut the door behind me, and froze in my tracks. Despite there being no sign of any activity inside this house, I could smell the very distinct and rancid odor of the undead.

The ground floor took me a few minutes to clear as I crept through the halls and peeked in a living room, dining room, kitchen, and what turned out to be a small office by the looks of things. That meant that wherever this zombie was "hiding" had to be upstairs.

As soon as my foot touched the bottom stair, I heard it: a soft moan along with a strange squeak. I crept up the stairs and stopped in front of a closed door where I waited until I heard the noise again. It was coming from the other side of the door. Gripping my hand axe, I braced myself and then threw the door open.

"Jesus H. Christ," I managed to breathe as I staggered back a few steps and threw my arm over my face.

11

Discoveries

I had no idea what had happened to this poor man, but a lot could be guessed. Judging by the small sizes of the bite marks I could make out up and down his arms, he'd been attacked by the child version of the undead. In my mind, there was nothing more horrifying.

I flashed back to that child with the large two-pronged fork. It had sat there regarding me and made no attempt to come after me. Yet, there had been something in the way that it watched me. I was certain that it was studying me and waiting for…something.

This man was middle-aged, and had thinning blonde hair that clung to the fringes, but had mostly abandoned the top of his head. He was wearing baggy shorts and a sweatshirt with the sleeves cut off and looked like maybe he'd just come back from the gym.

His left arm was torn up between shoulder and elbow, and you could see several bites up and down his right arm that either barely broke the skin or just left a nasty bruise. Only one bite on the apex of the right bicep looked to have torn away any meat.

The worst injury was on his face. The left cheek had a nasty rip and I could see his teeth gnashing through the hole. Sinews of flesh stretched and retracted as the creature opened and shut

DEAD: Onset

its mouth in frustration at my arrival. A single flap dangled but seemed to have gone slightly stiff.

The man had obviously retreated to this bathroom before actually dying. He'd had the presence of mind to zip tie his stockinged feet together and then slip his head through a belt that he'd secured to some kind of vertical handle mounted on the back wall of the shower.

I imagine that his shedding of his shoes had something to do with trying to hasten his obvious suicide. Maybe he did it in order to prevent being able to gain any solid footing in the tub when he'd hung himself. He now sat at an awkward angle in the tub with his body cocked to the left as I faced him.

This pathetic creature would swipe at me, try to regain his feet, then tumble one way or the other since he had no use of his legs to remain steady. I moved to one side and got a look at that handle. My best guess was that it was to help a person stand up if they were seated in the tub. As somebody who worked in construction and had built my share of homes, I was sort of impressed with the mounting job the builder had done on this single feature. If not for all the gore and stench, I might've actually been able to enjoy the craftsmanship a bit more.

All the various bodily fluids and seeping blood had fouled the bottom of the tub's basin and then dried into a sticky coating that allowed this zombie to almost struggle to his knees; albeit precariously with his bound feet. I could not imagine the nightmare this poor man had endured. All I could do for him was step up and end his existence. I pulled the knife from my belt and plunged it into the side of the head. The body slumped forward, the belt tightening one final time around the throat of the inert corpse. I quickly grabbed the few things of any use before leaving.

I exited the bathroom and shut the door. That was when I heard the scrabbling on one of the doors at the end of the hall. Besides the sounds of nails scratching on wood, I also heard low growls, hisses, and moans.

I approached the door, and my eyes went to the crack between the bottom of that door and the floor. I could see dark

Discoveries

shadows flitting about. After a brief moment of consideration, I decided that I could forgo whatever might be behind that door. I had no doubt there was more than one zombie on the other side. I glanced back at the bathroom door where I'd left that poor man's body. Something told me that his killers lurked here. If there were children in there, I wanted no part of it.

I headed down the stairs and exited out the back. The next three houses were uneventful due to them being empty. I was now approaching the end of what the sign told me was SE Scott Park Circle. Next would be the four houses along SE Scott Park Lane. The ones in the middle were all devastated by the fires that had burned here and they would not likely offer up anything useful. Plus, since they were mostly burned all the way down, there was little cover to be had. It was best to stick to the houses along the edge. At least that was my conclusion.

Making my way up the gradual slope, I saw a single zombie pause and then turn to look in my general direction. For a moment, I believed that it would just go about its business. When it began to trudge towards me, its arms reaching and its mouth opening and closing like it was warming up for some serious ripping and chewing, I knew I'd been spotted.

I needed to take this one down before it drew too much attention to me. This would be a job for my axe and I deftly brought it to bear as I rushed over. One swing and a loud thud and crack put this creature down for good. I planted my foot on its shoulder and pulled my weapon free just as a chorus of moans erupted from my left in the direction I'd been heading.

"You might've just saved my life," I whispered to the corpse at my feet.

Coming down the street were several of the walking dead. They had no apparent goal or destination and were simply moving along, following the easy curve of the road. I waited until the tail end of the small mob was past before coming up to a crouch and rushing to that group of four houses on the right.

This group had no actual backyard. They had nothing more than back decks a floor above the dead-end street that ran behind them. The first one had a door on the ground level and I rushed to it.

The door had been pried open at some point and I entered very cautiously. Sticking my head inside, I gave a sniff. Nothing jumped out at me to make me think there might be zombies inside, but I wasn't going to take that for granted and start making assumptions.

I found myself in a dark stairwell. There was a narrow and very dark hall with a door at the end and one on each side. Since it was so terribly dark, I chose to pass on being that brave.

Moving up the stairs, I reached another door that had a nasty smear that looked like somebody's bloody hand had swiped down it diagonally. I gave another experimental sniff, but still did not get even a hint of the awful stench seemingly unique to the walking dead.

I eased the door open very carefully and found myself in a hall running to the left and right from where I stood. To the right, I saw a kitchen. To the left, I saw an intersecting hallway. Since I was confident of what I was likely to find in the kitchen, I decided to go left.

In moments, I had cleared out a downstairs bathroom that had little more than a few soft soap dispensers and hand towels. I glanced in the living room and saw nothing that caught my eye, so I ventured upstairs. I was only halfway up when I began to smell something nasty. It wasn't the stink that I knew from the zombies. This was much heavier with feces and a coppery hint that I was certain had to be blood.

I peeked over the lip as soon as my eyes were at a point where I could scan the area from floor height. I saw nothing and heard not so much as the tiniest creak that might be somebody moving. There were four doors up here. One was open and I saw a larger bathroom.

What I did not want to have happen was for me to snoop around and have something occur that made me run for my life. If I had to bolt suddenly, I might leave behind all the potential goodies in there. I went in and emptied out the medicine cabinet, the drawers with toothpaste, toothbrushes, mouthwash, and fem-

Discoveries

inine products that I almost left until I remembered that we had one grown up and one tween version of a female in our little band of survivors.

Now that I had the important stuff, I felt okay with exploring further. I let my nose lead me to what I figured to be the source of the smell up here. I turned the knob, my free hand cocked back and ready just in case my theory on the unique smell of zombies proved to be inaccurate.

I winced at what I discovered. This had once been a young girl's bedroom judging by the abundance of Disney princesses and overwhelming pink color scheme. Sitting on the floor just to the right of the window that looked out at the neighborhood sat a man. More precisely, what remained of him. Most of his head was sprayed up the pastel pink wall from where he'd blown his brains and most of his head away.

I walked in and looked around to make sure there were no surprises and then pried the double-barrel shotgun from the stiff hands that held it in their dead grip; that accomplished, I grabbed the box of shells that sat beside the man.

Glancing out the window, I stood there for several seconds. Eventually I realized that I was standing with my mouth open, so I shut it. My eyes continued to track the group of zombies as they moved along with slow steadiness. I almost laughed at what I was seeing.

The zombies were rounding the corner to my right, and I could see the entire group from this vantage point. I could also see the trail they were leaving behind. Bits and pieces of loose meat fell to the road and was trampled underfoot, creating a nasty, dark stain. What had me so amused was the fact that this particular group was simply following the road as it wrapped around in a circle.

They were doing laps.

"Coming from the inside, we have Bubba One-arm...right on his heels is Spandex girl and then the rest of the pack. It looks like we have a battle for third between Girl-who-needs-a-sandwich and Gas Station Attendant. And...oh...Spandex girl has taken a tumble. This could be the big one. Yes, three more

DEAD: Onset

stumble over the body and now we have zombies swerving everywhere to try and get around this terrible accident," I droned in my best race announcer's voice. I wasn't entirely sure what a race announcer sounded like, but that didn't stop me.

I watched as the zombies that fell eventually made it to their feet again and rejoined the pack. They all shambled past and eventually rounded the corner to my left. I tracked them as they came in and out of my sight while moving down the street that was parallel to the one out in front of this house. I noticed a street that, if they turned sharp left just before rounding the corner and coming back by my location, would take them out of this part of the housing complex. Apparently they were not so inclined and eventually rounded the corner to my right again and started along the street below.

I watched in morbid fascination until I realized that an incredible amount of time had passed as that pack did two complete revolutions of the development. I had no idea how long they would do what they were doing, but it was just another thing to catalog for further contemplation later.

I looked in my pack and tried not to feel discouraged. I'd been to a handful of homes and had barely managed to fill the pack to the halfway point. I could search the other houses along this strip, but Carl had made it clear that I had to be back before it got dark or he would come searching for me. I needed more than what I was finding in these homes. I guess it was time to make my move to that clinic we'd passed.

The best way to get there from my observations would be to go back down to that steep drive that led up to this house. I headed down and used the same degree of caution as when I'd entered.

There was a long and very steep driveway that took me to 92nd Avenue and I followed it down until I finally reached the main road. I would need to cross it and climb a fence to get to the parking lot for the Mt. Scott Medical Center. I knew there was a surgery center and a pediatric facility.

When I reached the main road, those two lanes seemed like an ocean separating me from my destination. Unable to put it off

Discoveries

any longer, I saw a good break in the undead that were scattered pretty thin from what I'd seen so far. I took a deep breath and then made my run for it. I heard a moan from off to my left, but I ignored it as I sprinted for the fence. I was less than halfway there when I noticed an entrance up here on the road. I considered going for it, but knew that I would bring zombies to it if I did so now. No, that would be an important set of doors to remember when I was ready to leave.

At last, I reached the fence and almost vaulted over it in one swift move. If not for the pack, I would've probably made it. As it was, I only got hung up for a moment before I could free myself and then basically fall to the other side.

I was now on a raised ledge above the parking lot. So far, the immediate area looked to be zombie-free. I hopped down and jogged to the corner of the building and peered around it. This was the main parking lot, and apparently, a lot of people had come here simply because it was a medical facility.

There were a handful of military vehicles in front and even two county sheriff's cars. I went to them first and found a treasure trove of supplies. I pocketed three sets of handcuffs, slung two pistol-gripped shotguns over my shoulder, along with three Glock 21s and a dozen loaded magazines. These took standard .45 caliber rounds—which should be relatively easy to find once we were able to look—and would be plenty durable. As it was, I managed to scrounge up over a hundred spare rounds when I stumbled upon one police officer who'd been opening the trunk of his car before being attacked. He'd obviously killed the five zombies that were scattered on the ground around him before eating a bullet himself. A box of bullets was sitting in plain sight in that open trunk along with an ASP expandable baton, and a flashlight that I initially thought was another club.

There was more stuff here than I could carry which meant that Carl and I would have to make a few trips once I returned. A find like this could set us up nicely. All this, and I hadn't even had time to scrounge through the military stuff yet. I would not have the time at the moment as I saw a few zombies had noticed me from out on the street above and were coming my direction.

DEAD: Onset

One of them leaned forward and fell awkwardly to the pavement. I watched in stunned horror as it rose with one arm bent in three locations.

It was time to at least duck inside and see what I could find. The good thing now was that if the few zombies coming for me all gathered at the main entrance, then I could slip around to that door on the opposite side of this place and escape from that direction onto the street above. Of course, that was provided that the inside of this place wasn't a death trap waiting for me to spring it.

What I had come to realize was that going inside would be riskier than I originally believed. I had made the assumption that, since it wasn't a proper hospital, it would be an easier target. Did I want to turn around and just return with what I had? I considered that very seriously for a moment and then decided that I could at least take a peek. I promised myself that I would abandon the effort if it seemed too risky.

Moving to the main entrance, I felt my hopes rise just a bit. I pulled on the doors and they opened. Even better, I did not see anything moving in the entry lobby.

As my eyes adjusted to the gloom I could make out a few bodies. I pulled out the massive flashlight and clicked on the button. The brilliant white light was dazzling. A lone zombie was highlighted by my beam. It looked up from where it was crouched on the floor, letting loose a terrible moan. I could see dark stains all over its face and realized that I'd caught this one while feeding as my light brought more of the grisly picture into focus. The body on the floor was twitching, its legs thrumming in final spasms of death. I hurried over as it tried to get to its feet and I stuck my knife in one eye socket. I then leaned over and repeated the move on the poor soul lying on its back.

I marveled for a moment at how easy that kill had just been for me. Moving to the sign on the wall, I scanned it for anything that might be helpful. At last I saw what I was looking for: post-op recovery and the on-site pharmacy.

I thought the pharmacy would be a better first choice so that was my destination. I headed to the stairs and pulled one of the

Discoveries

Glock 21s. I ensured that it was fully loaded and then stuffed it into my waistband. The ASP would be my weapon of choice unless absolutely necessary, but I wanted the comfort of carrying the handgun in an easy to reach location just in case.

I reached the door once I was fairly confident that I knew the general direction that I was headed. It sucked that the power was out in this neighborhood. I knew it would all fail eventually, but this little raid would've been much easier with the lights still on.

The door to the stairs was propped open for some strange reason. A corpse was on the floor just inside, her ankle caught in between the door and its frame. I toed her to ensure she was dead. Once I moved past and glanced back, I saw a neat little black hole in her forehead. It wasn't made by a gun, that much was for sure. It looked like somebody had hit her with an ice pick or something of that nature.

Once I was on the stairs, I could hear moans and shuffling from above. I was glad that this was a contained stairwell. There were actual concrete walls on both sides of me and that would keep some curious zombie from leaning over the rail and plummeting down on top of me. The bad side of that was the fact that I had no idea how many were above me or how close they might be.

I had to move from one wall to the other as I reached the switchback to have the best vantage, and it proved beneficial when a grimy and stained hand gripped the corner and a face poked out from behind it. The filmed eyes shot full of black tracers gave away the certainty that this was one of them.

He'd apparently been a doctor. He was wearing scrubs and had a name tag dangling from above a slim pocket that still held what might've been a pen light. His stethoscope had gotten tangled around his neck and was now dried into place by the blood from where his throat had been ripped open. I brought the ASP up and then down hard on the side of the zombie's head.

"Fuck!" I practically screamed.

The blow had connected solid, but the follow through caused me to lose my balance and stumble back a couple of steps. The problem there was that I was only about one step from the stairs. I teetered as my one foot found nothing but air, and I managed to grab hold of the handrail just before I toppled. My flashlight clattered to the ground but, miraculously, did not break. It ended up against the wall, the light still bright enough to give me some ambient light that let me make out the dark shadow of the zombie as it recovered from my blow and advanced.

I swept its legs out and then had to hit the thing twice more on the back of its head until it stopped moving. I looked at the extendable baton and, after wiping off the clumps of hair and other nasty stuff, I put it away and pulled out my trusty hand axe. If I got in a jam, I could use the pistol, but taking several hits to end a zombie was an easy way to find myself in just such a predicament.

After scooping up my flashlight, I moved up the stairs to the second floor and stopped at the door. It had a long rectangular window that allowed me to look in at the long hallway. There were doors lining both sides, but at the end of the hall, I could see an open area that would be the lobby. That would be where the pharmacy was located. Between me and it were five zombies just roaming around this narrow passage. The shades on the windows at the end where that waiting area was located were all open so that there was plenty of light, but this corridor was still shrouded in enough darkness that I would need to keep the flashlight on for at least half the distance.

I tried the handle on this door and felt my heart skip a beat when I went to push the lever and it made an audible click that sounded loud enough to be heard for miles. Every head in the corridor turned and they all started my direction.

Having no other option, I pulled the door open and stepped into the hall and then shut the door behind me so that my back was protected. The first one was a man in overalls and a sweatshirt. I could not see any sign that he'd been bit. Unfortunately, I didn't have time at the moment to investigate. I brought my axe down hard and fast, ending him and then preparing for the next one.

Discoveries

This one had been a lady that I guessed to be in her early twenties or late teens. She was a bit chunky, and her gait was awkward. It took me a moment to actually see the tubes dangling from her arms. Her left leg seemed to be the problem. When my flashlight hit it full on, I finally realized the reason. Obviously, she'd suffered a tremendous break in that leg. I could see some sort of contraption that actually looked bolted to it and there was even a section that was laid open bare to the bone.

I tore my gaze away and then buried my axe in the top of her skull. She dropped like a sack of potatoes leaving me with three more that were a bit bunched up together. They would be a quandary. I could only take down one at a time, and if one of them got their hands on me, I could be done for. I pushed away thoughts of running. I was too near my goal to run away now.

I was trying to figure out which one to take first when a figure rounded the corner at the end of the hall. It looked like something from a cheesy science fiction movie. This was no zombie; of that I was certain as soon as whomever it was in that getup waved at me.

This person was wearing a yellow HAZMAT suit, but it was reinforced with shin guards that looked like they might belong on a catcher in baseball. There was a set of football shoulder pads modified with two-inch spikes set along the top and front. The person had leather wrappings on both forearms as well as a spiked collar like you might see on a cartoon bulldog.

In his hand he held a rather small pick. It looked like the kind that rock climbers used, but I didn't know what its official name might be. It dawned on me as to what might've dealt the fatal blow to the zombie that I'd discovered in the doorway on the ground floor.

The individual came at a jog and took down the lagging zombie with a quick strike to the crown of his head. As that zombie fell, I moved in and dropped the other two in rapid succession. As soon as the last zombie fell, I drew back a few steps from this stranger; my desire to snatch the pistol from my waistband was almost bad enough to cause my hands to itch. Despite this person taking down the one zombie, I had no idea what intentions may exist in another individual's mind.

The hood to the HAZMAT suit was thrown back and I saw a man's face looking at me with a bemused smile. His long blonde hair was held back in a ponytail and his eyes were bright enough that I was pretty sure they were blue despite the poor lighting.

"Hey," the man said as he took a step back after wiping his weapon on the hem of the shirt of the zombie he'd just taken down.

"Hey back at'cha." I slowly let the arm where I held my axe settle at my side.

There was a prolonged and uncomfortable silence after that as we both sized each other up. I could see a great deal of dark splatter all over his yellow protective suit.

"Looks like you've run into a bit of trouble," I said, finally tired of the silence and ready to break it.

"Yeah, this place is actually pretty compartmentalized, but there were a lot of stiffs walking around in this particular section." His answer was a bit guarded, and I noticed that he was leaning back just a bit as if he wanted to make a run for it. Also, his weapon hand had come down, but it was still flexed and ready.

"Look, I am here to try and get some stuff from the pharmacy. I'm sure there is plenty in there if you are here for the same reason. I think we can both get what we want and be on our way without this having to be a thing." I paused for just a second before adding, "But if you aren't cool with that, I'll go elsewhere. Honestly I'm just trying to get some stuff for my dog."

"Was it bit?" the man asked, suddenly seeming interested.

"Yeah, but it has been a few days and she seems fine."

"Dogs turn just like people."

It was like he didn't hear what I'd just told him. I decided that he could think what he wanted. And despite what I'd seen in that backyard, I was confident that my Chewie was fine.

"So, can we agree that both of us can pick through things and get what we each need and be on our separate ways?" I just

Discoveries

wanted to be out of here. Not only that, but I wished that I had my Chewie with me now. This guy gave me the creeps. I didn't know what it was about him, but something gnawed at me. Maybe the way he was acting had me unsettled. He seemed to have a tough time keeping eye contact.

"Who's watching your dog?"

That question caught me off guard. That is the only explanation that I can come up with for why I blurted, "She's with my little group a few blocks away from here."

I wanted to slap myself. I was making some of those really stupid mistakes that get folks killed in the movies. Never divulge your numbers or location. And while I hadn't given specifics, I'd said what I considered to be more than enough.

"You got room for one more?"

"Umm…" I didn't know what to say.

"Look, I'm by myself. I've been on my own since last night and I honestly don't know how long I can do this all alone. I don't remember the last time I slept. Every time I close my eyes, I hear something that wakes me, and I don't want to go out that way." The man was silent for a moment and it took me a second to realize that he appeared to be crying. When he made eye contact with me, I had my suspicions confirmed. "I was actually breaking into the pharmacy to end it. I figured I'd find something that would send me off painlessly. I considered eating a bullet, but that just gave me the creeps. I couldn't get past the idea that it might hurt."

I thought it over. Unless this guy was one hell of an actor, he was just scared and alone. It would be good to have another person who could help us defend the homestead. I wouldn't be able to make the final decision, but I could at least bring him along and introduce him to Carl and Betty; of course, I would be paying attention to how Chewie reacted as well.

"Sure, why not." I stayed put for a moment and then finally gave his weapon a long glance. He started, and then hastily let it slip into a loop on the large leather tool belt he had strapped around his waist. "Name's Evan Berry." I extended a hand.

"Brandon Cook," the man said, taking my hand in a grip that was firm but not crushing. I hated it when people tried to show you how incredibly strong they thought they were by squeezing your hand until the knuckle bones ground together.

"Okay, Brandon, let's go empty out some stuff from this pharmacy." I started up the hall to the intersection and looked out into the open lobby area.

What I saw was equal parts impressive and disturbing. There were bodies sprawled all over the place. This resembled the zombie apocalypse version of Custer's Last Stand. I glanced over at the man who now stood beside me.

"You?" I asked, giving a slight nod of my head into the room of carnage.

"Some of it was done before I got here." The man edged past me. "We should get moving. I thought that I was so clever coming here, but if you're here, then my idea may not be nearly as clever as I initially thought."

I felt my cheeks warm. That had sounded almost like an insult. He hadn't really said it with a condescending tone, but there was an implication. I brushed it aside. Maybe I was just being hypersensitive.

"I was picking the lock on the door when I heard you in the stairwell. I almost ran for it, but then I thought maybe some zombie got lucky and figured it out."

The more this guy talked, the more I was wondering if I'd made a mistake in saying he could come back to the group with me. Oh well, it wasn't like he was officially one of our group yet. Carl and Betty would need to sign off on him as well.

I stood by as he got the door open. I was impressed with his skill and had to admit that it would be handy to have somebody around who could do that.

We slipped inside, shutting the door behind us and then began to roam the aisles. I didn't find exactly what I'd hoped to find. There were boxes of the sterile alcohol wipes in the foil packages, but I didn't actually find any bottles of it here. I did find some wraps and bandages, but again, not exactly what I'd hoped for.

Discoveries

On the plus side, I did grab a lot of antibacterial ointment as well as anything with -illin on the label. I also grabbed a few bottles of assorted pain killers and seven boxes with vials of morphine. Those were in a special locker that Brandon had to take a few minutes on but still managed to pick.

Once we were loaded up, I expressed my disappointment in the lack of antiseptics like alcohol or hydrogen peroxide. Brandon looked at me with no expression for a moment and then said he knew where we could snag some on the way out.

I noticed that he'd filled his bag as well, but I hadn't really paid attention to what he grabbed. I considered asking, but then decided we were still strangers and it wasn't my place.

He led the way and I quickly forgot all my misgivings when he led me to a door to a supply closet that was loaded with rows of assorted bandages, wraps, and bottles of chlorhexidine, and iodine. It was a treasure trove of all the things that I needed.

"You might want to hold off on using the alcohol on your dog," Brandon suggested as I scooped bottles off the shelf and into my pack. "I would suggest the chlorhexidine. A person understands that burn, I am not sure your dog would."

Again, he was just giving me advice—and good advice if I was being honest—but there was something about him that set my nerves on edge. He just had a quality that I did not care for.

At last, I had all I could carry. The pack was a bit heavier than I would have liked, but I could not part with one single thing that I'd put in it.

I explained to Brandon where we were heading. He winced when I told him about the zombie race track. Something passed through his eyes, but I was too happy to care about any misgivings he might have. I was bringing back something that would enhance my Chewie's chances of healing up better. Also, I had almost everything that Carl and Betty had put on the request list.

Now, all we had to do was make it back.

DEAD: Onset

12

The Children

We hadn't taken three steps out of my little rear entrance that opened onto 92nd Avenue when we were spotted by zombies. A small group of them were off to our right and already headed our direction. The others were to our left and must have heard us come out of the building. They were all turning around and coming with arms out and hands grasping at air.

I was just about to make a run for it when I saw something that froze me in place. Just beyond the group to our left were three children. While they were barely far enough away that I could not make out any details, I knew they were zombies without a doubt. The dark stains down their fronts gave that away past the fact that three kids were basically standing in the middle of the street with zombies everywhere.

Unlike all the other zombies around us that had caught sight or smell or whatever the hell zombies use to home in on us humans, these were just watching us. And I had no doubt that they were doing exactly that. The only difference was that they were not coming after us. They were simply watching.

And waiting.

"What are they waiting for?" I mumbled.

Brandon looked up and glanced around frantically. "Who?" I noticed a slight tremor in his voice.

DEAD: Onset

"Them." I pointed at the trio of children who were still standing there like statues.

By now, some of the other zombies in the distance that had been drawn to investigate what all the fuss was about were shoving past them. When the children began to actually move out of the way to let others pass, I knew something was different.

Wrong.

That word echoed in my mind as I started across the street with Brandon just ahead of me. I'd given him general directions towards where Carl and the others would be waiting. He was just starting up the long drive that would take us between the house I'd entered through the back—the one where I'd discovered the man who'd blown his brains out—and the first group of homes that I'd searched. That is when I spotted him.

There was a house just to the right of us. On the porch was a lone zombie child. He was standing there…watching. I saw the head cock first to one side, then the other as it tracked us. And I had no doubt that was exactly what it was doing as its head moved slightly with us as we hurried along towards that housing development that bordered the place that Carl, Betty, the kids, and I were currently calling home.

"Stop!" I hissed, but Brandon kept going.

I hurried after him and grabbed his arm, yanking him to a stop just before he ducked into the bushes that would take us along the fence line of those first houses—the ones where I'd spotted the dog.

"We can't just go straight home," I snapped when he spun on me, an exasperated look on his face. If I didn't know any better, I would've sworn that he was about to take a swing at me.

"Why not." His anger was replaced by something else as he apparently spotted the child on the porch.

"It's watching us. I'm afraid of what might happen if we go back now. We need to take a different route," I said hurriedly. Glancing back, I could not believe that the child was still just standing there staring at us with its creepy, filmed-over, black-shot eyes.

Things from the movies and everything that I thought I

The Children

knew were starting to crumble. This was all so much worse.

I looked around and figured that we had no choice other than to go right instead of left. We could loop all the way around the outer ring of this neighborhood until we ended up on Johnson Creek Boulevard again. From there, we would just have to play it as it came until we could make it back up the hill and to the house.

"This way," I said, already starting along the back side of the houses that bordered the zombie racetrack.

I glanced back once to ensure that Brandon was following me. I noticed him giving the house with the suicide-by-shotgun guy a strange look. Maybe he'd come this way already and knew what was inside the place. That really didn't matter at the moment, what did was our getting the heck out of this situation. If any zombies followed—namely the child variety—we would have to stay in their line of sight for a while and lead them on. Eventually, we could pour on some speed and lose them.

We hooked left after passing the fourth house. I looked back and spotted him. I'd been correct. The child zombie had followed us. Even worse, he seemed to be pausing and making noise every so often. He couldn't be calling others…could he?

"Why is he doing that?" Brandon huffed after we scrambled up a steep dirt incline that would put us between the four houses on the south side of the zombie racetrack and the four that made up the east "wall" of it.

"Calling for help?" It was a guess, but I was beginning to believe it. I really wanted to know why the children appeared to be so different from the adult versions.

A moan to my right was my only warning as a pair of the undead stumbled through the trees that acted as a border between the houses we were skirting behind and the neighborhood a block over. One of them was on me before I knew it and we both fell to the hard-packed ground. I landed solidly on my left side and my elbow smacked a rock, sending sharp pain shooting all the way to my fingertips.

I threw up my right hand instinctively and caught the creature by the throat as it was about to lean in and take a bite out of my face.

The teeth clamped together with an audible click and something cold and wet splattered on my cheek. I didn't even want to think about what that might be as I shoved the undead menace aside. I kicked out with all my strength to scoot it as far away as possible. I tried to get up, but my pack was a serious problem in that department.

I only had a few feet of room to regain my feet and struggled gracelessly to my knees. I spied the other zombie that had attacked us; it was sprawled on the ground with a neat hole in its forehead. I could just see one of Brandon's legs off to the side, but they did not seem to be moving.

Was he just standing there watching me struggle? I thought as I heaved myself up and into a kneeling position. As I reached a more upright position, I saw him stride over and swing his pick into the head of the zombie that had jumped me.

I was about to lay into him when I heard a chorus of moans from behind us. I grabbed a nearby branch that was jutting out and made my way to my feet. I was positive that I wasn't imagining things. He had not made any offer to give me a hand up before he turned and began to hurry along the route we'd been taking.

I was at least a good twenty feet behind him as I got moving. I'd paused to look back the way we'd come and saw the leading edge of a small group of zombies. Leading the pack was that kid from the porch. But I swear, as soon as it…he…whatever…as soon as the child zombie realized that I saw *him*, he fell back in the crowd. I caught glimpses of him from behind the legs of some of the first few rows of adult zombies.

I started after Brandon again, and now I was almost certain that I would not be allowing him to join our group if it were up to me alone. There was even a more primitive voice in my head suggesting much darker things. I shoved those thoughts away, terrified of what that might mean for me if I even considered embarking down a path like that.

We reached the fourth and final house, and Brandon had

The Children

pulled up suddenly. Maybe he realized that he'd been leaving behind the person that was offering him some sort of sanctuary. We would be passing between a fifth house as this row of houses continued on for a few more. But ducking in here would put as at the lone road that branched off from the zombie racetrack. We would need to cross it and then duck behind a house that was on the fringe of the burnt ones.

"I think we should go one more house up," I suggested.

Of course, at this point, I didn't care if he followed me or not. I started back down the narrow gap between these two houses and followed the back fence of the neighboring home. I heard the footsteps behind me that indicated Brandon was following. I really wanted to look back and check on the progress that the zombies pursuing us were making, but I was afraid of what my expression might convey to this stranger.

Reaching the end of the fence, I looked and saw that the coast seemed clear. Without bothering to say anything or communicate with Brandon, I made a quick dash up the side of this house's fence line until I came to the end and could look out onto the street. My first glance was to my left towards the zombie racetrack. I was in luck. The last of the herd was shuffling past and out of sight.

If I used the house across the street as a shield, I could pass through and hopefully come out on Johnson Creek Boulevard. From there, I would have to see how much traffic there was shambling about. If it was clear, then I would be home in a matter of minutes.

I could hear Brandon's footsteps getting closer. Once more, without so much as a word, I took off. Crossing the street was the worst part, and I felt totally exposed. I was halfway when I could've sworn that I heard a weak scream. I paused, but Brandon practically plowed me down when he ran into my back. I was really get tired of being run into and knocked over.

A hand reached out and caught my shoulder to keep me from falling, but just as fast, I was pushed ahead. "We need to move. We lost that group behind us. If we can get to the end of this house and around that clump of trees just ahead, we might actually lose 'em."

I started to glance back, but Brandon was in the way as well as shoving me forward. I staggered ahead and tripped over a corpse. Thankfully, it was completely dead. It was also burnt to a crisp. I glanced down at it, but once again, Brandon was ushering me along with haste.

At last we reached those trees. I almost dove around them in the hopes that we didn't get spotted by that pack of zombies we'd left behind. I leaned against a tree and caught my breath.

"What the hell is your problem?" I asked the man with his hands on his knees, sucking in great gulps of air.

He looked up at me, his face an empty slate with practically no emotion on it. The only color was his flushed cheeks from the exertion of the run.

"That was close," he said, but there was a mechanical sound to his voice.

I had way more questions than answers when it came to Brandon, but here and now was not the place or the time. And maybe we just got off on the wrong foot. There are people you meet who you sometimes take an instant disliking to, and that can cloud your judgement. I knew that we would eventually need to bring more people in, and I wasn't about to be the person who said somebody could not join us of my own volition.

I turned and started towards the compound. Despite the fact that I would not make a snap decision on my own about this guy…that did not mean I wouldn't be watching him like a hawk.

***

"…and then we just cruised down Johnson Creek. It was practically deserted," I said, finishing my narrative on the events, doing my best to stick to reporting the facts.

Carl nodded and then handed my pack to Betty. Apparently, she was a regular volunteer at a local animal shelter. She helped clean up new arrivals and assisted with little things during the staff vet's rounds. Again, I was learning something about her that made me reconsider my stance on her. It was that same

The Children

revelation that had me doubting my opinion of Brandon; who was sleeping in one of the bedrooms already after both Carl and Betty seemed to welcome the new arrival with open arms.

"I want to go back to that medical center," I said once Betty hoisted up my pack and went to sort through everything. She'd promised me that we would take care of Chewie's tail as soon as she sorted out the supplies.

"Check out that military stuff?" Carl sat back and took a sip from a water bottle. "You know we can just load out one of the rigs and bring it back here," he said. "Don't need keys with most military rigs. Push button start 'em and bring it all here pretty as you please."

"And have every zombie for miles march to our front gate?" I scoffed.

"Yeah," Carl's head drooped, "you got a point there." He paused and sat back in deep thought for a moment. "You think we can bring that stuff back on our backs…one trip after another?"

"You got other plans?" I chuckled. "Not like you gotta be to work tomorrow…or ever again."

"Then maybe you and I can head out first thing tomorrow morning," Carl offered.

"Yeah…about that. You think we can just leave Betty and the kids alone with the new guy this soon?"

"Can I say something about that?" Betty appeared from the hallway, a small plastic bag in her hand with what looked like a few bottles of some of the stuff I'd brought back as well as boxes that I could plainly see marked as being gauze.

"Sure," I answered, but she was already talking and pretty much cut me off.

"You two seem to think that I'm an invalid. That I need watching over and such. Well let me tell you both…I'm a grown woman who has been taking care of business for longer than I think you've even been alive, *Mister* Berry." She put a lot of emphasis on the word 'Mister' and I could tell she was just getting started on this little rant. "I may not be in very good shape, but I am very aware of the danger that a new person represents.

DEAD: Onset

If it comes down to this stranger and the children…you can be assured that I will put a bullet in that man's head before I allow either of those little ones to be harmed in any way."

Wow, I thought. *She is further along in the game than I am if she is that prepared to take another living person's life. I'd had chances to put the guy away a few times in our journey back here. I hadn't been able to do it even when I thought he'd left me out to dry.*

"You need to have somebody with you out there, Mister Berry. I may not know much, but I am very aware of the level of danger outside the walls of this house. I was with you out there. And in case you forgot, it was me that took care of that gigantic zombie man in the coveralls that had you pinned to the ground." Betty glanced over at Carl. "And unlike you, I have been by that man's side from the beginning. I was out there holding those children by the hand as we waded through the unthinkable after you abandoned us."

Planting her hands on her hips, I think Betty was prepared for our retorts. Personally, I didn't have anything to say. She was correct on all counts, and if she was already seeing our recent addition as something that needed watching and was not willing to accept him, then I guess she had her stuff together.

"I have something that I want you to put someplace you feel comfortable with. You need to be able to grab this the moment something goes wrong." Carl walked into the main kitchen on the ground floor. Betty and I followed. I was admittedly curious.

Carl knelt behind the big island counter in the middle of the kitchen and then re-appeared with a black case. He unzipped it and pulled out what I initially mistook as a pistol.

"This flare gun should be able to get our attention if you need us." Carl waved the gun before replacing it in the case, zipping it, and sliding it across the counter to Betty.

That seemed to settle the situation. Carl would be coming with me, Betty would be keeping my Ruger on her person, and if something went wrong while she and the kids were here alone with Brandon, she would have to get to the flare gun, fire it into the air, and then hold out until we got back. The funny thing was

The Children

that we would only be a few blocks away as the crow flew, but in this new world, that seemed like miles.

Betty returned to taking care of Chewie while Carl and I packed what we felt would be the best to bring along for our little expedition. The plan was to get one of the military trucks, load as much into it as we could and then drive it around to the main gate to this place. Despite my misgivings about leading the undead to our gates, it would reduce the number of trips exponentially. We could then use the trucks as an addition to our barricade. If we backed up the driveway, we could have the open cargo bay facing in for easy unloading. After that, we could disable the vehicle and it would help as far as keeping that weak point a bit more secure. Of course, my mind instantly went to the big finale of the original *Dawn of the Dead*. I swore that if I saw a motorcycle gang led by a guy with a bushy black mustache, I would shoot first and ask questions later.

Yeah, I chuckled to myself, *who was I kidding? I would probably run screaming and hide like a bitch.*

***

The sun was probably an hour from coming up. Brandon had not stirred or at least not made his presence known since we'd gotten here and he retreated to a room. I still could not get over my initial opinion of him, but I seemed to be the only one.

Chewie was sitting beside me as I cinched the straps on my pack a bit tighter. I had a Glock 21 on each hip and felt just a little bit like a badass. While I was familiar with all sorts of firearms and even had a permit to carry, I had never actually gone out with a weapon. To know that I was about to embark on something that was straight out of the movies was a bit scary.

I glanced down at my dog and could not help but feel more than just a little gratitude towards Betty. The remainder of the tail had been cleaned up and properly bandaged. I'd even been given a tube of some sort of ointment that she suggested I apply every other day which coincided with when she would be wearing the bandages. The alternate days would be so that she could get some air to the area and help with the healing process or something like that. All I knew was that she was still apparently fine.

My mind went back to that dog I'd seen in the backyard. There had to be something I was missing.

"You wanna get your head back into the game?" Carl hissed, giving me an elbow in the ribs.

"Sorry." I gave my head a good shake and went back to inspecting what I would be carrying.

In my pack were three bottles of water and some granola bars. While we only intended to be out for a short period of time, there was no need not to be prepared just in case. I had four spare thirteen-round magazines ready for the Glocks as well as having each one already locked and loaded. Hanging from my webbed belt was my hand axe. Also, Carl had given me an aluminum baseball bat.

"If things get too hairy, you may want to use the bat instead of that axe. At the very least, it will provide you with a bit more breathing room," Carl explained.

It seemed as if we were all set. All that remained was climbing over the wall. It was like that moment before you jump into a lake or river. You think you know how cold it will be. You think you are ready for it, and somebody has managed to convince you that just going straight in is the best way.

Carl actually seemed anxious to get moving. I'd just been out there; I was scared and not nearly as eager. I gave Chewie a scratch behind the ears, hugged her thick neck, and then went up and over.

The initial part was relatively easy. We had trees first, then, once we cleared those, we had plenty of waist high brush to crouch and travel through until we reached the road. We'd agreed not to just exit through the gate and be obvious. There was the possibility, no matter how slim, that somebody could see us and follow our trail back. We also did not see the need to make a huge detour; we would just be cautious. The fact that it was still the murk of pre-dawn would aid us in staying out of sight for the most part.

The Children

When we reached the road, I pointed out the side entrance to the medical center. "That place is still a gold mine. If we make another run on it, we could maybe load as much as we can find right at that door. We could grab a second truck and back it up the drive as well. Not like we could park it right against the gate, but it would be close enough to maybe be worth it."

Carl gave a nod and then pointed to the right. My blood chilled. It could not be possible. Standing in that intersection where I'd first spotted...no, it couldn't be the same kid.

I squinted to hopefully get a better look at the small figure. From this distance, almost two blocks away, in addition to the gloom, it was impossible to say that the exact same child I'd seen yesterday was the one standing there in almost the exact same spot. Still the coincidence was unnerving and had me doubting our chances on this mission.

"That is precisely where I saw that kid that led the pack after us the other day," I whispered. I knew it sounded lame, but I also knew that my hands were already starting to shake.

"I seriously doubt that is the same one," Carl replied with a dismissive wave of his hand.

"Seems like too much of a coincidence." I kept trying to get a better look, but I realized that I hadn't made it a point to really commit the child's features to memory.

"Let's go." Carl's voice snapped my head around as I realized that he'd already started across the street.

I ran after him, but I could not keep from shooting concerned looks back over at the child at the intersection. I was halfway across and nearing the parking lot of the medical center where the trucks would be when I shot one more look.

I almost tripped over my own feet as I skidded to a stop.

The child was gone.

I searched frantically for him, but there was no sign. That had to be a mistake. From how slow I'd seen them move, I knew he wasn't outdistancing us.

There! I actually found myself walking toward that intersection. A small head bobbed and appeared from behind one of the stalled vehicles.

"You're trying to hide," I breathed.

That did not seem possible. Zombies don't hide. Do they? I warred with that thought for however long it took for Carl to run back and yank me towards him.

"Are you trying to get us killed?" he almost yelled.

I noticed a few heads turn our direction from some of the dark figures that were now being cast in the first pale light of the morning. Before long, we would be able to make out details much clearer. Those figures wandering around would lose their humanity as light transformed them into horrific visages that meant death was no longer the final step.

We hustled to the fence, climbed over, and then lowered ourselves down to the parking lot. Already I noticed that there was more activity than before I'd first visited this place. Whether it was from my having been here, or maybe it was all random, it didn't really matter.

I stepped to the left to meet the three staggering towards us. I'd decided to give the bat a try. Setting my feet, I brought it around hard and fast, taking the closest one in the side of the head. The bat recoiled and the middle-aged soccer mom sprawled onto the pavement. I planted a booted foot on the back of her neck and drove the barrel of the bat down hard into the rear of her skull. It took two attempts, but the results were impressive.

I decided that the amount of time I took lining up the perfect shot with my axe and then wrenching it free if I didn't manage to snap my wrist back fast enough to avoid keeping it from being stuck in the skull was actually a bit slower. Also, with the bat, I could take them down, getting the bitey part away from me quicker.

Also, I noticed that the blade part of my little weapon was starting to get some nasty nicks and chips in it. Sure, it would be easy to replace, but a good part of me believed I'd built a sentimental attachment to the weapon. Perhaps it would be okay to allow a few of those strands to be snipped

I could ponder this later. The next two zombies were almost shoulder to shoulder. I choose the smallest, a little old man who

The Children

made me think of one of those grouchy old bastards from the balcony on the *Muppet Show*.

"Eat this, Statler," I whispered as I swung. The old man toppled. "Or were you Waldorf?" I grunted as I brought the bat around for a second swing to take down the unlikely companion.

This one was decked out like a skateboarder. He had a lip ring which caught the glint of that first ray of sun to peep over the horizon, and I used that little shiny spot to aim my swing. I heard a crunch and saw teeth fly as I destroyed his mouth.

With each of them down, I moved in and finished them both off. The old man was the easiest, and I now had another bit of information. Maybe he hadn't consumed enough calcium in his later years, but whatever the reason, his head burst open and vomited its chunky gray contents after just one pile-driver blow with the end of my bat.

I turned just as Carl was finishing off a pair of zombies on the ground that were struggling like turtles that had been flipped onto their backs. I jogged over and pointed needlessly at the military vehicles.

"Jack-freaking-pot," he whistled appreciatively.

We jogged over to the closest truck. As we did, I looked around. This was nothing like yesterday. Already I could see zombies staggering along and arriving at this parking lot in droves. They were using a driveway that came up from the road below. I rushed over to the fence that acted as a bit of a barricade and peered down onto 91st Avenue.

"Seriously?" I said to the heavens.

I'd had no idea that a massive townhouse complex sat right across the street. From the looks of things, the people living there had tried to barricade the entry driveways. They just hadn't been very successful. Zombies had apparently swarmed the place. There was an impressive number of corpses scattered about, and in a few places, they were actually stacked like they'd fallen and begun to build a bit of a morbid barricade.

"We don't have long, I whisper-shouted over my shoulder. The road below was heavy with the walking dead.

Maybe in a few weeks this area might thin out, but at the

moment, it looked as if a good portion of the population of this area, and maybe even some of the surrounding neighborhoods, were down there. Perhaps they wouldn't all come up here to the parking lot. But that was not a risk that I was ready to take.

Rushing along, I peered down the length of the large parking lot that served the two multi-story buildings of this medical complex. More were finding their way using the much flatter entrance nearest Johnson Creek Boulevard.

I rushed over to Carl who was already picking through things and stacking what I assumed were his priority items in one area central to the cluster of military vehicles. I saw a few things that I could not even begin to identify.

"You weren't kidding when you said this place was a gold mine," the man almost crowed.

"Super." I cast a look over my shoulder. I could see a row of bobbing heads starting to crest the lip of the parking lot as the zombies coming up that steep entry ramp made inexorably steady progress in our direction. They might be slow, but they didn't take breaks. "We gotta go. Maybe we can come back later, but I don't think now is the time for us to be doing this."

Carl stood up and eyed me like I'd just ripped one in the middle of church. "Are you out of your ever-loving mind, friend?"

I was beginning to think his use of the word "friend" might not adhere to the definition. Sorta like that little guy's use of "inconceivable" in *Princess Bride*. I may've even heard Mandy Patinkin voice saying as much in my head with his overblown Spanish accent.

"Look, Carl, I want this stuff just as bad as you…okay, maybe not as bad…but pretty bad." I hiked a thumb over my shoulder towards the approaching mob of undead. "But there are too many of them."

"We can outrun 'em without even trying."

"And head right into them?" I grabbed the man by the arm and dragged him past the trucks so that he could see the ones coming in down at the parking lot entrance of the building adjacent to the one we were in front of.

The Children

"If somebody finds this stuff, they ain't just gonna leave it here, friend."

Yeah, I was now certain he did not mean that word the way it was defined in *Webster's*. I craned my neck back and could now see heads and shoulders of the first couple of rows of zombies.

"Is this shit worth dying for?" I implored. "Because if we stay here, we have a good chance of that happening. There's just too damn many."

"You run if you want, but I'm gonna get what we came for." Carl jerked his arm away from my grip and trotted back to military vehicles.

I considered my options and then threw my hands in the air in frustration. Rushing over to his stack of boxes, I started heaving things into the back of the nearest truck. After I threw the third crate in, Carl called out, "You may wanna be a bit more careful with them boxes, friend. That last one had M67s in it."

"So?" I snapped back as I jerked the next crate from the stack.

"Yeah…those are grenades. They go boom. So, as I said, you may want to show those boxes a bit of respect."

I can't recall a point in my life where I wanted to punch a person in the face more than I did him at that exact moment. "You'd think maybe that is a warning you would've shared sooner," I mumbled angrily as I pushed the next crate into the rear of the truck.

I managed to load five more assorted crates into the back when Carl called me over. "Help me with this big mother." He tapped one side of the long crate with his foot. "There are a dozen M4s and over five thousand rounds of ammo in here, but I can't hoist it on my own."

I had to admit, that was an impressive find, but it wasn't going to do us any good if the zombies chewed us up. I could now see that the first few rows had reached the lot and were heading our way. We didn't have long.

Carl glanced back in the direction I was looking. "Don't worry…this is it. If we can come back for more later, we will, but this ought to do us for now."

I tried not to let my relief show as I helped him haul the heavy metal container over to the truck with all the other stuff that I'd loaded. We got it up and in and I was already making a run for the passenger side door of the truck's cab when I heard Carl swear.

"Get in the truck! Get in the truck!" he shouted.

"What? I am. What's the problem?"

I climbed in and flopped down on the uncomfortably hard seat. Carl had some apparent knowledge, because he flipped a few toggle switches and then pushed a button. The truck grumbled and resisted, but eventually turned over with a belch and rattle.

"Look." Carl pointed as he brought us around and started towards the exit located in the parking lot of the building adjacent to the one we'd been in front of.

The sputtering red light of a flare was drifting slowly to earth in the direction of our house.

13

Noise

The truck barreled towards the cluster of undead that were all hobbling and moving directly at us. I had a tight grip on the dashboard as I braced for impact. I knew that the zombies wouldn't stand a chance, but I also knew that hitting a body was going to jolt and jar us something fierce.

To his credit, Carl tried to avoid as many of them as he could. That was about to become an impossibility as we neared the location where the parking lot dumped out onto Southeast 91st Avenue. From there, we would have to make a right on Johnson Creek Boulevard, then another on 92nd. If we could get up the drive without bringing a few hundred of these monsters with us, we might not be too bad off.

Of course, as soon as we reached the gate, I was coming out with gun in hand. I was already berating myself for having left Betty and the kids with that stranger. I'd let Betty basically bully me into believing that she could handle herself.

"Here we go," Carl shouted as we clipped the last of the ones we could at least partially avoid.

When we hit the cluster of bodies, the truck shuddered violently and I slammed against the restraints, sending a bloom of pain across my entire chest. The truck lifted in front as we rolled over the first bodies that fell underneath us. I saw a face belonging to a little girl no older than ten slide past my window as she was lifted into the air by the front bumper and sent flying. This ride was not going to leave my nightmares any time soon, of that I was certain.

As we plowed through the wall of undead flesh, I was noticing without a doubt that the zombies were reacting to sound. I could see many to the right that were passing by on Johnson Creek Boulevard as they turned and oriented on us. Also, to the left in the direction of the townhouse duplexes, I could see more of them stopping as they'd started to head up that steep driveway to the medical center and turn towards us.

"Sound lures them," I said as we shoved violently through the worst of the mob and emerged into relatively open road.

"You positive?" Carl asked through clenched teeth as we smashed into Granny Zombie, her head slamming down hard enough on the concrete that it burst, sending gore and bone out in a fan as if a shotgun had been put to her head.

"Absolutely," I replied, trying to look away from the carnage, but simply not being able to as we left a trail of broken bodies in our wake.

"Okay, let's test it."

Carl reached inside his heavy jacket and produced what I initially mistook for a green ball. Then I made out the dangling ring attached to the pin that was in place as the safety to keep a person from mistakenly pressing it and starting the fuse of what I had to assume was an M67 grenade.

"Grab the wheel," he said as he opened the door on his side.

I didn't have time to think of what an idiot he appeared to be. I reached over and gripped the wheel, trying my best not to jerk it and possibly send him flying from the cab. Carl pulled the pin and gave the grenade a toss; then he scooched back in and took the wheel.

"These windows don't just roll down like they do in normal cars and trucks," he said.

There was a muffled blast a second later, and I glanced in the rearview mirror. It looked like a few bodies were now smoldering on the road. I was about to tell him that his attack had been a bust when I saw a whole bunch of the zombies pause in their pursuit of us and turn in the direction of the blast.

"Well, I'll be," Carl exclaimed as he peered into his rearview mirror. "We can definitely use that to our advantage in the future."

That was all well and good, but I just wanted to get to the house, kill Brandon, and hopefully do it in time to prevent anything from happening to Betty and the kids. That train of thought shocked me. I was preparing to kill a living, breathing human.

"You watch my back when we pull in," Carl said as he yanked the steering wheel and turned us right on 92nd Avenue. "I am gonna have to take us nose first up this driveway. We can turn the rig around after we take care of business."

"What do you mean?" I asked, a bit confused by Carl's statement.

"I mean, you aren't the type to just start killing folks. Make sure he doesn't get behind us or ambush us as we enter the grounds. I will take care of putting him down." I opened my mouth to protest, but Carl held up a hand to silence me. "Nothing personal, friend, but you are not a killer."

"And you are?" I shot back.

"No, but I am a realist who has prepared his entire life for the fall of Rome."

I had no idea what Rome had to do with this, and I wouldn't get an opportunity to ask. We turned hard to the left and roared up the driveway.

I was determined to prove Carl wrong and my hand went to one of the Glocks I had holstered on my hips. If I got the shot, I was going to take it and show this guy that I could handle anything that came our way.

We skidded to a noisy halt a few feet from the gate and I threw my door open, tossing off my seatbelt harness and jumping out with my gun coming up and ready for action. I sprinted to the fence, confident that I could easily out run some know-it-all woodshop teacher.

I reached the gate and saw Betty running for us, her arms waving frantically above her head. *Was she trying to warn us away?* I wondered.

Just as I got the wire that held the gate closed out of the way, Carl strolled up and swept past me. I was right on his heels and getting ready to take off again when I saw him.

The long, blond hair was a dead giveaway as it fluttered behind him in the early morning breeze. He did not look the least bit alarmed at our arrival.

Well, that is about to change, I fumed as I brought my pistol up and aimed it at the man's chest. Unlike a zombie, I didn't need a headshot. The body was a pretty large target for anybody with any degree of skill at firing a gun.

"Evan, no!" Betty screamed, veering into my path.

I saw both kids come out the front door. Selina had little Michael by the hand and it looked like she was ripping him a new one. Michael did not seem the least bit bothered and just stood there on the landing staring at the ground like he always did.

"Whoa!" Brandon was yelling, hands in the air and patting at his hips, looking for a weapon that was not there now.

"Get out of the way, Betty," I ordered as I tried to line up my shot.

"Put your gun down, Evan," Betty begged. "It was Michael. He found the flare gun and took it outside. We had no idea until Selina came in and asked what the smoking red light in the sky was."

I lowered my weapon and noticed Carl do the same. I shot a look over at the kids, unsure of what to say or do. I had no experience dealing with children—at least none that young.

"I'm so sorry, he just slipped away. The boy is so quiet, and hardly makes a peep when he is around. It is so easy for him to disappear without being noticed," Betty was saying.

I recalled how he'd gotten away from us back at the café. I couldn't hold it against Betty when the same thing had happened with me right beside him. Sure, we'd all supposedly been asleep, but the fact that he'd managed to get up and leave without waking any of us was proof that none of us were above reproach when it came to watching over the boy.

Noise

"We can deal with this later," Carl said, interrupting my train of thought. "We have a truck to turn around and supplies to unload."

"Isn't anybody gonna tell me what is going on?" Brandon yelped. He had the look of somebody who wanted to bolt at the first chance. I hoped he did.

"Just a case of some messed up communication." Carl walked over and patted the man on the shoulder. "Tensions are a little high right now as I'm sure you can imagine."

"You two had guns drawn and that guy looked like he would shoot me without hesitation." Brandon pointed at me and I couldn't help but feel a small swelling of pride.

So much for Carl's assessment, I thought triumphantly.

"He was just trying to protect Betty and the kids," Carl explained. "You gotta understand, ain't nobody quite sure who's who yet, and we barely know you."

Betty walked over to me and leaned in close. "I'm glad you're back. I don't know what it is, but I don't much care for that fella."

Great, I thought, *I was on the same mental wavelength as Betty.*

"I coulda swore that he was checking things out and sort of inventorying our supplies and the weapons you brought back."

"What?" I spun to face her, struggling to keep my voice low so as not to attract Carl and Brandon's attention as they headed for the gate, Carl's arm around the man's shoulder like they were old pals. "We stored those someplace the kids wouldn't find them. How did he find them?"

"That's just it," Betty said, guiding me to follow Carl towards the truck; apparently, she was savvy enough to know that we needed to avoid suspicion if this guy was indeed the kind of person we thought him to be. "I didn't even know he was awake until little Michael came and told me the…and I am quoting him here, "bad man" was in the guns."

I looked over at the boy standing beside Selina. Just maybe that flare being fired had not been a mistake or simple case of a curious kid and a gun. I wished that he would talk to me. There was something about the kid that was special. Not like he was some sort of supernatural psychic or anything like that. I just felt that maybe he understood on a deeper level than we gave him credit. The problem would be getting him to relate the information whizzing around in his brain.

By the time Betty and I reached the truck, it appeared that Carl had managed to calm Brandon for the most part and had the man in the cab of the truck, backing it down the long driveway.

I did not agree with that decision. All the firepower we'd risked our rear ends to bring back were in the cargo bay of that truck. If Brandon wanted to, he could just get out on the road and take off. I was about to approach Carl and make my position on this situation very clear when I noticed that the man had one hand on the butt of one of his Glocks as he walked backward and waved the truck back with him.

One hour, and about thirty zombies later, we'd positioned the truck with its cargo area open to our gate. I got the feeling that Brandon was not very comfortable being around me. I tried a few times to make casual conversation, but he wasn't having any of it.

Was it possible that I was the jerk in this scenario?

***

I stared at the calendar on the wall that Carl had tacked up. The individual X's through each day were a shock to me every time I saw them. It was hard to believe that eleven days had passed since we'd been in this house.

In that time, the city of Portland had apparently gone dark everywhere. I'd been in my room with Chewie. Her tail was healing nicely, but now it apparently itched a great deal and so I had to keep distracting her from it.

I had the windows open and was reveling in the silence when I saw the horizon start to go suddenly and frighteningly dark. *This is it*, I'd thought, *we are back in the times of the caveman.*

Not more than a few minutes later, there had been a knock

at my door. It had been Betty "I guess you saw the lights go out in Portland."

When I said that I had, she simply stood there in the hall for a moment holding one of the small, battery-powered lanterns we'd found three of in the camping supplies. I wasn't sure what she wanted me to say or do.

She nods and looked away, seemingly captivated with the barely visible outline of a bit of bad but surely expensive artwork down the hallway. After a moment, she said, "I guess that's it then. It's just gone now."

My own eyes were suddenly drawn to the intricate wonders of the toes of my shoes. "Yeah, I think so," I said after what felt like the world's longest minute. "I'm pretty sure there's no coming back from this now."

I forced my eyes back upward. In the dim light of the lantern, I saw Betty blink rapidly a few times, drawing in a deep breath that was only slightly shaky before turning back to face me with a tight grim smile. "Well…" she said, raising her chin. "…I guess that's that then." And with that she squared her shoulders and walked back down the hall.

My throat felt tight as I stepped back into my room and closed the door. I don't think either of us had been talking about just the lights.

As a group, we had done what we could to fortify the place. Having a wall all the way around the property was a great bonus. The fact that it was set far enough back that you could not see it unless you were well up the road and above us was another benefit.

We'd heard the occasional sounds of gunfire from just about every direction the first few days. Now, it was seldom and sporadic. More often than not, it was a single shot here or there.

One thing we had accomplished was proving the theory beyond a shadow of a doubt that sound attracted the zombie like moths to a flame. All we'd needed were a few empty soda cans filled with a bit of gravel for our initial tests.

Being up on this hill, we were able to move to a spot that overlooked Johnson Creek Boulevard. When we would spot a zombie, or even a small group, we would hurl one of those cans in the opposite direction the case subject would be moving. Uphill or down, the cans never failed to cause the walking dead to alter its course. Even more interesting—at least to me—was the fact that they did not actually stop to investigate the cans. Since they were usually no longer moving and making noise by the time that the zombie was turned around, I found it fascinating that the zombie would just trudge along. It did not stop to inspect the can unless it was still rolling and making noise. And even then, as soon as the can would stop, the zombie would just keep moving in the direction that we'd diverted it.

"They have the short-term memory of a goldfish," Carl had quipped.

I saw more than that in our little experiment. I saw a way to divert the zombies away from us. That also meant that there had to be a way to create some sort of noise trap that we could activate in order to distract the zombies from our location if they ever came in large numbers.

The most likely location that we would have them come from seemed to be from the south in the direction of the zombie racetrack. While there was plenty of tall grass and trees in that direction, it was also the way that offered the flattest terrain. The driveway coming up from 92nd had been blocked by three military trucks, including one at the very bottom of the driveway that made it difficult for a fully mobile and living human to get around because of the dense foliage the previous occupants had placed—likely to increase their level of privacy and isolate them from all us regular folks.

I'd found a strand of trees fairly close together as my first location to set up what I considered our most rudimentary defense. Using some of the abundant fishing line we'd located, as well as a dozen cans that were half full of gravel, I'd placed my first lure.

This had been a very popular plan with Selina. A pleasant surprise was how Michael also seemed eager to help. I'd let them be the ones to fill the soda cans with the pea-sized bits of gravel. Once I had what I needed, I'd simply hopped the wall

Noise

and strung my line with the attached cans. Another length of twine was used to allow us to trigger the lure from our side of the fence.

I'd been itching to test it out ever since, but Carl and Betty both out-voted me when I'd suggested having a zombie chase me through that area towards our wall. The object would be to see if it would turn around and head away once it lost sight of me after I came back over the wall.

My second lure would prove to be more difficult to place. This one would be down on 92nd Avenue. I would need to string it between a set of powerline poles. That would be hard, but then I would need to run a line up to the house from there. I knew there was probably an easier solution to all this, but I'd become focused on this single approach. Besides, I was working with the supplies we had. Maybe later, once we ventured out and could raid some other places, something else would avail itself.

I had my knapsack with all my gear. The night before, Carl and I had slipped out and set a ladder beside the pole I would hang the strand of cans from. That had been harder than it sounds. For one, the collapsible ladder was not very easy to tote quietly. It kept making metallic clanks and clacks as we made our way down to the road. Second, the streets had been totally empty of any activity when we'd scouted it out. Just as we were setting the ladder up against the pole, three of the bastards came out from the nearby bushes. Two of them were little kids between the ages of eight and twelve. The youngest was a little boy and again I was certain that this was the very same one I'd seen in the intersection.

The runner's headlamp I was wearing at least gave me something to use for identification should we meet again. He was wearing a soiled and bloodstained Seattle football jersey with the number three on it. His dark hair was actually blonde, but he had so much blood and filth that it looked black. The last and most identifying feature came in the form of his missing lower jaw. Just seeing him had made me wince. What terrible thing had led to that disfigurement? I didn't know, and I didn't want to know.

By the time Carl and I simply set down the ladder, making sure to be as quiet as possible to prevent possibly drawing more zombies to our location, he was gone. That left the girl and a woman in a skirt that was almost totally ripped away. Considering the fact that her injuries were all around the left shoulder, I had to think that it was probably getting snagged on things all the time and would eventually be gone except for the waistband.

Since the girl was closest, I went for her and Carl went for the lady in the tattered skirt. That was when I got my next surprise. I'd noticed that the child versions made it a point to hang back. Even now, the girl was not advancing from where she'd emerged, and, of course, the boy was gone. The woman was coming straight for Carl without any hesitation.

I stood still for a moment just to be sure. After what seemed like an hour but was likely five or ten seconds, I pulled out my axe and started for her. Just that fast, she turned into just another zombie.

The arms came up and her hands turned into claws as she reached for me. Her head twitched as she focused on getting ahold of me and ripping me to shreds. Fortunately for me, the child zombies are no more agile than any other type of walking dead.

Despite everything, I still had trouble splitting her head open with my axe. When the body crumpled to the ground, eyes shut and final death granted, a lump rose in my throat and I wanted to scream…cry…rage. I'd tried to convince myself that this would eventually get easier. A day would come when I could see these things as nothing more than zombies—the walking dead.

We'd placed the ladder and returned home. I would be making my run to set up this lure at first light.

And now, here I was, climbing the ladder with my gear. I reached the top and glanced over my shoulder. I raised an arm and waved it back and forth twice. That was our very basic signal that it was all okay so far. I saw Carl wave back. He was on the roof of our house with a scoped rifle that he'd found during a supply run at the Zombie International Raceway neighborhood.

Noise

I braced myself and tied off the strand of cans. Now was the hard part. I had to climb down, move the ladder over to the streetlight pole across the road and attach the other end. This part had caused a lot of debate. Betty insisted that somebody come with me, but Carl and I explained that it would be best if we stationed two people a block away in each direction. Carl could sit on the roof and act as my guardian angel.

I realized that I was putting a lot of faith in my supposition that sound would draw the zombies away if they arrived, but I'd seen it for myself. Unlike the pre-apocalypse when everything had to be tested and governmentally approved *ad nauseum*, things were now strangely simple: have theory; test theory to your level of satisfaction; operate under that proven theory until proven wrong.

I made my way back down to the ground and gently picked up the ladder, doing everything in my power to not let it rattle or clang. Once I was across the street, I started to feel giddy. Sure, this was a very primitive setup, but it was a start. We weren't doing anything foolish or cliché like trying to secure a massive shopping mall.

I started up the ladder with the loose end of my lure in my teeth. I was halfway up when I saw him. I was absolutely certain it was the boy. And now I was equally sure that this same zombie child had been the one I kept seeing. Again, it was a huge leap, but this was too big of a coincidence to actually be a coincidence.

He was watching me from down below in the parking lot of the medical center. There were a few other zombies wandering around—all of the adult variety. I stayed absolutely frozen in place. Maybe he wasn't looking at me. Maybe he was just looking this general direction. Then he stepped forward and cocked his head to the side. Now I was almost sure that I was his focus. I climbed another few rungs and watched as his head tilted with my progress.

"Dammit," I swore softly.

I continued to the top, my head rotating back and forth from my actual task and the boy. Every single time that I looked away, I was certain that I would look back and find him gone. Once I reached the top, I was starting to wish that I'd been correct. He continued to stand right where I'd first noticed him. His head was craned upwards so far that he was bending back at the hips just a bit. That was new; not that I'd been studying the flexibility of the average zombie.

I tied off the other end and then clipped on the line that we would use to trigger this lure. The next part was going to be kind of fun. Carl had rigged one of the M4s with a device that I called the plunger. It was a simple device that fit in the barrel. The line was attached to it and all I had to do was aim and shoot and it would launch back to our little home base. He said that he "stole" the idea from his time in the Navy.

Apparently, when ships refueled at sea, this was the method that they used to get the line from one ship to the other. Whatever the case, we'd taken it out and tested it with amazing success.

I unslung the rifle that I had over my shoulder and checked to ensure that the line was connected to the rubber piece that protruded from the barrel. Once I was certain that everything was exactly as Carl had shown me, I brought the rifle to my shoulder and fired. I watched with my breath caught in my chest as I waited to see if the plunger made it over the fence.

"Yes!" I exclaimed in a whispered hiss. It hadn't cleared by much, but it had made it. Now I had to move before all the zombies came out to investigate the huge noise I'd just made.

I slipped my arm through the strap to sling the rifle back over my shoulder. Having a background in construction, I was comfortable working on a ladder. I let go with both hands and leaned forward so that I could secure my rifle before climbing down.

I was just ducking my head through the strap when the sound of breaking glass came from right behind me. The sudden and jarring noise caught me completely off guard and I lost my balance on the ladder. I fell back onto the sidewalk and felt something in my right arm give with an audible snap.

I yelped in pain and just as quick shut my mouth knowing that noise would increase my chances of not making it back

Noise

home alive as I gave the zombies something more precise to focus on. Forcing myself to the sitting position, I looked around and saw that I had nothing close enough to me that I wouldn't still be able to get up and make it to the gate.

Sitting up on the sidewalk, I was facing the side of the medical center that looked out onto 92nd Avenue. Three of the building's four stories rose above me with huge picture windows lining the exterior. To my left was the one door that I'd used to exit the place that first time. To my right was the newly busted window. I had to work past the pain and get to my feet unless I wanted to be zombie chow. There was a nearby hydrant that I used to heave myself to my feet.

Once I was standing, I paused to look back at the window and stopped in my tracks. It was just a foot or so off the ground out here on the street but was apparently set about waist high if you were standing inside this zombie-filled room. Several zombies were climbing through the shattered window. They were actually crawling over each other to get out. I had no doubt that every single one of those monsters were focused on me. Looking at the other windows that were closest, I did not see any signs of activity.

I was moving away and had moved so that I was just a little bit above the busted window when something grabbed my attention. There was very little busted glass outside of that window's frame. That would indicate that it broke inwards and had not been busted out by a bunch of zombies that saw a wandering snack tray move past them.

As I started towards the drive that wound towards the military truck barricade and eventually the gate, I wondered where the hell my decoys were and why I hadn't heard anything from them. Fortunately, I was able to get out of the zombies' sight line as I climbed through the dense foliage and then rounded the easy bend that led up the driveway. I passed the second truck and heard something to my right. I knew I would not be able to use my axe with my off hand, so I drew my Glock and brought it up where the bushes were shaking.

I started to apply pressure to the trigger when I heard a

DEAD: Onset

voice squeak, "Don't shoot!"

14

"Hate to say I told you so."

"Jesus, Betty, I could've blown your head off," I snarled as I lowered my weapon. "And why the hell aren't you out there as my decoy. Didn't you see what was happening."

"I saw you fall off the ladder and I hurried over this way to see if you needed help getting over the wall," Betty replied. "It was clear that you weren't in danger of being caught unless you got up to the gate and couldn't get over safely."

"Okay." I looked around and a new question came to mind. "Where is Brandon?"

"He probably thought the same as I did. I am not as nimble on my feet, and my guess is that he is already up and over, waiting for us inside."

"Without even waiting to see if I made it here? Or you for that matter."

"You know the way things work. You take care of your own ass first and then worry about the others when and if there is time. Besides…" she pointed up, "…we have Carl as our guardian angel."

I opened my mouth to protest and saw perfect logic in her response. While the zombies had been numerous, they had not been that close. I hadn't been in any real danger of them catching me. Also, we'd had a conversation one night around the dinner table after the kids were asleep. We'd all agreed that people in the movies were always acting like idiots. What was the point in getting yourself killed so that another person could make it out of a nasty situation? Basically, none of us were willing to die for the other—at least not at this point in our collective relationships.

"Now, we need to get on the other side of the walls before that little pack gets here," Betty urged. A low moan sounded from down the driveway as if to emphasize that point. "And I will look at your arm as soon as we get inside." She guided me towards the rope ladder that was dangling from the wall.

I reached it and paused. I was not sure if I could climb it. Now that the adrenaline was starting to ebb, the pain was ramping up. Betty was behind me when I paused and gave me a little shove.

"I don't know how this is gonna work," I admitted. "You go first."

It wasn't like I was breaking the rule of self-preservation. I just wasn't going to be the reason Betty died as she waited for me to try and make it up and over. To her credit, I think I saw a flash of concern in her eyes before she went up and then vanished from sight.

I glanced back and saw the first of the walkers come around the bend. Part of me wanted to wait and see if that kid was with them, but a bigger part of me didn't want to be eaten. I had a good enough lead that I tried to make it over one-handed. The rope ladder was not secure on the bottom. We'd made that decision as a just in case sort of deal. We were pretty sure that the zombies couldn't climb, but it only took one of them to get lucky.

When the original argument against zombies being able to climb was raised by Carl, I reminded him of the scene at the very end of the original *Dawn of the Dead*. He'd thought it over for a moment and then agreed that it wasn't going to hurt us to *not* have the bottom of the rope ladder anchored. We hadn't considered a situation like this in our plans.

I started up, but it proved much more difficult than I'd ex-

"Hate to say I told you so."

pected. The pain was bad, but I decided being eaten would be immeasurably worse. I reached the top and threw one leg over. Secure in the fact that I'd escaped, I looked back again. I was oddly disappointed when I still saw no sign of that boy.

Lowering myself to the ground, I saw Brandon and Betty already talking to Carl. Brandon glanced back my way and I was almost certain I saw his lips curve in the slightest hint of a smile. That was enough for me, I would talk about this with Carl later. I wasn't being paranoid.

"…saw no reason to wait. He was already getting up before the first couple even fell through that window," Brandon was insisting. "Like Betty said, if he can't move faster than a walker, he doesn't belong outside the walls.

"I think we need to make it clear that, whether somebody can escape or not, the decoys have a job to do," I blurted.

"I agree," Carl said with a nod. He shot a scowl at both Betty and Brandon before continuing. "But we have a bigger problem."

"What's that?" I asked.

"Somebody shot out that window," Carl said coolly.

"What do you mean?" Betty gasped. "I certainly didn't hear a gunshot."

"There are other ways to shoot out a window." Carl's eyes flicked at me for just a second. "And whoever did it, waited until Evan was at his most vulnerable. They wanted him dead."

"I thought I heard something," Brandon offered. "But I didn't have time to do much because the window broke and all those zombies started pouring out."

"That is the other problem," Carl continued. "Whoever did this knew exactly which window to take out. That means there is somebody skulking around the area. They might've seen us making our runs on the military gear down in the parking lot."

"Which window?" Betty sounded confused.

"Even from up on my post, I could see a lot of activity behind that one window…like somebody lured the zombies to a single room and then shut them in," Carl explained.

"You know what I don't understand," I said as Betty guided

me to a bench where she started on the straps of my pack so that she could get a look at my arm. "That was the one part of the stories that I always had trouble with."

"Stories?" Betty glanced up as she set my pack down and then went to work on my leathers.

"The books, movies, and all that stuff with zombies in it," I clarified. "In the stories, people were often worse than the undead. Why wouldn't we all band together and try to survive?"

"People are greedy," Carl offered. "Once they don't have the morals and deterrents of a normal society, they are free to be exactly the kind of person that has always lurked deep down."

"So you are saying that we are all mostly just dirtbags deep down?" I challenged.

"Nope." Carl shook his head. "But I'd be willing to bet that a lot of the good folks in the world died or are dying as they try to help or save others. What you have left are all the folks…like us…living in that gray area where most of civilized society exists. The downside is that the worst of us that have been hiding under rocks are now free to crawl out and take full advantage of the chaos. Hell, just think back to the evening news. Every single day, there was a story about some creep or perv getting caught. Imagine a world where those types are free to do as they wish without consequence."

That made me shudder. Certainly the logic was all there. Heck, Carl and I had touched on that very idea just before he ran off that time. And then there were my own thoughts that continued to bubble to the surface. I saw the children as a hindrance and a drain on our supplies. They were too young to go out and scavenge and were next to useless when we worked on reinforcing our little home-turned-fortress. I'd also made the statement that, if faced with saving one of these people or my dog, I would choose my dog.

"I'm heading inside to get out of this stuff," Brandon said as he strolled off.

"Subject hitting a little close to home?" I muttered at his back as he headed up the stairs to the front door.

As soon as he opened it, Chewie bounded out past him, al-

"Hate to say I told you so."

most knocking him off his feet in her effort to get to me. I smiled until I noticed the man spin on my dog with his hand raised in a clenched fist. Chewie was already well past his reach, but I'd seen the gesture.

"I get it," Betty sighed. "You don't like him. But you are going to have to get over it. We all need each other to survive. Wasn't that the very thing you were just complaining about?"

Hadn't she just come to me the other day? She'd told me about how even Michael called Brandon a bad man. Was everybody losing their minds, or was I just too set in my head that Brandon was bad and so that is how I saw him?

"I wasn't complaining," I grumbled. "Hey!" I tried to jerk away as Betty found the spot on my right arm that hurt.

"Okay, we are going to need to set this. I just wish that we had something better than Ace wraps to secure it with once we get the set complete."

"Grit your teeth, friend," Carl advised. "This is gonna hurt some."

I felt Betty and Carl get a grip on me. There was a sudden jerk and I yelped in pain. Chewie's howl joined in on the chorus sending a bunch of birds in the nearby trees to the sky in a swirl of dark wings.

***

"Ten weeks!" I exclaimed as Betty went about setting the evening meal on the table. Two propane camping stoves sat on top of what had probably once been a very expensive oven.

"That just means we dial things back for a bit," Carl said as he brought the water pitcher to the table and poured everybody a drink.

"It's not like we can't operate without you," Brandon sniffed as he took his seat, walking right past the platter with the ham on it and not bothering to help by grabbing it from the counter and setting it on the table.

"You know, you didn't need to come here. You are free to leave any time you like," I shot back.

"That so?" Brandon didn't bother to even look my direction as he stabbed a potato from the bowl and set it on his plate. "Are we voting again?"

"Why don't you just—" I started to rise to my feet.

"Enough!" Betty snapped. "There are children present. Perhaps we can *act* like adults and set an example."

I looked over at Selina who was watching all of this with wide eyes. Michael, on the other hand, was staring at his plate, steering a green pea around it with his spoon and making car noises.

"Guess that means Evan won't be joining us when we go up to that neighborhood and scout for any signs of living folks like the ones who apparently tried to kill him," Brandon said around a mouthful of ham.

"No, he can stay here and watch from the roof," Carl agreed. "He won't be much help as a sniper, but he can at least signal us if he sees anything coming our way."

"I doubt we will be able to see him once we move up into that one neighborhood," Brandon said as he shoved a forkful of potatoes into his mouth.

"Can you not talk with your mouth stuffed with food?" I snapped. "The kids don't need to pick up that habit." I tacked that last bit on hastily when I noticed Carl and Betty both giving me funny looks.

Maybe I was just never going to like this guy. Perhaps I should dial back my interactions with him as much as possible. I didn't want to look like I was being a dick. Still, I could've sworn that Carl had shot him a few looks out of the corner of his eyes, as well as giving me what I'd assumed were meaningful looks of understanding during some of our disagreements.

The next few days were a lot of me just trying to help around the place as we tried to make it as secure as possible. For whatever reason, it just felt like time started to drag on with terminal slowness. I did manage to stay away from Brandon pretty much the entire time, but that did not do anything to improve my opinion of the man.

On the plus side, Chewie was responding wonderfully to

"Hate to say I told you so."

Betty's treatment. It still looked odd to me. I was so used to her big, bushy tail that she now almost seemed like an entirely different dog sometimes. Through it all, I continued to watch her closely for any sign that she might become one of those things.

Eventually, the day came when Carl and Brandon left for their supply expedition. It annoyed me way more than it should, but I took my position up on the roof of the house. They would hike through the field on the other side of Johnson Creek Boulevard until they reached the first buildings of a gated community that sat across the way. We'd already scouted it enough to know that the people there had not even bothered to try and secure the place and hold it down. It appeared that a mass exodus occurred with only bare essentials being taken.

Things had spiraled out of control so fast that, by the time the word was being put out as to the danger of what was taking place, it was too late. These people had likely fled to one of the FEMA centers and walked out of the frying pan and directly into the fire.

As I watched Carl and Brandon moving up the slope across the way, my mind wandered to that day that was just a short time ago, but seemed like a lifetime. There was mention of the Moda Center and PGE Park. My mind reeled at those locations and what sort of nightmare they must've become. If Franklin High School was as chaotic as I'd witnessed, then those two locations—an indoor arena and outdoor stadium respectively—would have been living nightmares. Add in their proximity to downtown and the sheer number of people that would have been there when things went badly; I shuddered at the thought.

But maybe they were better fortified, my mind chirped. *Perhaps the soldiers there were more vigilant.*

I shook off my daydreams and brought up the field glasses that Carl had given me so that I could scan the area they were heading towards. I saw very little movement. We'd managed to heave the entry gate to that community shut a while back when we'd done some simple recon of the exterior of the area. While that might prevent any of the roaming zombies passing through from entering, we had no actual idea of how many of them might be trapped inside.

I watched as Carl and Brandon slipped over the wall. From that point on, I was basically useless to them until they emerged. All I could do was watch and wait.

Down below, in the massive backyard, Betty was having the kids help her carve out rows for what would hopefully become our garden. With spring just around the corner, the big box home repair stores were stocked with plenty of seed packages and gardening supplies.

That had been another thing that Betty informed us of one evening when we were sitting around trying to come up with the best ideas that gave us a chance at survival. Apparently she'd been browsing the selection a few weeks ago. Unfortunately, the area around the nearby Home Depot was still thick with undead traffic. It was simply not feasible to hit that location…yet.

The morning dragged on forever as I stayed posted as the lookout. The one thing that I did discover as I kept watch was that there was actually something as boring as watching paint dry. The area around us was pretty clear of the walking dead. From the roof, I could still see them wandering around the parking lot of the medical center. As far as the area uphill from us, there was next to nothing.

I have no idea how long I'd been watching and drifting in and out of various daydreams—half of them pertaining to creative ways I could rid our group of Brandon—when I heard somebody calling out.

Bringing up the field glasses, I turned towards the direction I thought the sound was coming from and started a very slow sweep. The first pass yielded nothing. The second time, I spotted him or her. The distance was not as much of a factor as the filth this person was seemingly covered in from head to toe.

The individual was standing on the back porch of the house next to the one where I'd discovered the suicide. At first I assumed the person had noticed me and was trying to get my attention. I lowered my field glasses just to take in the entire scene and figure out the big picture, and that is when I spotted the other person.

"Hate to say I told you so."

I had no doubt this second individual was a woman. I was seeing this person from a profile which made her curves very apparent. The two were gesticulating to each other in some form of sign language or signal that I was not able to get a grip on from this far away.

I am not sure what these people thought they were doing, but I did not think they were aware that they'd attracted the zombies still circling the racetrack. Despite the fact that the numbers had dwindled since I'd been there up close, there were still a few dozen. I didn't see any weapons on either of these individuals; that did not mean they might not have some stashed away, but something told me they didn't.

I was still puzzling why they would be in that location when movement to my left brought me back to where Carl and Brandon had disappeared. I recognized Brandon's overblown HAZMAT suit as he dropped down on our side of the wall. What I did not see were any of our duffel bags loaded with supplies…or Carl.

Brandon took off at a run, coming our way. He was almost to Johnson Creek Boulevard and I still saw no sign of Carl. I glanced back over at the two individuals I'd spotted just moments before, and it was clear that the female had also spotted Brandon. She was waving to her comrade and pointing.

Bringing my glasses up to see Brandon again, it was plain that he now saw the two strangers. He'd stopped running and was looking back and forth between my position and theirs. He looked back over his shoulder towards where Carl still had not appeared and then again back to me.

He was close enough that I could see his face with the glasses when he flipped his HAZMAT suit hood back. There was a look on his face that I didn't really care for.

I was still trying to make sense of everything when I heard a scream. It was more of a yell, but there was definitely concern, a bit of fear, and perhaps even some rage mixed in to this vocal. If I hadn't been focused on Brandon's face, I would've missed it.

He smiled.

There was an evil to his expression in that moment that con-

DEAD: Onset

firmed every single thing that I'd thought about him almost since first meeting the guy. He looked right at me and then made a very pointed effort to look over his shoulder and then to the two individuals over by the zombie racetrack. Then…he started towards the woman and the filthy individual of indeterminate gender.

As he walked, he kept his gaze on me, knowing very well that I was watching him. He made a shrugging gesture and started down the slope at an angle that would bring him to the racetrack.

"Betty, grab the rifle. Meet me at my room," I called as I made my way down the ladder to the balcony outside my bedroom.

I ducked in, looking around frantically for what I could get away with as a bare minimum and decided that I didn't have time for anything. I was certain that I knew the source of that scream. If I wasn't already too late, this would be perhaps the only opportunity to save Carl.

I threw a holster with a Glock 21 and a three-magazine pouch over one shoulder and headed for the stairs. I met Betty on my way down.

"Brandon has done something," I started.

"Evan, we've been over—" she started to protest, her expression quickly changing from concern to exasperation.

"Shut up and get your ass on the roof!" I snapped. "I have to go after Carl." I started down the stairs.

"But your arm," Betty called after me.

"I don't have time to worry about that now," I shouted over my shoulder as I reached the bottom of the stairs and bolted for the door.

I exited the house and was making my way to the wall when Betty reached my balcony and once again, despite it being one of our biggest no-no rules, called after me. "Evan, what are you doing? You are going to get yourself killed."

I started up the ladder that Brandon and Carl had used to climb over when they'd left. I had one leg slung over and was already wincing at the fact that I would have to jump down from

"Hate to say I told you so."

here. It was only about eight feet, but the slope on the other side was pretty steep. If I fell, it would not be pretty.

"Keep your eyes open. My glasses are on the dresser. Sweep over by the racetrack. I don't have time to explain." With that, I sucked in my breath and jumped.

I landed better than I'd hoped, and the jarring was only enough to cause a dull thrum of pain in my arm. I was not able to call myself ambidextrous, but I could shoot as well with either hand. Granted, that was at a fixed target on a range at a distance of around twenty-five yards, but still, if the need arose, I could shoot.

The bigger problem was going to be dealing with any zombie that got close. I might be able to hold a knife in my left hand, but that did not mean I was comfortable. Any sort of close confrontation with one of them would be ugly and dangerous.

I scolded myself as I started down the hill towards Johnson Creek Boulevard. I was doing exactly what I'd deemed as foolish just a few days ago. I was risking my ass to save another person who might already be dead for all I know.

In that instant, I understood. In a situation like this, you simply did not think—you acted. The option was to do nothing and allow some person that you have a link to, no matter how tenuous or forced. I was not close to Betty or Carl, but I was about to risk my life to save one of them.

When I broke free of the tall grass and could see better, I glanced back and saw that Betty's eyes were not on me at all. She was looking over in the direction I'd seen those strangers. That was also the direction that Brandon was headed.

I reached the stone pyramid-looking structure by where Carl had first rescued me, Betty, and Selina. This was another tricky spot, and I opted to follow it as it eventually gave way to just a steep grass hill before making my way down to the street below. Now that I was down, I had to cross on the run.

The good news here was that this particular part of the road was a large bend. At the moment, there were no zombies from either direction that I could see. I crossed on the run and started up the hill on the other side. Going up was so much more difficult than coming down. It was made worse by the fact that I could only use my left arm to catch myself when I tilted or started to stumble forward.

As I hurried, I heard that shout of frustration twice more. Each time sounded more urgent than the previous. Considering the conversations we'd had about this sort of situation, I wondered if maybe Carl was feeling beyond hopeless at this point. After all, I'd told him directly that there was no choice if it came to any of them or Chewie. That was still the case, but I now knew I could not simply sit by and allow somebody to be killed and not at least do something if it were in my power.

I reached the wall to the gated community and felt my stomach twist. Not only could I hear the moans of the undead coming from the other side of this stone wall, but I could smell them rather strongly. They were close. That was also when I started hearing some odd metallic slaps. It was almost like cheesy, B-movie thunder, but the sound wasn't ending. It just kept going.

I turned for just a moment and located Betty. She hadn't moved from her post, but she was obviously not watching me at all. Whatever Brandon was doing, it was enough to keep her attention riveted to him. For all intents and purposes, I was on my own. I looked over towards the racetrack, but I'd moved up and along the wall enough that I couldn't really see anything. I'd had to move this direction so that I could get inside the development. There was no way that I could climb over, so I'd had to make my way to one of the gates that we knew existed. I decided that the screams and the metal thunder noise had come from the same general direction I was headed.

When I reached the gate's location, I had to climb over the cars that we'd parked up against it. Now I was faced with a new problem. The gate was chained and padlocked. Carl had wanted to at least make anybody who chose to loot this place work for their goods if somebody got to it before we did. I would still have to climb over.

Getting up was a chore, but I managed. I was swinging my leg over when I saw the first of them. There had to be fifty of them surrounding a small metal shed. From the looks of things,

"Hate to say I told you so."

that shed was not going to last much longer. One side showed signs of buckling already.

"Carl," I shouted.

There was a single moment where nothing happened; then, one at a time, zombies began to turn my direction. A handful of them even started towards me.

"What are you doing out here, friend?" a voice called from inside the shed.

Just that quick, all of the zombies that had turned toward me did a shambling about-face and returned to the mob gathered around the shed. Those closest resumed their incessant pounding and slapping against the metal sides of the shed, sending a roll of thunder my way. Looking up the street, I could see another ten or so coming from my right. As soon as my feet touched the ground, I would be committed. There would be no way I could make it back over this gate without help or finding a ladder.

I looked back again and saw that Betty was now looking my general direction. I wasn't sure if she actually saw me or not so I raised an arm and waved it. There was a moment's pause and then she returned the gesture.

Taking a deep breath, I let myself drop to the street. The pavement crunched underfoot and I noticed a lot of broken glass that had been ground into dust. Hurrying, I ran out into the road and looked first to my left towards the shed and then to my right. The ones to the right were definitely closer, so I moved away from them. The street I was on went for a long way until there was an intersection where you could turn right as I faced it. That intersection was a good thirty or forty feet past the shed.

"This is gonna suck," I breathed as I took off at a jog.

I had no idea exactly what I was going to do, but at least I had a good idea that Carl was still alive. Now, I simply needed to free him and then haul ass back to our little compound where Betty and the kids waited.

"I really hate being right," I huffed as I picked up speed. That wasn't exactly true. I loved being right; didn't everybody? It was just that being right in this instance was a scary proposition.

DEAD: Onset

I finally reached a spot that was pretty close to midpoint between the zombies on my heels and the ones gathered at the shed. Now I would put my plan into action and just hope that it worked.

"Carl, stay quiet in there," I shouted. "I am going to try and lead all these bastards away from you. I will fire my gun twice when I think you have a pretty clear path. Meet me back over at that rear gate to this place."

That had been the gate I'd climbed over to enter. That was the one I wanted to leave from since it would allow us the best way to return to our place without being seen by any zombies as it provided the best cover between this community's walls and Johnson Creek Boulevard. That same cover would hopefully keep Brandon from spotting us from whatever rock he had crawled back under.

Already, the zombies around the shed were turning my direction. Looking around, I spotted a duplex that had an immaculately landscaped front yard. Everything was brick walls and rock features. I snatched up a few golf ball-sized stones and made my way towards the opening between another set of what I was now realizing were upscale townhouse apartments.

As soon as I was close enough, I lined up and hurled one of the rocks at the closest window on the side of one of those houses. I was glad that nobody was around to witness my feeble left-handed throw, but it accomplished what I set out to do as the window shattered. The sound was magnified by the relative silence of this dead world. A few zombies answered with their low moans, but a majority simply oriented themselves on this most recent stimulus and kept plodding along as they reached for me across that several feet of open space I maintained.

I decided to just start talking a lot of nonsense and taunts directed at my undead pursuers. It would've seemed childish and stupid to anybody who just happened to stumble upon me at that moment, but I didn't care. I just needed the horde to keep following me and moving away from Carl.

At last, I saw the trailing end of them filing in between the two buildings and into this somewhat narrow alley. I was almost

"Hate to say I told you so."

at the end when a terrible realization struck. It coincided with the sound that made the hairs on the back of my neck stand on end.

I'd been so focused on the zombies that I was leading away that I hadn't really been paying attention to what was behind me. Whether it was overconfidence that the majority of the undead denizens of this place had been clustered around that shed, or just not thinking of the big picture, I'd committed a potentially fatal flaw.

I shot a look over my shoulder and saw no less than five zombies filing in from what was supposed to be my exit from this little alleyway. Looking around, I realized I had little choice. I could absolutely bring my pistol into play, but I would need five perfect headshots in a row to prevent all of the zombies coming from behind me to get their hands on my person. That was not the sort of luck you could count on in the real world. This was where I bemoaned being useless as far as hand-to-hand combat was concerned.

Hoping that I was not altering my course from certain doom to one of likely doom, I charged forward and threw myself onto the windowsill that I'd just shattered. I felt glass grinding into my skin and sucked in a breath as sharp stabs of pain came from my stomach, my uninjured—at least up to this point—left arm, and my left shoulder.

I had to flail around to get myself through, and did my best to protect my right arm against my body as I flipped up and in. I was barely on the floor when I rolled fast and came up to my knees. I almost gave myself whiplash as I tried to look everywhere at once. Thankfully, the bedroom I'd entered was empty.

I rose to my feet and crept to the door and simultaneously gave a sniff as I listened for anything that might be waiting on the other side. The coast seemed clear and I cracked the door open to discover a dark hallway. Once more I was rewarded with an empty space. I moved out and hugged one wall, my nose on overdrive as I sought out even the slightest hint that a zombie may be near.

I moved to what turned out to be the living room. All I could smell was rotten garbage and dust. While unpleasant, it was a good sign. I could see out the large living room window to the empty street beyond. This was actually a good thing.

I winced and glanced down to see blood soaking through from the three areas I'd stabbed or sliced myself up when I'd dove through the busted window. I heard the sounds behind me at the same instant the first waft of undead stench reached my nose. The pack was outside the window that I'd come through.

I could not help it, I hustled back and peeked around the corner to see them. Only some of them were trying to get in, and they were not having an easy go of it. I was struck with an idea and strode into the room.

"Hello, beasties," I sing-songed.

I watched most of the heads I could see outside make jerking bird-like movements as they oriented on me. That had done the trick as the undead surged forward with a renewed effort. I waited until it looked like the first few were about to tumble into the room. I debated on leaving the door open and decided it shouldn't be a problem. It wasn't like I planned on staying around long.

I hurried to the front door and threw it open. At almost that exact moment, Carl was shoving away what looked to be the last mobile zombie in the area. His arm yanked back to reveal the knife that he'd just sheathed in the top of that zombie's head.

"Brandon." That single word from Carl confirmed what I'd suspected.

"I hate to say I told you so," I started as we met in the street and took off for the gate.

"No you don't," Carl shot back.

A distant scream caused us to break into a sprint.

15

Bad Man

We reached the wall and Carl boosted me up. Once I had a leg slung over, he was right behind me. I had a hundred questions rattling around in my head, but now was not the time. As soon as we emerged from the trees and were standing on the hill looking down at Johnson Creek Boulevard, I knew just one thing for certain: Betty and the kids were safe.

I knew this at the expense of the one person I'd seen who had been so filthy that I could not determine gender. At the top of the hill across the divide created by the road below sat the housing community with the zombie racetrack. That had been the direction I'd seen Brandon headed. Apparently, he'd arrived.

Dangling from one of the powerlines was a figure that swung on the breeze. It looked like that person had a few knotted together power cords wrapped around his or her neck. Another scream came and then ended abruptly. A moment later I saw a second figure being hoisted into the air beside the first one.

I was so fixated on that woman being strung up that I had forgotten about Betty. The sound of a rifle being fired made me snap around to our home. Betty was on the roof still, but she now had a rifle in her hands. I saw her looking in the direction of the woman being strung up. She brought the weapon to her shoulder again and fired.

DEAD: Onset

I looked just in time to see the woman plummet out of sight. There was another shriek from that direction followed by another shot from Betty.

"You head back to our place," Carl said as he took off down the hill.

I started to argue, but then realized that he was probably right. Like it or not, I was more of a liability. My arm was throbbing despite all the adrenaline pumping through me. I watched Carl take off at a pace I could not begin to match. Add in the fact that he was going down a rather steep hill and a fall might damage my arm beyond repair and there was no way I could follow him.

I headed away from Carl and down the hill in the direction of our place. As I neared Johnson Creek Boulevard, I spotted a few of the undead rounding the corner from the direction of Interstate 205. If I went straight home, I would be leading them to our walls. While a couple would not be a problem, a large swarm would become a concern over time. If we ever ended being surrounded by thousands of those things, we could very well starve or die of thirst. We'd been making it a point not to lead the undead to our doorstep if we could help it.

I was considering my choices when another gunshot rang out and the closest of the undead heading up the road towards me fell over. I glanced up and I saw Betty still sighting in Carl's direction. If she hadn't just fired, then who had?

I didn't have time to wonder when another shot rang out and the second zombie fell. This time I was paying attention. I turned back up the hill towards the place I'd just left. It was in that general direction, but not quite.

My eyes shifted towards movement and I saw a figure in hunter's camo step out of the woods just south of where Carl and I had exited. By this person's position, it was possible that we'd just run directly past the individual that was now waving at me.

I waved back and the person ducked into the trees. As curious as I was at the moment, I did not want to waste the gift I'd been given. I headed across the road and started up the hill towards home.

When I reached our own wall, I saw that Betty was no longer

on the roof. She'd come to meet me. She was staring down from the other side of the wall, the rifle jutting up over her shoulder. Her face was red and puffy and it was obvious that she'd been crying.

"He...he...he..." she tried to speak, but then broke down sobbing.

She had to set down the rifle in order to hand the step ladder over to me. I hadn't even gotten both feet on the ground when a large, furry, black shape loped across the yard. Her front paws bounced up and down on the ground as she woofed her enthusiastic greeting to my return.

"Hey, girl," I said as I knelt and allowed her to coat most of my face with slobber.

"She doesn't like it when you leave," a small voice spoke up and I looked to see Michael emerge from behind a decorative pine tree. He stared at the ground, but for just an instant, his face turned up to mine and he made eye contact. "She is afraid you won't come back." His head dropped once more.

Next to arrive was Selina. She appeared more confused than anything. It was obvious that she knew terrible things were happening around her, but she didn't know what exactly.

"Let's get everybody inside," I suggested.

Part of me did so because I wanted to down about a half a bottle of ibuprofen, but the other half needed to get up onto the roof. Carl was still out there, and this was far from over until he was safe and sound on our side of the wall. As we walked, I again noticed that, now that she seemed satisfied that I was okay, Chewie stuck to Michael's side like glue.

Once inside, I hurried up the stairs and told Betty I would meet her as soon as I downed a few pills to take the edge off the pain. I glanced over my shoulder and saw Michael sit down on the floor in the large entry. Chewie plopped down beside him and rested her head on his lap.

A few minutes later, I was out on the roof with the field glasses searching for any sign of Carl...or Brandon. Betty joined me and I was glad to see that she still had the rifle. Although I was not confident in her ability to do much considering the fact

DEAD: Onset

that she'd already gotten in a couple of shots. If she'd scored a hit, I think she would've said so by now.

"He's a monster," she whispered, finally breaking the uncomfortable silence that was growing between us.

"What did you see?" I asked as I continued to search.

"He ran up the hill and I lost him for a minute. When I spotted him, he was coming around the side of the house where that poor person was standing on the back porch. As soon as the person spotted Brandon, they ran inside and I lost sight for a moment. That girl took off for the house and vanished inside as well."

Betty paused and I could hear her voice crack as she related the story to me. I'd never believed she could sound so fragile and broken.

"He came out dragging the one person behind him on the ground and tossed the extension cord he'd tied around their neck up and over that power line. As soon as I thought I had a good shot, I aimed and fired. I should've hit him. I know I had him in my sights. He paused and looked right at me for a moment and then just continued to haul the person up. It was awful the way those legs kicked and flailed. I guess he had something to tie the cord off to around the side of the house, because that is where he vanished for a moment. When he reappeared, the person was almost done struggling and he actually did a strange sort of skipping dance back into the house."

Disgust and venom started to replace the grief and horror. As she spoke, I narrowed my search to a pair of houses that had zombies stumbling all around them. While not absolute, it was likely that one or both of the people I was searching for were inside those houses.

"When he started to haul that poor girl up, I swear I could hear him laughing…I know it is impossible, but…" Her voice trailed off and I wasn't sure if she was done or not. After a deep, steadying breath, she continued. "I fired again and there is no way I missed. But he only turned to face me for a moment before returning to what he was doing. I had to prove it to myself, so I sighted on the cable where it was knotted above the girl's head and fired. I don't think I could make that shot a second time, but I'll be damned if that girl didn't plummet to the ground. By then, I think Brandon knew you guys were coming because he took off at a run towards the houses that are just out of sight behind that grove of pines."

Just as she said it, I spotted something moving along a row of waist-high hedges. It was Carl. He moved in a fast crouch as he slipped past a small cluster of zombies gathered at the head of a nearby driveway. I saw something dark arc through the air and then watched as a huge picture window shattered. A second later, I heard the crash of glass breaking.

Many of the zombies turned to this new sound and began heading for the house with the newly busted window. Carl slipped down the side of a truck and stayed in a crouch as he hurried to the front door of the house where the suicide-by-shotgun person would be.

From my perch, I was able to see the rear of the house clearly. I knew instantly before he even popped out from the doorway that it had to be Brandon. There was no way that Carl could make it through that house and out the back so quickly.

"Betty," I snapped. "Get him."

The woman stepped up beside me and brought the rifle to her shoulder. I felt a surge of annoyance that she wasn't already prepared. That couple of heartbeats that it took for her to locate and come to bear on her target gave him time to slip down the dead-end street that ran behind this row of homes. He'd broken into a run as soon as he exited, obviously aware that we would likely be trying to snipe him from here.

I saw a puff of dirt a few feet behind him as Betty fired off a round. He was around the corner and once more out of sight before she could fire a second time.

"Maybe it's for the best," Betty sighed. I could hear the emotional exhaustion in her voice.

"Until he comes back and kills us in our sleep," I retorted.

A moment later, Carl emerged from the same door at the rear of the house. He looked our direction and gave a wave. I pointed in the direction Brandon took off, and through the glasses, I saw him glance that way. He looked back at me and made an exaggerated shake of his head.

I didn't like it. He was coming back and that lunatic was still out there. He knew where we lived and how we were set up. Not killing him was almost more dangerous than the zombies.

I was just about to drop the glasses when a second figure emerged from the house behind Carl. It was the woman that had been miraculously saved by Betty's one-in-a-million shot. She slung an arm around Carl and the pair began to limp our direction through the tall grass of the open lot.

I saw a few zombies falling in behind them and was almost embarrassed when I felt a surge of excitement rush through me. I started down and headed in the house. Only then did I realize that Betty had already abandoned me.

I hurried through my room and out to the hall that led to the stairs. It didn't really surprise me to see that Michael was right where I'd left him and Chewie. The only difference was that he seemed to be leaning down next to one of her big ears like he may be telling her a secret.

I hurried down the stairs past the pair and paused at the door. There was no sign of Selina or Betty. We needed to do something about giving people specific assignments when we were faced with a crisis. Sure, there was no way to plan for every eventuality, but at the moment, we all seemed to be doing our own thing. We needed to be a team. Maybe we'd get lucky and some kickass Marine would stroll into our little compound and whip us into shape. He wouldn't be the dickhead type from the movies. He would be the real type…the hero that had volunteered to put his life on the line for his country.

I exited the house and rushed over to where my trigger for the strand of cans I set up out in that field was positioned. Climbing the ladder, I looked over and soon spotted Carl and the female moving through the grass towards the wall. I grabbed the rope ladder and tossed it over so they could climb to safety, then I waited.

It felt like an eternity passed. Again, I warred with the guilt that I was feeling for being able to try out one of my kooky plans. This was a defining moment. We would know right here and now just how effective my lure would be in the future. Sure, not every situation is the same, but this would give us at least some idea.

Carl finally arrived. By now, I could see at least twenty zombies stumbling and staggering in pursuit. I scanned for any possible child versions and breathed a sigh of relief when all of these appeared to be of the adult type.

"Up you go," Carl said to the woman. She paused and looked up at me.

Her left eye was swollen shut and she had a nasty bunch of bruises and rope-type burns around her throat from the cord that had been used in the attempt to hang her. Her lower lip was split, but I couldn't tell if that was due to dehydration or being assaulted. She had dark hair, a naturally tan complexion, and brown eyes that hinted at Hispanic or some sort of South American heritage. She reminded me a bit of Selma Hayek in *From Dusk 'til Dawn*.

Once she climbed up and over, I realized that she was also above average when it came to height. She might even be an inch or so taller than my five-foot-nine-inches. She was curvy and, while not skinny, she wasn't heavy either. She looked like she might even be some sort of athlete.

"Evan, this is Amanda Rivera," Carl said as he climbed over after the woman. "Amanda, this is Evan Berry."

She mumbled something and waited patiently for Carl to reach the ground. She looked like she might bolt at the slightest provocation. Since I didn't know exactly what she'd been through, the only thing that I could think of was that perhaps it might help ease her mind if she saw Betty and the kids. It was a guess, but it was the best I had at the moment.

"Go ahead and take her in. Maybe Betty can check her out and make sure that she is okay," I suggested.

Carl nodded and led Amanda away by the elbow. I watched her walk and noticed that she was limping on her left leg. Betty checking her out was absolutely a good thing.

I turned my attention back to outside our walls. I saw the

zombies continuing to stagger towards us. Their numbers were such that it would not be any problem to dispatch them once they reached me, but I was itching to try out my lure. My gaze kept flicking between the oncoming little pack of undead and the rope suspended in the air between the trees.

As soon as I felt they were all a few yards past my lure, I slipped out of sight and gave my line a tug. In the distance, I could hear the rattle of gravel inside the suspended cans. There were moans that almost seemed to be in response. I had to fight the urge to climb up and look. It would be stupid to pop up and perhaps get the attention of a few stragglers and bring them back. Again, I gave the rope a few tugs and smiled when I heard moans that sounded distinctly different. If I had to guess, I would say that they were pretty much facing the other direction, but I waited a few more seconds.

It felt like an eternity passed until I eventually crept up the ladder and peered over the wall. I felt my heart do a flip in my chest.

"It works!" I hissed, actually clamping my hand over my own mouth despite the fact that the zombies were already starting to disappear through the trees.

Satisfied, I turned and headed for the house. I walked in and looked around. The entry was empty. Michael and Chewie had vanished someplace. I had no idea what had become of Selina and Betty, and I hoped that Carl had found them. I wanted Betty to give that woman a good exam. If she was bitten, it would be nice to know in advance that we would have to put her down soon.

I wandered around until I heard the low drone of voices. Eventually, I found Carl, Betty, and Amanda downstairs in the pool room. The water didn't look gross yet, but it wouldn't be long. I felt guilty that I'd allowed Chewie to just go swim in the swimming pool. While the water wouldn't have been drinkable due to the chlorine, it might've been better used by us humans to get cleaned up.

Betty was at the far end of the cavernous room with Amanda. The two had stepped behind a partition and Carl was just standing there, a grimace on his face. As soon as he saw me, he headed over.

"We have to go after that guy," he said by way of greeting.

"I agree." I glanced down at my wrapped-up arm and felt a surge of frustration.

"You may not be able to fight hand-to-hand with them things, but having a second set of eyes would be well worth it. If we go now, we have a chance. I imagine he scurried someplace and is hiding, hoping for darkness. That's what I'd do."

"We have a general direction," I offered hopefully.

"Then I will go grab a few things and we will go now." Carl had his mind made up and I agreed with him.

I glanced over at the little partition that hid Betty and Amanda from view. Time was definitely of the essence, but I had to know.

"You grab what you think we'll need and I will be upstairs and ready in just a minute." I didn't wait for any questions. I turned and walked quickly over to the women.

"…gonna sting a little," Betty was saying.

I heard a hiss and guessed that some form of antiseptic had been applied to one of Amanda's injuries. I didn't want to keep Carl waiting, so I tapped my hand on the top of the partition.

"Betty, can I talk to you for a sec?"

The woman stuck her head out, her face a hard scowl that seemed natural and reminded me of the woman that I'd met in the parking lot that first day. "What?"

"Any signs of bites or scratches?"

"Don't you think I would've told you if there were?" the woman shot back. "Now, if you don't mind, I need to finish getting her cleaned up and bandaged."

I raised my hands and backed away. That gave me a small sense of relief. Satisfied that Betty had things under control, I headed up to meet Carl.

He looked like a background character from a *Road Warrior* movie. In the brief time since I'd spoken with him, he managed to slap on a set of spiked gloves that I had never seen, a motorcycle helmet with a tinted visor and a runner's headlamp

DEAD: Onset

strapped to it that was similar to the one I was wearing, as well as a set of shin guards that I was pretty sure had belonged to Brandon. This was all in addition to his steel-toed boots, denim jeans, and a leather jacket over the heavy flannel shirt he wore. He had his big knife on one hip, a pair of Glocks in a pair of shoulder holsters that he'd fashioned, and the handle of an aluminum baseball bat jutting up over one shoulder.

"Let's go get this guy," Carl said with a grim voice.

"I'm ready."

That was a lie. I was about to go hunt down and possibly kill another person. Despite anything the man had done, I was simply not programmed to be okay with killing a human being. I thought back to the incident with the flare. Somehow, I'd hyped myself up to the point where I wanted to kill.

I dug down and tried to find that same resolve. The only thing that I found was that I was tired and felt like maybe all of this was hopeless. Would this be the shape of our existence from here on out?

We headed for the ladder and nothing that I could do mentally was working. I just hoped and prayed that my participation in this endeavor would be limited to keeping the undead at bay while Carl finished the deed.

"It's okay to murder this time," a voice startled me as I was about to climb the ladder and exit our little compound.

I looked down to see Michael walking beside Chewie; the pair were coming up the path and Michael was looking up at me as he spoke. Such a small change in his stature was enough to cause me to do a double-take.

"You called Brandon a bad man," I said, hoping that I would not break whatever spell was weaving around this moment. "Why is he a bad man, Michael?"

"He was stealing."

"Evan" Carl hissed, "we need to get moving."

"Just a sec," I called over my shoulder.

"What was he stealing?" I turned back to the boy. He was no longer looking up at me. He was petting Chewie who sat dutifully at his side.

"Bags of stuff. He took it last night."

I didn't have time to run inside the house to where we'd been stockpiling our food, medical supplies, and weapons. Something told me that I would be very upset if I checked.

"He went to the doctor's office."

I had no idea how the kid knew this stuff. What I did know was that he had a knack for not being seen. If Michael said that he had taken whatever he stole over to the medical complex, I believed him.

I threw my leg over the wall and was preparing to jump. Carl was already on the move, apparently not interested in waiting on me.

"You should say thank you," Michael said in his creepy flat tone.

I shot a look over my shoulder. The boy and the dog were already turning to leave.

"Thank you, Michael," I called after the pair.

"Welcome." The word drifted to me as I dropped to the ground.

I jogged after Carl. "We need to loop around to the medical center," I said just as we reached the trees.

"What?" Carl spun to face me.

"Brandon took a bunch of gear out of our place last night."

"And you're just telling me now?" Carl fumed.

"I just found out."

"How?"

"Michael. He just told me that Brandon stole supplies and took them to the medical center."

"That kid *told* you this?" Carl's voice oozed skepticism. "He doesn't talk to anybody except your dog."

"Well, that is probably why we need to take this serious."

Carl considered it for a moment. "If you can live with the consequences when this turns out to be a wild goose chase and that piece of crap gets away, then so be it."

Carl shoved past me, but I knew that there was no way he would change his path if he didn't think that this was a possibility. I fell in behind as we made our way down the hill towards

92nd Avenue. To our right, through the trees, I could see the outlines of the trucks we had parked in the driveway.

When we reached the road, Carl crouched in the bushes and brought his field glasses up. I scanned the front of the building and something caught my attention.

The zombie child missing his lower jaw was peering out at me from the window that had been busted when I'd been stringing my lure. Despite the fact that I was crouched down and trying to stay hid, his eyes were locked on me. He stood there for several seconds, his gaze giving me chills. Suddenly, his head snapped around. The boy turned away and vanished from view.

"If he circled around, he could already be inside," Carl whispered.

"He is," I replied, rising to my feet. Something told me that zombie heard something, which is why he departed so abruptly. I knew it was little more than a wild hunch, but I was ready to go with it.

"And you know this how?"

"Trust me…you don't want to know, but let's go before he manages to escape."

16

A Time to Kill

Hurrying across the street, Carl and I started at a jog, but when we heard the sounds of a tremendous crash from inside the same building where I'd seen the child zombie, we shifted to a sprint. I glanced both directions and saw a few zombies on the street, but we were across before any seemed to really take notice.

We arrived at the busted window and I knew we would be facing at least a couple of zombies just by the smell. Sure enough, there were three zombies wandering around in this large reception area. I could see the desk where people had checked in for whatever they came to this place for. The glass or Plexiglas partition was a busted mess and one zombie had gotten caught on a nasty shard.

From the looks this thing had tried to climb over the counter and lost its balance. A dagger-like shard had gone in the belly and came out the back. Its feet were off the ground and both arms were out in front swiping at the empty air. I imagine it would rip free in time if left to its own devices as well as the continuous effects of gravity.

Since it was closest, I stepped over and drove my knife into the side of its head. Carl was busy taking down a man wearing a shirt with a gas station logo over the left breast and so much of his throat missing that his head tilted forward to where his chin rested on his chest.

That left the soldier with no left arm. I let it approach me, and as soon as it closed to within range, I swept its feet out from under it by kicking it in the ankles. It fell and I moved in to finish it off.

"Next time just stay out of the way," Carl snapped.

"I had that one easy enough," I protested.

"I don't need you to *have* them."

He shoved past me to the doorway and his headlamp illuminated the face of a woman in scrubs standing just outside the doorway and staring in at us. His body blocked my view, but I heard the corpse fall to the floor with a smack of flesh on tile.

"I need you to be watching for the ones that are going to come up from behind and bite us in the ass." Carl poked his head back out the door. Without another word, he exited the reception area.

I followed and discovered that there was an even larger waiting area through the doorway. This one looked like maybe it was some sort of hub. There was a circular desk in the middle with multiple stations set up for people to come walk up to and maybe ask questions. There were also three doors leading away from this hub. We'd come through one. A second one exited into an actual hallway. I could see through the smeared and slimed glass to the dark hallway beyond by the glow of my own headlamp. A lone zombie was on the other side. It was staring in at us, but not reacting in any way. I kept expecting its hands to come up and start slapping at the glass, but it just continued to stand in place and stare at us with its blackshot eyes.

Carl trotted to the other door and tried the knob. It was locked and he hurried back to me. The sounds of moans were muffled by the glass, but it was clear that there were a good number of zombies in this place.

"As soon as we step out of this area, I need you to have your head on a swivel, you got me?" Carl asked as he cocked his head towards the door exiting to the hallway where the single zombie stood its lonely sentinel.

A Time to Kill

"Yeah," I said with a nod.

He was obviously taking point on this little mission. That wasn't necessarily a bad thing as I still had not been able to tap into that part of me that was ready to kill a living person. It was sort of like grabbing a wet melon seed. The tighter you squeezed, the easier it shot from your grasp.

He stepped to the door and gave it a shove. It opened easily enough and the zombie reacted by turning its head. Strangely, it did not try to turn its body yet and stayed almost motionless until Carl started for it. As soon as he did, it appeared to reluctantly face the oncoming warm body.

I followed and something struck me as soon as I managed to get a clearer glimpse of this zombie's facial features. I had a friend with Down's Syndrome and so I was very familiar with the facial features somebody with that birth defect would express. I was already coming to believe that children who turned acted different than the run-of-the-mill zombie—at least to a certain age. Could there also be something different in this particular zombie? Before I could ponder further, Carl stuck it in the eye socket and shoved it back and away.

Now that we were out in the hallway, I suddenly felt exposed and vulnerable. I followed Carl, my entire body coming around in a full three-sixty every few steps as I watched for anything that might try for us.

"Got one," I whispered as a single zombie appeared in the beam of my headlamp about a dozen feet up a hallway on our right.

It must've heard us approaching because it was emerging from a doorway and its head jerked first one direction and then the other. As soon as it spied us, it moaned and started our way. Carl had to backtrack to me, but as soon as he saw it, he hurried over and took it down. I glanced down at my arm, scowling at how it had betrayed me and reduced me to this ridiculous role.

Carl returned and swept past me to continue his trek up the hallway. His own headlamp was scanning to the left and the right as we moved along. It didn't take long for us to get the attention of the zombies that were like an infestation here inside the heart of the clinic.

I have no idea what happened here or how it went down, but by the looks of things, people came here after being attacked despite this not being an actual hospital. The staff probably did their best to treat these folks, and then the turning began and nobody could believe what was happening until it was too late.

That made me think about the military vehicles out front. I had to wonder what had brought *them* here. Again, this was not a proper hospital. Something was nagging at me about this place. All of a sudden, things didn't feel right, and it had nothing to do with Brandon perhaps being here as he attempted to scoop up the gear he'd taken from us.

We rounded a corner and discovered a set of double doors that were basically torn from their hinges. This was also when a few pieces fell into place. Carl had come to a sudden halt and I ended up directly beside him. Both of our headlamps shone into a massive ward. There were rooms along both sides, but this center location was probably a place where families sat together and visited a patient, or maybe waited while the person they'd brought here was being treated.

This room had toys strung about it, most of them stained and darkened with dried blood. There were a handful of soldiers here, all of them torn apart to varying degrees. They were not the problem despite the fact that they all basically turned as one and started for us.

At least twenty faces peered at us from around the room. Heads cocked and titled as we were regarded with what looked like a gross caricature of curiosity.

"A pediatric hospital," I breathed.

"Yeah...it says so out front," Carl replied absently as we both took a step backwards to maintain the distance between us and the approaching soldier zombies.

There was no time to try and explain what I'd seen from the child versions of the walking dead. Hell, I wasn't sure just exactly what I'd seen.

"Just back up slowly," I whispered. A memory flashed in my head and I added, "And don't make any sudden moves with

A Time to Kill

your weapon."

We backed up until we came to a corridor that led off from the one we'd been travelling and took it. The sounds of the soldiers could be heard as they shuffled along in pursuit, but we took a hard left the first chance we got and they faded.

We finally found one of the emergency stairwells. Carl tried the door and it opened much to my surprise. He took care to open it as quietly as possible, perhaps recalling my recounting of how loud the door had been when I'd come here before. We stuck our heads in and heard moans from above and below.

"Which way?" he mouthed.

I shrugged. I honestly had no idea where Brandon might be skulking about. A loud bang from below made up our minds for us. We headed down the stairs as fast as we dared. Carl had to stop twice to grab a zombie, pin it to the wall with one hand and then stick it in the head with his blade.

We reached the ground floor as we heard a yelp from through that doorway. It sounded close. I looked down and was surprised to see a Glock in my hand.

I followed Carl through the door and checked for anything coming at us to the right as he had the left covered. Three zombies who looked to be in their teens were on the other side of a large window that looked into what might've been another waiting room. They were all pressed against the glass, clawing at it and trying futilely to bite the smooth surface.

We were at the junction of a tee-intersection. The zombie kids behind the glass were on the right—my side—to the left was a long hallway lined with what appeared to be offices, and straight ahead were rooms. I was making a guess here based on being able to see through the nearest doorway where a bed sat beside a window. A chair was knocked over and the floor was a Jackson Pollack painting with the dried blood splattered everywhere.

"This way." Carl gestured and started off to the left.

I turned so that I was basically walking backwards behind him. We had gotten about twenty feet when I heard a voice. The words were unintelligible due to the echo, but I was almost certain that it was Brandon. Carl must've felt the same because he picked up the pace. When he started to jog, I had no choice but to turn around and follow.

We reached another corner and stopped. Now I could hear the person and was certain that it was Brandon.

"If you would've just done what I told you and hidden in that damn gated community across the way, we could've pretended that you were a lone survivor. Once we got in, it would be easy to knock those idiots off. They don't stand watch or anything," he was explaining.

"I still don't know how you fucked up the other place. And you are sure that everybody got killed?" a stranger's voice asked.

"Things got a little out of hand. Dizzy got loaded and he and a few of the guys started doing stupid shit. Apparently Dizz got off on hearing people scream. It brought a freaking wave of those zombies. They just rolled up on us and started ripping people apart."

As I listened, I was finding that I was getting as many new questions as I was answers. No…actually, I was now coming up with a lot more questions.

"I shoulda just stayed with Pierce," the other voice moaned. "He found a great spot, and we even rescued a few honies that are so grateful they do whatever we ask."

"No, you guys shoulda been back when you said," Brandon retorted.

"I told you, we got trapped in that house."

"Yeah, and somehow you and Pierce were the only ones who made it out alive." There was a skepticism in Brandon's tone that fought with the sarcasm for control of each clipped word.

"I could say the same to you," the other man shot back.

I heard what sounded like shuffled movement. "I told you, Dizzy caused this."

"And I told you we got trapped in a house and that Pierce and I barely managed to make it out alive."

Carl glanced back at me and held up a fist. Was he really

signaling me to stay put? Did he think I was an idiot? If this little discussion continued, those two might take care of our job for us. I wasn't an idiot.

I looked over our shoulder. With all the arguing going on in there, and the fact that the volume level was not being kept in check, I figured it was only a matter of time before the zombies showed up. So far, the coast was clear.

"We need to get this stuff and get out of here the moment it gets dark. I figure we can grab one of the police cars. Those dumbasses didn't even bother to strip the cops. I found a set of keys on one of the dead cops. Even know which car it starts. Most of the stuff I've been cherry-picking is already in that car's trunk, but last night I swore somebody was following me so I ran in here and stashed the last bags."

"Why are we waiting until it gets dark?" the other person asked, sounding mildly amused.

"Because that jerk with the busted arm went against everything he had been preaching about leaving people behind if something goes wrong. He went after the redneck and got him out. If that guy is on the roof with a rifle, he won't miss," Brandon explained.

"That fat chick didn't miss either," the other guy said with a laugh which was followed by a muffled curse and yelp from Brandon. My ears perked up at that. Betty swore she hit Brandon, but he hadn't gone down. That made her lucky shot that cut Amanda down from where she'd been hanging seem all that much more improbable.

"Kevlar can stop a bullet, but it still doesn't keep a person from getting bruised," Brandon hissed. "You poke me there again and I will cut your throat."

"Ease up, hero," the other person said flatly. "Let's not forget that it was me who showed up with the location to a really good place to ride this out."

"I can just as easily hang out around here and pick those idiots off in their little compound," Brandon replied. "I would have a safe place all to myself."

"And miss out on those bitches willing to do anything we

say just because we keep them alive? Not how I would want to ride out the apocalypse, but if you wanna go solo, that is fine with me."

Carl turned back to me and then hiked a thumb over his shoulder. He had one of the Glocks in his hand and then nodded to me and shot a questioning glance at my own. I smiled and then switched the gun back and forth between each hand as I nodded. I hoped that he understood my meaning that I could shoot with almost equal competence from the right or the left.

He moved to the very edge of the door frame and held up his free hand. Three fingers extended, he gave the countdown.

...two...

...one.

He ducked low and came around quickly. I was on his heels with my own pistol in my left hand. Brandon was seated against the wall opposite the entry and the other man was to his left.

This had been some kind of office, and a large desk dominated the floor. Whether it was due to his apparently bruised ribs or just slow reflexes, Brandon was still staring, wide-eyed and open-mouthed, when Carl shot him in the face. There was a neat dark hole just below the right eye, almost touching the nose where the bullet entered. The wall behind him instantly bloomed with crimson.

The other man was equal parts quicker as I was slow. While it was certainly true that I was a good shot with both hands, that did nothing for my reaction time or hesitation. I knew what had to be done. I even understood why. Yet, there was still a part of me that fought with the idea of taking another person's life. That is my only real excuse for why the man was able to dive behind the desk before I got a shot off. My bullet hit the wall and sent up a small cloud of dust...and that was all.

I adjusted my aim and fired a round into the desk in the general direction that I thought his body might be lying. That was always something that amazed me when I watched a movie or television show and a shootout took place. People would shoot the hell out of a wall after somebody ducked, but it was like they felt some flimsy pressboard desk would be able to act as a shield against bullets. They might not pack as big of a punch, but I was willing to bet they would still draw blood.

Carl moved around to circle the desk and dove forward just as a barrage of return fire came his direction. I took my opportunity and rushed the desk. Reaching it, I decided to come over versus go around. From my belly as I slid just far enough to look over the edge, I found myself staring down at the stranger who'd been sitting with Brandon. He barely had enough time to look up before I fired three shots into his body from almost pointblank range.

I stared down at the man. He could've been a guy standing behind me at the grocery store just a short time ago. I didn't know anything about him or his story other than some out-of-context conversation that I'd managed to overhear.

My brain wanted to take in every single detail, but for some reason, nothing would stick. It was as if my subconscious was refusing to allow this person to take up residence in my memory. Maybe it was trying to block out everything.

All I could register was the fact that his eyes were staring up at me and his eyebrows were still raised in surprise. There might have been just a pinch at the corners of his eyes as he had just a moment to register the pain before he died.

This was nothing like I could ever imagine. I knew right then that I'd been part of a lie my entire life. All the books, movies, and TV shows made it seem like you could take a life from another person and be okay with it in these situations. And who knows, maybe you can. Maybe Carl was standing just a few feet away from me and feeling none of what I felt. It was possible that he was feeling no sense of self-loathing like what was oozing into every pore of my soul and staining it black forever. There would be no absolution from this. I had taken the life of another person. It didn't matter the circumstance.

I was a murderer.

Michael had been right.

Then I vomited.

"Okay, time to go," Carl's voice made it through the buzzing in my ears and the pounding in my head. "We have to get out

DEAD: Onset

of here now."

I could hear them. The gunfire had drawn them to us. Maybe every single one in this building was coming to punish me for my sins.

I stood up and wiped my mouth with the back of my hand. One step was all I managed before I felt my knees buckle. I collapsed into a heap and dry heaved.

"Do this later, Evan," Carl's voice cut through the fog and acted as a line to pull me back from the brink of the breakdown I could feel coming.

I climbed to my feet and took one unsteady step and then another. We reached the door and Carl turned to face me.

"You need to screw your head on, Evan. We have to get out of here, past those things out there, and then make it back home. I need you not to fall apart."

"I'm good." I heard the words, but I did not recognize the voice.

"I mean it." Carl's face was right in mine now. "You need to tighten up. There are a lot of them out there."

I think I nodded. "I'm fine."

I saw the look of doubt clear in his eyes as he regarded me. "If you get us killed, I am gonna be so pissed," he mumbled as brought his pistol up and tapped his own forehead with it.

That must've been his signal to move out. He stepped into the hall. I was about to ask why he wasn't going with his knife, but I realized just how stupid that question was when I stepped out into the hallway and saw that it was packed back the way we'd come. If we continued along the hall past the room we'd just killed Brandon and his friend in, it was only marginally better, but at least we could see daylight between the oncoming zombies.

Carl fired off a few shots and dropped the leading zombies. He hit the release and let his magazine clatter to the floor and swapped in the next one.

"You take the next few," he said, stepping a little to the side. "One of us should always have a loaded weapon. And as soon as we close in, you take my gun."

A Time to Kill

"What are you gonna do?" I asked as I raised my left hand and sighted on the closest walker, a man with blonde hair. I pretended it was Brandon as I fired.

"Use my knife as soon as we get close enough. We ain't got nearly enough bullets for this. And no matter what, we gotta keep moving forward. If that pack behind us catches up, we are done for."

I wasn't sure we weren't just delaying the inevitable. I looked back, and it was clear that we were moving much slower than they were approaching.

Carl stepped forward and shoved the closest zombie back. It toppled and knocked two down with it. He struck like a cobra, his knife rising and falling with fierce precision. I stepped over the third body that he was putting down for good and shoved my pistol into the open mouth of the nurse that had her eyes locked on the vulnerable man. A dark spray of brain and bone made an audible clatter as it hit the wall, creating a constellation of gore.

Carl was already back up and rushing past me to drive his shoulder into the next zombie—a rotund woman who had been shot up and sported at least fifty dark holes on her large torso. She toppled easily and was stilled by one thrust of steel into her left eye.

I had to move to the right and take down two more that were almost within reach of Carl. Part of me wanted to marvel at how fast the man moved while not seeming to even realize or care how close the next zombie might be. If he was putting that much faith and trust in me, we would have to talk later. He would need to reassess his mindset.

I lost track of how many he killed. Just as I could not even begin to tally my own. It was just one undead face after another, each one gnashing its teeth and reaching with cold hands for me or Carl as we carved and blasted our way down the corridor.

"Last magazine," I warned as the empty one clattered to the floor and I slammed in the replacement.

"Just keep moving," Carl grunted as he kicked another zombie back to give himself enough space to take down one of the trio that were all converging on him at once.

I shoved my arm past him and brought the pistol up under the chin of one zombie and squeezed the trigger. Another pair down almost simultaneously and Carl hopped over to the one he'd kicked and planted his foot in its chest before sticking it.

I brought the Glock around and was struck by the realization that the way in front of us was clear. We were almost to the end of this corridor where it emptied into what I recognized as the entrance lobby.

We jogged the rest of the way and emerged into a day that still seemed gloomy despite the sun. I fell in behind Carl as he walked over to one of the police cars. I stood a few feet away and turned in a full circle as I surveyed the parking lot. Even though a handful of the walking dead were coming our direction, it seemed like nothing after what we'd just escaped.

The sound of an engine turning over made me jump. I spun to see Carl emerge from one of the green and white county sheriff's vehicles. He waved me over and I started across the open lot.

He was already in the driver's seat by the time I opened the door on my side and joined him. I didn't care to ask why he was bothering with taking the car. I had to guess that dealing with the few zombies that wandered up to our driveway would be a small price to pay.

"I thought you'd be happier," Carl said as we exited the parking lot and started on our short trip home.

"Why is that?"

"We can do this because you proved that your noisemakers work. We park the car, hurry to the wall and climb over, then you wait for a moment or two and activate your lure. The zombies all wander away and we slip out and bring our stuff back in."

"Sure, I guess." I was having a tough time feeling excited about anything.

My thoughts were returning to that day of the flare. I'd been set on charging in and killing Brandon. I was ready to prove to Carl that I could do what it took to deal with the rough situations. What a bunch of crap that had been. I'd been fooling myself.

Carl was right. I was not a killer. At least, it wasn't something that fit comfortably in my nature. I sat back and watched the empty buildings and straggling undead pass by without really seeing any of it.

We pulled in and Carl exited the vehicle. I looked up and saw him heading the rest of the way up our driveway. We reached the wall and Carl climbed over first. I followed, only slightly aware of the pain in my arm.

It was just a few minutes before I saw the first of the zombies coming up our driveway. I waited until I felt the time was right and gave my line a few tugs. I the distance, I heard the cans of gravel make their rattling sound. It took a little longer for the undead to turn around in the driveway that was already crowded with the military trucks. At last, the moans were distant enough that I risked a peek. The last of them was just vanishing around the slight bend in the drive.

I crossed the open yard and broke off from following Carl as I headed up the stairs to my room. I glanced down when I reached the top of the stairs to see Michael and Chewie in the huge circular entry hall. I considered calling my dog, but then decided against it.

I walked into my room and shut the door behind me. I have no idea how long I stood with my back against the door without moving. Eventually, I pushed off and crossed the room to the huge closet. I had blood, and bits of all sorts of things I tried not to examine that closely, splattered all over my clothing. I needed to strip down, sponge off in the basin, and then sleep for a month.

Never in all my years doing construction had I felt so exhausted as I did this minute. I ended up seated on the floor as I undressed because I kept erupting into shaking fits that prevented me from removing my clothes. By the time I'd gotten naked, I was over most of the shaking.

I grabbed a sponge and dunked it in the bin that Betty had placed in everybody's room. I scrubbed my face first and then cleaned up the rest of my body as fast as I could. As soon as I

DEAD: Onset

was done, I headed into the closet, threw on a set of sweats and staggered to the bed where I collapsed facedown.

At some point, I fell asleep.

I awoke to darkness. I shifted slightly and felt Chewie's massive body curled up next to mine. The boy must've brought her to my room at some time during the day and let her in.

I ruffled her fur and tried to go back to sleep. Eventually I gave up on that. The growling in my belly was insistent that I eat something.

I sat up and looked outside. A bright moon shone in through the window, and for just a moment, things could be normal. I swung my legs over and tried to get up. My feet tangled and tripped over something and I hit the floor with a thud that made me cry out. I'd partially used my injured arm out of reflex to try and break my fall.

A soft cry got my attention and I made out a dark figure on the floor beside my bed. "Michael?" I whispered needlessly. Already I could hear shouts and calls from outside my room.

The door flew open and Betty rushed in with Selina. The woman hurried to the child and scooped him into her arms, her shushing noises much louder than his soft whimpers.

"What is he doing in here?" I winced as I stood up. My arm hurt, but I didn't think I'd rebroken it.

"The dog wouldn't stop pawing at your door and Michael won't leave your dog's side," Betty said through the boy's hair as she kissed the top of his head. She headed out my door without another word, carrying Michael in her arms. Chewie followed, glanced back once as she went through the doorway, and then was gone.

Once I was alone again, my hunger reminded me as to what I'd gotten up for in the first place. I started for the kitchen, and as I descended the stairs, felt an itch on my left arm. I scratched it and paused when I felt a sting as well as something hard and scaly.

I moved to the shaft of light coming in from a kitchen window and hiked my sleeve up past my elbow as my mouth went instantly dry. There it was, about three inches long down the in-

A Time to Kill

side of my forearm: a scratch.
   "Damn," I whispered.

Where do zombies come from?

When a daddy zombie and a mommy zombie love each other very much…they nibble on each other and then that makes baby zombies.

Okay, so that is not really true. At least not in my DEAD world. For the most part, I stick to the tried and true Romero style. Sure, my universe has a few of its own quirks, but I would say I am mostly traditional. Still, when the characters in my books encounter zombies, every so often, one stands out. One of the zombies in DEAD: Onset (Book 1 of the New DEAD series) actually has a story of his own. I present to you "Paul Stokes is DEAD".

Paul Stokes is Dead

Paul Stokes pulled into the entrance of his Happy Valley community. He still marveled at what his career afforded. He'd grown up in a modest home, but just over eight years ago, his love for brewing beer changed his life. Nobody had been more surprised than Paul when a major brewery wanted to purchase majority ownership of his small microbrewery.

Overnight, he'd gone from renting a mid-level apartment to owning a home in an exclusive neighborhood on the outskirts of Portland, Oregon. He still walked around his home sometimes just touching things and soaking in the wonder.

This must be how it feels to win the lottery, he'd thought on more than one occasion.

He'd also told himself more than once that it was too good to be true. All good things come to an end. Today felt like just that sort of day. As his luxury SUV rolled onto Southeast Scott Park Circle, the changes were immediately apparent.

"Not even the Bradford or Coatney kids are outside," he mused as he aimed the nose of his vehicle for his driveway.

The first thing he noticed was that his front door was open. Marjorie never left the door open. During the summer, her reason was that it let the air conditioning out as well as allowed flies to migrate inside. During the winter, it let all the warm air outside. Period.

He turned the key and sighed as the vehicle shut off. An eerie silence fell now that not even the gentle purr of a motor gave him a soundtrack for distraction. He'd shut off the radio just a few minutes into his drive home. What he was hearing just did not seem possible.

DEAD: Onset

Unable to delay it any more, Paul opened the door and climbed out. A strange noise drifted on the air to his ears. He looked around. Was somebody hurt? Even worse…was it Marjorie? The sound had come from the direction of the side of his house. He started that way just as another of those peculiar moans came from *inside* his house.

"Marjorie?" he called, a tingle of fear shooting pulses of uncertain energy up and down his spine.

I am going to wake up and this will all just be a bad dream, he thought as he hurried up the walkway to his front door.

Maybe it was time to take those warnings seriously and head to one of those FEMA shelters that everybody was being directed to. When only two of his thirty-seven employees showed up to work this morning, he'd made the call to send everybody home to "ride this out" until things returned to normal. And they would, of that Paul had no doubt.

"Are you headed to one of the shelters?" his shipping foreman had asked.

"And leave my house?" Paul had scoffed. "I think I can ride it out better there than in some high school gymnasium or sports arena. This isn't Hurricane Katrina. It's just some sort of peculiar illness."

When the report that Japan and most of Asia had gone silent…he'd reconsidered his options. The military was supposedly securing the perimeter around these locations as rumors of groups of these infected or sick individuals were being reported all over the city. For the first time since purchasing this home, he envied the community on the other side of Johnson Creek Boulevard. Their community had a brick wall all the way around it as well as steel gates at the entrances.

Paul had liked the idea of living in a luxurious community with well-to-do neighbors, but a fence and a wall had just seemed too uppity and snobbish for his comfort level. Right now, a gated community sounded like just the thing.

Reaching the door, a smell wafted out of the house that made Paul pause. It was unlike anything he'd ever experienced.

Paul Stokes is Dead

That was saying a lot considering some of his early attempts at brewing beer.

"Margie?" Paul called.

Pushing the door open, the smell almost caused him to stagger. Throwing his arm over his mouth and nose, Paul stepped into the entry hall and gave his eyes a moment to readjust to the change in light. Already he knew there was something terribly wrong. The wall of his entry hall had a nasty smear along it that ended just before the stairs going up to the bedrooms. Looking up those stairs, he saw that there were bloody handprints as well as dark stains on the carpet.

A sound made him jump, and it took him a moment to realize that the sound had been a moan that escaped his own lips. In a rush, he bounded up the stairs calling his wife's name again. He just crested that point where his eyes could see the open bathroom door at the top. That was another indication that something was wrong with his Marjorie. She had a very strict rule about bathroom doors remaining shut.

All of this was just adding to the apprehension and fear that rooted itself in Paul's mind. He'd insisted that all this nonsense on the television was just a bunch of overblown media madness. Surely it could not be as bad as the reports were saying. It just wasn't possible.

Paul froze.

The boy stood in the doorway to the nursery that the baby would occupy in just five months. It had been decorated the day after the sex of the baby was revealed by the doctor. Paul had wanted to go with yellows, saying that pink was the old-fashioned color given to girls. And just maybe his little girl would be a bit of a tomboy. Marjorie had won that argument just as she had most others.

It was that background of soft pinks and hints of purple pastels that framed Toby Bradford. Only…it just barely resembled Toby. No child could look the way Toby looked at this moment. The blood…so much blood.

The nine-year-old boy was a caricature of Dennis the Menace. His blonde hair and sparkling blue eyes were enhanced by his gap-toothed smile that never seemed to fade. Dennis the Menace was his well-known neighborhood nickname. He wasn't a bad kid. Just a bit rambunctious.

"Toby?" Paul managed around a mouth that had suddenly gone dry.

As his eyes took in more of the picture, he felt his gorge rise. There was a dark stain just outside the bedroom where Toby now stood staring at him. His head cocked first one way, then the other. The figure on the floor behind Toby was sitting up. That caused something else in the room to move and the sound of something crashing to the floor made Paul jump.

First one, then a second face emerged from the unlit gloom of the pink bedroom. Two of the three Coatney children emerged and stood behind Toby, one at either side. Skye Coatney was the youngest child in the neighborhood and had just started kindergarten this year. Her hair was still in braided ponytails that stuck out from each side of her head like a pair of antennae.

Jenna Coatney's appearance was what shattered everything for Paul. At nine years old, she was the middle Coatney child. She was also the one who could outshine Toby Bradford in the mischief department. Her Minnie Mouse sweatshirt was in tatters. The once white shirt was now an ugly dark reddish-brown. Her belly was exposed and had been torn open. A ragged strand of intestine dangled from that rip—dark, viscous fluid dripping from it.

The eyes. That is what finally pulled Paul's focus from assorted injuries suffered by the three children who stood across the room from him. They were coated with a film that was shot full of dark tracers. When the next figure emerged, Paul thought it would be the teenage Coatney boy, Joshua. It wasn't.

"Margie?" Paul took the last few steps to reach the second floor of his home.

Marjorie Stokes was the stuff of nightmares. Her lower lip had been ripped away, leaving an ugly raw flap of meat dangling from her chin. Her nose was also gone. The right arm looked like it had been dunked in a piranha tank. One section of the forearm was almost stripped clean to the bone. Her throat was an ugly, gaping hole. A little blood trickled from the wound when her head twitched and jerked as she appeared to search and then focus on Paul. Her belly was a mess. It had been ripped open and a dark sac dangled from it, suspended by a fleshy cord that was almost black. Before he could look away, he was certain he saw something move inside that semi-opaque bulb.

"No," he whimpered.

All the reports came to his mind at once. The news stories about a small town in Kentucky that had been placed under quarantine. Then there were the peculiar attacks happening all over. People swearing that the attackers were the dead returned. Of course, the CDC had instantly discredited and dismissed that notion as nothing more than a juvenile fantasy.

Here it was. Right before his eyes. There was no way possible that any of those children or his beloved Marjorie could be alive. The visible wounds aside, there was enough blood soaked into the carpet that a squishing sound could be heard as Marjorie stepped past the children and began shambling towards him.

He'd reached the top of the stairs and froze as he felt his mind peeling away to its core. Madness was threatening to overwhelm him as the pain that scalded his soul touched every part of his being. He was still standing frozen when Marjorie reached him. She leaned forward as if to embrace him and despite the odd sensation of her cold hands on his arms, he did not move until her teeth clamped down on his left cheek.

Pain broke all the spells that had been preventing Paul from reacting outwardly to this terrible horror. He tried to scream, but the side of his mouth being ripped away caused him to choke on the blood. He gagged as he shoved Marjorie away, and that action seemed to trigger the three children into motion. He backed away and tripped over his own feet, his head smacking hard into the wall and causing his vision to momentarily flash bright and then dim.

Fighting to remain conscious, Paul felt something fall on him. He faded for a moment and snapped back when the pain sent a shockwave through his body. His right arm was agonizing fire from the shoulder to the elbow. He looked down just as Toby bit into his left arm right above the elbow and ripped away a strip of meat that brought Paul fully back to awareness of what was happening. Jenna and Skye had joined in and seemed to jockey for position on his bleeding right arm like a litter of puppies to their mother's teat. All three children had blood smeared across their faces—his blood.

Using one foot, Paul kicked Toby away first. The boy collided with Marjorie and sent her tumbling backwards. Skye was the smallest, and Paul winced when he shoved her away with ease and the little girl smacked into a table with her face. The crunch could be heard as her nose flattened. Yet, despite that impact, the child did nothing more than roll over and start to her feet again.

Jenna managed another bite as Paul wrestled her off his body. She had slipped across his midsection and was now on his right side. He looked down just as blood bloomed around where her mouth was latched to his bicep.

Paul screamed.

It was rage, sadness, and pain all rolled together. His scream changed to a roar and he rose, his mind fighting to not topple over the edge of madness and plunge into its crimson embrace.

Skye was closest, and he physically lifted her in the air and hurled her into the pink-themed room that had once been a sign of hope and a future filled with joy. Spinning, he caught Toby as the boy tried to clamp down on his right forearm. There was a tingle of pain, but the boy was not able to gain purchase as Paul heaved his small body into that same room.

Something grabbed his leg and Paul instinctively kicked out. He barely registered that it was the face of his Marjorie that he'd kicked. He might've lost his heart if he'd seen her jaw snap to one side and a few teeth break off leaving jagged remnants that snagged at her lips as she moaned in what might've been frustration at losing her grip on her prey.

Jenna was on her feet and stumbling for him. Paul moved to one side at the last moment and the child staggered past, unable to stop her momentum. Paul slammed a booted foot into the girl's back, sending her sprawling into the room with the other two children.

He yanked the door shut, fighting through the pain in his arms from the savage attacks. By now, Marjorie was slowly rising to her feet. He wanted to cry as he saw that the sac dangling from her open wound had burst. A small figure now writhed and spun at the end of that cord.

Staggering back, Paul led the thing that had once been his wife into their bedroom. She followed him, and when she tripped while rounding the corner of their bed, he rolled across the bed, came up on the other side and left the room. He slid down the door and wept.

When the clawing and pounding came from his bedroom as well as where he'd thrown the children, he tried to tell himself that the merciful thing to do would be to put them down. These were not his neighbors' children nor his wife.

Monsters were real.

Unable to do it, Paul finally got up and made his way to the bathroom. He looked in the mirror and gasped. It wasn't his torn cheek, the blood all over him, or condition of his arms that caused him to stagger back from his own reflection.

His eyes.

They were showing those dark tracers. While not as pronounced, he knew it was the same thing he'd seen in Marjorie and the children. He would become one of...*them*.

"Like hell," Paul croaked around a mouth that was swelling on one side to the point where speech was becoming impossible.

He knew what had to be done. At least he knew what *he* had to do. He also feared that he did not have the resolve to follow through.

Stumbling downstairs, he made his way to the garage. He returned upstairs kicking his shoes off when he reached the top. He would do everything in his power not to back out, but he also needed to hurry. He could feel the infection...taste it in the blood that ran down his throat as he found it increasingly difficult to spit it out.

DEAD: Onset

Grabbing the handle that was mounted to the wall of their large shower, Paul was grateful that this simple safety measure had been installed. He doubted the shower nozzle's ability to perform the task at hand. This metal handle was supposed to allow a person to step up and into the shower with more stability. Personally, he'd never once touched it, but Marjorie loved it and made a big deal of reminding Paul that it would come in handy once he was old and gray.

Removing his belt, Paul tied it to that vertical metal handle. There was just enough of a loop remaining that he could slip his head through when the time came.

The next bit would be difficult; especially since his vision was beginning to blur. Bending down, he produced one of the zip ties he'd fetched from the garage. They'd been great for securing the Halloween and Christmas decorations. Forcing his feet together as close as they would go, Paul paused as he watched his blood draining all over the basin of his large bathtub. At last, he felt his feet were secured.

His hands kept betraying him as he tried to grip the belt and slip his head through it. The fit was tight until he got it past his chin. Also, he was forced to remain hunched over the entire time. That was edging him towards a blackout. He had enough time to think a blackout might not be so bad when his legs buckled.

Paul slumped to his knees, already unconscious. The noose proved to be unnecessary as the blood loss became too much and he slipped into cardiac arrest. With a few spasms and shudders, Paul Stokes died.

Ten minutes later Paul's eyes opened

MAY DECEMBER
Publications

**The growing voice in horror
and speculative fiction.**

Find us at www.maydecemberpublications.com
Or
Email us at contact@maydecemberpublications.com

TW Brown is the author of the ***Zomblog*** series, his horror comedy romp, ***That Ghoul Ava***, and, of course, the ***DEAD*** series. Safely tucked away in the beautiful Pacific Northwest, he moves away from his desk only at the urging of his Border Collie, Aoife. (Pronounced Eye-fa)

He plays a little guitar on the side...just for fun...and makes up any excuse to either go trail hiking or strolling along his favorite place...Cannon Beach. He answers all his emails sent to twbrown.maydecpub @gmail.com and tries to thank everybody personally when they take the time to leave a review of one of his works.

He can be found at www.authortwbrown.com

The best way to find everything he has out is to start at his Author Page:

You can follow him on twitter @maydecpub and on Facebook under Todd Brown, Author TW Brown, and also under May December Publications.